NEVER TELL

This Large Print Book carries the
Seal of Approval of N.A.V.H.

NEVER TELL

LISA GARDNER

THORNDIKE PRESS
A part of Gale, a Cengage Company

Farmington Hills, Mich • San Francisco • New York • Waterville, Maine
Meriden, Conn • Mason, Ohio • Chicago

**LIBRARY OF CONGRESS CIP DATA ON FILE.
CATALOGUING IN PUBLICATION FOR THIS BOOK
IS AVAILABLE FROM THE LIBRARY OF CONGRESS**

ISBN-13: 978-1-4328-6025-7 (hardcover)

Published in 2019 by arrangement with Dutton, an imprint of Penguin Publishing Group, a division of Penguin Random House LLC

Printed in the United States of America
1 2 3 4 5 6 7 23 22 21 20 19

*In memory of Wayne Rock,
exceptional detective and human being.
We miss you, my friend.*

CHAPTER 1
EVIE

By the time I pull my car into the garage, my hands are shaking on the wheel. I tell myself I have no reason to feel so nervous. I tell myself I've done nothing wrong. I still sit there an extra beat, staring straight ahead, as if some magic answer to the mess that is my life will appear in the windshield.

It doesn't.

With a bit of care, I can still slide out of the driver's seat. I'm bigger, but not that much bigger. I fight more with my bulky coat and the strap of my oversized purse, as I ease out from behind the steering wheel. Conrad bought me the purse as a Christmas gift last year. From Coach. Real leather. At least a couple hundred dollars. At the time, I'd been so excited I'd thrown my arms around him and squealed. He'd laughed, told me he'd seen me eyeing the bag in the store and had just known he had to get it for me.

When I'd hugged him then, he'd hugged me back. When I'd laughed that day, and giddily opened up the huge, gray leather bag to explore all the compartments, he'd laughed with me.

Christmas morning. Nearly one year ago.

Had we hugged since? Laughed since?

The bulge in my belly would argue we'd found some way to connect, and yet, if not for the streams of bright colored lights and gaudy decorations covering my neighborhood, I'm not sure it would feel like the holidays at all. As it is, we're one of the last undecorated houses on the block. A wreath on our door; that's it. Each weekend, we promised to get a tree. Each weekend, we didn't.

I take my time hefting my purse over my shoulder. Then I turn and face the door leading from the garage into the house.

Dead man walking, I think. And something crumples inside me. I don't cry. But I'm not sure why.

The door is open. Cracked slightly. As if on the way out, I didn't pull it hard enough shut. Letting out all the heat, my father would say, which causes me a fresh pang of pain.

I push through the interior door, close it firmly behind me. That's it. I'm home.

Standing in the mudroom. Another day done. Another night to begin.

Hang up the purse. Shrug out of the coat. Ease off the boots. Jacket on the coatrack. Shoes on the mat. I fish my cell phone out of my bag and set it up on the side table to charge. Then, I take a final moment.

Breathe in. Breathe out.

Listening for him.

The kitchen? He could be sitting at the table. Waiting in front of a cold dinner. Or pointedly taking the last bite. Or maybe he's moved into the family room, ensconced in his recliner, feet up, beer in hand, eyes glued to ESPN. Sunday is football. Go Patriots. I've lived in Boston long enough to know that much. But Tuesday night? I never got into sports. He'd watch; I'd read. Back in the days when we spent so much time glued together, it seemed natural to also have some time apart.

I don't hear the clinking of silverware from the kitchen. Nor the low rumble of TV from the family room.

Door open, I remember. And my left hand flattens on the relatively small, but noticeable, curve of my belly.

The hall leads me to the kitchen. A spindly table sits in front of the back window. No sign of dinner. But then I notice a rinsed

9

plate lying neatly in the sink.

Breathe in. Breathe out.

I should have a story, I think. An excuse. A lie. Something. But in the growing silence, my thoughts churn more, my brain spinning wildly.

Dead man walking. Dead woman walking?

I'm going to vomit. I can blame it on the baby. You can blame anything on pregnancy. I'm sick, I'm tired, I'm stupid, I lost track of time. Baby brain, pregnancy hormones. For nine whole months, nothing has to be my fault. And yet . . .

Why did I come home tonight? Except, of course, where else do I have to go? Ever since I first met Conrad ten years ago . . . He noticed me. He saw me. He forgave me.

And I loved him.

Ten whole years, I have loved him.

I leave the kitchen. It's small and, like the rest of the 1950s house, still in desperate need of updating. We purchased the place with hope and aspiration. Sure it sat on a postage stamp yard, and each room was tinier than the last, but it was ours. And being young and handy, we'd fix it up, open it up, then sell it for oodles of money.

Now I walk down a narrow hallway where half the wallpaper hangs down in pieces and do my best not to notice.

Family room. Den, really. With Conrad's beloved La-Z-Boy, a modest sofa, and of course, an enormous flat-screen TV. The recliner is empty. The TV is off. The room is empty.

Door open, I remember again.

Our garage fits only a single vehicle, and even that is a perk in a Boston neighborhood. Conrad parks his Jeep on the street. Which I check now. Because I'd spotted it pulling into the driveway and, yes, there it is. Black Jeep. Situated at the curb straight outside. A prime spot I can already imagine he was thrilled to get, as even with parking permits, there's more demand than supply. Hence his kindness in giving me the garage.

It's okay, honey. I don't want you walking down the street alone at night. I like knowing that you're safe.

Dead woman walking. Dead woman walking.

Don't vomit now.

And then . . .

Then . . .

"Door open," I whisper. And I finally notice what I should've noticed from the very beginning.

Smell. I'd been listening for the sound of

my husband. The clatter of silverware in the kitchen. The thump of his recliner banging back in the family room. But there aren't any sounds. No sounds at all.

The house is hushed. Quiet. Still.

As if it were empty.

Smell.

The stairs leading to the second floor are like the rest of the house, narrow, confining, creaky. Conrad tightened the bannister three months ago. When I broke the news. When we both stood in our bedroom and stared at the little stick. My hands had been shaking so hard he'd had to take it from me.

I remember feeling ill then, too. Willing myself not to vomit, though it had been the near-constant queasiness that had led me to take the pregnancy test. A marriage is a mosaic of a thousand moments, a hundred precious memories. That day, watching his hands close around mine. Strong fingers, seamed with calluses. Steady, as they took the pregnancy stick away from me, held it closer to him.

I had that surreal feeling I sometimes get. Where I'm not present in my own life, but even all these years later, standing in my parents' kitchen again. Holding the shotgun. Smelling all that blood.

And Conrad, being Conrad, looked right at me. Looked right *into* me.

"Evie," he said. "You deserve this. *We* deserve this."

I loved him again. Just like that. In that moment, I adored him. We held hands. He cried. Then I had to pull away to vomit for real, but that made us both laugh, and afterward he'd wiped my face with a washcloth and I'd let him.

A thousand moments. A hundred memories.

That pain again, deep inside me, as I lean heavily against the wall, away from the bannister I no longer trust, and work my way up the narrow staircase.

Smell.

The odor hits me hard now. Nothing faint, teasing, ambiguous. This is it. Had I known all along? Turning into the drive? Pulling into the garage? The interior door open, open, open.

What had my subconscious suspected, long before the rest of me had paid attention?

Upstairs, not the bedroom, but the second tiny room, Conrad's office, looms to the left. That door is open, too.

Sounds to go with the smell. Sirens. Down the street. Growing louder. Coming closer.

But of course.

My parents' kitchen.

My husband's office.

Blood.

Dark, viscous. A spray. A pool.

I can't help myself. I'm sixteen. I'm thirty-two. I reach out. I touch the spot closest to me. I smear the red across my fingertip. I watch the way it fills in the whorls of my fingerprints.

My father. My husband.

Blood.

More noise. Banging. So far away. Shouts and demands and orders.

But up here, none of it matters. There is just me and this final moment with Conrad. His body fallen back into the desk chair, the back of his head sprayed on the wall behind him.

I fear what I will see on the computer screen before I even look. But I force myself to do it. Take it in. Register the images. This is my husband's computer. This is what my husband was looking at before he died.

Harder banging now. The police. Responding to reports of shots fired. They will not be denied.

"It was an accident," my mother whispers urgently in my ear. *"Nothing but an unfortunate accident."*

I reach over to the computer. I close out the images. Then, because I have enough experience to know it won't be enough, I pick up the gun from my husband's lifeless hand. I curl my palm around the checkered grip. I slip my finger into the cold trigger guard.

And I start shooting.

When the police finally burst through the door, I stand at the top of the stairs, both hands up, gun in plain view, while turning slightly so that the curve of my stomach can't be denied.

"Drop the weapon, drop the weapon, drop the weapon!" the first officer shouts from the base of the stairs.

I do.

He scrambles up the stairs, cuffs in hands. I hope for his own sake that he doesn't stumble against the bannister.

A marriage is a mosaic. A thousand moments. A hundred memories.

The officer twists my arms behind my back. He cuffs my wrists tight, pats me down as if expecting even more weapons, as more uniforms pour through the door.

"My husband," I hear myself say. "He's been shot. He's dead."

"Ma'am, is there anyone else present?"

"No."

A thousand moments. A hundred memories.

"Ma'am, you have the right to remain silent. Anything you say can and will be used against you in a court of law. You have the right to speak to an attorney, and to have an attorney present during any questioning."

The officer escorts me down the stairs, out of the house, away from my husband's body.

"Do you think I'll be allowed to plan the funeral?" I ask him.

He looks at me funny, then deposits me in the back of the patrol car on a hard plastic bench seat.

More cops. More sirens. The neighbors appearing to watch the show. I know what will come next. The trip to the police station. Where my hands will be swabbed for blood, tested for GSR. Fingerprinting. Processing.

Then, when my past appears on the computer screen . . .

An accident, my mother whispers again in the back of my mind. *"Nothing but an unfortunate accident."*

I can't help myself; I shudder.

She will come for me now, I think. And

because of that, as much as anything else, I curl my hands around my belly and tell my baby, this fragile, fluttery life that hasn't even had a chance yet, how sorry I truly am.

CHAPTER 2
D.D.

"Okay. Just like we've done before. I'll head straight. Alex will cut left. Jack, you ready?"

Jack nodded. Sergeant Detective D. D. Warren took a steadying breath. Three of them. One target. How badly could things go wrong?

First step forward. Light tread, heel, toe, designed not to make a sound. Alex utilized the same strategy, heading sideways to intercept the line of retreat. They'd done this enough times to know that silence was the key. Alert their opponent too early, and that was it. She was both faster and — D.D. was beginning to suspect — smarter than the three of them put together.

Which made the situation particularly dire, given that it was D.D.'s favorite black leather boot at stake.

She eased into the dining room, where Kiko had wisely retreated beneath the table with her prize. So far, the best spotted dog in all the land was lying contentedly on the rug, chewing on the heel of D.D.'s shoe, as D.D. and Alex made their circular approach.

Five-year-old Jack had taken up position in the family room. His job: catch Kiko when she inevitably bolted from beneath the cherrywood table. They expected the dog would run toward Jack, her partner in crime. The two adults of the household, on the other hand . . .

A floorboard creaked beneath D.D.'s foot. She froze. Kiko looked up.

Time stood still. Detective and dog locked eyes, D.D. wearing one boot, Kiko holding the second between her paws.

Alex appeared in the left-hand doorway of the dining room. "Kiko! Release! Bad dog!"

Kiko grabbed the boot in her mouth and ran for it.

D.D. lunged to the right. An act of desperation, and she and the dog both knew it. Kiko, a Dalmatian–German shorthaired pointer mix who was all long legs and high energy, dodged the move effortlessly. Alex came charging from behind.

Kiko galloped straight for Jack, who cried out in boyish delight, *"Roo, roo, roo!"* right before he tossed Kiko's favorite toy straight up into the air.

True to form, Kiko dropped the boot and

leapt up for her stuffed hippo.

D.D. snatched her boot. Kiko caught her toy. Then Kiko and Jack were off, tearing around the family room in a whirlwind of puppy-boy energy.

"Damage?" Alex asked, coming to a halt beside her. He was still trying to catch his breath. For that matter, so was D.D.

She inspected her boot. The bottom of the heel showed signs of chewing. But the leather upper was still intact.

"You gotta remember to put them in the closet," Alex said, eyeing the teeth marks.

"I know."

"She's going to grow out of it, but not overnight."

"I know!"

"So who do you think is going to take longer to train, her or you?"

D.D. growled at her husband. He grinned back.

"Roo, roo, roo!" Jack added from across the room. He was now standing on the sofa, springing up and down on the cushions, while Kiko matched him jump for jump from the floor. It had been Alex and Jack's idea to adopt a dog from the local Humane Society. D.D., as sergeant detective of Boston homicide, had argued they weren't home enough. To which Alex had ruthlessly

replied that *she* wasn't home enough. His job teaching crime scene analysis at the academy had set hours, and Jack's schedule as a kindergartener was hardly grueling. A boy needs a dog, he'd told her.

Which, from what D.D. could tell, seemed to be true. Because God knows Jack and Kiko were already inseparable. The black-and-white-spotted one-year-old pup slept in Jack's bed. Sat next to his feet at the kitchen table. And did everything the boy did, from leaping across the furniture to racing around the yard.

D.D.'s son was happy. Her husband was happy. In the end, a chewed boot heel seemed a small price to pay. That said, Kiko and Jack were now racing laps around the room.

"I gotta get to work," D.D. said.

"Take me with you," Alex tried.

"And rob you of this magic moment?"

"Pretty please?"

"Sorry." D.D. was already sliding on her damaged boot. "Wife shot and killed her husband last night. She's been arrested, but I want to check out the crime scene. Clearly, you'd be biased."

"Woman's already been charged," Alex asked, "and you still need to visit the scene?" Following an on-the-job injury two

21

years ago, D.D. had been moved to a supervisory position in homicide. As her fellow detectives would attest — and Alex would agree — D.D. took a much more hands-on approach with her management style than was strictly necessary.

"I have a personal interest in this one." D.D. made it to the front door, eyed the crystalline sheen to the half-frozen ground outside, and grabbed her black wool coat. A month ago, the air had been crisp but the sun warm. And now this. Welcome to New England.

D.D. spared the twin racing streaks of her son and dog a second glance from the entryway, and despite the chaos — no, because of the chaos — felt the corresponding warmth in her chest. "They really do love each other."

"Heaven help us," Alex agreed. He stood close. They'd just had four whole days off together, a rare treat. As always, they both now felt the pull and pang of D.D.'s demanding job. Alex had always respected D.D.'s workaholic ways. But there were times, even for her, when disappearing down the rabbit hole that was a homicide investigation became difficult. Especially lately.

"Why is this case personal?" Alex asked.

22

D.D. buttoned her coat. "The woman in question, Evelyn Carter, née Hopkins, I investigated her for murder once before."

"She killed a husband before this one?"

"Nope. She 'accidentally' shot her father. But, seriously, how many shootings can one woman be involved with?"

Alex nodded sagely. "You're going to get her this time."

D.D. smiled, stepped into her husband's embrace for a quick kiss, then waved goodbye to her crazy kid and dog. "Totally."

Evelyn Carter and her husband, Conrad, lived in Winthrop, one of the smallest and oldest towns in Massachusetts. Dating back to 1630 and positioned on a peninsula just miles from Logan Airport, the area offered views of the Atlantic for the lucky and up-close-and-personal contact with densely packed homes for everyone else. The Carters' residence was located on a street of modest, distinctly 1950s Colonials that had probably once been strictly working-class. Now, given property values in Boston, especially this close to the waterfront, God only knew. As it was, D.D. was surprised to see so many of the original homes intact. These days, it felt like every neighborhood in Boston was being gentrified, developers coming in, razing the old, and replacing it with bigger and better. Personally, D.D. preferred a little character in a home, but then again, on a detective's salary she wouldn't be living in any of these neighborhoods anytime soon.

Her former squad mate and onetime mentor Phil had contacted her first thing this morning to fill her in on the shooting. Pretty straightforward case, in his opinion. Neighbors had called in reports of shots fired. Uniformed officers had responded to find the wife standing at the top of the stairs, gun still in hand. She had surrendered without incident and been taken to the South Bay House of Correction.

Pregnant, Phil had added. Far enough along to be noticeable, while not yet huge.

D.D. couldn't yet picture that. The Evie Hopkins she had known had been a sixteen-year-old girl. Thin, dirty-blond hair, huge, doe-like brown eyes as she'd sat at the kitchen table, mere feet from her father's blood-soaked body, shaking uncontrollably.

She hadn't cried. D.D., a new detective back then, had thought that odd. But there'd been something to the girl's flat expression, combined with her hard tremors, that had been compelling. Shock. A sort of delayed reaction to grief that made D.D.

believe the girl was honestly in pain, only of such an extreme magnitude she couldn't comprehend it.

They hadn't been able to get her out of the kitchen and down to the station for proper processing. At the time, it hadn't seemed such a big deal. Evie, covered in blood, hadn't denied anything. The gun had gone off. Yes, she'd shot and killed her father.

And now her legs didn't seem to work. She couldn't stand, move. Short of physically picking her up, D.D. and her partner, an older detective, Gary Speirs, couldn't get the girl out of the kitchen. Speirs had made the judgment call not to push it. He'd been afraid the girl would give over to hysterics, ending their interview once and for all.

So they'd all sat feet from the body, the spattered cabinets, the smeared refrigerator.

The mom had stayed in the front room. An actual parlor, which D.D. had found strangely mesmerizing. She'd heard of such things, but to actually see one . . . The Hopkinses lived in a beautiful historic Colonial in Cambridge, as befitting the father's position as a Harvard professor. Perfectly tended, everything in its place. Except, of course, for the crime scene in the kitchen.

Had it biased D.D. at the time? The

upper-class home? The well-groomed mom? The obviously shell-shocked sixteen-year-old suspect, her thin shoulders shaking?

The mom, interviewed separately in the front parlor, had corroborated everything her daughter had reported. The shotgun had been a recent purchase given a rash of break-ins in the area. The father had been showing it to his daughter. She'd picked it up, had been trying to figure out how to clear the chamber, when the gun had gone off, blasting her father in the chest from mere inches away. A tragic accident. Follow-up interviews revealed no reports of any ongoing rancor between the father and daughter. In fact, the entire family was described as good people, great neighbors. The daughter a gifted pianist. The wife active with literacy causes and aid for battered women. As cases went, it wasn't even one D.D. had wondered about in all the years since.

Now this.

Yellow crime scene tape roped off the front yard. Several open parking spaces had been secured, probably for the detectives who'd worked most of the night before finally taking off for home in the hours since. Only two official vehicles remained.

All in all, the house appeared quiet. No

neighbors lurking outside. No crime scene techs bustling about or uniformed officers working the street. As Phil had said, a straightforward case. A man had been shot and killed. His wife was now sitting in county jail.

D.D. got out of her vehicle. She approached the front door, noting the splintered frame and skewed Christmas wreath. The police had had to force their way in. Interesting.

She entered. Like a lot of the homes hastily constructed postwar to accommodate the boom in young families, the house had a simple layout. Narrow staircase leading straight up against the wall to the left. Front-facing family room to the right. Tight hallway leading to a modest eat-in kitchen. Downstairs bath to the right. Mudroom area and garage access off the kitchen to the left.

The kitchen showed signs of recent updating. Fresh-painted pale-gray cabinets. New, solid-surface dark-flecked countertops. Stainless steel appliances. The hallway, on the other hand, with its ripped yellow wallpaper and scuffed wooden floors, was deeply in need of care.

Clearly a fixer-upper, though given modern tastes for open-area living, a tough one at that. Had the Carters been doing the work themselves?

Had they already started in on the nursery?

D.D. found herself with her hand resting on her belly. Hastily, she dropped it. Lately, she'd been thinking too much about the days she'd been pregnant with Jack. A child she'd never expected to have. Her greatest miracle and deepest love. Usually . . .

"Hey, there you are."

D.D. turned to find Detective Carol Manley standing in the hallway behind her. The petite investigator, just over five feet tall and barely a hundred pounds soaking wet, had taken D.D.'s place on her squad after D.D.'s injury. Manley was a perfectly good detective. Both Phil and Neil seemed to like her and accept her as part of their three-person team. D.D., on the other hand, still didn't trust any cop named Carol.

Completely unreasonable, but there it was.

Now D.D. carefully schooled her features and reminded herself that part of her job was to play well with others. It was the part of her job she was worst at, but hey.

"Body was found upstairs," Carol was saying now. "Looks like she shot him sitting at his desk. Then shot up his laptop as well."

"Do we know motive?" D.D. fell in step

behind Carol as the woman headed for the stairs.

"Wife isn't talking. Phil said you knew her."

"I questioned her regarding another shooting sixteen years ago. That one was ruled accidental. Though now I wonder."

"Watch the bannister," Carol commented as she headed up. "It's pretty loose. One of those things they must not have gotten around to fixing yet."

D.D. gave the wooden bannister an experimental shake; yep, it was definitely less than stable. "Don't suppose murder weapon was a shotgun?" D.D. asked.

"Nah. Sig Sauer P-two-two-six, registered to the vic, Conrad Carter. Looks like he kept the nine-mil in the top drawer of his nightstand."

"Where anyone could grab it."

"Ah, but the ammo was in a shoebox in the closet."

"Because clearly that provides security. Love 'smart' gun owners."

"And yet where would our job be without them?"

D.D. conceded the point. They arrived at the top. The landing was tiny. Only three doors to pick from. Two bedrooms and a bath, most likely. But D.D. didn't need to inspect all three to find the scene of the crime. Smell directed her enough.

Conrad had converted the smaller bedroom into a personal office. Massive executive-style black leather chair, the back now smeared with dark splotches of gore. A wall of waist-high laminate filing cabinets, covered in piles of paperwork and stacks of what appeared to be catalogues. Across from the filing cabinets, the room held a massive oak desk, currently riddled with enough bullet holes and metallic rubble to qualify it as a war vet.

Small space, D.D. thought, huge carnage. Clearly, the wife hadn't been messing around.

"The remains of the laptop?" D.D. asked, gesturing to the debris-strewn desk.

"Yep. Techs have it. Woman closed it up, then emptied her clip into it. Not a huge target, meaning our gal knew what she was doing."

"What do the techs think?"

"They need time to take the laptop apart and inspect the damage. There's a lot going on inside a laptop — battery, RAM, motherboard, Wi-Fi card, hard drive, thin hard drive, et cetera. So lots of things to hit, but in theory, also some things that could've been missed. Unfortunately, a dozen forty-caliber rounds to a target that small . . ."

D.D. arched a brow. "How many bullets to the husband?"

"Three."

The Sig P226 held fifteen rounds. Meaning: "Three to the husband, twelve into the computer? If we view the laptop as a second victim, certainly seems she hated the computer more."

"Or was a woman with something to hide."

"Trying to eradicate something on the laptop," D.D. followed. "Do we know if it was strictly the husband's computer, or did both of them share it?"

"Don't know."

"And she didn't say anything to the police when they arrived? No 'I had to do it,' 'he started it,' 'the voices in my head . . .' Anything?"

"She wanted to know if she could plan her husband's funeral."

D.D. shook her head. "What about her demeanor? Did the arresting officer describe her as appearing shocky, grief-stricken, relieved?"

"Calm and cooperative. Allowed herself to be cuffed and led to the patrol car. Was taken to the station and charged without incident."

D.D. frowned, still not sure what to think. She studied the blood-smeared chair, the spatter across the far wall. "What did the husband do?"

"Sales. Worked for one of those custom window companies." Carol pointed to the pile of catalogues on the filing cabinets. "According to the neighbors, he was on the road a fair amount, speccing out jobs, that sort of thing. But when he wasn't traveling, he worked out of this office."

"The contents of the filing cabinets?"

"Phil went through them. Seem to be customer files. Nothing out of the ordinary."

D.D. nodded, returned to studying the damage. She should've brought Alex, she thought. This was how they'd met, analyzing spatter at the scene of a brutal family annihilation. What did it say about her life that studying a crime scene made her miss her husband?

"And Evie?" D.D. asked. "Her occupation?"

"Evelyn? She teaches algebra at the local high school."

D.D. had to smile. "Her father was a prof at Harvard. Some kind of mathematical genius who taught classes where the names alone hurt my head."

"She's pregnant. Five months along."

"Were they close to their neighbors? Get any good dirt?"

Carol shrugged. "People on the block had nothing bad to report. Couple bought the house four years ago. Been working on fixing it up as time allowed. Apparently in the summer, Evelyn liked to work in the yard. She'd wave when neighbors walked by but wasn't exactly the chatty sort. *Quiet* was the word people used a lot. Conrad, on the other hand, was the social half of the pair. Much more likely to stop, hold court. But then again, uniforms couldn't find any neighbors who'd been invited over for dinners, barbecues, drinks, whatever. Neighbors didn't seem to take it personally as much as there was an assumption the Carters were a young, busy couple."

"So by all appearances, a happy couple?"

"No reports of domestic disturbance calls or loud arguments."

"And Evelyn, when she was arrested, bore no signs of a physical confrontation between her and the husband?"

"Not a mark on her."

"Rules out self-defense."

"But not battered woman's syndrome," Carol pointed out. "Some guys know how to hit where it doesn't show, and if it was ongoing . . ."

"Never know what goes on behind closed doors," D.D. agreed, thinking of that first crime scene, the stately Cambridge Colonial, the impeccably decorated front parlor. Again, had she, a rookie detective, let herself see only what outsiders were meant to see?

She gestured now to the gory wall before her. "Tell me about the husband's body. Three shots fired?"

"Two to the chest, one to the head. Torso shots lodged somewhere inside, probably ricocheted around his ribs. Head shot was a through and through."

Which would explain the far wall and the ongoing stench in the room.

"Close range?" D.D. asked.

"We're still working on the trajectories, but yes, stipling around the entry wounds suggest a distance of less than two feet."

D.D. considered the room, number of feet between the doorway and the desk chair. "Chair had to be facing the door, right?"

"Yep."

"No defensive wounds on his hands, any sign of a previous altercation?"

"Negative."

"Evelyn retrieves the gun from the bedroom," D.D. thought out loud. "Loads it using the ammo from the closet."

"We found the shoe box with ammo open

on the bed, loose slugs next to it."

"Walks into the office, maybe calls her husband's name."

"He turns around in his chair," Carol filled in.

"She steps closer, opens fire. Quick. Has to be, for him to never even get a hand up. Just, 'Hey, honey,' then, boom, boom, boom."

"Or, 'You bastard,' boom, boom, boom."

"Something like that," D.D. agreed. "Three shots. Enough to make sure she definitely got the job done, but not so much that it's a crime of passion. That, she saved for the laptop." D.D. frowned. "I'd really like to know what was on that computer."

Carol shrugged. "What would motivate a wife to kill her husband? Porn? E-mails from a girlfriend? Online gambling addiction? Plenty of things out there that would justify shooting up a husband and his laptop. Hell, maybe he was just that into video games, or she was just that hormonal from her pregnancy."

D.D. gave the childless detective a look. "If pregnancy hormones led to homicide, there wouldn't be a husband left alive. Plus, you said it yourself. Evelyn knew what she was doing during the shooting, and she was calm and cooperative afterwards. That's not a woman on a rampage. There's something else going on here. Something more."

"How'd she look sixteen years ago?" Carol asked.

"Young and traumatized. I'm surprised, given that tragedy, she'd allow a gun in her home. You'd think she'd want to stay as far away from firearms as possible. And yet . . ." She glanced at Carol. "Two shots to the torso, one to the head, a dozen straight into the laptop. Even at such a close range, to never miss . . ."

"Sounds like a woman with some training," Carol agreed. "Maybe the ol' face-your-fears sort of thing? After the last shooting, she wanted to make sure she never had an 'accident' ever again. Took some classes, joined a local firing range?"

"Definitely worth pursuing. Her hands were tested for GSR?"

"Absolutely. Tested positive. Not to mention the flecks of blood we found on her clothes, more on her hands."

"She did this," D.D. stated. "Evelyn Carter shot and killed her husband."

"Open-and-shut. Police responded to sound of shots fired. Found her standing at the top of stairs still holding the Sig. Never even denied it."

"The police forced their way into the

house. Why?"

"They heard more gunshots."

"But the initial call out was due to neighbors reporting gunfire. How long did it take police to respond?"

"Eight minutes."

D.D. tilted her head. "So fifteen shots were fired over the course of eight minutes?" She eyed the detective.

Carol merely shrugged. "We're still gathering facts. But my guess, first round was Evelyn killing her husband. Second round — when the police arrived — was Evelyn taking out the computer."

"With a gap in between. While she was doing . . . ?"

"Who knows. Closing out files on the computer, maybe? Trying to cover something up? Then, when she heard the sirens, realized the police were closing in . . . she decided on a more definitive approach."

It was possible, D.D. thought, but also a lot of conjecture. "Covering something up?" she murmured, more to herself than anyone. "Or backing something up?"

"What do you mean?"

"Clearly the laptop held something significant. Did she just want it destroyed, or was there also data she wanted to retrieve? E-mail address of her husband's alleged

lover, I don't know. But eight minutes . . .
It doesn't take eight minutes to close out
files or shut down a computer. It could take
eight minutes, however, to back up desired
data."

Carol nodded slowly. "All right. I'll check
on it. If she copied data, it'd have to be to a
thumb drive. She didn't have anything on
her when she was processed at South Bay.
So maybe she stashed it around the house?
I'll take a look."

"Something else you should know: Evie's
father, the Harvard prof, was known for his
photographic memory. It was part of the
reason for his success in his field. All he had
to do was glance at something once, and he
retained the image forever."

"Meaning Evelyn . . . ?"

"Maybe she didn't have to back anything
up. Maybe she just had to look."

"Lovely," Carol murmured.

D.D. smiled. "Nothing to worry about,
right? Like you said. Open-and-shut."

Carol muttered again. This time, the word
was not *lovely.*

D.D. left the detective to take a fresh look
at the crime scene. She'd just exited the
house when she noticed the person standing across the street. A lone female. Blond
hair. Gray eyes. Deceptively slight build.

Flora Dane. Onetime kidnapping victim. Current survivors' advocate/vigilante. Also D.D.'s newest confidential informant. Just a month ago, they'd worked together to find a sixteen-year-old girl who'd disappeared after the murder of her entire family — if *working together* was a phrase that could be used for either D.D. or Flora.

Now D.D. frowned, stared across the street.

"What?" she called out. Because where Flora appeared, trouble usually followed.

Flora didn't approach. She shifted from foot to foot, hunching her shoulders inside her oversized down-filled jacket. If D.D. didn't know any better, she'd say the young woman looked nervous.

Another moment passed. D.D. sighed, crossed the street herself. Flora was staring at the Carters' house as if she were trying dissect all the contents while peering straight through the exterior walls. The girl had many talents — including lock picking and chemical fire — but D.D. didn't think X-ray vision was among them.

"What?" D.D. asked again.

"I saw his picture, on the news."

"You mean the victim? Conrad Carter?"

"His wife shot him?"

"Appears to be the case. Why?" asked

D.D. "You know Evie?" Flora ran a support group for survivors. Maybe, after the death of her father at her own hands, that was how Evelyn saw herself. Anything was possible.

"No. Not her. Him. I recognized him." Flora glanced at her, and D.D. knew that her notoriously hard-edged CI was indeed nervous. "I met him before. In a bar. When I was with Jacob."

Jacob Ness was the man who'd kidnapped and raped Flora for four hundred and seventy-two days. He'd died six years ago, during the FBI raid to rescue her.

D.D. had that feeling again. Of knowing only that she didn't know enough. That Evie Carter had reappeared in her life, and it was going to bite her in the ass.

"Flora —"

"Jacob knew him," her CI whispered. Flora stared at D.D. with stark gray eyes. "Conrad Carter. Jacob Ness. I think . . . I'm pretty sure they might have been acquaintances."

CHAPTER 3
FLORA

Every day, I work out. I run. I hit various stations set up along the Charles River for fitness enthusiasts such as me. Pull-ups on bars. Triceps dips on wooden benches. Knee tucks, hip twists, calf raises, chest flies, lunges, lunges, lunges. It doesn't matter if it's December and below twenty, or raining, or boiling. I'm a woman who needs her morning serotonin the way others demand a double-foam latte.

The truth is, like a lot of survivors, I've been taught the hard way to ignore physical complaints. Basically, spend enough time starving, beaten, isolated, and you can teach yourself to ignore most anything.

It's true that what doesn't kill you makes you stronger.

But no one says that strength doesn't come at a price.

After my morning endurance event, I return to my tiny one-bedroom apartment with its multiple bolt locks and very kind elderly landlords who charge me only a fraction of the going rent. I make some money working at the pizza parlor down the street, but it isn't much. I have a fund, however, that my mom set up when I first returned home. Filled with checks, some large, some small, sent by total strangers because they felt sorry for me. In the beginning, I hated that money. All these years later, no college degree, no real life plan, it's come in handy. Still, I try to draw from it sparingly. It won't last forever, and so far my only calling — helping other survivors — is more of a volunteer gig. Oh, and now I'm a CI for one Sergeant Detective D. D. Warren, using my street savvy to help solve crimes. Turns out, that pays nada as well. Figures.

I shower. Forever. Cleanliness, after all those months of lying in my own filth, is everything to me. After showering comes coffee.

I turn on my TV. Local news because that's part of my morning routine. Amber Alerts, missing persons, developments on national crime cases, this is what I do — much to my mother's dismay. But six years later, we've agreed to disagree.

I don't look at the TV, the talking heads more of an audio backdrop as I bang around my tiny kitchen, searching for food that still hasn't magically appeared because my mother hasn't driven down from her farm in Maine to bake for me lately. I both dread and long for her visits. My mother fought for me. I went to Florida, a stupid, naïve Boston college student, giddy with the limitless potential of spring break. I got drunk. I got kidnapped. And for the next four hundred and seventy-two days, my mother and my brother went through hell, appearing on national news shows and orchestrating major social media campaigns to beg for my safe return.

Then when it happened . . .

I think we can all agree that the Flora who went down to Florida isn't the same Flora who came back. My brother, Darwin, eventually took off to Europe. It hurt him too much to be around me. My mom is built from sturdier stuff. All these years later, she remains convinced that her sweet little girl who ran around the wilds of Maine and tamed the local foxes is inside me somewhere.

I admire my mother's courage. I'm still never sure what to think of her optimism. Though right now, I really miss her blueberry muffins.

Behind me, the TV is talking about a local

murder. Pregnant wife shot and killed her husband last night. Fussing with my coffee maker, I shrug philosophically. Nice to have the pregnant wife come out on top, is my first thought, after all those years when it seemed that every other homicide was some cheating husband murdering his pregnant spouse just to avoid alimony and child support.

It's not until the coffee is percolating that I turn, glance at my tiny flat-screen TV sitting on the far wall cabinet.

And I start to shake. My hands, my shoulders, my entire body. My feet are rooted. I can't move. I stand in the middle of the kitchen. I shake and I shake.

Sheer terror. From a woman who's not supposed to feel such emotions anymore.

Cheap hotel. Too-tight hot-pink tube dress, barely held in place. Jacob smacking me across the face. "Stop fidgeting. For fuck's sake, you look like shit. Is this any way to show some appreciation? Get back into the bathroom and try again."

I do what I'm told, retreating to the dingy bath, where I stare at my reflection in the mirror. My orders are to "look like something worth coming home to." My cheeks are sunken. My eyes bruised. Jacob had left me in the cheap motel days ago, maybe even a week. Nothing to eat. Only tap water to drink. In the beginning I'd expected him to return at any moment. By the end, I was curled up in a ball on the floor, half unconscious from sheer starvation.

Then: Jacob returned. Just like that. No bags of food in his arms. Just this awful dress and instructions that we were going out. Now. Time to clean the fuck up.

I rouse myself long enough to bang on the wobbly faucet. I'm still weak from hunger and definitely not firing on all cylinders, but when it comes to Jacob's demands, failure is not an option.

I shimmy out of the micromini, do my best to rinse my bony arms and sweat-encrusted skin with a wet washcloth. I take a bar of soap to my stringy hair. There's only a hand towel for drying off. Then I pull back on a dress only a hooker would wear.

This time when I exit the bathroom, Jacob grunts his approval. I follow him out the door.

I don't know where we're going, but any-place has gotta be better than this.

Fresh popcorn. I smell it the moment we walk into the dimly lit bar, and my stomach growls. Fortunately, a jukebox blaring out Montgomery Gentry covers the sound. I'm not sure what town we're in. Maybe someplace in Alabama? I'm only allowed out of my box at night, so I miss long stretches of the road. But we're definitely someplace rural. The locals, clad in tight jeans, worn boots, and way more clothing than me, mill around pool tables, trading shots, guzzling beer, tossing back handfuls of free popcorn.

My stomach growls again. I press a hand to it self-consciously, but Jacob just laughs. His eyes are too bright. He's definitely riding high on something, which only makes him more dangerous.

He didn't bother to clean up. His thin hair is a greasy cap on his too-shiny face. The snaps of his western-style shirt strain around the bulge of his swollen stomach, made more obvious by his skinny arms and legs.

Once, I never knew men like Jacob Ness existed. Once, I thought life was fair and being good meant I would always be safe and secure and loved. Then I went on spring break, had a little too much fun slamming back shots at a Florida bar with my college friends. And now this.

Jacob finds us a spot at the bar, gesturing for me to take the seat, then standing behind me. Protectively, some might think. Possessively. He orders two beers. One for him, one for me. A rare treat.

I pick up my beer, sip nervously.

Popcorn. Delivered in a red-and-white-checkered container. My whole body clenches but I don't make a single move; I glance at Jacob, knowing the rules by now.

He nods. I grab the first few kernels. Warm and salty. I want to devour the entire tray, dump the contents in my mouth. I catch myself just in time. If I act out, if I draw attention . . . I force myself to slow down. Couple of kernels here. Couple of kernels there.

Crunch, crunch. Salty goodness. My eyes close . . .

And for a moment, I could be a little girl again, sitting in my mother's kitchen, swinging my legs, waiting for the air popper to complete our after-school snack: "Darwin, what are we gonna do today . . ."

When I open my eyes again, a guy has appeared beside Jacob, and he's staring straight at me.

Jacob nods at the man, almost . . . congenial. He doesn't even protest when the man pulls up the neighboring barstool and orders a beer.

I grab another handful of popcorn. Have to pace myself. I've learned by now that eating too fast after forced deprivation leads to vomiting. Jacob will kill me if I get sick in public. But the man sitting next to us continues to stare at me.

And Jacob continues to let him.

Something bad is about to happen. I know it, even if I don't understand it.

Sip of beer. But only a sip. I'm on guard now, desperately trying to pay attention.

"Girlfriend's a skinny thing," the man says.

Jacob shrugs. "Chicks these days. Think if they're any bigger than a shadow, they're fat."

Single popcorn kernel. Pick up. Chew, chew, chew.

"Come here often?" the man asks.

"Sure. I'm a regular," Jacob says, and both men laugh, though I don't understand the joke.

"I'm on a business trip," the man offers. "Sales. Good excuse, you know, to move around."

"What the wife doesn't know," Jacob suggests.

"Yeah. Sure she doesn't mind?" The guy nods toward me.

My next warning light goes off.

"Nah. My girl's a good girl. She does what she's told." Jacob turns to me abruptly. "Ain't that right, Molly?"

I look away. Don't say a word.

I understand then. At least, have an inkling of the threat. Jacob had tried getting me to pick up random men in bars before; testing the level of my obedience. Each time, I'd managed to avoid the situation. Because I understood, somewhere deep inside of me, that while Jacob might make a game of forcing me on someone else, he'd still never take me back. And not because he's big, bad Jacob Ness. But because he's a man. And no man wants used goods.

The part I still don't understand — before, the men had been strangers, maybe a cowboy caught eyeing me from across the room. Whereas this man, he'd come straight over. And the way Jacob is turned toward him, engaging with him . . . It's almost like they'd been expecting each other.

What has Jacob done? What exactly has he promised this not-quite-stranger?

I shake out the last of the popcorn, then grab my beer. No more sipping. Chug, chug, chug. I'm desperate now. Thinking fast, but maybe not fast enough.

The man buys a second round for us. Jacob doesn't protest, though he's eyeing me suspiciously.

Nachos. A plate goes by, heaped high with melted cheese and sour cream. I follow it with huge eyes, never saying a word. The stranger man immediately orders us a platter. Jacob jabs my thigh. I gaze up at him innocently and swallow the last of my second beer.

Then we're off to the races. Food. Drink. Jacob and the man talking in low voices about things I can't hear and don't care about. And maybe Jacob is suspicious, but he's a fast-food addict himself and the nachos, followed shortly by sliders, then chicken wings — all at our newfound companion's expense — are too good for him to pass up.

Except the new man doesn't act that new. And Jacob, who never interacts with anyone, is talking, laughing, slapping the man on the back.

Eat. Drink. Faster, faster, faster. Not much time left. Whatever is going to happen is going to happen soon. The man is staring at me now, his eyes nearly as bright as Jacob's.

The bartender flashes the lights. Closing time. Our new friend pulls out his wallet. Throws down a hundred as casually as a ten. Jacob's smirk grows.

No more beer, nachos, wings, popcorn. My stomach hurts. My legs are wobbly. Jacob grabs my arm, dragging me forcibly off the barstool and toward the door, the man falling in step behind us.

Come on, come on, come on.

I can feel a pale sheen of sweat on my brow. I hesitate, trying to drag my heels even though I know better. Jacob digs his fingers into my bony arm, giving me a stare that promises further pain if I don't knock it off. Right now.

Foxes. Gators. Florida beaches. So far from

home. The way Jacob is the evilest person I've ever met. The way all men are the same.

Jacob yanks me into the parking lot, close to a vehicle that isn't his own. The night wind hits my bare arms, my sweaty brow. Then, finally, thankfully, what I've been planning on, waiting for . . .

I turn, and in a move of sheer beauty, projectile vomit all over Jacob's newfound friend.

"Jesus Christ!" The man leaps back.

It doesn't save him. Seven days of starvation followed by three hours of binge eating. I lurch forward and hit him again, a thick stream of barely digested food.

Crowds gather. People gasp. I barely notice, falling to my hands and knees, dry heaving onto the warm asphalt. My stomach cramps painfully, sour bile gathering in the back of my throat. I'll pay for this. Oh, in a million different ways.

But right now, the man's eyes widen with disgust. Then he turns and hastily walks away . . .

Jacob has his games. But I have my rebellion. He might always win in the end. But I'm not completely broken yet.

"All right, all right," Jacob announces to the milling people. "Girl never could hold her beer. Come on, now, not the first time any of you have seen someone puke outside a bar. Move along."

He grips my arm. I'm shaking uncontrollably, too weak to even stand.

But the not-quite-stranger is gone. The immediate threat is over.

Which leaves me with just Jacob.

"You did that on purpose!" he growls low in my ear.

"I had to. The thought of leaving you . . . Please. You've been gone for a week. I just want to be with you. Only you."

He narrows his eyes, studies me hard.

"Bitch," he says, but there's no heat left in his voice.

He pulls me to standing. I lean against him heavily. After a moment, his arm goes around me.

And for one more night, I survive.

Six years later, Cambridge, Mass. I'm still standing in the kitchen of my apartment. Images of the murdered husband's face appear, disappear, reappear, on the TV across the room. Followed by snapshots of his wife, the outside of their home, miles of yellow crime scene tape. I'm shaking. As hard as I shook that night, so long ago.

Now, I fist my hand and force myself to focus. Deep breath in, deep breath out.

Jacob is gone. Jacob is dead. Jacob can never hurt me again.

The man on TV, Conrad Carter, I never saw him after that night. And now he's dead, too. More power to his wife.

Except that so many thoughts hit me at once, I have to grab a chair for support.

It takes me a bit, but I finally get my legs to move. I retrieve my cell from the coffee table. I make a single call.

"Samuel, it's me. You know how I said I'd tell you about my time with Jacob once and only once, and then I'd never speak of it again? I lied."

CHAPTER 4
EVIE

It's after midnight when they take me to the police headquarters. I have a brief impression of a monstrous glass building; I think I've seen pictures of it on TV. The officer leads me through a vast lobby, then through a warren of hallways. First stop, fingerprints. I was never printed the first time. Ironically enough, it's my job as a schoolteacher that finally put me in the system. I had to have a background check to chaperone field trips, after-school activities. I'd been nervous then. What if they ran my prints and the previous incident — *"nothing but an unfortunate accident,"* my mother whispers — popped up for all to see? You'll be fine, Conrad had kept telling me. You were just a kid; no charges were even filed.

In the end, that's what saved me — no charges were filed, meaning I had no criminal record, versus a sealed juvie record,

54

which could come back to haunt a person later.

After scanning each fingertip into the digital machine, the uniformed officer — Bob, someone calls him — leads me to a clinical-looking room where a woman in a lab coat swabs both my hands with some kind of substance, then uses a metal file to remove scrapings from beneath my nails. "I'm going to require her clothing," she informs the officer, who nods as if this is no surprise.

If they're taking my clothes, what does that leave me with? But no one bothers to tell me, and I can't bring myself to ask.

I'm tired. The shock, adrenaline, something wearing off. Mostly, I feel like a pregnant woman, up way past her bedtime and deeply self-conscious that it's not just me the police are arresting, but my unborn child.

I haven't even met my baby yet, and I'm already filled with so many regrets.

Upstairs. A new floor with miles of blue carpet. I don't get a chance to look around. My escort leads me straight to a small room with two chairs, one table, and a mirrored wall. Interrogation, I realize, and can't help but think it looks much nicer than the rooms you see on TV. Then Officer Bob dumps me in the chair, releases my left wrist from the handcuff, only to attach the bracelet to a ring on the table, and any positive impressions I have of the room are over.

Officer Bob exits. At least I still have my clothes, I think, then move my free hand to rest on my rounded belly. As if that can protect my baby from what will happen next.

The door opens. An older gentleman with thinning brown hair walks in. He's wearing a brown-and-gold-flecked sports jacket over a light-blue shirt. Pleated khakis; the kind that went out of fashion a decade ago, and yet are still favored by people of a certain age. He has a nice face. Serious, but not harsh. Never the bad cop, I think, more like the stern father figure.

I'm grateful I don't recognize him. Then I wonder if they picked him because, given my history, stern father figure is exactly the right approach to take.

"Evelyn Carter?" he asks. "I'm Detective Phil LeBlanc."

I have this ridiculous impulse to wave. Years of social training kicking in. I constrain myself to a short nod.

"I understand you're pregnant?" he says.

I nod again.

"Can I get you anything? A glass of water?

Ginger ale? My wife always loved ginger ale."

Definitely the concerned father. I smile at him. I can't help myself. He doesn't understand. They never understood. And now . . . My baby. My poor unborn child.

"I would like my phone call," I say. "And I'm not saying another word until I get it."

There are two people I could call. Option A is the most obvious and the call I can't bring myself to make. Option B will inform Option A of the situation anyway, so it hardly matters. Plus, Option B was my father's best friend. He has plenty of reasons to doubt me, which is why I trust him more.

He doesn't seem to be surprised to receive my call in the middle of the night. Because of his job, or because of how well he knows me? I walk him through the evening's events, at least the bare bones. Conrad shot dead. Me in police custody.

"Have they arrested you?" Dick Delaney, one of Boston's top criminal defense attorneys, asks me over the phone.

"I think so." The events of recent months, let alone the past few hours, are starting to weigh heavily on me, dragging me down till everything has taken on a surreal quality. They never handcuffed me the first time.

Never put me in a squad car, never drove me to the station for fingerprinting and processing and interrogation. I don't understand these steps. It's like watching an old movie, except the story line has been changed.

I don't know how this story ends.

"Where are you?" Mr. Delaney asks.

"Police headquarters."

"What did you tell them?"

"Nothing."

"Keep it that way. They're at the house now, working the crime scene?"

I nod into the phone, then remember I have to speak. "Yes. I've been fingerprinted. And my hands were swabbed. Blood. I had blood on my hands."

"Probably testing for blood and GSR — gunshot residue," Mr. Delaney mutters, but he seems to be talking more to himself than to me. "How are you holding up?"

"I'm tired."

"Are you in pain, do you require medical assistance? How is the baby?"

"I'm okay."

"You could be in shock. Perhaps you require medical observation."

"I'm okay," I say again.

Maybe that's not the right answer. Maybe he's trying to tell me something and I'm not getting it, because he falls quiet for a full minute or two.

"Evie — you're going to have to spend at least one night in jail."

I don't know how to process that. Again, the story line is all wrong. I know shootings. I know blood and horror and loss.

The aftermath is not supposed to go like this.

"It's the middle of the night," Mr. Delaney is saying. "Nothing can happen till tomorrow, when the charges against you are formally presented in court. At that time, there'll be an arraignment. I'll be there to represent you, and hopefully get you released on bail. But again, none of this can happen before tomorrow."

"They want my clothes," I hear myself say. "Can they take my clothes?"

"Yes. They're going to try to question you, Evie. Your job is to say nothing. Next, you will be taken to the county jail for overnight admittance. Given the severity of the charge, you'll be held in isolation. But you'll be formally processed. Your personal possessions will be taken and inventoried."

I don't have any. It occurs to me for the first time. I'd taken off my coat, set down my purse. I don't have my cell phone. Not even my wallet. I feel a rising bubble of hysteria.

"They'll take your clothes as evidence," Mr. Delaney continues, "and hand them over to a waiting officer."

My escort, Officer Bob.

"In return, you'll get an orange jumpsuit."

I don't speak, but I feel a giggle rising again in the back of my throat. A prison jumpsuit. Like *Orange Is the New Black.* I'll be the new girl. Fresh meat. Until I win them over with my story of woe. And get a cool new lesbian roommate. Or maybe I'll be the muscle, taking some delicate, fragile thing under my wing. After all, two shootings to my credit. I can get double teardrop tattoos on my cheek, swagger across the prison yard with my soon-to-be enormously pregnant belly. Mess with that, bitches.

I'm not doing well. I'm going to start laughing. And once I do, I'll never stop.

My poor baby, my poor, poor baby.

Conrad.

Mr. Delaney promises to meet me at the courthouse. He reminds me to say nothing. He tells me I have medical rights, as well as the right to speak to my attorney at any time. "You're going to get through this," he says gently. "Hang tough. Be smart."

Like last time?

When the call ends, the older detective

returns. He gives me a disappointed look. I've ruined his interrogation, proven that I'm no fun at all.

Then Officer Bob returns, unshackles me from the table, and off we go. Suffolk County Jail.

I sit in the back of the patrol car, my eyes drifting shut with exhaustion. Conrad, face breaking into a smile as he sees me for the first time. Conrad, fingers shaking uncontrollably as he tries to slip the simple gold wedding band on my finger at the courthouse. Conrad, the look on his face as we both stare wide-eyed at the pregnancy stick.

Conrad, collapsed in his desk chair, half his head sprayed across the wall behind him.

A thousand moments. A hundred memories. Some that felt completely right. Some that I know by now were totally wrong. And yet . . .

I loved you, I think, and my hand curls once more around my belly. Not just *my* baby — *our* baby. The best of both of us, at least that's what all parents hope for.

Even my parents, once upon a time.

The patrol car stops, slows, turns, comes to a halt. Outside the windows, I can see nothing but the harsh glare of too many lights. The kind designed to rob even the purest soul of all secrets.

South Bay House of Correction.
This is it.

I grew up in a beautiful home in Cambridge. A historic Colonial with dark-stained wood trim, a gorgeous curved bannister, and bull's-eye molding around a matching set of front bay windows. My mother is partial to richly colored oriental rugs, silk-covered wingback chairs, and decorative tables that hold cut-crystal decanters and silver serving trays.

Do not touch was one of the first phrases I ever learned. Followed shortly by: *No running in the house. Comb your hair. Chew with your mouth closed. Sit straighter. Stand taller.*

Do not embarrass your father was never actually said, but always implied.

My father wasn't merely a Harvard professor. By the time I was born, he was already considered one of the greatest mathematical minds of his generation. Bachelor's in psychology, master's in computer science, doctorate in statistics. He held honorary degrees from universities all around the world and his office was wallpapered in various awards. We didn't just have dinners at our house; we had standing Friday night poker games where my father and his fellow geniuses traded discourses on chaos theory, data mining, and string theory, all while vying to see who could count cards.

To the best of my memory, very few women ever attended these nights. There were female mathematicians, of course, as well as physicists, computer scientists, engineers, but not that many. Or maybe my mother didn't go out of her way to include their company. Accomplished, brilliant females rubbing shoulders with her husband . . . ? I don't know. For most of this, I was just a kid.

I understood my father was a great man. I assumed, judging by the quality of our home and the size of my mother's pearl necklace, that we led a life that others envied. Certainly, I spent my days in an elite boarding school where my teachers were suitably impressed by my own intelligence, while having to break the news to my father that I was no mathematical prodigy. Gifted, definitely. I had a fighting chance at understanding a fraction of the conversations I greedily eavesdropped on every Friday night. But my father, his mind, his intellect . . . he was a mystery to me till the bitter end.

He loved me. He took pride in my straight-A schoolwork. And he would sit for hours in the front room, his eyes closed as I ran through Bach, Mozart, Beethoven. He said when I played the piano, he could hear the math pouring out. There is a high degree of correlation between math and music. So maybe for me, math wasn't the classroom. Math was the piano, and the notes, scales, tones I found without even trying, and played obsessively day after day.

My father told me I was brilliant.

Back in those days, sitting at the baby grand in the front parlor, I believed him.

I had my own wing, an only child in a home built for when families had eight kids and three servants. My suite of rooms occupied the front of the second floor, with a pillow-covered seat built into the bank of windows that overlooked the street. I had lavender-painted walls and a wrought-iron canopy bed covered in yards of gauzy fabric. A private bath, of course, not to mention a smaller room, perhaps originally intended as a nursery, that had been converted to a walk-in closet with built-in mirror and makeup table. The adjoining sitting room, however, was my favorite. Bookshelves lined all four walls, filled with everything from Nancy Drew to musical compositions to historical fiction. I loved to read about faraway people living in distant times. Their fathers were never world-renowned geniuses. In fact, in most of these novels, both parents were dead — but no worries; the plucky heroine would make it on her own.

I had more than enough space for slumber parties and playdates. But somehow, other kids didn't want to hang out with a professor's daughter. Especially one more comfortable playing the piano for hours at a time than engaging in common discourse. Fashion, gossip, popular music? I felt like my father in those moments. I wished someone would break out some poker chips and tee off a discussion of the ten most useful mathematical equations (my father loved Euler's identity, but I spent plenty of Friday nights listening to passionate arguments for all ten entries). Sometimes, my mother would set up little mother-and-daughter teas, where she and her cohort-in-crime would cast glances in the direction of me and my obviously unhappy assigned companion, waiting for us to magically hit it off.

What I learned from those teas was that other mothers feared my mom, and that no one really wanted to be friends with a girl as strange as me.

My mother was big on appearances, meaning my bedsheets were of only the finest Egyptian cotton. When not in private school plaid, I could wear Laura Ashley, Laura

Ashley, or Laura Ashley. My mother considered me too young for my own pearls, but I was allowed to wear a tasteful heart-shaped silver-and-diamond pendant my father gave me on my thirteenth birthday.

To judge by the look on his face when I opened the Tiffany box, my mother had done the actual picking out of the pendant, but I still hugged my father gratefully, his beard tickling my cheek. And he still hugged me back enthusiastically. Geniuses are geniuses, you know. You can't expect them to waste their brilliance on such trivial matters as a daughter's birthday gift. That's what wives are for, my mother would tell you.

If everything had stayed on track, I would have attended Radcliffe, married some up-and-coming genius, maybe one of my father's own research students, and gotten a string of pearls of my own to wear in a neighboring Cambridge home, where I would teach piano, or something equally respectable.

If everything had stayed on track.

"Squat," the nurse says now.

I am completely naked. My clothes stripped off and taken away as promised, even my underwear. I stand alone with a female nurse, who — given my rounded

66

belly, or maybe the lack of needle tracks on my arms — is doing her best to appear kind.

I still have that surreal feeling. This can't be me; this can't be my life. It's three A.M. I should be home. With Conrad.

I don't know what to do with my hands. Cover my belly, as I've been doing for months now? Or my bare breasts? My exposed pubis? I settle on my stomach. The rest of me already feels too long gone.

"Nothing but an unfortunate accident . . ."

She will come. She will come for me next. Then, the real adventure will begin.

"Honey," the nurse says, snapping the glove on her right hand. "The sooner you do this, the sooner both of us get on with our lives."

I nod. I squat. She inspects. Next order. I bend over, best that I can. She inspects.

I don't cry. I've never been good at tears. My mom, she breaks into hysterics at the drop of a hat. Sixteen years ago, she did enough crying for the both of us. But me — under stress, loss, extreme pain?

I never cry.

I just . . . hollow out. A pit of anguish.

I feel it now, for my baby. Who will never grow up in an impressive Colonial in elite Cambridge, or even a well-intentioned fixer-upper in Winthrop.

Then I take it back. Because if I'm found guilty of shooting Conrad, if I go to jail this time, when my baby is born, they will take him or her from me. And there's only one person they'd give my baby to.

I start shivering then, and I just can't stop.

The nurse thinks I'm cold. Given my unclothed state, I don't blame her. She produces the promised orange jumpsuit, along with voluminous panties. She steps back a few feet as I wrestle the clothing on. The underwear are just plain wrong, like granny panties met men's boxers and tried to mate. The orange jumpsuit is also overly large, and scratchy from harsh chemicals. I can get it over my belly, but it swims around my upper body. The shoulders land somewhere around my ears. The leg length is intended for someone twice my height. The nurse takes pity on me and helps roll up the hems before I trip and fall.

We've already run through all my vitals. Physical description, date of birth, identifying tattoos. Foreplay before this main event.

Now it's done. I'm in the system. Not a prisoner, yet, I'm told, as I'm in jail, which is considered temporary. It all depends on how good my attorney, Dick Delaney, is and what happens at the courthouse a mere few hours from now.

"You'll be in your own cell," the nurse tells me now, throwing away her gloves, picking up her clipboard. "How do you feel?"

She nods toward my rounded belly.

"Tired."

She hesitates. "You're entitled to a medical hold. If you have any concerns about your health, the baby's health."

I have a sense of déjà vu. Mr. Delaney asked me all these questions. I didn't get it then. I don't get it now.

"Your pulse rate is fine," the nurse says now, looking straight at me. "Surprisingly strong, all things considered."

I don't have tears. Just an endless void of anguish.

"Your vitals are stable. In my honest opinion, I would stick to your own cell. But of course, you have rights . . ."

"What happens in medical?" I ask finally.

"The infirmary is a different ward. More like . . . a hospital. You'd get your own room there, as well as access to medical staff, twenty-four seven. Are you depressed?" she asks abruptly.

"I'm tired," I say again.

"If you have concerns, any thoughts of harming yourself, your baby . . ."

"I would never do anything to hurt my child!"

She nods. "This place, it's loud. The pipes, the walls, the inmates in the wards above you. You're going to hear noise, all night long."

I smile; there's not much of night left.

"But the infirmary . . . let's just say, it's its own special kind of shrill. It's not populated by inmates with physical injuries as much as by prisoners with mental ones. The screazies, the other inmates call them — screaming crazies. But again, if you have any concerns for your or the baby's well-being . . ."

I get it now. They all think I'm going to kill myself. Or the baby. Mr. Delaney, this nurse, they don't want me on their conscience. Even if that means assigning me to a night surrounded by frothing lunatics.

"I'm okay," I say again.

That's it. A female CO reappears, leads me out of the medical exam room. I have a little baggie of toiletries; a clear toothbrush the size of a pinky; a small, clear deodorant; clear shampoo; and white toothpaste. On my feet, I wear the world's ugliest pair of flat white sneakers, but at least they're comfortable. Around my wrists, the CO has once again fastened the restraints.

The hall is wide and cold. Cinder block. Thick, but the nurse is right; I already hear the towering prison moaning and groaning around us. Thudding pipes, booming mechanicals, distant murmurs of hundreds, if not thousands, of caged humans, trying to get through another night.

We arrive at a cell. Cream-painted cinderblock walls. A molded stainless steel toilet, no seat. Thin foam mattress with single beige blanket.

I say nothing. Walk inside. Hold out my wrists. The female CO removes the cuffs.

She closes and locks the heavy metal door, with its cutout window so they can monitor me at all times.

I sink onto the hard platform bed. I pull up my legs with my tennis shoes still on. Then I close my eyes and wish it all away.

My father. Conrad. Beautiful Cambridge. Hard-fought Winthrop. Choices made. Cycles repeated. Around and around and around.

And now, growing determinedly in my own womb, the next generation of tragedy.

I need to do better. I have to do better.

Yet, locked inside jail, waiting to be formally charged with murder . . .

I don't have any answers. Just distant notes from piano pieces I haven't played in at least ten years.

Once upon a time, there was a little girl in

a big house who loved her father so much she was sure he would never leave her.

But he did.

And now this.

I close my eyes and, curled around my baby, will myself to sleep.

CHAPTER 5
D.D.

Flora Dane was driving D.D. nuts. Which was why, D.D. thought for the umpteenth time, a smart detective should never recruit a wild-card vigilante to be her CI. Because D.D. had to follow rules and procedures, whereas Flora had absolutely no interest.

"You're saying you recognize the victim, Conrad Carter. You spotted him in the company of Jacob Ness during the time of your captivity. Furthermore, you believe they might have had some sort of relationship. At least knew each other."

"I already told you that!" Flora was agitated. Pacing the sidewalk, rubbing her arms. D.D. had never seen the woman so rattled before. All the more reason to get her on the record.

"I need you to come down to the station and make a formal statement."

"No!"

"Flora —"

"I will talk! But we both know it won't be to you."

Which was the other issue. Flora might have been a Boston college student at the time of her kidnapping, but she'd been on spring break in Florida when Jacob snatched her. Meaning, from the first taunting post-card Jacob had mailed from a small town in the South to Flora's mother in Maine, Flora's abduction had fallen under FBI jurisdiction.

The feds had done right by her. Eventually identifying Jacob as a long-haul trucker. Tracking his rig to a cheap motel. Storming the room with a dozen SWAT team officers and enough bullets and stun grenades to take out a small village. Jacob hadn't survived the raid; Flora had.

To the best of D.D.'s knowledge, it had been at the hospital, still waiting for her mother to fly down, that Flora had given her official statement. She'd made a deal: She'd speak of her kidnapping one time to one person. Then she'd delivered her story, word by painful word, to FBI victim specialist Dr. Samuel Keynes.

The rumor was that Keynes — who had a long history of interviewing international kidnapping victims — had barely made it to the bathroom before vomiting.

Since that day, Keynes and Flora had maintained a relationship that was beyond D.D.'s understanding. She doubted it fell strictly within the guidelines of the FBI's Office for Victim Assistance. Not that it was romantic at all — in fact, last D.D. had heard, the famously reserved psychologist had finally expressed his true feelings for Flora's mom, Rosa, who was an organic-farming, homemade-muffin-baking, free-spirited yogi. What they actually talked about, D.D. had no idea, but having person-ally seen the spark between them . . .

At least something good had come from Flora and her family's ordeal.

The problem remained; Keynes was Flora's confessor of choice. But he also worked for the FBI. Meaning, the moment Flora started talking to him about seeing D.D.'s murder victim in the company of Jacob Ness, D.D. now had the FBI involved in her case. Or worse, taking it away.

"How many times did you see Conrad?" D.D. tried now. If Flora wouldn't agree to a formal statement, D.D. would settle for an informal one.

"Just once. At a bar."

"How long ago?"

"I don't know. I'd been with Jacob for a

while. Weather was cooler." Flora rubbed her arms. "So maybe it was winter in the South."

D.D. nodded, working some mental arithmetic. Winter of Flora's abduction would mean they were looking back basically seven years. Detective Manley had reported that Conrad had traveled for his job, which could mean he'd had a good cover for many activities.

"What about the wife?" D.D. tried now. "Evelyn Carter look familiar to you?"

"She wasn't there," Flora said. She stopped pacing abruptly. "Was she married to Conrad then? What do you know of their lives?"

"I don't. Not yet."

"She shot him, that seems to signify less than happiness. Could she have been abused? Maybe a victim herself? The news said she was pregnant!"

Flora's voice had grown strident.

"I think we're getting ahead of ourselves. Investigations are a series of steps, and we have many left to take. For the record, the neighbors describe them as a normal, happy couple."

Flora snorted. "Neighbors don't know shit."

D.D. shrugged philosophically. On that,

they could agree.

"Do you know what bar you were in? Where Jacob met Conrad?" D.D. tried to refocus her CI.

"I don't . . . Jacob had left me for days." Flora's voice dropped. "I was very, very hungry but I didn't dare leave because Jacob would track me down and kill me. That's what he told me every time he left, and I believed him."

"Okay." D.D. made her voice equally soft. This was the most she'd ever heard Flora say about Jacob. There were questions she'd love to ask, of course, but Flora had never deviated in her onetime, one-telling policy. Mostly, D.D. was left to admire the monster's handiwork, because if Jacob had been the worst of the worst, then the woman who'd survived him was the toughest of the toughest. Whether he'd known it or not, Jacob had served as a particular kind of forge. And the Flora who'd emerged four hundred and seventy-two days later was solid steel.

The detective in D.D. admired the woman's resilience. The mother in her was saddened by the loss.

"You were in the South," D.D. continued now. "Jacob's trucking route?"

"Yes."

77

"You said he left. You were at a motel."

"Yes."

"Can you think of the name? Letterhead on the stationery in the room?"

"Jacob didn't stay in places that had stationery."

"Okay, flashing neon sign? Work with me here."

"Motel . . . Motel Upland." Flora frowned. "I think. Maybe."

"Motel Upland." D.D. nodded. "Sounds regional. We can work with that."

Flora rubbed her arms and resumed pacing.

D.D. hesitated. In for a penny, in for a pound, she decided. "Flora, I don't think Evelyn was Conrad's victim. She's from around here, has family in Cambridge."

"You know her?"

"Let's just say, I'm not terribly surprised to hear about what happened. When I last spoke to her, it was right after she 'accidentally' shot her father."

Flora's head popped up. D.D. had the woman's full attention now, including a hard gray stare designed to force someone to hand over all their valuables or confess all their sins. D.D. finally got it then — Flora's real fear. That she hadn't talked enough about Jacob. That with her onetime, one-tell policy, she may have left some other victim behind.

As someone who now dedicated her life to helping other survivors, such a thing would devastate her.

"Flora. I think you should come with me. I think there's something you should see."

"What? Where?"

"Come with me to the courthouse. Evelyn Carter is due to be arraigned this morning. I think you should see her in person. I think you should know exactly who it is you're so concerned about."

Courthouses were their own special kind of madness. D.D. tried to avoid them as much as possible, though that was difficult in her line of work. Actual trials weren't so bad. They involved a set number of players in a predetermined room — if anything, they were much more boring than anything seen on TV.

The morning arraignment rush, however, was a sea of harried lawyers and wide-eyed — or completely hungover — defendants. The accused piled up, while overworked public defenders tried to identify which handcuffed prisoner would be their date for the party. The front steps were littered with bored reporters waiting for something interesting to happen, small groups of briefcase-wielding lawyers playing let's make a deal, and neck-craning loved ones trying to catch a glimpse of the spouse, kid, friend, whatever, who'd spent the night in the slammer and might not be coming home again.

Inside was worse. D.D. had to shoulder her way through the throngs, reading the signs to determine the proper room. Flora stalked alongside her, head up, gray stare lasering a path forward. At one point, a tattooed and muscle-bound gangbanger paused beside his escorting officer long enough to give Flora a second glance.

Two alphas, sizing each other up? D.D. wondered. Predator to predator? She was never sure with Flora, but half a heartbeat later, the big guy looked away first.

"You like that," D.D. murmured, having finally spotted Phil outside the assigned courtroom.

"Yes," Flora said, no explanation necessary.

"Still working our way through the docket," Phil said by way of greeting. He was the lead detective on the case, which explained why he was in the courthouse. D.D. could already tell from the look on his face that he was exasperated by her presence. Strictly speaking, supervising sergeants didn't need to personally visit crime scenes or arraignment hearings. And having Flora with her hardly helped matters. Both of D.D.'s former squad mates, Phil and Neil, had opinions about the vigilante, much of it having to do with how they'd all first met: Flora, naked, hands bound in front of her, standing over the charred remains of a would-be rapist; Phil and Neil arriving to arrest . . . someone . . . in the case.

Phil, who considered himself the voice of reason to D.D.'s more aggressive ways, hadn't been thrilled when she'd announced she'd recruited Flora to be her new confidential informant. Clearly, his opinion on the matter hadn't changed.

"Flora recognized the victim," D.D. announced bluntly, in order to cut off Phil's arguments at the pass. "She met Conrad Carter at a bar, when she was with Jacob."

Her strategy worked. Phil went from fatherly disapproval to immediate investigative interest.

Flora didn't like Phil any more than Phil liked her. "That's as much as I'm saying on the subject," she said.

Phil returned to fatherly disapproval, for both Flora and D.D.

"I want her to see Evelyn," D.D. said. "Maybe that will jog something. Or help her know what exactly we're dealing with here."

Phil accepted that. "Her mom's here," he said.

"But of course."

"Real lawyer, too. No public defender. Criminal defense attorney Dick Delaney."

"Great." D.D. rolled her eyes. She'd been involved in cases represented by the silver-haired lawyer before. He was very good.

Phil opened the door. They were hit first by a heat wave of humanity, then by the harsh pounding of the judge's gavel as she sought to keep some semblance of order in what was by definition an assembly line of procedures. Already two court officers were leading a young woman, gaunt, stringy hair, wild eyes, from the room, as a door opened to the side and two more officers appeared.

No prison clothes this time. Instead, Evie Carter appeared, pale, slightly trembly, clad in black slacks and a demure cream-colored button-up cardigan that strained slightly over her rounded belly. The Evie D.D. had met sixteen years ago had been a scared teenager. The woman she'd become still had the same dirty-blond hair, but cut short, in a fringed style that emphasized her large brown eyes. The clothes, D.D. was already guessing, had been supplied by Evie's mother, Joyce, who sat in the front row, every frosted blond hair in place as she gazed at her only child.

Evie, D.D. noticed, didn't look at her mother at all, but took her place beside her lawyer at the defense's table. Her hair was mussed, her eyes bruised. For all the dress-up clothes, nothing could change the fact she'd spent the night in the slammer.

"That's her?" Flora whispered in D.D's ear. "She doesn't look anything like I expected."

"Her mother dressed her," D.D. whispered back.

Flora nodded, as if that explained everything.

"Your Honor," the Suffolk County ADA Danielle Fitzpatrick began. "The people are pursuing charges of murder one against the accused, Evelyn Carter, in the shooting death of her husband. We request she be held without bail, given the severity of the charges."

"Your Honor!" Delaney was already on his feet. "That charge is ludicrous. The people lack sufficient evidence for a charge of premeditated murder, let alone given the delicate state of my client —"

"The 'delicate client,' " Fitzpatrick intoned drolly, "shot her husband three times. As for evidence, the police found her at the scene, still holding the murder weapon. In addition, her hands tested positive for GSR as well as human blood. We are confident in our case, Your Honor, and that's without delving into Mrs. Carter's previous history —"

"Objection! Inadmissible and not even relevant. Continue to make such underhanded references" — Delaney glared at Fitzpatrick — "and I'll be forced to demand a change of venue given your deliberate contamination of the jury pool."

The judge banged her gavel again. "Sustained, though I'm not sure what underhanded references you two are bickering about. Feels to me we have enough to discuss with the case at hand."

Flora looked askance at D.D., who murmured in the woman's ears, "Evie shot and killed her father when she was sixteen. It was ruled accidental at the time and no charges were ever filed — I should know, as I was the investigating detective. Delaney's right: Given that, the incident is inadmissible. But Fitzpatrick isn't playing to the judge. She's playing to the press, who I can guarantee you are right now scrambling to figure out what about 'Mrs. Carter's previous history' is worth such a fuss."

"Your Honor," Delaney was saying. "My client does not deny being at the scene of the crime, nor even holding the murder weapon. In fact, she'll even concede she fired the gun. What ADA Fitzpatrick has failed to mention is the slight problem with the police's timeline of events."

The judge turned, regarding ADA Fitzpatrick with interest, while on the other side of D.D., Phil stiffened. D.D. got it a second later. "Oh shit."

"Your Honor," Fitzpatrick began, but Delaney was already on a roll.

"Eight minutes, Your Honor. There's an eight-minute gap between the time neighbors first called in the report of shots fired, and the police arrived on the scene and *also* heard shots fired. That's because there was not one shooting last night but two. The first was the fatal shooting of my client's beloved husband and father of her unborn child. We can prove, in fact, Your Honor, that my client wasn't even home at the time of her husband's death. She arrived minutes later, discovering the dead body. At which point, she did pick up the gun. She fired the weapon.

"She committed the second shooting, Your

Honor. Except her victim was a laptop. Which, let's face it, we've all wanted to shoot at one time or another. So, yes, my client handled the murder weapon and, yes, she had GSR on her hands. But she did not kill her husband. We demand the dismissal of all charges as well as my client's immediate release at this time."

The judge regarded Delaney, then the ADA, whose face was now set in a grim line, then Delaney again. "Well," the judge said, "it sounds like we have plenty to discuss at trial. Given there is sufficient evidence worth presenting, charges are not dismissed. However, I will grant bail. Five hundred thousand, cash bond."

The judge banged her gavel. Evie Carter, who'd never looked left or right, was led from the room. A moment later, every reporter in the place had leapt to his or her feet and was racing to the door.

Phil, D.D., and Flora stood to the side to let the rush pass.

"I'll be damned," D.D. murmured. "She's gonna do it." She glanced at Phil, who nodded his agreement.

"Do what?" Flora demanded.

"For the second time in her life, Evie Carter's gonna get away with murder."

CHAPTER 6
FLORA

My father died when I was young. Traffic accident. So long ago, I no longer really remember him. The images in my mind are less from real memories than from the photos my mother still has up around the house.

Jacob, on the other hand, the man who kidnapped me, raped me, tortured me . . . six years later I still dream about him three or four nights a week.

Samuel Keynes, my victim specialist and a trained psychologist, has done his best to explain it to me over the years. Something about the omnipotence of an abductor. It wasn't just that Jacob snatched me off a beach or locked me in a coffin-sized box for days on end. It was his total control over every facet of my life. I ate when he willed it. I drank when he permitted it. I lived, second by second, day by day, because he decided, for that instant, to allow it.

Stockholm syndrome is when a victim starts to bond with her captor, partially due to the captor's role of complete power over her life. Did I bond with Jacob? The question isn't as simple as I'd like it to be. I hated him. I still hate him. I worked hard every day on my own survival. Counting backward and forward in the long hours I was trapped in a box. Wiggling my toes, moving my limbs as the space would allow. Then, when he finally let me out, I observed, I learned, I adapted.

I don't think I ever truly liked Jacob or saw him as a human being. He was a monster, plain and simple. But he was a monster who held the other end of my leash, so I tried to understand him. Anything to survive another day.

But not all days were awful. Not all moments torturous. After weeks turned into months, Jacob would sometimes show up with little surprises. DVDs of a favorite TV show I'd mentioned. Movies for both of us to watch. There's a lot of time to pass in a long-haul rig. We'd look for license plates from all fifty states, play the alphabet game.

I never believed Jacob was human. But sometimes, like a lot of predators, he did a decent impression of one.

And to this day, he remains the single-most powerful relationship of my life.

Which is why I do my best to talk about him as little as possible. But if I'm being totally honest with myself, I'm not angry to finally be breaking my onetime, one-tell policy. I'm simply relieved to finally get the monster out of my head.

Samuel agrees to meet me after lunch. He's an incredibly busy victim specialist, working for the FBI's Office for Victim Assistance (OVA). A lot of his cases involve high-level executives kidnapped in various far-flung countries. Samuel's job is to help the families understand the process, from the law enforcement steps involved in locating the evildoers to what it might be like when their loved one finally returns home. He also works with the victim him- or herself. Among other things, he generates a "strategy for reentry." It's to help guide both the family and the victim as they transition back to the real world.

Eight years ago, I had no idea such plans existed. Eight years ago, I didn't understand that anyone would need a ten-point plan for reentering the "real world."

Final step of being a victim specialist: supporting the family and victim through what can be a very long legal process, where they will still be asked to make statements, revisit statements, testify in this hearing, testify in that hearing. Part of the FBI's impetus for creating the OVA is the modern trend of high-profile crimes (say, a five-year abduction case) and mass-casualty events (shootings, bombings, arson) that can take years to wind through the legal system.

See, one day, you're a normal person with an ordinary family. Then, in a single instant, you're not. You're a young girl, waking up in a coffin-sized box. You're a mom, back on her farm in Maine, getting a call from her daughter's friends, asking if maybe her daughter has unexpectedly returned home from Florida.

It begins. The onslaught of local, state, federal investigators. The media camped out in the front yard. Maybe even taunting postcards from the predator himself, stoking fears, inflicting fresh terrors.

My mom had to learn how to work national media. Samuel is one of the people who prepared her. What to wear, what to say, the necessity of humanizing her daughter to an unknown kidnapper in order to increase the chances of his keeping me alive. My brother, Darwin, returned home from college to run the social media campaign. Again, with Samuel's guidance. Posting pictures from my childhood. Quotes from friends. I don't know how they did it, to tell you the truth. It's one of those things we still never discuss. I don't describe my time with Jacob because I don't want to hurt them. And they don't mention the four hundred and seventy-two days they lived in constant fear of letting me down or maybe, through their own inexperience, making it easier for my captor to kill me.

Samuel helped them. I know that. And some kind of relationship was forged between him and my mother. They left it alone for years. Samuel's doing, my guess, given the man has the emotional core of carved granite.

But my own plan for reentry was much shorter than many. Dead Jacob meant no trial. Samuel checked up on me for a good year after I came home. Made sure I understood the resources available to me, prodded me to utilize all my "tools," as he liked to put it. He should've cut me off ages ago. I'm six years back to the real world, hundreds of pages, at least, beyond my "strategy for reentry" plan. But Samuel has always taken my calls, and this morning, when I reached him nearly hysterical, he never even batted an eye.

So here we are again. All these years later,

and still about to hash out the same old story.

"Have a seat," Samuel tells me, having met me in the lobby of the FBI building and escorted me upstairs. His office isn't huge, but he does have windows, which I guess makes him a feebie of distinction.

I can't sit. I pace. Five feet this way, three feet that way. He really needs a bigger office.

I left D.D. at the courthouse. She's not happy with me, having wanted to accompany me on this visit. But we both knew that was never going to happen. I might be her CI, but I still live by my rules. Besides, her crankiness is nothing new to me.

"I want to read the file," I say now, cutting straight to the chase. "The FBI must have a file on Jacob. I want to see it. Every word."

"Have a seat," Samuel says again.

"Is he a suspect in other crimes, murders, disappearances? I talked about the things I saw — I told you. But I was only with him for a year. And we both know, there's no way I was his first victim. He'd been busy way before me."

Samuel stands behind his desk. He's known for his wardrobe: Today's perfectly tailored suit appears to be Armani, dark charcoal, and paired with a light gray shirt with white collar and cuffs, topped by a rich blue silk tie. How Samuel pays for his wardrobe, let alone his Lexus, is one of the many things he never discusses. I have my secrets. He has his. It's what I like about him.

Since I won't sit, he joins me, walking with his hands clasped behind him, dark-fringed eyes perfectly serious, black-is-beautiful bald head gleaming beneath the lights. I imagine it takes him serious time to get ready every morning. Trimming his sharply etched goatee. Picking out the suit, the shirt, the tie for the day. Let alone his collection of bespoke shoes and cashmere coats. Samuel is a scarily beautiful man. He uses his wardrobe to further enhance his skills. If others are stupid enough to get distracted by the packaging, that's their problem, not his.

In contrast to my victim specialist, I wear jeans, worn combat boots, and a hoodie, the uniform of disenfranchised urbanites everywhere. When I first returned after my kidnapping, my mother would bring home bright summer dresses, which I never wore. She only recently stopped shopping for me. I wonder now if that's because she finally figured out this is the new me, or if Samuel intervened on my behalf. Either was possible.

"You're sure this Conrad Carter is the same person you saw in a bar?" Samuel asks now, pivoting at the wall, heading back toward me. He goes to one side of the twin chairs; I head for the other.

"Yes."

"And he was there to meet Jacob?"

"Yes! He didn't just sit down next to us; Jacob turned toward him. Jacob, like . . . talked to him. Jacob didn't talk to others."

Samuel tilts his head to the side, regards me steadily, as we reach opposite sides of the tiny office.

"I think they had a deal," I say. "I think Conrad was there for me. Like . . . Jacob offered me to him or something. Some predators do that, you know. Trade around their victims. Or, hell, Jacob sold me for fresh drugs. He'd clearly been on a bender."

Samuel nods. "Had Jacob done such a thing before?"

"No. But sometimes he'd pick out some random guy at a bar, then tell me I had to make the new guy want me."

More nodding. More staring. Samuel has eyes like molten chocolate. When he uses his weapons like this, it always makes me wonder: If Jacob Ness made me, then who made Samuel?

"Some predators talk," I say now. "In chat rooms, on super-encrypted sites, predators have been known to share tips."

Samuel nods.

"So maybe this Conrad guy was another monster. He and Jacob connected somehow — Jacob had his laptop in the rig. And in some chat room, they made arrangements for the evening. Jacob promised me to Conrad. In return for what, I don't know. Drugs, a fresh girl of his own."

"But you didn't go home with Conrad."

"No. I ate and drank till I vomited. That put a damper on the evening."

"You made yourself sick intentionally?"

"Yes."

"Because to directly disobey Jacob would mean punishment, if not death. And to have sex with Conrad would mean punishment, if not death?"

I hadn't thought of it that bluntly, but now I nod.

"You read the situation. You trusted your instincts. You survived."

I sigh, whack the back of the chair. "Samuel! I'm not here for a fucking pep talk. I want the file. You're FBI. The FBI loves files. Give me my fucking file!"

Samuel smiles. It's a devastating look on

him. Good luck to my mom, I think, because no man this beautiful can be easy to manage.

"No," he says.

"What do you mean —"

"No. Big *n*. Little *o*. No. I will not give you the file."

"That's total bullshit —"

"That's FBI policy. You're neither an agent nor a member of law enforcement —"

"I'm a CI, working with the Boston police!"

He continues, "You have no right to the file."

"Bullshit! You wouldn't even have Jacob Ness if it weren't for me. Half that file is my life story. Mine!"

"Technically, we wouldn't have Jacob Ness if it weren't for SSA Kimberly Quincy, who tracked him to the motel where he was holed up with you. She put together the data in the file. She organized the SWAT team that rescued you."

I remember her. Not well. Those first few moments, hours, after the hotel room door blew in . . . I think I stood outside my body. I watched it all as a movie, happening to someone else. When she first approached me, asked me my name, I stared at her blankly. My name? It took a shockingly long time to answer that question.

Later, I read accounts of other survivors going through the same thing. First thing any captor does is take away your identity; Jacob forced me to go by Molly. Meaning SSA Quincy wasn't just asking me a question; she was making me take the first step toward the person I used to be.

And have never been again.

"It's my file," I say, and there's a tone of pleading in my voice. I realize I'm on the edge of tears. Me, who never cries. I don't know what's wrong. Since waking up this morning, since turning on the news, seeing the dead man's face . . . I'm not myself. I don't know who I am. I churn, I churn, I churn.

"Flora," Samuel says at last, "please sit down."

This time, I do. I collapse in one of the leather chairs. They're hard and slippery and I hate them. Yet having sat, I feel like I'll never get up again.

This is why D.D. couldn't come. This is what she still doesn't know.

I'm not always Flora Dane.

Sometimes, even all these years later, I'm still Jacob's victim. Now I put my head in my hands and I don't look at Samuel, because I don't want him to see me like this either. Like I've been undone. Turned inside out. And there's no me again, just this terrified girl, desperate Jacob will return at any second, even more terrified he won't and that will be it. I'll die alone in a coffin-sized box and my mom will never find my body.

The way my mom looked on TV. In clothes that weren't her clothes. But her voice, never breaking. So strong. The silver fox charm resting in the hollow of her throat. A fox to show me, hundreds or thousands of miles away, how much she still loved me.

I'm rocking back and forth. Not making a sound, because I can't afford to wake up Jacob. Except he's dead. Except he's still in my head. Except I want it to be over. Except I want it never to have happened. Except I'll never get over him.

Samuel sits down. I'm aware vaguely of his movements. Most likely, he has his elegant fingers steepled in front of him. His position of patience. If I'm a void of darkness, then he has a well of serenity. I hate him for it. But then, I hate everyone right now. Myself most of all.

"There are other victims," I whisper at last, still not looking up.

"Yes."

"Their information, it's in Jacob's file."

"Yes."

"You don't want me to know. You think I'll use it to torture myself more each night."

"Yes."

"How many?"

He won't answer.

"Could I have made a difference? If I'd escaped earlier? Cooperated more with this Quincy agent?" My voice is nearly breaking.

"No."

"Then let me see the file."

"No." He unsteeples his fingers, leans forward. "Because me knowing you couldn't make a difference isn't the same as you *believing* you couldn't have made a difference."

I know what he means. Survivor's guilt. The toughest affliction for people like me.

"I should've told her about Conrad. SSA Quincy. I should've mentioned some of the times Jacob took me out to bars."

"When did he take you out?"

"Nighttime."

"Day, week, month?"

"I don't know. Winter. Someplace in the South."

"What bars? Do you have a list of names?"

I shake my head.

"And the men. Did you know Conrad Carter's name?"

I frown. "I think . . . maybe he mentioned his first name."

"And the others?"

"I don't . . . I don't know."

"So sometimes Jacob took you to some bars in some places to meet some men. Does that about summarize it?"

I flush. "I could've warned her that he was networking with others. She should check his computer."

"You didn't know that much about predators then, Flora. That kind of criminal psychology you only learned after you came home, as part of your coping mechanism. SSA Quincy, on the other hand, happens to be the daughter of one of the FBI's most legendary profilers. She did check Jacob's computer, I assure you."

"What did she find?"

"I don't know. I'm a victim specialist, not a special agent. Her job was to save you then. My job is to save you now."

"Bite me."

He smiles again, and maybe it's just my imagination, but he appears relieved at my returning rancor.

"Flora, what's the biggest enemy for survivors?"

"The coulda, woulda, shouldas," I mumble. We've had this conversation before.

"Whatever happened, happened. You won. Jacob lost. Don't replay the game."

"You're not going to give me the file."

"No."

"But you also know I won't just walk away."

"It's possible I've met you before."

He smiles again, but now it's somber. He and I both know I'll pursue this. I understand that in his professional opinion, this is a bad choice for me. I understand that in his personal opinion, it's also not good for me. Or, for that matter, for my mother. And yet . . .

"I'm sorry," I say. We both know what I'm apologizing for.

Maybe he thinks I'll personally call up SSA Kimberly Quincy. I haven't spoken to her since that day. I barely remember her face. And yet, saving me was probably one of the highlights of her career, meaning she'll more than likely take my call. Maybe even give me a few kernels of information.

But I've spent a lot of time researching both criminals and law enforcement in the years I've been home. The FBI is a stodgy, conservative, rigid institution, where talking out of school is one of the quickest ways to get fired. Whatever SSA Quincy tells me won't be enough for me, while still potentially damaging for her.

Sergeant Detective D. D. Warren recruited me for a reason. Law enforcement officers have their resources. And I have mine.

I know then who I'm going to call. A man who's been waiting six years for this moment. Sending me countless e-mails, from the sweet, to the bragging, to the nagging, to the just plain whining.

I've always ignored him.

Now, thanks to one shooting, I'm going to make his day.

I don't need the FBI after all.

I just need the right true-crime nerd.

I rise to standing. Samuel can tell from the look on my face that I've made a decision. We know each other that well. He cares about me that much.

"Be careful," he says softly.

"Be there for her," I say, because what I'm going to do next will definitely break my mother's heart.

CHAPTER 7
EVIE

Do you ever feel alone in a crowded room? That when other people laugh, you don't get the joke? That everyone knows something — the secret to life, the true meaning of happiness — that you will forever fail to understand?

That is the way I have always felt.

Even when my father was still alive.

My mother drives me home. She is talking excitedly, completely oblivious to my lack of answers. That's okay. My mother has never required my thoughts or opinions, and most of her questions are rhetorical anyway.

She is nearly sixty years old, I find myself thinking. The age of a grandmother, which makes sense since I'm carrying her first grandchild. She doesn't look a day over fifty. In fact, today I'm willing to bet she looks younger and better than me. The frosted Jane Fonda hair, not a strand out of place.

Her signature pearls around her neck. She wears a spring-green cashmere sweater with camel-colored slacks. She looks like Cambridge. She looks like what, in her mind, she'll always be: a professor's wife.

She paid half a million dollars, cash, for the pleasure of my company. I don't ask where she got the money. Mortgaged the house? Probably couldn't do that in a matter of hours. Maybe she extracted it from a Swiss bank account, remains from my father's life insurance. Hell if I know.

We've stayed in touch over the years. Kind of. She'd tell you whatever coldness exists between us is of my making — assuming she admits there's any strain in our relationship. My mother is one of those women who don't have problems. Or really, problems wouldn't dare to bother her.

She's never moved from her and my father's house. She spent a year in black, *widow's weeds*, I believe they used to be called. She played up the tragedy. Her loving husband, killed in the prime of his genius life. Her poor daughter, who would surely never recover from the horror of the experience.

One year. Exactly one year. Then, like some heroine from a Victorian novel, she put away the black Chanel and returned to her signature spring palette. And took up the very important role of preserving her Husband's Legacy.

My father's legacy? Again, hell if I know. He was active in many projects. Most likely, he had unfinished theorems, theories, research projects, research papers. I'm sure his various assistants rushed to fill the gap. What my mother with her cashmere sweaters and Mikimoto pearls had to add to that, I have no idea.

But she continued to be the hostess with the mostest among the Harvard crowd. I think people came in the beginning, attracted to the drama. Unfortunate accidents such as shotgun blasts don't happen much among the academic set. Best I can tell, however, my mother's charm has prevailed. Sixteen years later, she continues to hold court among the intellectual elite.

Only I keep my distance.

Conrad tried to fix us. In the beginning, when he viewed my relationship with my mom as something salvageable. She's such a lovely woman, he'd tell me time and time again. I'd nod, because my mom is a lovely woman. And charming and smart. Can't argue with any of that.

She's also a fucking wack job.

No one wants to hear that sort of thing,

but my father got it. During her more trying times or dramatic tirades, he'd offer me a conspiratorial wink. I think, however, that her kind of crazy fit him.

My mother isn't mean, at least not intentionally. She's neither violent nor cruel. She's just — herself. She sees what she sees, she knows what she knows, she believes what she believes, and nothing is going to change that. I think for my father, who lived in the land of the abstract, she was refreshingly tangible. You always knew exactly where you stood with her, which was mostly on the outside, looking in. She also worshipped my father's brilliance, took genuine pride in being the wife of one of the greatest minds in mathematics. Last but not least, I heard some noises as a kid that — later, as an adult — I realized meant my parents had a very robust sex life.

Together, they worked.

Meaning our issues aren't that my mother didn't love my father. Or that that I didn't love my father. It's more like each of us, for various reasons, wanted him all to ourself.

My mother pulls into the drive. Same stately Colonial. Historic gray paint, black-painted shutters, white trim. My mother adheres to a strict maintenance schedule — her hair, her face, her home. I believe the exterior paint is on a five-year plan. Many wait seven to ten, she'd tell you. But why have three to five years of a tired-looking home, when it can appear clean and fresh always?

The front porch has a pair of whitewashed Adirondack chairs framing the huge solid black-painted door and leaded side windows. This time of year, the door is draped with a holiday garland of various greens and festive berries. Beside the Adirondacks sit enormous pots of spruce branches, white-frosted twigs, red bows, and pinecones.

Conrad and I hadn't even gotten to a tree yet.

I feel that pang again. Will myself not to think of the stair bannister, the study, the smell. My husband. My father. Too much blood.

The story of my life: too much blood.

Now this.

My mother turns off her Lexus. Turns to me. And smiles.

"I did the best I could without you," she says as we walk into the house. "Of course, since you're here, you can help with the final decisions. When will you find out the sex of the baby? Soon, right? I don't remember exactly when they can tell you that sort of thing, but it seems with today's technology, anything's possible."

I have no idea what she's talking about, only half listening to her prattle as I enter the childhood home I've done my best to avoid for the past sixteen years.

Like many historic homes, the house doesn't have a garage. My mother parks on the driveway; in the winter, some college student will get paid to shovel out and clear her vehicle. As family members, we use the side door off the kitchen. For the full effect, however, my mother prefers to greet even longtime friends at the front door, which better showcases the full impact of the home, including the huge oil portrait of our family. I was four when my mother had it commissioned. Too young to realize no one should ever be painted in a marshmallow-shaped white dress with a giant white bow in her hair. My mother is sitting in a wing-back chair, which was custom-upholstered to be nearly the exact same shade of blue as her eyes. My father stands behind both us, his hand on his wife's shoulder, smiling benevolently at the painter. He is wearing a gray tweed jacket over a dark green sweater-vest. His face is slightly rounded, his sandy beard perfectly trim. He looks kind and powerful and maybe just a tad bemused by the whole production.

When I was little, and my father worked late, I used to climb onto the wingback chair just to touch the portrait and my father's curving smile.

I would whisper, "Love you, Papa," then scramble down before anyone (my mother) caught me.

I don't enter the sitting room, though the front parlor, across the way, is just as bad. The baby grand piano, where I used to sit and play for hours while my father relaxed on the settee across from it. The piles of music still sitting on the closed cover. The faint smell of wax and pipe smoke. In the corner sits the octagonal game table that would be dragged out for poker nights.

I imagine given my mother's busy social life, it's still in use, but I don't like to think about it. In my mind, it's my father's table. My mother's house, but my father's table, my piano.

Then there's the kitchen, where my father died.

My mother reaches for my coat, before remembering I don't have one. She hangs up her own in the hall closet. She is still talking. I nod absently.

We pass my father's study, neither one of us looking. I don't have to peek inside to know the walls remain plastered in awards and honorary degrees, that his favorite pens are still scattered across the desktop, along with a yellow legal pad still scribbled with last-minute thoughts. For the first few years after his death, I could smell him every time I walked in. The whisper of his aftershave. Something expensive my mom imported from England just for him. Sandalwood, a hint of lemon, something else.

It used to be how I knew he'd come home. I'd catch a whiff of his aftershave floating through the house.

I don't catch it now. Sixteen years later, scent fades, no matter how much both my mom and I are loath to let it go.

"Your rooms are ready for you, of course."

I nod again. With the exception of the kitchen, my mother hasn't changed anything about the house. *Anything,* which cracked Conrad up the first time he visited.

"Is this, like, your childhood bed?" he said, bouncing up and down on the obviously girlish comforter. *"I feel like I'm corrupting a minor. Maybe I can be the handsome bad boy, sneaking into your room after your parents have gone to bed. Ever fantasize about the local rebel without a cause?"*

I'd merely smiled. The girl I'd been in high school hadn't attracted the attention of boys, bad or otherwise. I'd been quiet and awkward, then after my father's death, just plain freaky.

Meeting Conrad . . . He'd been the first person to truly see me. To tell me I was sexy and attractive and the girl of his dreams. For him, I'd come alive. For him, I'd started believing in second chances.

I should've known better.

There is moisture on my face. Am I crying? I don't want to cry. Mostly, I'd like to shower.

My mom is headed up the vast, sweeping staircase that dominates the center of the house. I follow her up to the second floor, where, yes, my suite of rooms is exactly as I left it.

"This is where the nursery will be," my mom is saying. "I'm sure you want it closest to you. But I didn't want it so far away from me that I couldn't help out."

For the first time, I register where we are standing. In one of the rooms that used to be part of my suite. I believe it had been a sizable dressing room, designed to hold the dozens of dresses my mom had been so sure I'd one day love wearing.

Now the room is devoid of shelving, makeup trays, and shoe trees. Instead, it has been painted a pastel green and contains a lovely white-painted crib and matching diaper table.

I stare at my mother. I'd only called her with the news of my pregnancy a few weeks ago. And not just because I had to gear myself up to make contact, but because Conrad and I had wanted to keep the news to ourselves for the first three months. Our baby. Our family. Our accomplishment.

We would sleep spooned together at night, his hands splayed on my still-flat belly. Everything looking the same but feeling different.

"How did you . . . when did you?" I don't know what to say.

"I don't love the sage green," my mother announces briskly. "It's the top gender-neutral color, but it feels plain to me. The room itself has no imagination, and that won't do. You have to consider that from the very beginning, Evelyn, your baby may have extraordinary intellect. How best to stimulate and nurture such a mind must be integral to the nursery's design. Are you listening to Bach? Reading to the baby in the womb? Better yet, what about playing the piano? That kind of auditory, and yet also kinetic, experience would be deeply beneficial."

My jaw is still hanging open. I don't know

what to say, what to do. Even by the standards I've come to expect from my mom, this has caught me off guard.

I find myself already wondering — did she pay bail to get me out of jail, or to save the next family genius? And if I'm found guilty of murder and sent off to prison, leaving her alone to raise the baby, would that even bother her?

"I need to shower," I hear myself say.

"Of course. I took the liberty of stocking up on some maternity clothes for you. You'll find them all hanging in the closet."

Again, when? How? Do I want to know?

I find myself studying my mother. The elegantly coiffed hair, the perfectly made-up face. She really does have beautiful blue eyes. Now, she regards me guilelessly, which makes the hairs rise on the backs of my arms, because nothing about my mother is without guile. As if reading my mind:

"Don't worry about your job," she says. "I already phoned your principal and said you wouldn't be back."

"You *quit* my job?"

"What did you think was going to happen? There's going to be a murder trial, you know. You certainly can't be showing up at a public high school every day through that. And by the time this nonsense has all wrapped up, you'll be ready to have your baby. Might as well let the administrators know now."

She makes it sound so matter-of-fact. The job I loved gone, just like that. Indeed, what did I think was going to happen?

"Do you want to know?" I hear myself whisper.

"Know what, dear?"

"Did I kill him. Did I shoot my own husband."

She pats my arm. "No need to stress yourself out, honey. Other people will judge. Other people will wonder. Which is why family is so important. We understand each other. I know everything I need to know about you and Conrad."

"And what is that?"

She regards me directly with those big blue eyes. "That it was an accident, of course. Nothing but an unfortunate accident."

CHAPTER 8
D.D.

"We need to find out everything about this couple, ASAP," D.D. said. She and Phil had returned to BPD headquarters. Phil sat in his office chair, leaning way back, his hands tucked behind his head. D.D. walked small circles. They both had their way of thinking things through.

"Conrad Carter," Phil rattled off now. "Thirty-nine years old. No criminal history. No living family."

"Shit," D.D. said.

"Worked for a major window corporation. Already talked to the head honcho. Guess what?"

"Everyone liked him, no one knew him well," D.D. intoned.

"Exactly. Guy worked out of his home. Had an excellent reputation for sales. Kept up on his quotes, bid sheets, on-site specs. Manager had nothing bad to say about him. Then again, he saw the guy once a month at management meetings. He didn't even know Conrad and his wife were expecting a baby until he heard it on the news."

"Pregnant wife accidentally shoots husband. Three times," D.D. muttered. "Press is going to have a field day with this one."

"So much for open-and-shut," Phil agreed. He yawned.

She glared at him.

He shrugged. "Hey, I was the one working the scene half the night. *Sergeant.*"

"And I was fighting an evil canine for the safety of black boots everywhere. We all have our problems."

Phil smiled. He was used to D.D. in this mood, was probably one of the only detectives who could handle her, which is why she liked him so much. And missed her original investigative squad terribly. Managing sergeant her ass. Who wanted to sit at a desk all day anyway?

"Wait, there's more," Phil said now, in his best TV infomercial voice.

"Should I be sitting down?"

"You'd only pop back up and pace. Before moving to Mass., Conrad lived in . . ." Phil dragged it out.

D.D. closed her eyes, already seeing the answer. "Florida."

"Yep."

"Same state as Jacob Ness and where Jacob kidnapped Flora."

"Yep."

"Jacob and Conrad could've known each other prior to meeting with Flora at the bar."

"It's possible," Phil agreed.

D.D. shook her head. She could not believe this case was spinning so far out of hand. "Okay, what do we know of Conrad? Don't suppose techs have anything back on the computer?"

Phil gave her a droll look.

"Cell phone?" she tried.

"Can't find it."

" 'Can't find it'? What does that mean? Everyone has a cell phone, especially a guy in sales."

"Agreed. Except we don't know where his is."

"You ping it?"

"No, we were waiting for it to walk home on its own." Phil gave her that look again. Sometimes, his mood matched her own. "Of course we pinged it. Nothing, nada. Wherever it is, it's shut off. Carol contacted the mobile carrier. Working on getting their copies of texts, voice messages now."

D.D. studied Phil. "You think Conrad hid his own phone? Turned it off, stuck it somewhere before his wife shot him?"

Phil shook his head. "Guy didn't even get his hands up."

"Someone took it," D.D. said.

"That'd be my guess."

"The wife? She hides his phone, shoots up the computer? What exactly is she trying to hide?"

Phil shrugged. "You heard her lawyer. We have an eight-minute gap. It's possible someone else shot him, that person grabbed the phone, that person ran away."

"Please. One shooter runs away just in time for the wife to return home —"

"Or her arrival is what scared him away —"

"At which point, Evelyn enters her own home, discovers her husband's murdered body and . . . doesn't dial nine-one-one, doesn't run to the neighbors for help, doesn't scream for the police. No, she picks up the same gun and fires a dozen rounds into the laptop?"

"The mysterious-first-shooter theory loses something right around this point," Phil agreed.

"We need to know everything there is to know about this couple," D.D. repeated.

Phil shrugged, yawned again. He probably had been up all night. Welcome to homicide.

"Old school," D.D. announced. "If we can't trace Conrad through electronics, then what about personal files, credit card receipts, banking info?"

"Neil's digging through it now," Phil reported. The youngest member of their original three-person squad, Neil had joined the force after serving years as an EMT. He used to be the one in charge of autopsies, but lately he'd been expanding his wings. With D.D.'s promotion out of the unit, and Carol Manley's entry into the squad, he was also no longer the rookie, which seemed to suit him.

"Nothing extravagant has jumped out yet, Neil said. Lotta charges to Lowe's, as you might expect from a couple with a fixer-upper. Between Conrad's sales job and Evelyn's teaching assignment, they pulled in low six figures. Not bad. Course, Boston's an expensive town. Two cars, taxes, mortgage, cable, cell phones. They weren't drowning, nor were they living in the lap of luxury."

"Life insurance policy on the husband?" D.D. asked.

"Hundred grand. That we know of. People have killed for less."

D.D. nodded, but she also registered Phil's lack of enthusiasm on the subject. A hundred grand might be a lot of money to some people, but for Evelyn Conrad, who'd grown up in a multimillion-dollar home in Cambridge while attending the finest private schools and socializing with the city's best and brightest, a hundred thousand wasn't enough.

"What was her father insured for?" D.D. thought out loud.

"Half a mill." Phil spoke up. "Thought you might ask."

"Better motive for shooting him."

"If you're Mrs. Hopkins, sure. You thinking Evelyn didn't do it after all? Her father's death wasn't her fault?"

"I don't know what to think anymore." D.D. gave up on pacing, leaned against the doorjamb. "There are too many strange coincidences here. A woman who may or may not have been involved in two fatal shootings in the past sixteen years. A victim who may or may not have had ties with an infamous serial rapist. It's like this giant Gordian knot. I can't figure out which string to pull first."

"Conrad Carter doesn't have significant ties to this community. No coworkers, no family, no electronic devices. Until the computer geeks can make some progress, there's not enough string there to pull."

"Which leaves us with Evelyn Carter. The quiet one, according to the neighbors."

"She has a mom," Phil said.

"Who just paid half a million cash to get her daughter out of jail. Good luck with that interview."

"Evelyn has a job."

D.D. nodded slowly. "Coworkers. Principal, fellow teachers. All right, let's start there."

" 'Let's'?" Phil asked, arching a brow at her use of the contraction.

"Let's," D.D. repeated firmly. "I already worked one shooting case involving this woman. Like hell I'm missing something the second time around."

Phil sighed. "Let's," he agreed.

The principal of Evelyn Carter's school was more than happy to speak with them. Unfortunately, Principal Ahearn had nothing useful to say. She'd hired Evie four years ago. The woman was an excellent math teacher — did they know who her father was? The school was lucky to have her; the kids were lucky to have her. Evie was notoriously shy, of course. Pleasant but reserved. Some teachers — especially of the advanced math variety — could be like that.

Yes, Principal Ahearn knew Evie had been

expecting. Best she could tell, Evie was very happy. Never in a million years would Principal Ahearn have expected last night's incident. They were making counselors available for the students. Everyone was in a state of shock. There had to be some kind of logical explanation. Or maybe it'd been a terrible accident —

Principal Ahearn caught herself, flushed slightly.

"You mean the way Evie's father died?" D.D. asked helpfully.

The woman turned redder. "Evie's never mentioned it. But of course I had to run a background check before hiring her."

D.D. found this interesting. "She was never charged in her father's death. There wouldn't have been anything in her background reports."

"Well, not hers . . ."

D.D. got it. "Her father. You Googled her father. A famous mathematician, you're looking to hire his daughter. Makes sense. You check out his Wikipedia profile, ending with how he died, accidentally shot by his teenage daughter in his own home."

"Not many Harvard professors come to violent ends." Principal Ahearn shrugged. "And Earl Hopkins was considered to be one of the best minds in his field."

"Did Evie know you knew?" Phil asked.

Principal Ahearn nodded. "It was one of those things. None of us ever spoke of it, but in this day and age of immediate access to information, how could you not? Every now and then, one of the students would figure it out and rumors would start flying. Evie herself . . . She never spoke of it. She showed up. She did her job. And she gave the best of herself as a teacher to her kids. Again, never in a million years . . ."

"Anyone ever threaten her? Try to make a big deal about what happened to her father?" Phil pushed.

"How could they? His cause of death was public knowledge. Tragic, absolutely, but not scandalous. Evie herself had been cleared of all charges. It's a sad family history, one of those things people are bound to whisper about. But other than that?" The principal shrugged.

D.D. nodded. She wondered what it was like for Evie, trying to move forward with her life while being forever shadowed by such a dark past. The principal was right; thanks to the internet, nothing was secret anymore. And having chosen to go into mathematics, even as a high school teacher, Evie Carter was bound to be connected with her father. Did the fact that no one talked to her directly about his death make things easier or worse?

"What did you know of Conrad Carter?" Phil was asking.

"I didn't. I met him once or twice at after-school functions. He traveled a lot. Sales, I believe."

"Any sign of trouble in the marriage?"

"Not that I could see." Principal Ahearn hastily shook her head.

"But you wouldn't know, would you?" D.D. pushed. "You respected Evelyn, but you weren't close to her."

Apologetic shrug. "I wouldn't say we had a connection. But I'll miss her."

"You'll miss her."

"Yes. I got a call, just an hour or two ago, from her mother. She said given the circumstances, Evie wouldn't be returning to work."

D.D. arched a brow. "Her mother quit her job for her? And you accepted that?"

The principal flushed. "Well, given the circumstances . . . At the very least, Evelyn would have to take a leave of absence to handle the legal charges. Then there is the matter of the pregnancy . . ."

D.D. got it: The principal was happy enough not to deal with either situation.

"Did she have a friend among the staff?"

Phil spoke up. "A fellow teacher, mentor, someone?"

The principal had to think about it. "Cathy Maxwell," she volunteered at last. "She's one of the science teachers. They often sat together at lunch."

"And where is she now?" Phil asked.

The principal glanced at her watch. "Given that closing bell is in five minutes, finishing up her lecture."

D.D. and Phil waited for the students to stream out of the classroom and down the hall. A few of the kids gave them suspicious glances, their gazes going immediately to the gold shields clipped to their belts. Sadly, the presence of two detectives in a Boston public school wasn't that unusual, so most just moved along.

Which sparked a thought. Why public school? Someone with Evelyn's background, not to mention parental legacy, could've most likely written her ticket to a number of the area's prestigious private schools. Better hours, better pay.

But Evelyn had chosen public education. Because she wanted to give something back? Or because she hoped it would keep her one step removed from her past? The more elite the school, the better the odds she'd meet someone who hadn't just Googled her father but had known him personally.

Which led to the next question: Why stay in Boston at all? Her husband was a transplant with a job he could've done from anywhere. Why not move to Florida, or the Midwest, or anyplace where the tragic shooting of a famous Harvard prof didn't still linger in people's memories? Was she that close to her mother? Because Evelyn wouldn't even look at the woman in the courthouse. More and more curious.

D.D. didn't like sitting at her desk in BPD headquarters, but she did like a case where nothing was as it seemed. Meaning she was currently quite happy. Phil, standing beside her, shook his head in exasperation.

Cathy Maxwell was cleaning the dry-erase board when they walked in. The classroom held rows of desks up front and long tables with lab equipment in the back. D.D. recognized Bunsen burners — after that, she gave up. She'd never cared for high school science, though she had no trouble following the latest advancements in forensics. Her educational issues had never had anything to do with her intelligence — it was more her inability to sit still for long periods of time. Much to the chagrin of her academic parents, who were content to sit quietly, discuss politely, and ignore their rambunctious only child pointedly.

D.D.'s parents had retired to Florida. They visited once a year. If D.D. was really lucky, she spent their stay working a major case. They were all happier that way.

"Cathy Maxwell?" Phil spoke up. "We're detectives with the Boston PD. We have some questions regarding Evelyn Carter."

"Oh dear." Immediately Cathy stopped wiping. She clutched the dry eraser with both hands, gazing at them blankly. "Is it true she's not coming back? She really quit?"

"That's not for us to say," D.D. stated.

Phil added: "Would you like to have a seat?"

"Okay." The woman sat at her desk. Stared at them again. Probably around fifty, she was dressed in brown wool slacks and a forest-green sweater. She had long brown hair clipped in a barrette at the back of her neck. Several strands had escaped and were drifting around her face. Between the eraser in her hands, the smudges of ink on her hands and the wire-rimmed glasses perched on the tip of her nose, she looked very much like a teacher to D.D. But a well-put-together one.

"We understand you and Evelyn were

friends?" Phil prodded.

"Evie? Sure. We often lunched together. Two females, one math, one science." Cathy Maxwell lifted a single shoulder. "You know, anyone will hang with the lit department, but tell someone you teach math or science, and it's like you're personally reminding them of every test they ever failed. People have a tendency to be intimidated, without ever giving us a chance."

Phil nodded sympathetically. He excelled at the good-cop role. Already, Cathy Maxwell was leaning closer to him.

"How long did you know Evie?" Phil asked. D.D. helped herself to a student desk, willed herself into the background.

"Four years. I was already working here when she was hired."

"And you became friends . . . immediately?"

"Pretty close. Evie's quiet. Keeps to herself. Of course, once you learn what happened to her father . . ." Cathy waited expectantly.

"We know," Phil assured her.

"She was just sixteen." The science teacher sounded genuinely empathetic. "To have something that terrible happen, then have to live forever with the guilt. Of course Evie isn't the most outgoing personality. Who could blame her?"

"Did she ever talk to you about it?" D.D. spoke up.

"Never." Cathy hesitated. "Though she'd mention her father from time to time. Randomly. Something he once said, a piece of advice he gave. She always sounded admiring. I think she loved him very much."

Cathy flushed, shrugged slightly. She set down the dry eraser. "From time to time, someone at the school would figure out Evie's role in her father's death. The whispers would start up again. Evie never said anything. But you could tell it took a toll on her. How could it not?"

"Any one person more vocal than another?"

"No. Evie might not be the warmest person around, but everyone respected her. She's a great teacher. And she supported her fellow educators. Didn't have any Harvard airs or anything like that. Academics" — she leaned forward conspiratorially — "can be the worst kind of snobs."

"What do you know of her husband, Conrad Carter?" Phil asked. "She speak of her home life much?"

"Sure. Their latest house project. And of course, now that they were expecting, she'd speak of the baby. Where would they put the nursery, that sort of thing. She was very excited. At least . . ." That slight hesitation again. "In the past few weeks, I haven't spoken to Evie much. She seemed distant, preoccupied. Morning sickness, holiday stress, I don't know. I didn't worry about it too much in the beginning; everyone gets busy from time to time. But now, in hindsight . . . I wonder if there was something on her mind. Maybe something was bothering her."

"But you don't know what something?" D.D. spoke up.

Cathy shook her head. "She started eating lunch in her own classroom. Catching up on work, she told me. I didn't question it the first few days. But, again, in hindsight, it's been nearly a month. That's a long time to be holed up in a classroom."

"You ever stop in, check up with her?" Phil asked.

"Sure. She'd wave me off and I'd let it go. I mean, this time of year, with the holidays coming, the kids are crazy and we're all losing it a little."

"Do you know how she met Conrad?" D.D. asked.

"Um." Cathy seemed to have to stop and think at this sudden change in topic. "Through a friend, when she worked at her first school. One of the teachers there had a cookout at his house and Conrad was there. They bought their house in Winthrop four years ago. That's what made Evie apply here; it's a much better commute."

"She struggle with her marriage?" Phil asked.

Cathy shook her head. "She wasn't one for that kind of talk."

"What do you mean 'that kind of talk'?"

"Personal. We talked teaching mostly. About being females in our respective fields. About how to get more students excited for two subjects a lot of kids already think they don't like or can't do. We talked shop, I guess. We ate in the teachers' lounge, after all."

"You never went out after work? Ladies' night at the martini bar?" D.D. pressed.

"Evie always went home. Even when Conrad was traveling. I don't know. She seemed the homebody type. Plus, many of the projects going on at their place she did herself. It wasn't that *he* was fixing it up. They both had talents."

Which, again, D.D. found interesting. Where had a rich girl who grew up in Cambridge learned home improvement skills?

"What about her relationship with students?" Phil asked now.

"Her students loved her."

"All of her students?"

Cathy shook her head. "Nothing stands out. We're nearly halfway through the school year now; Evie didn't mention having problems with any particular teen."

"What about a student who might've needed extra attention? Been unusually demanding of her time."

Again, the science teacher shook her head. "You might ask Sharon — Principal Ahearn. I hadn't heard of anything."

Phil and D.D. exchanged glances. The principal already seemed like a dead end when it came to learning more about Evelyn Carter. Asking for detailed information about students probably wasn't going to get them any further; school administrators were naturally disinclined to share those kinds of records.

"Did Evie have a computer?" Phil asked now, nodding to the one on Cathy's desk. "One assigned for her by the school, or she would've used to contact students."

"Sure. We all have school-issued laptops. Though much of what we do is handled by apps now, on our personal cell phones. Attendance, school grades, you name it. The modern era."

In other words, Evie should have a computer in her classroom. Which, once they had the proper warrant, might prove a useful bread crumb given their total lack of a digital trail right now. E-mails with students, other staff, maybe even Google searches Evie had felt safer doing in the relative privacy of her workplace, rather than in her own home, just down the hall from her husband . . .

Phil's cell rang. He glanced at the screen, frowned. "Excuse me a moment."

He put the phone to his ear. D.D. could tell it was one of his fellow detectives, probably Neil or Carol, based on the fact that Phil didn't speak as much as grunt. *Uh-huh, uh-huh, uh-huh.* Then, turning toward D.D.: "We gotta go."

Cathy was already rising to standing. Phil handed her a card. "Thank you for your time, we'll be in touch."

He didn't give the bewildered educator time to reply or ask any other questions. Instead, he was already turning on his heel, heading toward the hall with D.D. in his wake.

"What, what, what?" she demanded as she finally reached his side.

"You're never going to believe this. Evie and Conrad's home, *our* crime scene . . ."

D.D.'s heart sank. She didn't need to hear what Phil had to say next.

"It's on fire."

CHAPTER 9
FLORA

This is what I know about Jacob Ness:

He was old and ugly and disgusting, the kind of guy that a pretty blond college girl like me never would've given the time of day. His hair hung in greasy hanks. He had a mouth full of crooked, tobacco-stained teeth. He was built like a scarecrow, all massive belly and four scrawny limbs.

He wasn't partial to showering or any other kind of hygiene. He not only looked repulsive, he smelled that way, too. Every smell that ever made you want to vomit, that was his personal cologne.

He was strong. You wouldn't think it to look at him, with his flabby gut and flaccid limbs. But he had that skinny-guy thing going on — arms like bands of steel. I tried to fight him. As he dragged me back to the coffin-shaped box, as he forced me into various acts of depravity. I'd been a strong, athletic girl in the beginning. But I never

135

won. Not once.

Jacob had a family. Those details are sketchier for me. A father he referred to only as Dickhead or Asshole. The father had been a trucker as well, but Jacob implied that he only came home long enough to smack his kid around. Is he still alive? Did he ever read about what his son did? Mourn his death? Shake his head that Jacob had been stupid enough to get caught? I have no idea.

Jacob was raised by a chain-smoking mother who worked two jobs. When he was little, he talked about a grandmother who helped watch him during the day. According to Jacob, when he was five or six, he found his father's stash of porn, and that's when his obsession with sex began.

Jacob was a sex addict. He was very honest on that subject. He also made it clear he had no intention of reform.

I don't know what happened to the mom. The police or Samuel once mentioned to me that Jacob had been using his mother's address in Florida as his permanent address. That's one of the things that helped them make the connection between him and my disappearance. In the beginning, however, he hadn't kept me in Florida, but in some cabin in the mountains of Georgia.

The kind of place with no neighbors and few witnesses.

He was married once. He told me about that. He tried to do the traditional thing. Have a wife, spend night after night in the missionary position. That went so well he beat the crap out of the woman and ended up arrested for domestic abuse after the docs in the ER called it in. He went to jail for a year; he told me about that, too. How prison was no place for a man with his appetites. How when he got out, he vowed he'd never go back. On that, he kept his word.

Jacob raped a girl. That girl had a daughter. The girl died. The daughter, too. This bit of the family tree I know better. Which leaves us with? A father? A mother? Aunts, uncles, cousins? Did any of them care about him, or blame me for what happened?

I have no idea.

What about friends? I considered Jacob to be a loner, and not just because his job was to trawl the highways of the southern United States, but because I never saw him talk to anyone. Except, of course, that one night in the bar. Conrad.

Jacob spent a lot of time on his laptop. I assumed he was looking up porn, but knowing what I know now, it's also possible he was hanging out with other predators, comparing notes, even bragging. Many perverts do. Is that how he met Conrad? Were there others? I was never granted access to the computer. Maybe Jacob had a whole online community, even a fan club.

I wasn't allowed secrets, but Jacob kept plenty from me. Especially during his benders, the days, entire weeks, he'd disappear, only to return, high, wasted, whatever. He never talked about where he went, what he did. I never bothered to consider, how did he score the drugs? Surely that implies some kind of community right there, a dealer, other addicts, a means of contacting such people. He never mentioned names — and whatever the FBI recovered from his laptop, they never shared with me.

To the best of our knowledge, Jacob never posted my picture online. For that, I'm grateful, as once those images are out, you can't get them back again. Jacob e-mailed some videos and images to my mother; he wasn't beyond taunting. But he seemed to understand that sharing too much might get him caught. Or maybe, in his own Jacob-like way, he didn't want to share.

For the first year we were together, Jacob forced me to call him by my dead father's name, Everett. He referred to me as Molly.

We were like characters in a play. Or maybe short-timers in a relationship we both knew would never last. Except one month, two months, twelve months later, Jacob still hadn't gotten around to killing me. And whether I meant it to happen or not, we turned a corner. I stopped fighting. I stopped running. I made myself Jacob's friend and confidante.

A man that lonely certainly wasn't immune to a little female charm.

The last day, SWAT pouring through the door, tear gas exploding everywhere, Jacob crawled to *me.* Jacob draped the water-soaked towels around *my* mouth to block the stinging smoke. Jacob handed *me* the gun.

No one wants to be a monster, Jacob used to tell me. None of this was his fault. Abduction, rape, assault. Four hundred and seventy-two days of hell.

No one wants to be a monster.

It didn't stop him from being my monster. But now I wonder, did my monster know others? Did my monster leave behind other living victims besides me?

I can't ask Jacob these questions anymore. That final day, after he gave me the gun, I did exactly what both of us wanted me to do. At the time I had no doubts.

But welcome to the world of being a survivor. You make it out alive, and yet you spend the rest of your life wondering woulda, coulda, shoulda. I swore I would never look back. Samuel has advised me not to second-guess decisions that can never be changed.

Yet here I am.

Keith Edgar first contacted me six years ago. I'd barely returned to my mother's farm, was still trying to get used to the textures and smells of a childhood home that now felt totally alien to me. Keith initially reached out through the Facebook page my brother had set up during my abduction. When that got him nothing, he turned to snail mail. Back in those days, our local postman would deliver mail by the boxload. My mother would stack up all the plastic bins in the kitchen. She never expected me to go through them — no one expected me to do anything but heal, rest, recover. Every night, though, I'd see her sitting at the kitchen table, opening each envelope, skimming the contents, sorting them into piles.

Many of the envelopes contained money. Small checks. Five dollars, ten, twenty. Donations from total strangers who were moved by my story and wanted to help. My mother established a savings account in my name. All deposits went into it. She'd give me updates I refused to hear. I didn't want the donations; they felt like blood money to me. And I definitely didn't want everyone's pity.

My mom wrote a lot of thank-you notes. Diligently, religiously, night after night. My mom is good that way.

But not all letters were nice. Some writers wanted to forgive me. As if getting kidnapped and raped was somehow my fault. In the beginning, my mom dashed off hasty words to correct their misunderstanding. But over time, those notes earned a bin of their own — the trash can. "Can't change narrow minds," she'd mutter.

Forgiveness. My mom is good like that, too.

Then came the other letters. Fan mail, I'd guess you call it. From predominantly male writers. Many with marriage proposals. Some wanted to save me. After all I'd been through, they wanted to sweep me off my feet, promising me I would never suffer again. My mom would set those letters down gingerly. Like she didn't know what to make of such madness, wrapped in good intentions. Pretty soon, they joined the trash pile, too.

Then came the less subtle notes. Men who, having followed every detail of my ordeal, had decided that I'd be perfect for them. Submissive. Pretrained. With tastes as depraved as their own.

My mother didn't throw away those letters. She burned them.

I learned about the various correspondence piles because I didn't sleep much in those days. Meaning that after my mom went to bed, I would take up her position at the table. Driven by morbid curiosity more than anything. Why would any of these strangers want to write to me? What about my terrible story spoke to them? Turns out the answers to those questions are many and varied.

Which brings us to the last category: the Keith Edgars of the world. True-crime buffs. They wrote to request personal interviews. Maybe one-on-one, maybe with their entire Sherlock Holmes geek squad. They wanted to learn from me. Have the opportunity to hear firsthand what a serial predator was really like. The notes were earnest. But again, they essentially wanted me to turn myself inside out, relive my own victimization, so they could indulge their clinical fascination and boost their own stature within the true-crime community. Some offered financial compensation. Some promised to provide me with information in return.

They didn't stop with one letter. They wrote and wrote and wrote. Keith Edgar still delivers a note probably every six months, even though I've never responded. I did look him up. He runs a whole true-crime blog. The group meets in Boston to study a case-of-the-month. Keith lists himself as a specialist in sexual-sadist predators. In fact, according to his blog, even without my help he has managed to become the foremost expert on Jacob Ness.

Why you'd want to be an expert in such a thing, I have no idea. But this is what Keith Edgar supposedly does in his free time. Which makes me wonder just what kind of cave dweller I'm going to meet as I get off the T, make my way up the street to the address I found online. There are no photos of Keith on the site, which I find suspicious in this age of selfies.

My best guess? I'm about to meet a pale, moon-faced geek still living in his parents' basement. Someone who spends all his time hunched in the glow of his computer monitor, surfing crime/horror websites, while chugging Red Bull and plowing through bags of Doritos. Is it really fascination with criminal minds that keeps someone like him coming back for more? Or do the images and stories of such violent acts serve as their own kind of stimulation? I'm suspicious. True-crime geeks can claim all they want that they're attracted to puzzles and driven by the need to find the truth; I still don't believe them.

I climb up the stairs to the Boston brownstone. It's in a nicer neighborhood than I would've thought. A street of well-tended town houses, all nestled shoulder to shoulder with matching wrought-iron railings and freshly painted white- or black-trimmed windows. Wreaths hang on front doors. Many of the porches are decorated with festive ribbons and fresh holiday garlands.

Keith's parents, I decide, must be very successful.

I climb the four steps to the dark-green door, where a huge Christmas wreath encircles an impressive brass knocker.

What the hell. I knock.

It takes a bit before I hear footsteps. Fair enough. I didn't call first. I'm running on adrenaline and shock, same emotional state I've been in since I turned on the news and saw the dead husband's face. I don't want anything like rational thought slowing me down now.

Footsteps drawing closer.

A pause. Someone looking through the peephole no doubt. Life in a big city.

The door opens. I stand face-to-face with a six-foot, thirty-year-old white male, with short-cropped dark hair, startling blue eyes, and definitely a runner's body. He wears a blue Brooks Brothers sweater exactly the same shade as his eyes, coordinated with sharply pressed charcoal slacks and perfectly buffed brown leather shoes. I open my mouth, but no words come out.

On the other hand, his face is already changing, his eyes widening in wonder.

"Flora Dane," he whispers.

"Ted Bundy, I presume?"

His answering smile lights up his entire face. And I realize I've just made a major mistake, as I shoulder my way past Keith Edgar and enter the home of Jacob Ness's biggest fan.

CHAPTER 10
EVIE

My mother tells me to rest. I should. For myself. The baby. The days to come. But I can't get comfortable. Everything feels wrong. The too-soft mattress, the sheets that aren't my sheets, the pillow that's filled with feathers because my mother loves all things European, whether my dad or I agreed or not. Even as a child, this room was never my room. Just another stage setting for the drama that is my mother's life.

As a grown woman, an adult with her own house, own husband — the pang hits me again — I can't sleep in this place. I just want to go home.

I shower. That at least feels good and allows me to think I'm taking care of myself and, by extension, my unborn child.

Boy or girl. That's what my mother wants to know. I don't have the answer. We were going to be surprised. At least, that's what we'd been thinking. Five months along, still plenty of time to change our minds.

Conrad died never knowing if he was going to have a baby girl or baby boy. Which would he have preferred?

The thought sends a fresh jolt through me, and for a moment, standing under the sting of the shower spray, I can't tell if I'm going to cry or vomit or both.

My hands are shaking so badly, I can barely handle the soap. I move on to shampoo, lathering my hair. I've never seen myself such a mess. Not even the first time. My father splayed back against the refrigerator. The weight of the shotgun. The blood the blood the blood. It had all felt like a terrible, surreal dream. This . . .

This is a judgment I can't escape.

I get out of the shower. Pat dry my swelling abdomen. Do what pregnant women have been doing since time immemorial: I turn sideways and stare at my changing profile in the mirror. In the beginning, being pregnant had felt miraculous, but also not quite real. We'd been trying. Long enough we'd both given up hope, without actually admitting it out loud because that would bring us to discussions on infertility treatments or timing cycles, or some other kind of external intrusion into a relationship that was already fraying.

Except after days of nausea, I gave in to my own curiosity. Peed on a stick, then stared at the results in complete shock.

Conrad's beaming smile. My own lightening chest. For one moment, we were united again. We loved each other. This new life was proof. Despite ourselves, we would do this and live happily ever after.

For six weeks, eight weeks, we floated long, all fresh promise and forgotten regrets. Except I'm not my mom. I don't live in a fantasy world of European pillows and exquisitely cultured pearls. I'm my father's daughter. I see puzzles everywhere. Then I must solve them.

And as any mathematician will tell you, once you've worked the equation, numbers don't lie. What you get is what you get. There's nothing left to do but accept that truth.

And what is a marriage except adding A to B and hoping it equals an amount greater than the sum of its parts?

Briefly, the promise of a new life almost made the math work. Except A was still A, and B was still B. We could create a new life, but we couldn't stop being ourselves.

The bathroom in my mother's house is fully stocked, including a coconut-oil concoction formulated specially for stretch marks. After seeing the nursery, nothing surprises me. I rub the tropical-smelling lotion onto my belly and breasts. I find more products for my face, imported brands way too expensive for a math teacher at a public high school. Generally, I avoid my mother's generosity, as it definitely comes with a price. Given the past twenty-four hours, however, I figure what the hell. If anyone could use some rejuvenation from a five-hundred-dollar French cream, it's gotta be me.

In the closet, I find a full lineup of maternity wear, arranged by size and going all the way up to the final trimester. I have a brief, dizzying thought. I'm trapped now. My mother's going to keep me here, has clearly been planning it all along. I bathed with her soap, used her lotions, and will now put on her clothes. I'll never get out. I'm like that girl in the Greek myth who ate pomegranates in Hades, then could never fully escape.

Except my mother doesn't want me. I already know that.

My child, on the other hand, this final addition to my father's legacy . . .

I lean against the closet door, trying to figure out once more if I'm going to cry or vomit. When I manage to pass a full minute without doing either, I pull on soft gray stretch pants and a matching gray top. Cashmere, probably.

Conrad would laugh if he could see me now. He'd grin and tell me to enjoy the ride. Not having any family left, he couldn't understand my ambivalence about mine. Clearly she loves you, he'd tell me again and again, which only proved he never understood my mother at all.

Downstairs, my mother is in the kitchen. There is a heaping plate of fresh fruit on the kitchen table and she has the Cuisinart whirring away. She turns it off when she sees me.

"High-protein smoothie," she announces cheerfully. "Full of antioxidants and healthy fats for the baby."

Only my mother can work a blender while wearing pearls.

There's no use fighting it. Years of training kick in. I sit at the table. I pick at the fruit. I obediently sip the green sludge.

I don't look at the fridge. I never look at the fridge. Not that it's the same one, of course. After the "tragic incident," my mother had the kitchen gutted. New cabinets, marble countertops, high-end appliances, custom window treatments. It's all creamy and soft and Italian. Not at all like the original dark cherrywood cabinets, green-and-gold granite tops. Meaning nothing in here should remind me of my father or that day.

But it does. It always does. I don't care that the flooring has been ripped out and replaced. Or that the stainless steel refrigerator was exchanged for a wood-paneled model. I see the spot where my father died. I recall the smell. I remember looking at his face, so waxy and still, and thinking it didn't look like him at all.

I don't know how my mom still lives in this house. But I guess I'll get to figure that out for myself now. How to go back to the home Conrad and I shared. How to pick up the pieces of a life, where I'm still not sure where we went wrong.

I notice for the first time that all the lights are on and the curtains drawn, though it's only midday. I don't have to think about it for long.

"The press?" I ask.

"You know how they are." My mother waves an airy hand. At least on this we're united. The media descended the first time, too. Harvard math professor killed in his own home by his teenage daughter. How could they resist? Initially, my mom had thought she could control the story, the way she controlled every other facet of her highly fictionalized life. Needless to say, the reporters ate her alive.

She retreated. Took up the tactic of letting her grand silence speak for her. As a minor, at least I wasn't subjected to such abuse. But it was weeks, maybe even months, before we could leave our house in peace. I learned to hate the sight of news vans. I learned not to believe anything I saw on TV. At least I got that education early in life, because I'm definitely going to need it now.

Knock on the side door. The one used only by close confidants. My mother bustles over.

Dick Delaney, my lawyer, is standing there, still wearing the same sharply pressed gray suit from the courtroom. He's a handsome man with his silver hair and closely trimmed beard. I have countless memories of him. Poker nights with my father. Laughing indulgently at all the math jokes, as one of the only nonacademics in the room. How did he even know my father? What had earned him a seat at the poker table? I don't know. But he was always part of our household, brilliant and successful in his own right, a fellow Harvard alum, which maybe was all the credentials he needed. I never even thought of him as a defense attorney.

Until, of course, sixteen years ago. Again,

the smell, the look on my father's waxy face.

I have this terrible sense of déjà vu. Here we are again, the three of us, this kitchen.

My mom doesn't say a word. She simply steps back, allowing Mr. Delaney to enter. In an echo of my own thoughts, her right hand is already clutched protectively to her chest, fingering her precious pearls.

He looks from her to me to her again. The expression on his face isn't good. "After picking up Evie from the courthouse, where did you go?" he asks my mother.

Her brow furrows. "Here. Straight here, of course. Poor Evie needed to rest."

"No stops along the way?"

"Of course."

"Not even a drive by her old house so she could pick up personal possessions, items of clothing?"

"Absolutely not. Evie has everything she needs right here."

Mr. Delaney stares at me. Slowly, I nod, though I already understand I don't want to hear what he'll say next.

"Your house is on fire." He announces it bluntly.

I try to absorb the statement. I hear the words. I just can't seem to process them. My house. Conrad's and my home. My husband's death scene.

"Total loss," he continues.

The future life I was going to lead. The photos and personal items that tied me to the past.

"I'm sorry," he says. "You're sure you were together all afternoon? Both of you? Right here?"

"Of course!" My mother is outraged.

"The police will be coming," my lawyer says. Then he takes a seat at the table, and together, we wait.

This time, the knock comes from the front door. But we were already alerted to the detective's arrival by the sudden spike in noise from across the street — the media spotting the official vehicle and descending with a crescendo of questions. No comment, the police will say. That's what they always say. After all, it's not their lives being torn apart.

Mr. Delaney gets up, does the honors. My mother and I don't look at each other. We can't. I fix my gaze on my half-finished green smoothie, the piece of uneaten pineapple on my plate. Under the table, my hands are shaking furiously on my lap. Again, I've never felt myself such a mess. Shock? Pregnancy hormones? My heart is racing like a hummingbird's and I suddenly want to blurt out everything, anything. Except I honestly don't know what to say. I just want whatever magic words will give me my life back.

Dead woman walking. If that's what I'd felt like twenty-four hours ago, then what am I now? Corpse walking? The ghost of a never-realized dream?

I recognize the first detective who walks into the kitchen. The father figure who attempted to question me last night. He still wears his very stern, yet somehow equally concerned expression. Standing next to Mr. Delaney, who is wearing a thousand-dollar suit, the detective appears both slightly frumpy and more human.

My mother is already sitting up straighter, her eyes zeroing in on a target. An older male, reasonably attractive and clearly out of his socioeconomic league. She will devour him alive. And relish every bite.

Behind him comes a second detective. Female. Chin-length curly blond hair. Killer cheekbones. Nearly crystalline blue eyes. She's wearing slim-fitting jeans and sleek black leather boots that match her swagger.

I have that sense of déjà vu again. Her gaze goes straight to me, narrowing slightly.

Smell hits me first. The memory of gunpowder and blood. The refrigerator. Don't look at the streaked stainless steel. Don't stare at the wax-doll version of my father on the floor. Sitting at the table. Except not this table. That table. And not in this kitchen, that kitchen.

She'd been the one sitting across from me. Younger. Softer. Kinder, I think. Except maybe because I'd been younger and softer, too. Questions then, questions now.

I look at my mom, Mr. Delaney, the detective, my hands still shaking on my lap. And I can't help but think, the gang's all here.

The blonde, Sergeant Detective D. D. Warren, doesn't speak right away. She lets the older detective, Call Me Phil, run through the particulars. Warren prowls the kitchen. I wonder if she's noting all the differences — new cabinets, countertops, appliances. Does she think it's strange my mother still lives, cooks, eats, in a crime scene? That we are sitting, even now, mere feet from where my father died?

My mother is talking. With Mr. Delaney's approval. She's also turning her head a certain way — her best side, while periodically fingering a strand of frosted blond hair above her ear, French-manicured nails lingering on the graceful curve of her neck.

I've never seen my mother interact with a

man without batting her eyelashes. She remains an attractive woman. Slim, graceful, good bones. Not to mention she's a fanatic for green smoothies and organic this and organic that. In lieu of yoga, she prefers triple-distilled vodka, served straight up. Still seems to work for her.

My father never minded her flirting. He'd watch, a knowing gleam in his eye as she worked the room. I think he liked the way she sparkled. Others admired her. Others wanted her. But she always belonged to him.

I feel like I can't breathe. Time is collapsing. I'm sixteen. I'm thirty-two. My father. My husband.

The same detective. Still prowling the expansive kitchen while most likely thinking, *How many "accidents" can one person have?*

I have a question for her: How many losses can one person take?

My mother is swearing she was with me all afternoon. The detective, politely but forcefully, wants to know if anyone can corroborate. Mr. Delaney intervenes smoothly that if the police don't believe his client's statement, the burden is on them to prove otherwise. Do they have anyone placing my mother or myself at the scene of the fire? For that matter, the city is filled with cameras and prying eyes. Surely, if the police had something more concrete, they wouldn't be wasting everyone's time with these questions.

Mr. Delaney is fishing. Even I can tell that. Do the police have anything substantial? That's what he really wants to know. The older detective doesn't take the bait.

I find it interesting that my own lawyer is curious if the police have evidence that contradicts his clients' statements. Do all lawyers believe their clients are lying to them? Or is it merely because he's been a family friend for decades and knows us that well?

"What caused the fire?" When I finally interrupt, the sound of my own voice startles me. I sound hoarse, like I haven't spoken in years.

The blond detective halts, stares at me. Neither investigator offers an answer.

"You think it was intentional, right?" I continue. "Otherwise, why would you be here? But why would I burn down my own home? I left last night without even a toothbrush. Everything I own . . . everything I had . . ." My voice breaks slightly. I force myself to continue, though I sound hollow even to me. "It's all gone. My entire life . . . it's all gone. Why would I do that?"

The blonde speaks for the first time. "This doesn't look like such a bad place to land."

Just like that, I'm pissed off. I shove back my chair. Rise to standing. "You of all people should know better. You of all people!" I'm almost yelling at her. Why not? I certainly can't yell at my mom.

I stalk out of the kitchen. I can't take the room, with all its creamy wood and expensive marble. A fucking stage setting.

My father was real. His smile, his booming voice, the way he pursed his lips when working a particularly difficult problem, the way he'd sit with his eyes shut and listen to me play the piano for hours.

He loved me. He loved me, he loved me, he loved me.

And Conrad had loved me, too.

The blond detective is following me. Mr. Delaney, too, clearly concerned. Emotional clients are probably a danger to themselves and others. My mother stays behind. With Call Me Phil. She's probably offering him a glass of water, while briefly touching his arm.

I don't know where I'm going. I can't exit the house. Whatever is overwhelming me here is nothing compared to the media that's waiting to pounce outside. I move into the formal room with the baby grand.

Black and gleaming. I spent so much of my childhood sitting on that bench, working those keys.

I haven't touched it since.

I can't be in this room. I move into the front parlor instead. I never liked this room. What kid cares about a formal parlor?

"My client needs to rest," Mr. Delaney is informing the detective.

She doesn't listen to him but regards me instead. "You remember me, don't you?" she asks.

I nod. Not sitting, but walking around the small space. It's taken me years to realize that most people do not live like this, with carefully placed silk-covered wingback chairs and antique sideboards and crystal-line decanters.

"Yes." I finally glance at her. "You looked nicer then. The sympathetic cop. Not any-more."

The blonde smiles, not offended at all. "I was younger then. Still learning."

"What did you learn?"

"To ask more questions. To accept fewer answers. That even the most honest person will tell a lie."

"My client —" Mr. Delaney tries again.

I hold up a hand. "It's okay. You can go help my mom. Or rather, save the other detective."

Mr. Delaney gives me a stern look. Though he's already torn. He does know my mother, and sometimes her manipulations, even done with the best of intentions, can backfire.

I feel stronger now, more certain. I address Sergeant Warren directly. "You're not going to ask me about Conrad, are you?"

Slowly, she shakes her head.

"Will you tell me about the fire?"

Another pause. She nods. We have a deal. Maybe my lawyer doesn't understand the terms, but we do.

"It's okay," I tell Mr. Delaney again. "Give us a moment, please."

"As your lawyer —"

"I know. A moment."

He's not happy. But I'm the client, he's the lawyer, and he is worried about my mother. As he should be. Finally, he retreats, leaving Sergeant Warren and me alone. Last time, it had been her and me in the kitchen. My mom and the other detective in the parlor. I like this change of venue. I need it.

She does look harder, as if the past sixteen years haven't been entirely kind to her. Or maybe she'd been right before; disillusionment was part of the job. After all, sixteen years ago she'd believed me in the matter of my father's death. And now?

I wonder what she sees when she looks at me. Am I harder? Disillusioned? Angry? I don't think I feel any of those things.

I'm sad. I'm lost. I am my father's daughter, and I always saw the truth even when others didn't. But that doesn't mean I've known what to do with the information. Especially when it involved the ones I loved.

"How are you feeling?" Sergeant Warren asks me. She doesn't take a seat in one of the washed-silk wingbacks. Neither do I.

"I don't know."

She tilts her head to the side. "Are you excited for the baby?"

"Yes."

"Conrad?"

"We'd almost given up hope. We'd been trying for a bit. Nothing, and then . . ." I don't have any more words to say. I place my right hand on the gentle swell of my abdomen. Another silent apology. I already have the same relationship with my child as I do with my mother.

"I have a son," the detective offers. "Five years old. We just got him a puppy. They're both crazy."

I smile. "We were waiting to be surprised. It feels weird now. That Conrad died, never knowing if he was going to have a boy or girl. One of those silly things, because it's terrible enough Conrad will never get to meet his child, what does it matter the gender?" A pause, and then, in the silence, because it's weighing so heavily on my mind I just can't help myself: "I still miss him."

"Conrad?"

I look at her. Shake my head. "Do you think it will be any better for my baby? That maybe by never knowing his or her daddy, she won't miss him as much?"

The sergeant doesn't say anything.

"I didn't shoot him."

"Conrad?" she asks again.

Again, I shake my head.

She doesn't move anymore. Neither do I. We study each other across the small space. Two women who barely know each other and yet are intricately bound by the tangle of so many questions, the weight of too much unfinished business.

"We came home to him," I continue softly, my voice very low, which is the only tone appropriate for confessing sins. "I walked through the back door into the kitchen, and there he was."

"Your mother was with you?" The detective asks, her tone as hushed as my own. She glances at the open doorway. Mr. Delaney will return soon enough. We both know it.

"Yes, standing outside."

"You had blood in your hair," Sergeant Warren states firmly. "Gunpowder on your hands. If you didn't shoot your father, how do you explain that?"

"It rained." I can barely get the words out. Sixteen years later, and still the horror seems fresh. "I walked through the door, and it rained on me." I touch my short hair self-consciously. "Hot blood from the ceiling."

"What did you do?"

"I picked up the shotgun. It was on the floor in front of me. I picked it up. I don't know why. To get it out of the way. Then I saw him. He was half hidden behind the island. But turning the corner I saw . . . all of him."

Another glance toward the foyer. Footsteps, did we hear them in the distance? A tinkle of laughter. My mother flirting with Detective Phil.

"What did your mother do?"

"She screamed."

"What did you do?"

"Nothing. He didn't look real. Not like himself. I kept waiting for him to get up."

"Who called the cops?"

I look at her. "We didn't. I checked the shotgun. Made sure the chamber was empty —"

"You knew how to work it."

"I always knew how to work it. My father wouldn't bring a firearm into the home without teaching us basic safety."

"What did you do, Evie?"

"Whatever my mother told me."

"And she told you to confess to killing him? Not, 'let's call nine-one-one,' 'good God our loved one has just been shot'?"

I know how crazy it sounds. Back then. Today. All the hours in between. I don't have the words.

The sergeant's eyes narrow. "Are you covering for your mom, Evie? She and your father got in a fight. She shot him. You, being a minor with no criminal record, took the blame to save the parent you had left."

"She was with me. She couldn't have killed him."

"Then why such a crazy story? Why not call the police?"

"There would be an investigation. So many questions. The potential for . . ." I couldn't articulate the words back then, but I understand them now. "Scandal. I don't think my mom knows who or why my father was shot. But she didn't want to risk the answer to those questions. Not if they might tarnish his legacy. You have to realize, my father is more than just a man to her. He is . . . everything."

The sergeant eyes me skeptically. "So she threw her sixteen-year-old daughter under the bus rather than seek justice in her husband's murder?" A pause. "Or rather than a risk an investigation into his possible suicide?"

I don't have to answer that question. The sergeant is finally starting to understand. My mother's true fear. The real reason I did what I did. Sometimes, the danger isn't from outside, but from inside ourselves.

"Gonna blame your mom for your husband's death, too," the sergeant asks at last, "or this time did you finally get it right?"

I hesitate. I don't want to. I think of my mother as crazy and manipulative, sure, but not homicidal. And yet the closet bursting with maternity wear, the fully stocked nursery . . . It's almost as if she knew about today. Has been waiting all along.

"What did you think back then?" I ask the sergeant now.

"I thought you were scared. I thought you were in shock. And I thought, based on the physical evidence alone, that you did shoot him, but you were sorry about it."

"And now?"

The detective shrugs. "Looking at your husband's crime scene? I think you're the shooter again. Except this time around, you're not sorry about it."

"It would be stupid math," I say.

She gives me that look.

"Having been involved in a shooting before, to repeat the same equation . . . Stupid math."

"Except the equation worked for you the first time."

"You think so? Sixteen years of murmurs and whispers and innuendos. Sixteen years of loss, and I'm not even allowed to grieve because, supposedly, I'm the one who killed him?"

The sergeant doesn't answer that right away, just continues to study me.

"Besides." I speak more briskly. "I wouldn't burn down my own house. I've now lost everything. My baby has lost everything. No mother would do that."

The sergeant merely shrugs, gestures to our luxurious surroundings.

She leaves me no choice but to play the only card I have left. "I've lied for my mother. Made excuses, enabled her bad behavior, curtailed my own hopes and dreams just to make her happy. But I would never willingly move back in with her. And I would never happily grant her this much access to her first grandchild."

"What are you trying to say?"

I shake my head. This time, I'm the one eyeing the doorway nervously. "I don't know. But don't you think it's curious, a mere twenty-four hours later, how few choices I have left?"

CHAPTER 11
D.D.

"Get anything out of her?" Phil asked as they headed back to the car. They'd parked on the family's driveway to get some distance from the reporters yammering on the sidewalk.

"She didn't magically confess to killing her husband," D.D. said as she slid into the passenger side. "But just to make things interesting, she changed her story about shooting her father sixteen years ago."

Phil, firing the engine to life, stared at her. "What would be the point to that?"

"I don't know. Maybe just to muddy the waters? Evie has to know one of the reasons she looks guilty in her husband's death is that she already confessed to accidentally shooting her father. So rather than address her husband's murder now, she's recanting sixteen years ago."

"No statute of limitations on murder," Phil murmured. He twisted around, got to the business of backing down the driveway into the street without taking out any overly aggressive newspeople.

The days were short this time of year; the sun had set while they were inside the house, interviewing the family. Fortunately, the huge spotlights and the blaze of flashing media cameras helped light their way.

"So who shot her father?" Phil asked.

"Evie claims she doesn't know. She and her mother walked into the scene. Her mother convinced her to take the blame, rather than risk an investigation that might tarnish the man's 'legacy.' Still sounds fishy to me. Who discovers their loved one's body and doesn't immediately call nine-one-one? Opts for let's play make-believe instead?"

"The mother's scary," Phil stated. He shuddered slightly.

"Really? Because she seemed quite taken with you. A wealthy widow, and a rather well-preserved model at that."

Phil gave her a look. D.D. already knew the score. Phil was madly in love with his childhood sweetheart and longtime wife, Betsy. Their marriage was one of the few things in life that gave D.D. hope.

"She's scary," Phil said again.

D.D. smiled, turned to studying the view out the window. They'd cleared the reporters now and were cruising through Cambridge, past row after row of gorgeous Victorians and historic Colonials, all decked out for the holidays with shimmering icicle lights, garland-wrapped bannisters, impeccably decorated shrubs. In an enclave this wealthy, D.D. had no doubt the inside matched the outside, towering Christmas trees covered in delicate antique ornaments, decked-out staircases, pots of overflowing greenery. She and Alex were still working on a Christmas tree. Given the modest size of their home compared to the staggering amount of Jack and Kiko's energy, they'd probably have to put up their tree the night before to have any hope for it to still be standing on Christmas morning.

"How much money can one dead math professor be worth?" D.D. muttered. She hadn't really thought about it at the time. Everyone said Earl Hopkins had been a genius, he was also a tenured Harvard professor. That had seemed worthy of the grand home. But all these years later, he was gone, and to judge by the kitchen renovations alone, the family's lifestyle hadn't suffered. Half a million in life insurance didn't go that far. Did that mean there were other sources of income, more tangible benefits of Hopkins's brilliance his wife hadn't wanted to risk to a murder investigation? Phil was right: There was no statute of limitations on homicide, which meant Evie's changing story line raised all sorts of interesting questions. Though despite what she might have intended, they still centered mostly on her and her mom.

"My partner and I were the first to interview Evie and her mother," D.D. said now, gazing out the window. "At the time, she had blood spatter in her hair and tested positive for GSR on her hands. That kind of physical evidence has gotta mean something."

"Did you ask her?"

"Sure. In her new and improved memory, she walked in when the blood was still fresh. It dripped down on her from the ceiling. Then she picked up the shotgun and checked the chamber, which would contaminate her hands with GSR. The GSR can go either way. But the blood evidence, I'm less convinced."

"I worked a scene once," Phil provided. "Kid was arrested standing in his best friend's apartment, covered in blood, holding a shotgun. His friend's body was slumped in a chair, missing most of its head. Kid was arrested for murder, of course. His story: He'd gotten a call from his friend, claiming he was about to commit suicide. The kid had run right over, heard the shotgun blast, and raced inside just in time to find his friend's body. The blood was from all the spatter dripping down from the ceiling."

"The verdict?" D.D. asked.

"Forensic experts proved the friend was telling the truth. The directionality of the spatter on the ceiling indicated the shotgun blast had blown up, while the directionality of the spatter on the friend revealed the blood had dripped down. Friend was exonerated. And I believe they still cover the case at the academy. You should ask Alex about it."

D.D. nodded. Given that her husband Alex's specialty was blood evidence, she'd definitely run Evie's new and improved story by him. And while suicides by long guns weren't as common as suicides by pistols, they did happen, meaning Evie and her mom might have been right to worry about the results of a full-on death investigation.

"Here's the problem," D.D. said now. "I can pull the file, but my memory of the Hopkins case is that we didn't exactly work it to the letter. We had a body. We had a confession. We had a witness, and we lacked any evidence of motive. Everyone said Evie loved her father, et cetera, et cetera. At the time, all the elements matched the given story line of a terrible family tragedy, versus any whiff of something criminal. Let's just say the senior detective, Speirs, took a more efficiency-based approach to his case management. Close the ones you can, so you have the hours to work the ones you can't."

"Versus your own obsessive, take-no-prisoners approach?" Phil asked.

"How Speirs and I ever survived five years of working together, I'll never know," D.D. agreed. "Except I was the rookie, and in the beginning, everyone gets to do as they're told."

"Did you have doubts about Evie's confession back then?"

"Honestly, no. The way she presented. The physical evidence at the scene. There are cases I still wonder about. But Earl Hopkins's shooting death wasn't one of them."

"And now?"

"I don't like it." D.D. turned away from the window. "I don't like any of it. Evie's husband's death. A fire at their house and our crime scene. Evie's new statement, which frankly makes less sense than her old statement. I mean, who confesses to a shooting just to appease her mom?"

"Scary woman," Phil provided again.

"Questions. I have lots and lots of questions. And you know how I feel about questions."

"I'm never going to see my wife again, am I?"

"I think we have our work cut out for us."

"Making our next stop?"

"Where all confused detectives should go: back to the crime scene. Arson fire and all."

They could smell the charred remains of the scene before they arrived. Phil navigated the narrow street, made tighter by the rows of parked cars on both sides. This time of night, people were home for the evening. The small, boxy homes glowed with cozy kitchen scenes or flashing flat-screens. D.D. thought it interesting that as the homes grew smaller, the outdoor Christmas displays grew larger. Entire rooftops covered in Santa and his sleigh. Blow-up snowmen that ballooned across entire yards. Miles of twinkling lights.

Alex had trimmed their front porch with icicle lights, then wrapped the lone tree in their front yard. Not quite keeping up with the neighbors, but certainly more effort than D.D. had ever made. Then again, they had a kid now, and Jack was obsessed with anything related to Santa.

Phil turned the corner, and the Carters' former home became immediately visible as a black void in the midst of a sea of festivity. Not to mention, the smell of burnt wood and melted plastic grew significantly stronger.

They'd left Evie's school and gone straight to the Carters' residence after receiving news of the blaze. The scene had been too hot to approach, however, with the fire crews still working. In the end, it had made more sense to head directly to the source of their problems — Evie Carter — than wait around.

Now Phil turned in enough to park at the end of the driveway, just beyond the crime scene tape. His headlights illuminated a gutted shell. Collapsed roof. Blown-out windows. While a fair amount of the single-car garage appeared intact, only the front wall of the two-story residence remained, and even that was barely standing.

"All right, this is what we know." Phil pulled out his notebook. Many cops now worked off tablets, or even their smartphones. Phil, however, was a traditionalist. D.D. appreciated that about him.

"According to the arson investigator, Patricia Di Lucca, fire most likely started in the kitchen in the rear of the home. Definitely arson. Looks like a pot was left on the kitchen cooktop, filled with highly flammable materials. Then an accelerant was doused liberally around the house — most likely gasoline — with the largest concentration dumped in the upstairs bedrooms. Range was turned on. Arsonist exited stage right, and once burner achieved proper temperature, poof. Initial spark caught and fire was off and running. These old structures don't take much to burn, but the extensive nature of the damage, particularly given the fire department was here in under six minutes, meant someone really wanted to get the job done."

"Whole house was intended to be a loss," D.D. provided.

"Yep, except the garage, which, as you can see, is relatively intact."

"The arsonist didn't care about the garage."

"Apparently not."

She tilted her head to the side, contemplating. "Seems like a fairly blatant attempt to eliminate the crime scene. Except, if you really wanted to be precise, why not start the fire in the office where Conrad was shot?"

Phil shrugged. "This stove-top system allowed the perpetrator adequate time to get out of the house. Safer than having to outrun a fire, down a flight of stairs you've already covered in gasoline. Di Lucca should have more information on the accelerant and fire-starting device by tomorrow. She'll also run the details through the arson database to see if it matches any established MOs."

D.D. nodded. True arsonists were a lot like serial killers. They didn't — couldn't — deviate from form.

"For now, she'd say it was nothing too sophisticated. Maybe even a single-Google-search-away sort of thing. But Di Lucca is excellent. She'll figure it out."

"Witnesses?"

"Nada. Fire started shortly after two. Not that many people around. Those that were . . . no one saw a car parked in the driveway or anyone dashing from a smoking home. Then again, given the time delay, the person may have exited more like one thirty and simply strolled down the street. This isn't one of those neighborhoods where everyone knows everything and everyone. Too big for that."

"What about cameras?" D.D. asked. Because Evie's lawyer had been right; Boston was a city lousy with surveillance systems, and a good detective knew how to use them.

"Couple of home security systems in the area, but none that capture the Carters' residence. As for traffic cameras, closest one is at the major intersection a mile back, where you make a left onto these side streets. Not terrible, if we knew who we're looking for. But without a target, too many subjects. Plus, there are side roads leading into this neighborhood as well; that traffic cam covers only the main drag."

"Meaning anyone, including Evie and her mom, could've arrived using one of the lesser-known byways?"

"True. Except Dick Delaney came up with quite the alibi for those two."

"When?"

"When you were talking to Evie. It's Joyce Hopkins's custom to park on the driveway."

"I know. We parked behind her."

"Exactly. Meaning her car was in plain sight most of the afternoon. As Delaney pointed out, there are about two dozen rabid reporters who can vouch for it."

"The meddling media as alibis?"

"Told you it was interesting."

"They could've taken an Uber, or a taxi, or whatever."

"Again, without the hordes noticing?"

D.D. scowled. Evie's attorney made a

good argument. The media had had the house under constant surveillance pretty much since this morning. The chances of Evie or her mother doing anything without some cameraman or reporter noticing were slim to none.

"I have to admit," she said at last, "I see Evie's point. Why would she burn down her own home, especially without having picked up some personal belongings first?"

"Women are that sentimental about their favorite sweater?"

"I was thinking more along the lines of her baby. Five months along, Evie's probably bought at least one item or two, let alone ultrasound photos, personal snapshots of before and after. I can't see any soon-to-be mom willingly destroying such items. Unless, of course, she removed them before she ever shot Conrad. During the initial crime scene walk-through, did you notice any baby items?"

"I wasn't really looking," Phil confessed. "But we have plenty of photos of the house. Easy enough to look again. I have another thought regarding the fire."

"Which is?"

"Evie shot the computer. Over half a dozen times, right? Seems to me the computer was what she wanted to eliminate.

And did. So why risk returning to set a fire?"

"You think she already covered her tracks. The destroyed laptop."

"I think we've established she's partial to firearms."

D.D. couldn't argue with that. She stared at the gutted home again. "Again, from the top. What do we know? Sixteen years ago, Evie's father was shot and killed in his own home."

"Evie now says she didn't do it. But her story is still subject to debate," Phil provided.

"Could it have been suicide?" D.D. postulated. "That would certainly be something the mother might feel compelled to cover up. Evie didn't report seeing anything other than her father's body and the shotgun, however."

"Again, if she's telling the truth." Phil looked at her. "Even if you don't have spatter evidence from Evie, you gotta have crime scene photos of the body. Have the criminalists rework the angle of the blast. That'll tell you where the shooter was standing and whether or not Hopkins could've shot himself."

"Good point. Okay, so one shooting death sixteen years ago that was probably covered up in some manner. Fast-forward to yesterday, when Evie's husband just happens to also meet death by firearm."

"Conrad Carter," Phil intoned. "The kind of guy everyone liked but no one seemed to know. Except maybe your CI, Flora Dane, who claims to have met him in a bar with Jacob Ness."

Phil's tone implied he still had his doubts. D.D. shrugged. With Flora, anything was possible. On the other hand, D.D. had never known the woman to intentionally lie. Omit truth, yes, but deliberately lie . . .

D.D. picked up their story line: "No history of domestic disturbance calls or tension between Conrad and Evie. But according to Evie's fellow teacher, some signs of recent stress in Evie's life."

Phil nodded. "Which brings us to Evie Carter, five months pregnant and tied to one accidental shooting that happened when she was a juvenile. Clean record, however, since then."

"They bought the house together four years ago. Both have day jobs during the week, home renovation projects on the weekends. Ordinary," D.D. said at last, frowning. "By all accounts, a normal if not boring young couple building a life, starting a family. Until last night."

"Three rounds into the husband. Twelve

into the computer. Eight minutes in between."

"That time gap is gonna kill us at trial."

"What about your theory Evie used the eight minutes to retrieve something off the computer before destroying it? Which she then must have hidden somewhere in the house, or it would've been recovered from her person during processing."

"And the house was then torched to eliminate whatever she recovered?"

Phil shrugged. "That would imply someone else had to know she hid something. We're still processing phone records for her and him. It's possible something will come up."

"A phone call right after that shooting?"

"Would be pretty damning. And certainly, eight-minute gap or not, we have a tight timeline of the evening. Neighbors called in the first sound of shots fired. Uniformed officers were standing on the front porch for the second. Can't argue with that."

D.D. sighed. "I wish Conrad's laptop was still intact. Seems like the key to this puzzle was on that laptop."

"We know Evie has access to a computer at work. We'll grab that next. Amazing what the browser history can reveal about a person."

"How to burn down a house and still have time to get away?" D.D. intoned dryly.

"Exactly. And we still do have one last item of consideration: if there was . . . is . . . a connection between Conrad Carter and Jacob Ness . . ."

D.D. followed his train of thought perfectly. "Lots of perpetrators use the internet."

Phil sighed heavily. "I can't believe I'm going to say this, but . . . your crazy CI? She may be able to help us yet."

CHAPTER 12
FLORA

The inside of Keith Edgar's brownstone is as surprising as the man himself. An open floor plan that yawns way back. Miles of dark wood flooring beneath a stark-white tray ceiling. A slate-covered fireplace that rises like a granite column in the middle of the distinctly modern space. The fireplace boasts gas flames, which dance across highly polished stones. In front of that sits a low-slung turquoise sofa, bookended by orange chairs. Some kind of shag rug covered in bright splashes of color gets the hard job of tying it all together, while above the fireplace, a massive flat-screen TV belches out the evening news, including an update on the fire at the Carters' house. I already caught some details on my phone. Yet more questions about a shooting, a couple, a man, I have yet to understand.

I remain rooted in the entryway of the brownstone, my back to a wall. Now that

I'm in the house, actually face-to-face with Keith, I'm not sure what to do.

Keith springs to life first. He darts forward, grabs a remote from the glass coffee table, and turns off the TV. "Sorry, just catching up on the news. Can I get you something? Water? Coffee?" He glances at his watch, notes the hour. "A glass of wine?"

To judge by the furniture, I would've pegged him for a dry martini. And lots of hours spent viewing *Mad Men.* In between his time on the true-crime boards.

"Have a seat," Keith tries now. He gestures to one of the orange chairs. "Umm, welcome, thanks for coming. Is this because of the last letter I sent? I didn't actually think you'd respond. I mean, it's not like the other notes worked. But you can't blame a guy for trying."

He smiles, blushes slightly, and for a moment looks as self-conscious as I feel. I can't decide if this guy is for real or if he's already the most accomplished psychopath I've ever met.

"Is this your place?" I ask at last, moving toward the chair.

He nods.

"Wife? Kids?"

He shakes his head.

"What do you do?"

"I'm a computer analyst. Most of the time I work from home. And don't look anything like this." Again, the charming tinge of color to his cheeks as he gestures to his upscale wardrobe. "But I happened to have a meeting with a client today. You're lucky that I'd just returned home. Or I'm lucky. Something like that."

"I'll take that glass of water now."

He turns immediately, striding past the fireplace and heading to the rear of the house, which must contain the kitchen. I take the moment to compose myself, reassess the space. Front door behind me. Most likely patio doors straight back. An open-bannister staircase to the left. A door at the base of the stairs. Coat closet, most likely. Another door directly across from that. Downstairs powder room.

Otherwise, a very open, expansive space, decorated like a page out of a West Elm catalogue. But in my second survey, I catch what I missed the first time around. No photos. No wall art. Nothing of any personal nature at all.

According to Keith Edgar, he not only owns this house, but also works out of it. And yet this space might as well be a showroom. Perfectly appointed and completely devoid of personality.

We all wear masks. And the more we have to hide, the more accomplished the veneer.

Keith returns with a tall glass of water. I take it from him carefully, not standing too close, making sure our fingers don't touch. Then I do take a seat. My inventory has restored my sense of paranoia. I have all my survivor's instincts kicking in now.

Meaning I'm relaxed for the first time since I knocked on the door.

"Why true crime?" I ask him. I hold my water glass but don't sip it. I notice the glass coffee table has a perfectly clear top. Not a single spec of dust or water ring. I wonder if he cleans it obsessively, or pays someone to do it for him.

"I've always been fascinated by puzzles." He takes the orange chair across from me, leaving the table between us, as if he understands I need the barrier. He leans slightly forward, arms resting loosely on each leg. He's still smiling, clearly delighted by my unexpected presence in his house. I decide then and there that if he takes a selfie, I will kick him in the balls.

"Doesn't explain true crime."

"I particularly enjoy puzzles that haven't been solved. True crime one-oh-one. You start with Jack the Ripper, then the Black Dahlia, and next thing you know, you're reading everything about every notorious homicide, because the only way to get fresh insight into the unsolved murders is to learn from the killers who did get arrested. Why did they do what they did? And how can they be caught?"

"What's the nature of evil?" I ask dryly.

He shrugs slightly. "Most people debate whether evil is born or made. Nature versus nurture. Based on my research, I think of it more as a spectrum. All of the above, but with some predators leaning more one way or another. For example, Ted Bundy —"

"By all means, Ted Bundy."

That quick grin, proving he knows just how much he resembles one of the nation's most feared super-predators. "I think he's an example of evil that's born. Bundy claimed that he was affected by his unconventional upbringing — being raised by his grandparents as his mother's younger brother, versus being acknowledged as her illegitimate child. But I think we can all agree that as traumas go, that doesn't quite rise to the level of spending your adult life hunting and killing young women — particularly given evidence he was playing with knives by the time he was three. Him, Dahmer, they were always going to be killers. Just a matter of when."

I say nothing.

He clasps his hands, continues quickly. "Then you have Edmund Kemper the third. Raised by an abusive, alcoholic mother who was severely critical of him. Forced to live in the basement because she didn't want him near his sisters. Then sent as a teenager to live with his grandparents, whom he hated."

I can't help myself: "He was sent to live with his grandparents because he'd already murdered the family cats."

I earn a quick nod of approval. Whatever game we're playing, I'm at least living up to expectations. Or was just stupid enough to take the bait.

"But here's the deal with Kemper," Keith says now, totally serious. "He shot and killed his grandparents when he was fifteen. That got him sent away to a facility for youthful offenders where he was diagnosed with paranoid schizophrenia. So, sure, you could argue brain chemistry, born bad —"

"He shot his grandmother just to see what it felt like."

"Exactly." Another earnest nod. "And upon getting released, he murdered six young women, even liked to drive by police stations with their bodies stuffed in the trunk of his car. But this is what makes

Kemper so fascinating: He was also incredibly intelligent and reflective. Smart enough, he realized one day that the person he really wanted to kill was his mother. So he did. He went to her house, murdered her —"

"Stuck her larynx down the garbage disposal so he'd never have to listen to her again."

"And then he *turned himself in.* That was it. His mother had tormented him most of his life. He'd finally addressed the issue. Then he was done. Compare that to Bundy, who broke out of prison, what — two, three times? Swore each time he'd clean up his act, only to devolve into larger and more horrific crime sprees. Bundy was born evil. Kemper had some of the necessary starting ingredients, don't get me wrong, but his upbringing at the hands of his mother was the deciding factor. So again, there's not one answer to the question of what's the nature of evil, just as there's no one answer that defines anything about human behavior. Evil is a spectrum. And different predators fall in different places along the scale."

"No one wants to be a monster," I murmur.

"What?"

"Nothing."

"You have questions," he says abruptly.

He's not smiling anymore. His expression is serious. He steeples his hands, rests his fingertips against his chin. "You didn't come to talk. If you were going to do that, you would've contacted me in advance, made arrangements to meet the group. Asked about the speaker's fee."

"Cashed the check?"

Another nod. "This isn't about what you have to offer us. It's about what we can offer you."

I don't answer right away. I study the glass of water. The way the condensation has beaded up, heated by the flames from the gas fireplace.

"Why don't you have any personal photos in this room?"

"This isn't just my home, it's also a professional space. I don't care to give that much away to clients."

"Your reading has made you that paranoid?"

His turn to fall silent. I know then what I should've suspected from the beginning.

"How old were you?" I ask.

"Six. And it wasn't me who was victimized, but my older cousin in New York. They never caught who killed him; it's one of those open cases. But the details of his murder match four other unsolved homicides from the same time period. My aunt and uncle . . . They've never quite recovered. You grow up seeing the impact such a crime has on a person, a family, a community, it leaves a mark."

"You work his case?"

"I have for the past twenty years. I'm no closer to solving it than the police are."

"A string of related murders that simply ended?" I raise a brow.

"Exactly. Predators don't stop on their own. But sometimes, they get arrested for other crimes. Or change jurisdiction. In this day and age of nationwide law enforcement databases, it's harder for that trick to work. But international travel . . ."

"A killer with means."

"My cousin was strangled with a silk tie. There was evidence of sexual intercourse, but not necessarily assault. He'd told some friends he'd recently met an older, wealthy gentleman. He was excited about the potential for the relationship."

"You think he was seduced, then murdered?"

He nodded.

"I'm sorry," I say at last.

"I was too young to understand the nuances of his death. Later, when I was fifteen, I happened to look it up. Imagine my surprise to find my cousin's murder linked to a series of strangulations on various websites. But it was the true-crime sites, groups like the one I run now, that captured my attention. They'd given it serious thought and in many cases done some real work. We're not all just armchair detectives. Some of our members are retired police, medical professionals, even a coroner."

"And *your* skills?"

"I'm a computer nerd. Trust me, you want to do any kind of meaningful research these days, and you're going to need a geek."

"Why Jacob Ness?"

"Local case. Received a lot of coverage when you were recovered." He pauses slightly and I can tell he's trying to figure out if he should've used such clinical terms. Then he shrugs. It is what is, and we both know it.

"But Jacob's crime is known," I say. "Well documented. Where's the riddle?"

Keith cocks his head to the side. "Do you really call him Jacob?"

"I just did."

"When you were together?"

"Well, 'Rat Bastard' had a tendency to earn me negative consequences."

"You still think about him."

"You're the expert, you tell me."

He shakes his head. "I only know the perpetrators. I don't know . . ."

"Me? Other survivors? The ones who, unlike your cousin, got away?" My words are harsh. Unnecessarily so. I can't seem to help myself. I still can't figure out if this guy is for real. Successful computer analyst by day, brilliant true-crime solver by night. Or something darker, more sinister. Does he study predators because he wants to stop them, or because like always calls to like?

Across from me, Keith has carefully reset his features. He taps his steepled fingertips against his chin, once, twice. Then: "I think Jacob Ness remains an unsolved riddle. I think we know about *a* crime — his abduction of you. But the sophistication of his operation, the box, the sensory deprivation, the brainwashing techniques —"

"I don't need a recap."

"You couldn't have been his first victim. These guys, by definition, they escalate. They build to the kind of premeditated, well-planned, sustainable operation that was your abduction."

"The FBI looked into it. I'm told they couldn't find evidence of other crimes."

Keith regards me intently. "That's not correct, strictly speaking. They found other evidence. Just not enough to build additional cases."

I can't speak. I study my water glass again. I get the distinction he's making. After all my years with Samuel, I know how the FBI thinks. Of course they would make a distinction, and Samuel would split those hairs in delivering that news to me. *We aren't looking at additional cases at this time.* Not because there wasn't any evidence. Just not *enough.*

I can't look at Keith. "How many?" My voice is quiet.

"The group . . . We have been looking at six unsolved missing persons cases. All young women. None of them ever seen again. All during the time Jacob had his truck route in the South. We've been trying to see if we can establish a firm connection. For three of the women, we have been able to place Jacob in the same town as them at the time of their disappearance. The police, of course, want more."

I inhale. Exhale. Six women. I'm waiting for the news to surprise me, but it doesn't. I've always known I couldn't have been Jacob's first. He talked about at least assaulting others. But had he actually kidnapped them? Eventually killed them? I hadn't allowed myself to consider it. That maybe there had been others in the coffin-sized box before me.

"The police would have forensic evidence," I say at last. "From his rig. He had a special compartment. They could study it for DNA."

"The police recovered multiple strands of hair and fibers, as well as additional DNA evidence from Jacob's truck. Most of it, however, was connected to various prostitutes, including two that were murdered in Florida. Gutted after walking off with a beautiful young woman."

I don't say a word.

"With dark hair," he adds.

I still say nothing.

"But there's also evidence that the box where he held you in the truck was new. A recent insert, probably prepared especially for you. Meaning . . ."

"He could've had other inserts for previous girls."

"In your statement, you talked about being held in a basement of some cabin in Georgia. Jacob told you he had to vacate it because the owner died, so he allowed you to join him in his truck."

I shrug. I know this already.

"The police have never been able to locate the cabin. Which is stranger than you might think. While the mountains of Georgia are vast, the number of cabins whose owners died the year you were abducted isn't that big. From there, it's simply a matter of visiting the local community, floating pictures of Jacob and his vehicle, as well as checking Jacob's financials for gas receipts — anything. The FBI should've found a connection between him and one of the towns or cabins easily enough. But they didn't. Haven't. Ever."

I frown. Rub my right thumb along the water glass's condensation. "You think I was wrong? I lied to the police?"

"Actually, I think Jacob lied. To you. He wanted to keep your initial location secret. Even from you. That way, if you did escape, you couldn't give it away."

"His lair," I say the words softly. "That cabin. It was his monster's lair, and he didn't want to give it up."

"I think if we could find it, we'd learn a lot more about Jacob Ness. Maybe even find a link to the other missing girls."

"He's dead. If he did own such a cabin, it would've gone on the auction block by now. Foreclosure, repossessed by the IRS, whatever."

"I tried that. The property can't be in Jacob's name, or listed under any of his known associates because, again, the FBI would've found it already. So periodically, I run a list of all properties up for auction in northern Georgia, with a basement. Unfortunately, that list is longer than I'd like."

"You're serious about this."

"Yes."

"You've been working these other missing girls' cases, for what, six years already?"

"Samantha Mathers, Elaine Waters, Lilah Abenito, Daphne Passero, Rachel Englert, Brenda Solomon."

"Do the police assist you?"

A small pause. "Officially, no. But some of the group's members . . . have connections."

"With the FBI?"

"Not as good as yours," he says bluntly.

"And this is why you wanted to talk to me?"

"Not necessarily. You're a victim. We're the hunters. We don't expect —"

I hold up a hand. "Never call me a victim again. I'm a survivor. There's a difference."

He nods.

"I killed him," I say shortly. The words are hot and fierce. I won't take them back. "Does your group know that?"

"Yes."

"Do you blame me? If I'd let him live, you'd have your answers. These missing girls, their families, they'd have closure."

"Did you ever hear Jacob talk about other girls?"

"Specifically, no. But he was a sex addict, wife beater, and serial rapist. I already knew I wasn't his first. But I assumed that I was the first he'd taken such great lengths to keep."

"Why?"

"Fuck you."

Keith falls silent again.

I can't take it. I'm too agitated. I smack the glass of water on the coffee table. I like the sharp sounds it makes, as brittle as I feel. Water rings. I can already see them forming, and watch as Keith glances helplessly at the growing mess on his precious, shiny table. It gives me a perverse pleasure. Then I'm up, moving, walking, wishing I could shed my own skin.

I don't want to be me anymore. Not today. Not seven years ago. Never every single moment of the four hundred and seventy-two days Jacob kept me his prisoner. I hate to think of him. I loathe remembering what it was like to feel so helpless, so weak.

But I'm further disoriented to be here, in this place, with this man. Somewhere in the back of my mind, I get it. In this room, the two Floras collide.

The teenage girl I used to be. The beautiful blonde who could make any boy look twice. That Flora would've been impressed by Keith Edgar. His dark good looks, a swanky Boston town house. She would've been scintillated to hear of his murdered cousin, his heroic cause to catch other killers out there. She would've been thinking about kissing him.

Then there's the woman I am. Who looks at a handsome, charming man and thinks instantly of Ted Bundy. Who is too skinny and too hard and too tired after seven years without a single good night's sleep. Who doesn't think about dating, or men, or kissing . . . anyone.

I don't have romantic dreams or aspirations anymore. Some survivors do. They figure out how to compartmentalize, that was then, this is now. I can't. I live in a state of lockdown. I spent so long separating my mind from my body in order to survive another day, I can't get it back. My body is merely a tool. Jacob used it for sex. I use it for revenge. Neither of us respects the package.

And now I don't want to be here. I don't want to talk to Keith Edgar. I don't want to think of other missing girls. Whom Jacob might have kidnapped and held in his big rig. Did he keep some longer than me? Did he enjoy their company more? Dear God, is it possible to be jealous of such a thing?

"Flora?" Keith asks quietly. He hasn't moved.

"Did Jacob have a partner?" I say. "In your research, is there any evidence he knew other predators, maybe connected with them online?"

"I'm not sure."

"What does that *mean*?"

"It means I'm not the FBI. I don't have access to his laptop the way they do. Jacob was a loner. Yet, the amount he traveled, his ability to so completely cover his tracks . . . I wouldn't be surprised if he had some friends, associates helping him out. Why are you here, Flora? Why are you asking these questions now?"

"You said you don't have access to the FBI."

"No."

I finally look at him. "I do."

He regards me evenly. "Why here, why now?" he repeats. "What happened?"

"I need to know everything about Jacob Ness before I met him. Help me answer those questions, and eventually, I'll answer yours."

He doesn't even blink. "When do you want to start?"

"Right now. Get your computer. We're going to make a call."

CHAPTER 13
EVIE

What is the perfect marriage? When I first met Conrad, I felt like acceptance was the key. I was at a fellow teacher's cookout. A rare public venture, since even back then my past followed me everywhere. But it was May, a beautiful sunny day after another long Boston winter, and I wanted one afternoon of feeling like everyone else. So I showed up, a young teacher, hanging out, eating slightly charred chicken in a colleague's backyard.

I heard his laugh. That's what caught my attention first. Booming. Natural. Unencumbered. In my family, my parents' house . . . I don't remember ever hearing anyone laugh like that.

Conrad was standing in the corner near the fence, sweaty beer in hand, ketchup stain on a blue Hawaiian shirt. He was clearly holding court, regaling the gathering throng. So I drifted closer, still on the outskirts, but listening now.

Windows. He was telling stories of windows. Of five-by-three windows that arrived being fifteen inches by thirteen inches, and custom creams that showed up pine green, which he was then informed was merely a darker shade of cream, and even better the order he placed for a fancy home in Barrington, Rhode Island, that the factory claimed it couldn't deliver because Rhode Island wasn't a state — surely he meant Long Island instead.

More laughter. More swigs of beers. More stories from the road.

I don't know how long I stood off to the side before he noticed me. He glanced over once or twice, taking in the crowd, but surely not zeroing in on a slim woman with dirty-blond hair, still nursing her first beer, which was more of a placeholder than a beverage.

Then, suddenly, he stood before me. The crowd had disappeared and the man himself had appeared. Up close, he was compact, muscularly built, with light brown hair and deep blue eyes. His features were tan, and when he smiled his teeth were a flash of white against his sun-darkened skin.

He looked . . . strong and capable and funny and honest and like all my hopes and dreams rolled up into one package.

Then he shook my hand. Reached over and simply took it, and the feel of his calloused fingers against my skin . . .

I wanted him right then. In a way I'd already taught myself never to want anything. I didn't move. I didn't smile hello. I didn't offer my name. But it didn't matter. He did the talking for both of us. He did the laughing for both of us. Later, he asked for a walk around the block, just so we could get to know each other, and he asked me so many questions, that I found myself answering.

None of my answers fazed him. Not my job as a math teacher (*great, a woman with brains!*), not my legendary father (*that must be interesting, I don't have any family left*), and not what had happened one day when I was sixteen, that still left me gutted and reeling and untethered to real life (*I'm so sorry, I lost both my parents several years ago; you never get over the loss*).

By the time we hit the end of the street and were headed back, I was hooked. I wanted the boom of his laugh, the brightness of his company, the way he looked at me, truly looked at me. As if nothing I could do or say would shock him. Or make him not want me.

That's who I fell in love with in the beginning. A guy who seemed to accept me, unconditionally.

It wasn't until later that I realized that Conrad was also the kind of guy who seemed to get everyone. Strangers gravitated toward him in a crowded bar. Neighbors lingered just to talk to him.

It was his superpower, what made him so good at his job, traveling to job sites, speccing out high-end windows, soothing irate customers.

Everyone loved Conrad. Everyone felt heard and understood and acknowledged by him.

Yet how well did any of us know him? A guy who logged so many hours on the road with little or no accountability? A guy with no family to visit and tell stories about his younger years?

A guy who did all the talking but never really told you anything about himself.

Then there was the locked door.

Innocent enough. I ran out of packing tape in the kitchen. Walked up to Conrad's office, thinking he'd have a fresh roll. He was traveling, his office door shut. No biggie, I thought. I went to turn the knob only to discover that I couldn't.

Confusion. A locked door in my own

house? Followed shortly by disbelief. Why would Conrad even bother? There was only me hanging around and it's not like a custom window business involved state secrets. Followed shortly by . . . curiosity.

A locked door is a puzzle. And no self-respecting mathematician can walk away from a puzzle.

It became a game for me. Every time the door was closed, to wander by, test it. Conrad watching TV downstairs at night. Door unlocked. Gone for an afternoon meeting. Locked. Business trips, definitely locked. Two A.M. when I got up just because I had to know, locked again.

I never said a word, of course. That would imply that I didn't trust him — wouldn't it?

Anyway, I grew up with a mom who regularly manipulated reality to best suit her needs. I didn't want to be told an answer. I wanted to learn it for myself.

So I did what any dysfunctional adult who is accustomed to chronic lies would do: I waited till my husband's next business trip; then I picked the lock to his private office.

My hand shook when I first cracked open the door. My heart was pounding. I felt like Bluebeard's wife, stepping into the very room she'd been warned about. The next thing I would see would be the hanging corpses of past wives.

I discovered file cabinets. Stacks of window catalogues. A printer/ scanner. And a cleared spot on the desk where Conrad's laptop usually lived. I went through the files. Once you've committed B and E you can't just walk away. I found project files, various blueprints for homes up and down the East Coast. I found vendor files, handwritten notes on upcoming product changes, and new and improved color options.

In the end, I got on my hands and knees. I searched for documents taped under the desk, files slipped behind the cabinets, maybe even a computer code stamped to the bottom of the executive leather chair. I felt crazed. A woman having an out-of-body experience. It struck me that this was exactly what my mother would do. My poor husband was simply in the habit of locking up, and here I was, turning it into sordid drama.

Why couldn't I simply trust him? Or was it me I didn't trust? Did I figure that anyone who loved me the way he loved me had to have something wrong with him?

I crawled around the office on my hands and knees. I went through every single scrap of paper. If Conrad hadn't been out of town, if he'd returned home early, there's no way I would've been able to justify my behavior, the total gutting of his neat and almost hyperorganized professional space.

Except I'm a mathematician, raised by one of the world's best intellects. And part of brilliance isn't just solving a problem; it's seeing a problem no one else realizes is a problem yet.

A locked room, in the privacy of a man's own home, containing only files and not even a computer . . . Why? Why lock it at all?

A puzzle. I needed the solution.

Then I saw the lone piece of semivaluable equipment. The printer/ scanner. With a memory cache.

I fell in love with Conrad for his loud laugh, his smile, his personality. And, no, I didn't find any bodies of murdered wives that day. But in the end, I did find a bread crumb. An image of a scanned document, a record of a bank account that I never knew existed.

Not a crime. Not even anything I could mention without having to reveal how I discovered it. But a piece of a puzzle.

Which, of course, I churned and worried and worked. Until I waited for him to go on trips, just so I could once more rip apart his space. Except then he started regarding me through narrowed eyes upon his return, probably because I didn't put everything back perfectly, so he knew something was off even if he didn't quite know what.

I started taking pictures. Of exactly how the office looked upon entry, so I could carefully replace each item. Then, when he still seemed unsettled, I started checking the doorway for tricks I read about online — a piece of hair positioned across the doorway, which would be broken upon entry. Easy enough to replace with one of my own upon exiting. Or lint positioned just so on top of a slightly skewed open drawer. Which I photographed and returned to its exact location.

A duel of sorts. Months, years. A period of strain followed by a period of shame when I swore to myself I'd stop this madness. Conrad was a good guy. Conrad loved me. If he had financials that were his own, frankly, so did I. That made us independent adults, not government spies or nefarious criminals.

But eventually I would break again. And back into the office I would go, tearing apart my marriage in search of answers to a question I couldn't even ask.

What is the perfect marriage? Acceptance, I had thought. But I'd assumed it would be my husband's acceptance of me. I'd never stopped to consider that maybe I'd prove incapable of accepting him. That maybe my mother, via the lie that had become my adult life, had warped me even more than I'd understood.

You can't sneak around in a marriage forever. Sooner or later, no matter how careful you are, you're going to get caught. Yet I couldn't stop. It's almost as if I wanted Conrad to figure out what I was doing. I needed our marriage to fall apart.

Except, suddenly, two made three.

Then my mistakes truly came back to haunt me.

I don't know what to do. I can't go outside. Even this late at night, the media vans remain a solid wall of high-powered lights parked just across the street. I'm too keyed up for sleep, my brain jumping between images of Conrad's blood-spattered body and our home's burnt-out shell. I should rest for the baby's sake. I should flee my mother's house for my sake. I should do . . . something.

But I don't know what. Sixteen years ago, confronted by a similar tragedy, I'd simply done what I was told and taken the blame. Now?

I hate the lingering sense of déjà vu. And worse, the feeling of once more being helpless.

I hadn't lied to the detective. I still don't know what happened to my father. One moment, I had a dad, my hero, my rock, the man I could always count on. Then he was dead. Just like that.

My mom's response upon entering the kitchen . . . it wasn't horror; it was outrage mixed with hysteria. That he'd gone and died? Or that he'd gone and killed himself, which is what I've always wondered. At sixteen, shell-shocked and traumatized, I'd never thought to question my mom. If she said we needed to keep what happened between us, then we needed to keep it between us. Denial was what my mother did best.

I followed her lead that afternoon. It wasn't hard. A terrible tragedy had occurred. In my own mind, it was easy enough to substitute myself with the shotgun, maybe even easier than contemplating my beloved father positioning the gun beneath his ribs. Standing grimly in front of the refrigerator, which offered the safest backdrop for gunfire (when cleaning the shotgun, he'd instructed, always aim it at the stainless steel appliance). Then, upon hearing the crunch of my mother's car tires in the driveway, pulling the trigger.

No, it was so much easier to lie than to picture any of that.

For all my father's brilliance, I'd seen the dark shadows that lurked in his eyes. The way he sometimes smiled but still appeared sad. The times he squared his shoulders before walking into his office, appearing less like a gifted mathematician off in search of answers and more like a soldier burdened by a never-ending war.

The truth is, genius and depression have always gone hand in hand. Which was why I spent so many afternoons, sitting at the piano, playing and playing, because my father said my music soothed his spirit and allowed him to rest in a way a truly great mind could never completely be at ease. I did my best to music the sadness out of him.

And that day, walking into the kitchen, my father's hot blood dripping down into my hair, I felt the weight of my failure. That I had loved this man so much, and tried so hard, and it still wasn't enough.

Just like Conrad.

I hope my baby isn't a boy, I think now. Because I just couldn't take another such loss.

■ ■ ■ ■

I should marshal my resources, I decide. Money. I'm going to need some. Which is the first time I realize how lost I truly am. My wallet, cell phone, car keys, had all been in the house — which, according to the detectives, is now nothing more than a pile of charred ruins. I have a moment of growing hysteria: Next time you're arrested for the murder of your husband, grab your purse!

But of course, I hadn't, and the police certainly hadn't offered to fetch anything. Meaning I have . . . nothing.

Not completely true. I have a head for figures. Including bank accounts. Just because I don't possess a checkbook or debit card, let alone an unmelted driver's license, doesn't mean I don't know my accounts and their exact balances. The savings account has some money. Not a lot, as neither Conrad nor I had high-paying jobs and it seemed like most of our checks were spent on home renovations.

Then again . . .

My head starts spinning. Suddenly, I'm thinking about a lot of things. Including scraps of documents in a printer/scanner.

Conrad's news upon learning we were pregnant. Other forms of photo ID.

The house was burned to the ground. Including Conrad's precious office and all his customer files.

But some things he valued even more than his office. Some things he had made fireproof.

I am not helpless, I tell myself. I'm damaged and incredibly sad. But I'm not helpless.

And now, with a little help from my lawyer, I have a plan.

CHAPTER 14
D.D.

"I think I might have screwed up an investigation."

"You? Never."

It was after nine P.M. Jack nestled in for the night in his red race-car bed, Kiko curled up at his side and taking up nearly as much of the mattress as the boy. Alex had poured himself and D.D. both well-deserved glasses of wine. They sat side by side on the sofa, engaging in their own nightly ritual of catching up and winding down.

"So I'm investigating a pregnant woman who's accused of murdering her husband last night, and who also confessed to accidentally shooting her father with a shotgun sixteen years ago."

"I remember. You handled the father's shooting."

"Exactly. And I believed her. Bought her story, her mom's story, the whole kit and caboodle. This afternoon, she informed me she'd lied."

Alex paused, wineglass halfway to his lips. "Interesting defense strategy."

"According to her revised statement, she and her mother weren't even home at the time of the shooting but must've walked in moments later. The spatter in Evie's hair and clothing was from blood dripping down when she walked through the door. The GSR from her picking up the shotgun."

"Okay. But given that scenario, why confess?"

"Her mother didn't want to risk an investigation that might result in findings that would tarnish her father's intellectual legacy."

It didn't take Alex long. "Suicide. She assumed her husband had shot himself."

D.D. nodded. Took a sip of her own wine. She waited. She did her best thinking out loud. Alex, on the other hand, had a tendency to compose himself. Then, a true teacher, deliver his lecture.

"Suicide by shotgun happens," he said now. "Generally the end of the barrel is positioned under the chin or against the ribs, pressed against the skin in order to help stabilize the long gun while the victim reaches down for the trigger. Though I did read about an enterprising young man who used his toes to pull the trigger. Then there's the Australian case of the triple-shot suicide, where the victim's first attempt ended up being clean through the chest cavity, missing major organs. Then he set up for under the chin but flinched upon pulling the trigger — which happens more than you think — destroying half his jaw, but again, not incapacitating himself. I don't remember his third choice — maybe that was the same guy who finally sat down and used his toes — but the third shot got it done. Now, from an investigative perspective, can you imagine walking into a scene of a man hit by three shotgun blasts and thinking even for a second that it was suicide? In our jobs, anything is possible."

D.D. gave him her best scowl. "I don't want theoretical. I need practical. I'm drowning here in half lies, past assumptions, and a family with a whole new brand of crazy. I think Phil is actually scared of the mom. Probably for good reason."

"Interesting. I like it. And you know you do, too."

She rolled her eyes. Another sip of wine for them both. Then Alex set down his glass on the coffee table and grew serious.

"All right. Let's take it back to the evidence."

"By all means."

"I'm assuming a pump-action shotgun?"

"Yes."

"Contact point?"

"The chest. Evie's official statement was that she'd picked up the shotgun, was trying to figure out how to clear the chamber when it went off mere inches from her father's torso."

"Okay. We can work with that. So the issue with suicide by long gun is trigger access; it's a reach to get it. Given that, like I said, most victims balance the tip of the barrel against their own bodies to help hold it in place. In a head shot, the most common contact point is the underside of the chin. In a chest shot, the ME should have evidence of a contact burn — against the ribs, if not right below the rib cage."

"I'll pull that report."

"Just to play devil's advocate — victims sometimes recoil as they're pulling the trigger, flinching away from the barrel. In which case, you'll get soot markings on the skin, versus an actual sear pattern. Soot means the barrel of the shotgun was held between three-quarters of an inch and a foot from the skin. Unfortunately in your case, such stipling could still go either way, as the girl testified she was standing just inches from her father, right?"

"So searing means the gun was definitely pressed against him — contradicting her statement. Soot means it still could've been suicide but he flinched, or that indeed she shot him from a close distance. I'm going to need more wine for this."

"Ah, but now we need to factor in trajectory. One hallmark of a suicide with a long gun is that there's nearly always a sharply angled trajectory, the bullet having tracked up, with the entrance wound distinctly lower than the exit wound. Think of trying to hold out a loaded shotgun level in front of you with one hand and pull the trigger with the other. It can't be done naturally. I mean maybe if the butt of the weapon was wedged against a wall or some other object, or some machination was in place to hold the barrel level, but you have no sign of that, right?"

"He went down in front of the refrigerator, open space in front of him."

"Toppled chair, by any chance?"

D.D. had to think about it, then shook her head. "I honestly don't remember. I've put in a request to pull the old file, which should have photos."

"If you are thinking suicide, one scenario is that he positioned the butt of the gun on a kitchen chair, placed the tip of the barrel against his torso, and pulled the trigger. Depending on how tall he was —"

"Six feet."

"Then you're still going to have a fairly angled trajectory versus the daughter's scenario, where she's holding the gun up, messing with the chamber, and accidentally pulls the trigger, shooting her father square in the torso."

"Okay."

"Which brings us to the last point of consideration: directionality of spatter."

"Ah yes, what would an evening in our house be without a discussion of spatter?"

Alex picked up his wineglass, clinked it against hers.

"There can be blowback from shooting directly into a torso. But the directionality of that spatter on skin and clothes is not at all the same as what might happen from the suicide scenario, when again, the force of the blast is going to be up and out of the body, distributing a pattern higher up on the wall behind the victim, possibly even on the ceiling."

"She said it dripped down on her when she walked into the room. She could feel the heat of it."

Alex's face was serious. "Wouldn't be the first time. But again, the two scenarios —

her shooting her father from mere inches away square in the chest, and her walking in after he's fired an upward shot through his chest cavity — lead to very different blood evidence. Very different."

"So review the photos, and whatever spatter evidence we still have from the scene."

Alex nodded.

"Okay. Got it. Thank you."

"There is a third possibility, you know."

D.D. sighed heavily. Because in this case, why not? "Which is?"

"There is searing on his skin, the trajectory is a steep angle passing through his torso, and the blood pattern from the blast is up and out."

"I thought that meant it was suicide."

"Or someone placed the barrel against his chest and pulled the trigger from a position beneath him. Forensics gives us position and angle, but it still can't tell us everything that might have led up to such a scenario."

D.D. eyed her husband. "As in, there could be other possibilities. Say, a struggle. Two people vying for the shotgun. Other person got it first. Hopkins stood up, tried to step back. Second person jammed the shotgun into his ribs and pulled the trigger. Self-defense. Or possibly murder. Wait a minute! I've lived with you long enough. In that scenario, we'd have a void in the spatter evidence, basically a blank spot where the shooter stood, got hit with blowback, and then exited out the door, removing that piece of the puzzle."

"But didn't you say the girl and her mom walked in right afterwards? Picked up the gun, mostly likely rushed to the body, even fell to their knees beside it?"

"Contaminated the scene," D.D. finished for him.

"I have a feeling your crime scene photos aren't going to be as revealing as you'd like."

"So I'm back where I started. Sixteen-year-old shooting death that could be either suicide or murder."

Alex shrugged. "It can always be murder, D.D. Where would our jobs be without it?"

CHAPTER 15
FLORA

"SSA Kimberly Quincy."

"Hi, um . . . This is Flora Dane."

There's a pause. I'm not surprised. What does catch me off guard is the sound of my own voice, shaky and faint. SSA Quincy and I are hardly BFFs. She organized the raid that eventually led to Jacob's death and my escape. But we haven't exactly spoken since.

Sitting across from me, Keith eyes me uncertainly. Nine P.M., I've just called a federal agent on her personal cell, and she isn't exactly responding with gushing enthusiasm. But I know how these things work. The raid on Jacob's motel room didn't just save me; it also boosted Quincy's career. One way or another, our lives are intertwined. I also know from Samuel that Bureau types don't exactly keep regular hours. This isn't the SSA's first late-night call, just her most unexpected.

"How can I help you, Flora?" Quincy's

voice is perfectly neutral. Apparently, she's decided to give me enough rope to hang myself. Fair enough.

Now it's my turn to collect my thoughts. Keith sits up straighter. He has his fingers poised over the keyboard of his laptop as if he's ready to record every word of the call. Maybe he is.

"I need information on Jacob Ness," I finally announce.

"I see."

"It's come to my attention he might be a person of interest in some other missing persons cases."

Another pause. "Flora, it's nine P.M. You're calling me at home. You're going to have to do better than sudden interest in a bunch of cold cases."

"So you *do* think he's connected to other missing women?"

"You have till the count of three, then I'm going to hang up. Future requests can go through official channels. One, two —"

"There's been a development!" I get it out in a rush. "A murder. Here in Boston. I recognized the victim. He met Jacob in a bar. It wasn't random. They knew each other."

Keith's eyes widen. I hadn't told him this part yet, but he doesn't make the mistake of gasping audibly or distracting from the call.

This time, the quiet on the other end of the phone is thoughtful. "Name of the murder victim?" SSA Quincy asks finally.

It occurs to me that Sergeant Warren is probably going to kill me. I decide it's a small price to pay. "Conrad Carter. Now I have questions of my own."

"Of course." Quincy's tone is droll.

"Do you think Jacob kidnapped other women?"

For the first time, there is no hesitation. "Yes."

"Murdered them?"

"Yes."

"How many?"

Cool tone again: "The investigation is ongoing."

"Maybe I can help."

"Can you? Because you never have before."

I wince, the effects of my onetime, one-telling policy coming back to bite me in the ass. She's right. I'd declined all official requests for interviews, debriefing, whatever the agents chose to call it back in the day. I gave my statement to Samuel while still collapsed in a hospital bed. I watched him run off to vomit. Then I never spoke of it again.

"I want to help."

"Does Dr. Keynes know?" SSA Quincy is a clever one.

"Do you know what I do now?" I ask the agent.

"No."

"I work with other survivors. Run a support group of sorts. I'm not qualified, I'm not brilliant, but I am experienced. I teach others to stop surviving and start living again."

SSA Quincy doesn't say anything. Neither does Keith. His fingers are still waiting above the keyboard. He wants details, I realize, not pleasantries.

"I understand I'm late to the party," I say at last. "That by not giving a statement earlier, maybe there were other victims of Jacob's or their families that I've let down. Samuel tells me not to second-guess, but it has been six years. I like to think I'm not the same girl anymore. I like to think . . . I'm stronger now. I want to do better. I can do better."

"I can be on a plane to Boston first thing in the morning," Quincy says.

"I have questions now. Information I need right now."

"Flora, it's late —"

"You really think I sleep at night? You think I care about rest at *all* anymore?" My

228

voice turns hard. Quincy doesn't hang up the phone.

"There has to be quid pro quo," she begins. "Otherwise known as you gotta pay to play. Official department policy."

"I already paid. Conrad Carter. Shot Tuesday night by his wife in Boston. Look it up. Lead detective Sergeant D. D. Warren."

"D. D. Warren?" I can tell by the change in Quincy's voice that she knows the name. "Does she know you're calling me?"

"Not yet. But I'm also her CI, so if she decides on bodily harm, at least she'll feel conflicted about it."

Across from me, Keith's eyes are growing rounder and rounder.

"I want to know what was on Jacob's computer." I plunge ahead. There's no stopping now. "Did you find evidence of e-mail correspondence, chat-room visits, online associates? He spent a lot of time on his computer. In real life, he was a loner. I already know that. But on the internet . . . Some predators network. I know that, too."

Keith is nodding softly, leaning closer to his laptop. Both of us eye the phone positioned on the table between us. This is the heart of the conversation. I paid. Now, would SSA Quincy play?

"Yes and no," she says at last.

My shoulders sag. Keith rolls his eyes. We share an immediate and unplanned moment: feds. Good God.

Then, as if she could see our exasperation: "Ness's computer was curiously clean."

"What does that mean?"

"We know he took photos and videos; we have the images he sent to your mother."

I nod. Keith starts to type.

"But his laptop was clear. Not a single copy existed. And wiping a hard drive is no easy task. Most experienced computer techs can rebuild anything these days. Find ghost images, piece together fragments of a fragment. So how did a long-haul trucker with only a high school–level education know how to clear his entire hard drive?"

Keith opens his mouth. I immediately hold up a hand to silence him, vigorously shaking my head. I probably should've mentioned his presence in the very beginning of the call. Having failed that, I wasn't about to spook a federal agent by mentioning we had company now.

"You think someone must've taught him how to cover his tracks," I say.

Keith is scribbling furiously. He holds up a note.

I continue: "Maybe even told him about

particular apps that would assist in clearing his hard drive."

Keith nods.

"What did this Conrad Carter do?" Quincy asks.

"I don't know. He traveled. Spent time in the South, I know that."

"Where did you meet him?"

"A bar. Honky-tonk. He sat down right beside us. After a bit . . . I had the impression Conrad was there for me. Like, maybe Jacob had made a deal with him."

Keith starts typing.

"Did you leave with him?" SSA Quincy asks.

"No. I threw up on him. Then he went away."

There's silence. Keith is no longer typing. I refuse to look at him. I don't want to see what's in his eyes.

"Were there other such instances?" Quincy asks. "Other meetings with other men?"

"No. But soon after that . . . I realized I'd never make it if I kept fighting." I stare at nothing in particular. "I decided to become Jacob's friend. Make him need me a little, as my entire existence depended on him."

"You survived, Flora. That's what matters. You picked a strategy and it enabled you to come home safe to your family."

I smile; I can't help myself. But I know it's a sad expression, because both my mother and brother will tell you that I didn't come home at all. They just got a shell that looks like their beloved daughter and sister, except there's nothing left on the inside.

Keith is scribbling another note. He holds it out to me. I read his question to the agent. "When was the last time the computer was analyzed?"

"Six years ago."

I glance at Keith, already anticipating his next point. "There have been advancements in computer forensics since then," I say.

He nods vigorously.

"Given the new development, I could have the computer reexamined. Did Jacob strike you as techie?"

"No. But —" I catch myself. "He was clever. And mechanical. I mean, he could keep his rig running on his own. And you know, building the pine coffin and all. He prided himself on self-sufficiency. I can't imagine him in a classroom environment. But pursuing something that would help him get something he wanted, yeah, he'd do that."

"He still would've had to utilize resources," Quincy states. "We never recovered any books on computers, web surfing, or programming one-oh-one from his vehicle. On the other hand, he only made contact with your mother through internet cafés, which reveals a certain level of sophistication right there. He knew better than to use his own laptop, which we might have eventually been able to trace back to him via IP address, et cetera."

"You never found the cabin in Georgia."

"We've never found anything resembling a permanent residence for Jacob Ness."

"His lair," I murmur. "What about his mother?"

"He used her address for mail. According to her, she hadn't seen him in years. We did a full sweep of that house, mostly recovering clothing and porn."

"There should've been porn on his computer. He was always watching porn."

"We found DVDs in the front cab; nothing on the computer. Not even a history of porn-site visits or searches."

"That's not right. The guy was a sex addict. His computer should've been ninety percent smut."

Across from me, Keith is nodding. Predator one-oh-one, no level of murder or assault is ever enough for them. They all have to feed their appetites in between, even the ones who travel around the country with their own girls stashed in coffin-sized boxes.

"I'm going to get on a plane in the morning," Quincy says.

I nod, then realize she can't see me. "Okay."

"I want to know everything about Conrad Carter."

"Be sure to use your nice voice," I offer weakly, already picturing D.D.'s face when the federal agent shows up at HQ. Maybe I should warn her in advance. Or call Samuel and beg for safe harbor.

"I'm going to use my bright, shiny federal shield."

Yep, I'm a dead woman. "I want information on the other missing women," I say, because as long as my time on this earth is limited . . .

Keith nods adamantly.

"Flora —"

"I have more to offer."

"Than embroiling me in a pissing match against one of BPD's toughest detectives?"

"I want to find his lair. We need it. If we could find it, think of the evidence."

My voice is soft but certain. Keith regards me curiously. I can't decide if he thinks I'm incredibly brave or truly self-destructive. Quincy must think the same because she doesn't answer for a long time.

"We already checked for cabins in Georgia whose owners died the year you were abducted. We didn't have any luck," she says at last.

"Maybe it wasn't Georgia. Maybe the owner didn't die. Maybe he lied to me, another layer of protection in case I did manage to escape. I mean, if we're now saying Jacob was clever enough to wipe his laptop, what's a few lies to a girl he has locked in a box?"

Again the silence. Then, because I can't help myself: "Was there other forensic evidence in the box? Of, you know, of other girls?"

"We think he built the box for you."

There's something in the way she says it that catches my attention. "But it wasn't his first box," I fill in slowly. "There were others, for . . . other girls."

"An UNSUB doesn't achieve Ness's level of organization and sophistication overnight."

Which is nothing new. Keith had already told me the same. But it's starting to hit me now. Truly register. I might've been Jacob's last girl. Maybe his longest-surviving girl. But there had been others. Ones who, most likely, had been fed to the gators. Ones

235

who'd screamed and begged and still never made it home. Maybe they'd each slivered their fingers on the crudely bored air holes, then sucked their own blood to have something to do. Maybe they'd recited their favorite stories, the names of their childhood pets. Maybe they'd promised anything, everything, if they could just see their mom, brother, boyfriend, ever again.

Except it never happened.

And I'd failed them. Me, the one who did survive. I killed Jacob Ness. I put a gun to his head and pulled the trigger because it had to be done. Then I came home to my family and left all those poor girls behind. Never asked any questions. Never provided any answers. Simply abandoned them, faceless victims whose bones were moldering God knows where, whose own loved ones would never have the closure at least my mom and brother got.

I don't feel guilty. I feel ashamed. I can't look at Keith anymore, because I don't want him to see my eyes filling with tears.

"There are memory techniques," Quincy says at last.

"I know."

"Dr. Keynes," she begins.

"He'll help us," I answer for him.

"And if he recommends against it?"

"He won't. I'm a survivor. Survivors are tough. If I could endure the real thing, then I can handle the memories."

"I'll be on the first flight in the morning," Quincy says.

I nod. A tear splatters down onto the screen of the smartphone. Keith doesn't touch me. But he does reach over and gently wipe the moisture away.

I end the call.

CHAPTER 16
EVIE

The first thing that hits me when I get out of my lawyer's car is the smell. Charred wood, slightly smoky, and not unpleasant. It brings to mind Sunday afternoons cozied up before a nice fire, sipping tea, listening to the Pats game on TV.

I have to stand perfectly still before I can fully process that it's not a barbecue in front of me, but the remains of my home.

Mr. Delaney lets me be. He answered my call in the middle of the night without hesitation. No doubt used to odd hours, given his job as a defense attorney. And no doubt understanding that it took that long for me to finally be free from my mom, who had to complete her nightly martini ritual before turning in for bed.

It's seven thirty, the sky just starting to lighten given the short days this time of year. The temperature remains below freezing. We are both bundled up in wool coats, hats, and gloves. Half of my neighbors still have their Christmas lights on from the night before, twinkling borders around their roofs, windows, ornamental shrubs.

It gives the whole scene a surreal feel. *Merry Christmas! P.S. All that remains of your life is a charred shell of collapsing wreckage.*

Then the police arrive and it's time to get the party started.

Sergeant Warren climbs out of the car first, bundled up in a puffy blue down coat, embroidered BPD on the chest. She finishes wrapping a lighter blue scarf around her neck, then pulls on black leather gloves and a knitted hat. She still shivers slightly as she waits for the driver, a younger detective with a shock of red hair, to untangle himself from the front seat. He heads straight for the trunk, removes a rake and a shovel before pulling on a pair of heavy workman's gloves. Gotta love the Boston PD. Prepared for anything.

D.D. gives me a look, then heads for my lawyer. She addresses her opening comments to him, as if I'm nothing but a signpost. Posturing. As a high school teacher who spends my days working with teens, I'm unimpressed. She can only *pretend* I don't matter, whereas I have dozens of students who for months at a time honestly *believe* I don't. Till they fail their first test, of course.

"Your client understands that the terms of our initial search warrant still stand, meaning we have the legal right to seize any items relevant to the source of the fire, as well as any additional evidence the fire may have exposed relevant to the shooting which was missed the first time around," D.D. is rattling off.

Mr. Delaney's answer is equally crisp: "I've discussed the matter with my client. She understands that as owner of the property, she is entitled to anything that isn't considered evidence in the case. Furthermore, the police bear the burden of proving an item is evidence. Otherwise, it goes to her."

Mr. Delaney had walked me through it last night. I couldn't just return to my former residence and search for Conrad's firesafe filing box. The police would take exception and seize whatever I discovered as a matter of principle. So invite them over. Make a show of cooperating fully with the authorities. They would open the SentrySafe box, but the contents should belong to me. Not like the ignition source of the arson fire was in the middle of a fire-resistant safe.

All I wanted was our financial records,

including the copy of the life insurance policy Conrad took out when he learned I was pregnant, as well as our homeowners' policy. The box also contained our passports, which — in lieu of my now melted driver's license — I could use as photo ID.

As I told myself last night, I might be sad, but I will not be helpless. I have my unborn child to consider, and my crazy-as-a-fox mother to outmaneuver.

The redheaded detective heads for the pile of charred wood, rake in hand. D.D. refers to him as Neil. He looks like he's about twelve. Maybe the police are recruiting straight out of elementary school these days. I often thought about teaching the lower grades. My particular math skills, however, would be lost there. And for all my moments of sheer exasperation with high schoolers, every semester I have at least a few students whose potential comes to life. An equation that, for the first time, clicks for them. A test they thought they'd failed only to find they'd earned the A they always knew they could achieve.

You don't become a teacher without having some level of optimism. And you don't stay in the field if you don't believe that everyone, from bitter teens to burnt-out administrators, can change.

I used to think that was one of the things Conrad loved about me.

"Fire chief declared the scene safe," D.D. is saying now, taking up position beside me. "Still" — D.D. gestures to my bulging waist — "I would recommend you stay clear."

"The fumes?" I ask.

"A lot of nasty stuff burns up in any house fire."

I nod, well aware of the plastic pipes, glued laminates, cheap stains, fiberglass insulation, and metal appliances that went into home construction. Yesterday this scene would've been borderline toxic. Now . . . now it held the only hope I had of moving ahead.

"I smell gasoline," I comment.

D.D. eyes me. "So did the arson investigator."

I have to process this. "So someone killed my husband, then the next day, burned down our house?" My voice sounds surprisingly steady. Maybe because even as I say the words, I don't really believe them. Conrad and I . . . A schoolteacher and a window salesman. Surely, this couldn't have happened to us. This couldn't *be* us. "Do you know why?"

"I was hoping you could tell me."

"I didn't do this. I'm not just a wife, I'm a

mother." I shake my head. "No mother would do this."

D.D. simply stares at me. I lapse back into silence, but I am shivering slightly. Standing in front of the decimated remains of my life is no longer just sad; it's scary. Because a person who would murder a man, burn down a house . . .

I don't know what happened. Worse, I don't know what will happen next.

The redhead has started working the piles of rubble, using the shovel to lift off charred pieces of sheetrock, collapsed two-by-fours. Mr. Delaney had told them what we were looking for: a fire-rated lockbox for personal papers. It'd been upstairs in our master closet. Given its weight, it had most likely crashed down as the fire devoured the floor from beneath it. The firemen hadn't discovered it yesterday — but then again, they hadn't really been worried about personal possessions.

"Arson investigator will be returning this morning," Sergeant Warren says now, still studying me. "Di Lucca is one of the best. Do you know arsonists generally stick to the same MO? That we have a whole database of local firebugs and their preferred methods? It's only a matter of time before Di Lucca identifies who did this." She pauses, leaving the end of her sentence implied. *And traces that person to you.*

"Why in the world would I arrange to burn down my own home, especially with my cell phone, purse, and all personal possessions inside?"

"People do stupid things."

"Then I must be a real idiot," I finally snap, "to burn down my own home after already being discovered holding the gun that killed my husband."

"Maybe you decided shooting the computer — what was it, twelve times? — wasn't enough."

Standing behind us, Mr. Delaney clears his throat. D.D. isn't supposed to be asking questions about the shooting, and she knows it. She's just trying to rattle me, see what she can shake loose.

"Maybe this isn't about me," I say finally. "Maybe this is about Conrad. All spouses have secrets. Just ask your husband."

The redhead finishes clearing one pile, moves on to the next waist-high collection of rubble. At least the house didn't have a basement, given the high water table in the area. Some of our neighbors did, and the constant flooding drove them insane. Conrad had liked this house particularly for its slab construction, plus the one-car garage. I had liked its cozy size, the charm of the hardwood floors, even if they'd been trashed at the time.

We'd been happy the day we signed the papers on this home. Bought a bottle of champagne, which I'd clutched to my chest as Conrad carried me over the threshold. I'd been laughing, demanding that he put me down. It all seemed so ridiculous and silly and . . . perfect. A great day for a young couple, with so many great days ahead.

D.D. is still watching me. I shouldn't get emotional in front of her. I shouldn't let her know that standing here right now, looking at the destroyed remains of so many dreams, hurts.

The redhead shouts her name. She gives me one last look, then jogs into the debris field toward her fellow detective.

I will have my papers soon enough, I think.

Except a heavy black SentrySafe is not what the redhead has discovered.

This lock box is thin. Maybe an inch tall with roughly the same dimensions as a pad of paper. At first glance, it looks like a tablet computer, which gives me an unsettling thought — I'd shot up a computer, but had I shot up *the* computer? I don't know anymore, and this isn't the time or place to wonder.

The outside of the box is covered in soot and charred along the edges. It doesn't appear heavy-duty enough for a fire-resistant or waterproof rating; then again, I don't recognize the box at all.

The redhead detective clutches it tightly against his stomach. I'd sent the detectives for a file cabinet. They'd discovered a small lockbox. All parties are equally confused — and equally suspicious.

D.D. starts the negotiations: "You got a key?"

"Of course not. I don't even have a fucking cell phone."

If the profanity bothers them, no one says anything. "The key was kept in the lock," I lie eventually. "Dig a layer deeper. You'll find it."

"Neil," D.D. orders, taking the box from him.

The twelve-year-old returns to the blackened debris field, rake in hand.

"You said you were looking for a fireproof safe," D.D. states shrewdly. "You know, like one of heavily reinforced boxes discovered in airplane wreckages."

I ignore her, keep my eyes on the redhead: where he's digging, his approximate location in the house . . . He's standing under

Conrad's office, I determine. Which leads me to my next thought: all those wooden filing cabinets, chock-full of boring customer files. What if it wasn't the files that had mattered? What if beneath them had sat this flat, nondescript box?

I want to believe I would've seen it. On my many, many missions, working through the cabinets, shoving manila folder after manila folder aside in sheer frustration. Then again, a container this thin could've been tucked beneath one of the filing cabinets itself; I'd never thought to lift an entire thing. Given the size and weight of the broad, double-drawer units, I'm not even sure I could've. But Conrad, fit and muscular . . .

Would I have noticed the disruption? A slight change in positioning of the cabinet, a fresh scratch on the old hardwood? Or maybe I had, which is why I'd kept coming back. Because just like Conrad had sensed the disturbance in his locked office every time he returned, I'd also sensed something had changed every time *I* returned. And around and around we'd spun.

Secrets.

Had my husband ever loved me? Or had he married me because once he knew the true story behind my father's death, he'd assumed I would be the type to forgive and forget?

Shouting. The redhead Neil is now attacking a pile of rubble with renewed vigor, clearly having spotted something. Slowly but surely, I make out the compact shape of a fireproof safe. The filing box is not huge, but it is heavy as hell, as I can relate from personal experience. Dragging it out of the master closet was like dragging a boulder, only to stick in a few insurance docs, then — several deep breaths later — heave it back into place.

Neil tosses aside the rake and shovel. He's cleared the area around the box. Now he has both arms around it. Two or three staggering steps later, he's on the move, having to carefully navigate his way through the ruins with the bulky SentrySafe clutched against his chest.

As he approaches, I can tell the fireproof, waterproof safe has lived up to its heavily warrantied reputation. There's barely a scratch on it. In comparison to the flat metal lock box, the SentrySafe still has a key dangling from the front lock. The key is now black and singed, but a key is a key.

Neil drops the box on the driveway in front of us, breathing heavily. D.D. squats down beside it, also out of breath, but in her case, solely from anticipation.

"That looks like a file box," she says, gesturing to the SentrySafe. "So what's this other thing?" She has the charred lockbox at her feet.

"Overflow," I state without hesitation.

She gives me a look. I stare at her right back. This is what happens when you take the blame for your father's death at sixteen. After that, all mistruths are relative. I might have been honest once, even a Goody Two-shoes. But after what I saw, what happened next . . . Really, what's the point?

The SentrySafe has a key, so we start with it first. D.D. does the honors. Strictly speaking, anything recovered at the scene the BPD gets to inspect first, before passing it on to the rightful homeowner. I'm not nervous. I know this box. I've added to it many times. As the wife of a husband who traveled often, the business of personal finances and monthly paperwork was more my bailiwick than his. I'm grateful for that now. I'm not some helpless female who has suddenly lost her husband and has no idea how to hook up cable or find the life insurance policy.

Conrad was equally organized. His parents had died when he was in college, and though he never talked about it much, clearly he'd handled the estate. A family wasn't just a collection of love and well wishes. It was a physical asset to be protected and preserved. Auto insurance, homeowners' insurance, life insurance — he'd believed in all of it.

D.D. turns the key. It's one of those circular ones, distinct for safes. It takes a bit of jiggling, then gives. The lid of the box won't lift, however. The detective frowns, whacks the box, frowns some more. I finally squat impatiently, earning raised eyebrows from all. I grab both sides of the top of the box and shimmy hard, thinking the heat might have warped it. Whether my assumption is valid or not, the technique works. I lift the heavy lid, giving both the detectives a superior stare, before I rise to standing.

D.D. immediately goes to work, flipping through the manila folders labeled Auto Insurance, Property Insurance, Mortgage, Passports, Life Insurance, CDs, Savings Account. All the important papers you'd never want to lose in a fire.

Nothing terribly exciting, and yet my best hope of trying to figure out the next few months of my life. Or how to escape my mother's clinging grasp in the least amount of time possible — depending on your point of view.

D.D. removes each file, flips through the contents — not much, just the latest statements, policies, et cetera — replaces them in the box. When she gets to life insurance, she pauses.

"Million dollars?" She gives me a look. "This appears to be a brand-new policy. Seriously?"

"He took it out when we discovered I was pregnant. According to the insurance rep, it should be enough to pay off the mortgage of the house, cover eighteen years of the average costs of raising a child, plus four years of college."

"In other words, a million motives for shooting your husband."

"If I wanted a million dollars," I inform the detective, "all I have to do is phone home. Or better yet, move in."

She gives me a fresh look. "Which you just did."

"Yeah, and why don't you ask Call Me Phil what that's like?"

The redhead glances up. " 'Call Me Phil'?" Abruptly, he breaks into a smile. "*That's* what he was talking about yesterday. We should get him a T-shirt."

Now D.D. and I both scowl at him. He shrinks back, holds up a black, warped object. "I think I found the key to the other lockbox not far from this one."

"Hang on," I say. I look at Mr. Delaney. "I see personal papers and financial files. No source of arson fire. Nothing that rises to the level of evidence."

"Agreed," Mr. Delaney states. He stares hard at D.D.

"I want a copy of the life insurance."

"Snap a photo with your phone," I suggest. Because I'm taking the policy home with me. I need it.

"My client is being more than reasonable," my lawyer seconds.

Clearly, D.D. isn't happy. But she photographs the doc, closes up the file, sticks it back in the box. The SentrySafe has done its job admirably, saving its contents, surviving to tell its tales. Now Mr. Delaney picks it up, grunting slightly from the weight as he carries it to the trunk of his car.

Which leaves us with the thin metal lockbox. I have no idea what it is, but I won't admit to that because I'm dying to see what's inside. It probably doesn't matter anymore, but it might be what I was searching for all along.

The black key is warped. The redhead tries jiggling. D.D. tries jangling. I take it from them both, me, the experienced homeowner who must certainly know the quirks of this lockbox as well as I did the fireproof safe.

It still takes several tries. I coax, beg, plead. Please, after all this time of looking for you, don't you want to talk to me, too?

Then: *click.*

Just like that, the lock gives. The lid doesn't pop open, clearly warped along the edges. But I can feel the box relax, preparing to surrender its secrets.

I place it on the ground before us. I don't know what to expect. Ashes, charred ruins. The heat inside a house fire must be so extreme. And while Conrad clearly meant to keep these contents hidden, he didn't necessarily care if they were safe. An interesting distinction in its own right.

D.D. has to force the lid. Black flakes float down.

Inside the box, the metal is cool and gray, untouched. The first evidence that the contents came through unscathed. Then:

"What the hell?" D.D. stares at me.

The redheaded detective is already digging through the contents, equally mesmerized.

I don't have words. I don't have moisture in my mouth. Of all the things I thought I might see. Of all the secrets I knew Conrad had to have.

I'm staring at bundles of cash. Still in original wrappings, which is suspicious enough. But more than that, I'm staring at piles of plastic cards. Various drivers' licenses, covering half a dozen states.

All with Conrad's photo. All bearing different names.

"You need to start talking and you need to start talking now," D.D. orders intently.

Except I have nothing to say.

CHAPTER 17
D.D.

"You need to start talking and you need to start talking now." D.D.'s voice was hard.

She regarded the stacks of cash and fake IDs in the soot-blackened box at her feet and ideas raced through her head. Conrad Carter was some kind of secret operative. Except any decent undercover agent would also have a backup piece and ammo stashed with his cash. A criminal mastermind or serial offender? Carter was a man with no family whose job demanded long periods away and who was described as the kind of guy everyone liked but no one knew.

D.D. felt she was standing at a precipice. The next step would take her free-falling over the edge, the answers to dozens of questions roaring past her. Except it would be her job to frantically grab each piece and sort them into a meaningful explanation, all before crashing into the ground below.

In front of her, Evie was shaking her head

slightly. The woman appeared shocked, but by what? The contents of the box, or that the police had finally discovered her husband's secret?

Neil, God bless him, did the sensible thing. He snapped several quick pics with his cell phone, showing the box in situ. Then, donning a pair of latex gloves, he started sorting out the contents.

The cash was banded piles of hundreds. Neil organized them in stacks of ten to equal a thousand, then lined up the stacks. D.D. could practically hear Evie work out the math: twenty-five thousand dollars. Not much compared to the solid bricks of Washingtons seized during the average drug raid, but more than enough in a working-class neighborhood where Evie and her husband had probably considered that a solid year's renovation budget. D.D. took several photos of her own, to corroborate Neil's photos. Chain of custody over recovered cash was a big deal in policing. Good cops looked out for each other, dotted all i's, crossed all t's, so neither they nor their squad could face any scrutiny.

Five photo IDs. The first names were a mix of Conrad, Conner, Carter, Conroy — always good to stick with names that sounded similar. The last names repeated the trick. Conrad Carter from Massachusetts became Carter Conrad in Texas or Carter Conner in Florida.

Given the name game, D.D. doubted the IDs were professional grade — the kind of fakes that cost thousands of dollars and involved trolling death certificates for an infant who'd departed thirty-eight years ago, then stealing that identity. Such an alias could conceivably be used for decades, the holder acquiring credit cards, even a passport. This . . . Neil had lined up each slightly warped piece of plastic. These fakes reminded her of the kind underage kids used to talk their way into local bars. Good at a glance, but not great.

She could tell from the look on Neil's face he was thinking the same. Whatever Conrad Carter was doing, he definitely wasn't a pro. Which made him what?

D.D. rose and eyed Evie sternly. Evie was still staring at the cash and cards, but she didn't appear to be looking at them as much as *through* them. Seeing something only she could see.

"My client is tired," the attorney began. "Given her condition —"

"I don't know anything," Evie interrupted. Her voice sounded as far away as her expression.

"You said this lockbox contained the overflow of financial documents."

"I lied. I'd never seen it before. I wanted to know the contents."

"So you admit —"

"All spouses keep secrets, Sergeant. I already told you to ask your husband."

D.D. could feel her temper starting to rise. "Fine. Let's head to HQ, where we can talk about yours."

"Sergeant Warren, my client —"

"Is lying to the police and admitting it? Is possibly leading a double life of her own? Does your baby even belong to Conrad Carter? Or maybe it's" — D.D. nudged the closest driver's license with the tip of her boot — "Carter Conrad's baby? Or Conroy Conrad's?"

"Sergeant Detective!" Attorney Dick Delaney again, all outrage and bluster.

"I don't know anything," Evie repeated quietly. "I thought . . . He locked his office door. A room in his own house. Every time he went away. Except I was the only person around, and his business, selling custom windows . . . Why lock up customer spec sheets? And why protect such documents from your wife? Or was he protecting me from them?"

Evie glanced up. For a moment, she appeared as genuinely confused and puzzled as D.D. felt.

"You suspected something," D.D. stated.

Delaney made another noise in the back of his throat. D.D. nudged Neil with her foot, and he shot immediately to standing.

"We're going to need to see the file box again," Neil said.

Delaney gave them a look, Neil's bid at distraction not fooling him for a moment. "Then you can fetch it from the back of the trunk." He tossed Neil the keys.

D.D. kept her attention on Evie. She was on to something. She could feel it.

"You shot the computer. Why did you shoot the computer?" D.D. moved closer, keeping her voice low. "What did you suspect, Evie? What did you catch the father of your unborn child doing?"

"My client —"

"First your father. You loved him, didn't you? Idolized him. I conducted those neighbor interviews. Everyone talked about what a close bond you and he had."

"Sergeant Detective, I am warning you —"

"You thought he killed himself, didn't you? So acting on your mother's orders, you became the patsy. All these years, carrying that weight alone. Just so you could fall in love and discover . . . what? That your husband's sins were far greater?"

"This conversation is over." Delaney had his hand on Evie's arm. "Take the file box or don't take the file box. Either way my client is coming with me."

"No, she isn't." D.D. was staring directly at Evie. She knew she had the woman's total, undivided attention. She understood then the truth to getting at her prime suspect. Every person had a lever, the button that a good detective learned how to push. Evie had given her the key just yesterday; the woman was her father's daughter. She did work the math. And she couldn't walk away from an unsolved equation.

Curiosity. That was Evie's downfall. Which gave D.D. a slight chill because curiosity had always been her weakness, too.

"Come to HQ. Answer my questions," she told the woman now.

"She's going home!" Delaney snapped.

Evie said, "Why?"

"Because in return, I have photos. From sixteen years ago. Going through them, I can prove to you, your father didn't shoot himself."

Evie would come to HQ. D.D. never doubted it for a second. First her lawyer had to draw her aside and engage in frantic conversation. No doubt informing his client she was being foolish, letting the police get under her skin. If they had any real evidence, they'd be forced to disclose it prior to trial anyway. As for Evie, the woman seemed to have some strong words of her own. D.D. could've sworn she heard the woman state angrily, "I am your client and you will *not* call my mother."

How interesting.

After a few more minutes of terse exchange, Evie climbed into her lawyer's car, file box still planted in the trunk. D.D. couldn't justify seizing the papers as evidence, though she was happy enough to have a photo of Conrad Carter's life insurance for future reference. Neil bagged and tagged the metal lockbox and its contents as the BPD's share of the spoils. They loaded up their car, then led the way to HQ.

BPD's headquarters was an acquired taste. People either were sufficiently impressed by the modern glass monstrosity or, more likely, shook their heads at yet another example of their tax dollars at work. D.D. wasn't into architecture. As a woman who liked to eat, she appreciated the café on the lobby level. And the upstairs homicide suite was far bigger and more useful than the old

HQ had been, even if the blue industrial carpet, gray filing cabinets, and collection of cubicles made them look more like an insurance company than an investigative unit. Sometimes, like now, when she had a suspect she didn't want to spook, it was nice to pretend they were just hanging out at an office versus, say, starring in an old episode of *NYPD Blue.*

Given the circumstances, D.D. led Evie and her lawyer to homicide's conference room, something a bit more hospitable than the spartan interrogation rooms. Evie already had her attorney at her elbow. D.D. didn't want to spook her prime suspect before extracting as much information as possible.

After a quick sidebar, Neil disappeared to find Phil. Neil would handle processing the evidence they'd recovered at the arson scene. Phil would resume his role as family man/father figure detective. Again, interviews were strategy and while D.D. liked a good full-court press, that was never going to work with a lawyer in the room. This would be a finesse job. Fortunately, she was a woman of many skills.

And like Evie, of much curiosity.

D.D. played nice. She got Evie and her lawyer situated. Brought them both bottles of water; then, at the request of Delaney, who seemed to enjoy having one of Boston's finest waiting on him, she returned with a cup of coffee. By then, Phil had joined the room, armed with a heavy cardboard box. The outside of the box bore large black numbers: the case number for Evie's father's shooting sixteen years ago.

Phil set the box at the head of the table, away from Evie and Dick Delaney. He and D.D. had been playing this game for so long, they didn't need to speak to know how to proceed. D.D. sat directly across from Evie and her lawyer, engaging them in small talk about best brands of coffee in Boston, black versus cream and sugar, and, oh yeah, having to give up coffee while pregnant, which D.D. had never thought she'd be able to do, but in fact had come quite naturally.

In the meantime, Phil unpacked the box. Slowly. File after file. The murder book. Binders of evidence reports. Stacks of photos. Pile here. Pile there. Pile after pile.

Evie lost focus first. Nodded at whatever asinine comment D.D. was making while her gaze drifted to the head of the table, the growing stack of yellowing papers, frayed photo edges, dirty manila files. Records were all supposed to be scanned and stored electronically these days. And yet, if the average bureaucrat ever walked through the warehouse, saw the full magnitude of the job . . .

Walking the stacks to manually retrieve an evidence box wasn't going away anytime soon.

"That's evidence from my father's case," Evie said suddenly. The woman was agitated. Not even bothering to sip her water but spinning the bottle in her hand.

"That's right."

"You have photos?"

Delaney spoke up. "I would like to go on the record that I don't recommend my client be here today, taking these questions, Sergeant Warren —"

D.D. kept her focus on Evie: "Do you remember your statement from that day?"

"A little."

"Let me read it to you, from my notes: 'sixteen-year-old subject, female, white, appears in state of shock and/or traumatized. Subject states she had been in the kitchen with her father, Earl Hopkins, fifty-five-year-old male, white, after two thirty on Saturday. Father was showing her how to unload a recently purchased Model eight-seventy Remington pump-action shotgun. Father was standing in front of refrigerator when female subject, in her own words, picked up shotgun off the kitchen table and attempted to clear the chamber. According to female, shotgun discharged into her father's torso from a distance of mere inches. Female states father fell back against the refrigerator, then sank to the floor. Female claims she set down gun and attempted to rouse her father without success. Female further claims she then heard screaming from the doorway, where her mother, Joyce Hopkins, forty-three-year-old female, white, stood. Mother claimed she'd witnessed the shooting. Detective Speirs interviewed independently.' "

Evie didn't say anything while D.D. read, just kept staring at the box. D.D. set down her notepad. "Does that fit your memory?"

Evie finally looked at her. "What do the photos say?"

"Phil?"

Phil stepped forward with the first set. They were gruesome. A shotgun blast at close range did a tremendous amount of damage. Evie had sat through the real event. In theory, there was nothing here she hadn't seen before, though in D.D.'s experience, memory had its way with things over time. Meaning the photos could look far worse than Evie had allowed herself to remember, or more likely, given the woman's burden of guilt, far less awful than the images that replayed in her head night after night.

D.D. spread out the first three photos in front of Evie and her lawyer. Delaney inhaled sharply but didn't look away. He'd been there that day, too. A friend of the family, summoned by Evie's mom, who hadn't thought to call 911 but knew immediately to dial the family lawyer. Said something about the woman's mental state right there.

"Long guns are used in suicides more often than people think," D.D. stated now. She kept her voice even but soft. No need to play hardball just yet; that would come later. "This particular shotgun, the Model eight-seventy Remington, comes in two different barrel lengths for the twelve-gauge. Your father had purchased the slightly shorter version, but even then, the barrel length is twenty-six inches, the full length of the shotgun forty-six and a half inches. In instances of suicide, the victim will generally press the tip of the barrel against his own body to stabilize the weapon while he reaches for the trigger. Hence, one of the most common indicators of suicide by long gun is a clear burn pattern against the victim's skin from the heat of the barrel."

Evie glanced up at her. "I don't see a burn mark. It would be on his stomach, yes? I just see . . . soot."

"Scorch marks," D.D. provided, "indicating the shotgun was in close proximity to the victim at the time of discharge, but not actually touching the victim's skin. In fact, the scorch marks are consistent with your initial statement, a scenario of someone standing mere inches away from the victim, pulling the trigger."

"I don't understand."

"The second indicator of suicide by long gun is trajectory. It's nearly impossible to hold a long gun level and pull the trigger, meaning inevitably the impact of the blast should be up and out. The projectiles enter lower on the body, travel in an upward diagonal until exiting higher on the body. In this case" — D.D. tapped a photo — "we can see the entrance wound was beneath your father's lower ribs. But according to the ME, the shotgun pellets didn't follow any diagonal path. Instead, they traveled nearly straight through the body, shredding his organs and intestines along the way."

"Sergeant!" Delaney objected.

Evie, however, did not look away. "The gun was fired level. From someone standing directly in front of my father."

"Which, again, would be consistent with the story you provided. You picked up the shotgun. You were trying to inspect the chamber, and instead, you pulled the trigger while standing directly in front of your father. Hence no burn marks, no upward trajectory."

"Except I didn't! We'd been out. Myself and my mother. We parked on the driveway. I'd just opened the car door and I heard a noise. We entered the kitchen. And there . . . I saw . . . There was my father."

"The third thing we'd look at for a suicide," D.D. continued relentlessly, "is the blood spatter. If someone else was in the room, if someone else pulled the trigger, that person would be subject to blowback, or spray from the impact of the shotgun pellets entering the body. Meaning we should have at least one person covered in spatter."

She stared hard at Evie, who sputtered: "I walked in . . . the blood . . . it dripped down on me . . ."

"We'd also have a void in the spatter. A clean spot in, say, the floor or countertop, where the shooter's body blocked any droplets from landing." D.D. tapped a third photo, where, sure enough, bloody spray appeared above and to the sides of Hopkins's body, but directly in front . . .

"Your father didn't commit suicide," D.D. stated firmly. "The evidence has now been reviewed several times by several different experts. There was someone else in the room, and that person shot him."

Evie opened her mouth, shut her mouth. "You think I'm lying now," she whispered at last.

"I think your story sixteen years ago is a better fit with the evidence than the line of bull you tried to feed me yesterday."

"Sergeant," Delaney started again.

"Why would I lie? I only did it back then to protect my father."

"Your father, or your mother?"

"My mother was with me! We'd gone out shopping. Surely, you can find a witness, pull store security tapes. A credit card receipt. Something that proves we were together."

"From sixteen years ago?"

"I thought he'd killed himself! He'd been . . . off. Not himself. And genius and suicide . . ." Evie shrugged, sounding genuinely distressed.

"Your father did not commit suicide."

"I didn't shoot him!"

"So you're a liar, but not a killer. And Friday night, with your husband?"

"Sergeant! This line of questioning is over!"

"Not so fast, Counselor. Your client came

to me yesterday, recanting her story from sixteen years ago. She's the one who re-opened this can of worms. Based on her new statement, the case of Earl Hopkins is no longer being considered accidental. We're now treating it as an active homicide, and you know the statute of limitations on homicide — there isn't one."

"I didn't do it!" Evie, still aghast, pounded her water bottle against the table. "I would never harm my father!"

"But your husband? The guy with rolls of cash and nearly half a dozen fake IDs?"

"We're out of here." Delaney was already on his feet, pulling at Evie's arm. The woman, however, continued to resist. And it wasn't the allegations about her husband that had her agitated. Clearly, she was still distressed about her father. Even sixteen years later, it was all about her father.

She was gazing at D.D. wildly now. "My hair. You took photos of my hair. Samples. I remember that!"

D.D. nodded slowly.

"Test it. Have it reexamined. You can, can't you? I don't understand it all, but I watch crime shows. You can prove direc-tionality from blood spatter, right? Say, the difference between this blowback you're talking about, versus contact smear from someone entering the room right after-wards."

"I don't know if we have enough evi-dence," D.D. said, which wasn't entirely un-true.

"Test it. Do whatever you have to do. I didn't kill my father. *I didn't!* All these years." Her voice broke off. "I assumed the worst about him."

"Him, or your mother?"

"*She was with me.* I'm telling you the truth. My mom is crazy, I know, but she loved him. They loved each other. I don't know. Not all relationships are meant to be understood by outsiders —"

"Talking about your husband again?"

"My mom didn't do this," Evie repeated more firmly. She seemed to be pulling herself together now, allowing her lawyer to guide her to standing. "She, me, we didn't do this. All these years, we thought he shot himself. That's why we lied. Not to protect ourselves. But to protect him. If you'd met him, if you'd talked to him . . . My father was a great man. He deserved better than to go down in the history books as one more depressed genius."

"Then who, Evie?" D.D. rose to standing. "Who would have motive to shoot your father? Did he have professional rivals? Failing students? Jealous husbands? Someone pulled that trigger. If not you, then who?"

"I . . . I have no idea." Evie glanced helplessly at her lawyer. It was all he needed.

"This interview is over. You asked for answers from my client and she provided them. You want to learn anything else, Officers, I suggest you go out and — here's a thought — do some detecting."

Delaney guided his client around the table. But Evie's gaze was still glued to the photos as she walked by. Fascinated. Fixated. Frustrated.

That she finally realized all these years later she'd lied for nothing? Or because she'd just discovered yesterday's attempt at changing her story was never going to work?

D.D. still couldn't figure it. But there was something about the way Evie looked at the photos that tugged at her, made her wonder if that woman hadn't told her the truth yesterday after all.

Longing, she finally decided. Evie Carter looked at those photos like a woman who, sixteen years later, just wanted her father back.

It made D.D. wonder what other regrets the woman had, and how many might involve her husband and his own death just two nights ago.

Knock on the door. Neil poked his head in. He appeared nervous.

"Got something on the fake IDs?" she asked immediately, collecting her notes.

"Ah, no. You got a visitor."

"I have a visitor?"

"A fed. SSA Kimberly Quincy from the Atlanta office. She's here with Flora Dane and some other guy. Says she needs to talk."

"No," D.D. said.

"Too late," a female voice drawled from behind Neil.

D.D. sighed. "Shit."

CHAPTER 18
FLORA

Memory is a funny thing. There are moments that sear into our minds. If we're lucky, it's because we're happy — first kiss, wedding day, birth of a child. The kind of experience where you both have it and stand outside of it because your brain recognizes this is something so special that you're going to want to relive it.

I have some of those memories. Being asked to prom by the cutest boy in high school, practically floating home to share the news with my mom. The first time I got a baby fox to eat a piece of hot dog out of my hand. A particular bedtime ritual my mom used to have when I couldn't get to sleep. And the nights my brother and I turned it on her, giggling hysterically as we pretended to tuck her into bed, but really ended up in a giant mosh pile of limbs in the middle of her mattress, a tangle of family.

I have other memories, too.

The moment I woke up in a coffin-sized box. The sound the first woman made, when Jacob stuck in the knife, followed by the look in her eyes as she stared right into me, knowing he was killing her, knowing she was dying, knowing I was doing nothing to stop him.

Now I have to face the fact there could be six more of her out there, six more girls who never made it home. Maybe Jacob made good on his promise and fed them to the gators. Maybe they're buried on his property, if I could just help figure out where that is.

Memory. Such a fickle tool. And for better or worse, the best option I have left.

I don't sleep. After leaving Keith Edgar's house, I return to Cambridge, then pace my tiny apartment until my elderly landlords politely knock on the door and ask me if I'm all right. After assuring them I'm just dandy, I give up on walking continuous circles and debate calling Sarah. She's a fellow survivor who once held off a murderer by using the severed arm of her just-butchered roommate. She's also the closest thing I have to a friend.

She understood bad nights. How the brain

could spin for days, weeks, months at a time, an endless cycle of remembered traumas from falling off your bike at seven to being attacked by a knife-wielding maniac at twenty. Trying to sort out the experiences, Samuel had explained to me once. It felt like my brain was racing wildly, but really, it was searching for patterns, matches, order. Something that would give it context, so my mind could go, *Aha — that's what happened.* Then, presumably, people like Sarah and me would sleep again. Except some experiences defied definition. So our brains kept spinning long after the horror had ended.

If not Sarah, then I could call Samuel, who most likely was expecting to hear from me after this afternoon's discussion. Or my mother, who would be simultaneously honored and stricken to have me finally open up about what it's like to be me.

But I don't feel like talking. I pick up the clothes in my bedroom. I wipe down kitchen counters. I rearrange the four things I have in the fridge. Then, in a burst of inspiration, I try on my own to recall the original place Jacob had held me. The first coffin-sized box in a dingy basement of some house. Small windows, up high. Shit-brown carpet that I used to comb through with my fingers, marveling at how many shades of brown it took to make carpet the same color as dirt. I jot down notes. Ugly carpet. Moldy sofa. Stairs leading up. Pine trees. When he finally led me out of the house, I remember pine trees.

But my mind keeps ping-ponging, until I can't be sure anymore if I was remembering the first place, or that second motel, or what about that place in Florida? I grow light-headed, can feel the edges of the panic attack start to build, when it's been years since I've been humbled by such a thing.

Four A.M., sweaty, panting, and borderline feral, I opt for a different memory. The day I was rescued, an image that should be higher on the happiness scale. I force myself to sit calmly on the floor of my apartment, recall exactly the crash of the motel window. The canister of tear gas bouncing into the room, then releasing an ominous hiss. My eyes welling, my nose running. Then the front door blowing open, and a horde of heavily armored men pouring into the tiny room. They scream at me, yell at Jacob. Scream louder when I pick up the gun. Fall silent when I've done what I had to do.

Then, Kimberly Quincy. The fed. She'd been the first to greet me outside the room, her arm around my shoulders, telling me over and over again I'd be all right. Everything was okay now. I was safe.

I remember her voice clearly. Clipped, firm, in control. The kind of voice that inspired confidence.

But what does SSA Kimberly Quincy look like? For some reason, that piece of the puzzle keeps escaping from me. I work on it for an hour. The sound of her voice. The feel of her arm around my shoulders. Me, turning my head, looking straight at her.

I had to have seen her. My eyes had been red and swollen, my nose a snotty mess, but still . . . No matter how much I try, I still can't bring her face to mind. She remains a voice in the dark. Clipped. Firm. In control.

The kind of woman I'm going to need for the day ahead.

Five A.M., I give up on sleep completely and go for a run in the ice-cold dark, neon vest glowing, headlamp beaming. Then shower. Bagel. Black coffee. Still hours to kill.

I boot up my computer, check in on my new friend Keith Edgar, who, interestingly enough, has posted nothing from yesterday on his true-crime blog site. Trying to impress me with his restraint? Or just waiting for something more significant to share?

I decide not to worry about it for now. Instead, I cycle back to where I'd started my evening. Memory. Such a fickle tool.

I read anything and everything about how to handle traumatized minds, from EMDR to virtual reality simulations to old-fashioned hypnosis. Ten A.M., my phone finally rings. That familiar clipped voice: "My plane has landed."

I'm not nervous anymore. I'm ready.

Arriving at BPD headquarters, I spot Keith first. He is standing awkwardly to the side, gazing up at the glass structure as if he's not sure its existence is such a good idea. When he sees me walking toward him, his face immediately brightens and I feel an unexpected tug inside my chest.

He's dressed upscale metrosexual. Open dark wool coat. Black skinny jeans topped with a deep purple sweater over a lavender-and-pink-checked shirt. He looks like an Abercrombie model. Which is to say, an updated Ted Bundy. I wonder what SSA Kimberly Quincy will make of him.

Then I see her. Stepping out of an Uber vehicle. Long camel-colored coat to fight off New England temps that must feel shocking after Atlanta. A dark leather shoulder bag slung across her body. Nice brown boots, currently getting ruined by the wintry mix of salt and sludge.

I don't even have to hear her voice to know it's her. Something about the line of her body as she leans down to retrieve a smaller overnight bag. Then she straightens, turns.

And I realize why I blocked her face from my mind. Because for all intents and purposes, SSA Quincy looks almost exactly like me. Same lean profile, gray-blue eyes, dusty-blond hair, hard stare. Except she's a slightly older, wiser version of myself. No dark shadows under her eyes. Real muscle mass lining her frame. A woman who sleeps at night, eats three to five healthy meals a day, and knows exactly who she is and where she's going.

"Damn," Keith says, taking in the two of us, and I realize I'm not ready for the day after all.

Keith and I let Quincy take the lead. She shakes my hand, then his. If she wonders about his presence, she doesn't say anything. Maybe she thinks he's my boyfriend. Maybe I don't mind that impression.

She leads us into BPD, slaps down her credentials to announce her arrival, and crisply requests to see Sergeant D. D. Warren. Keith is looking all around the vast glass and steel lobby. I can already feel myself shrinking inside my down coat. As I'm a woman who'd once been confined to a box, you'd think I'd like large open spaces. But this kind of space makes me nervous.

A redheaded detective appears. I've met him before, Neil something or other. He chirps about do we need breakfast, coffee, anything? Quincy stares at him. He stops talking, leads the way up to the homicide unit.

Along the way, we pass an older man in a suit and a woman I recognize instantly from the news — Conrad Carter's wife. The woman who supposedly shot and killed her husband. My feet slow on instinct. I open my mouth, feel like I should say something, anything. How well did you know your husband? Would it surprise you to know he was hanging out with a known rapist in a honky-tonk in the South? But Keith suddenly has a grip on my arm. He drives me forward, till she's gone, and I'm left with a last impression of a woman who's as anxious and exhausted as I am.

D.D. greets us with her normal chipper self. "What the hell?"

Quincy smiles. "Sergeant Warren. Nice to speak with you again. Shall we?" Quincy gestures to the conference room behind D.D. D.D. looks like she's on the verge of arguing, probably on principle, but Quincy smiles again, says, "Not in front of the children," and that does the trick.

The two female investigators enter the conference room, closing the door firmly behind them. Keith and I remain in the hallway, still in the company of the redhead, who's fidgeting.

"Coffee?" he asks again. Most likely to have something to do.

Keith and I exchange a glance. "No," we state in unison. Which makes me feel warm all over.

From inside the room: "A Boston shooting is a Boston case!"

"I'm not interested in your murder. I'm interested in the victim's possible connection to Jacob Ness."

"This has nothing to do with Ness. We've already charged the wife in the shooting."

"Then my angle of inquiry won't conflict with your own."

"Like hell! You start digging in Conrad's past, raise the specter of some serial killer bestie, and you've just handed the defense reasonable doubt. Evie Carter didn't kill her husband. Clearly the ghost of Jacob Ness did it."

"Do you know for sure someone else didn't do it? Because a man who was known to go on frequent business trips, and at least spent part of them in the company of a serial rapist . . . As an investigator, these are questions I'd like to answer."

"Me too. Which brings us back to the wife. Who in addition to shooting her husband, plugged even more bullets into his computer."

"Anything recoverable?"

"Not yet."

"The FBI forensic techs are the best in the industry —"

"Bite me."

"Sergeant Warren, your case intersects with an ongoing FBI investigation. Period. You can invite me to assist gracefully. Or I can commandeer your case forcefully."

"What ongoing investigation?"

"The disappearance of six women believed to be additional victims of Jacob Ness. With his death, we've lacked investigative avenues. However, this new information, that he might have met with other predators, could prove promising."

"Conrad Carter can't help you, he's dead. And so is his computer."

"Jacob Ness's computer isn't."

For the first time, quiet. A long pause, where Keith and I lean forward. The redheaded detective as well.

"You have Ness's computer?" D.D. asks.

"In all its mysterious glory."

"What does that mean?"

"Invite me to play and I'll be happy to share."

"And Flora?" D.D. asks abruptly. "Why is she here?"

"She's also agreed to help."

"How?"

"A trip down memory lane. We've never found the house where Jacob originally held her. We have reason to believe it might be more significant than he let on. And that he took steps to mask its location."

"You think Jacob Ness still has property out there? A personal cabin, residence?"

"I think finding such a thing could provide a great deal of information regarding six missing women, and, who knows, one recently deceased husband. Do you have all the answers for your case, Sergeant Warren?"

"No."

"Neither do I. So, shall we?"

Heavy sigh. "You did help me with Charlene Grant."

"And you did keep her alive."

A change in tone. "How are the girls?"

"Amazing. Ten and seven. Ready to take over the world. Yours?"

"Jack is five. Has a new dog. They spring around the house going 'roo, roo, roo.' "

"Never a dull moment."

"Wouldn't change it for the world."

"Me neither."

"Fine. You want in. Let's do this. But I'm telling you now, there's more about this case that doesn't make sense than does."

"My favorite kind."

Just like that, the deal is struck, the hunt is on.

Quincy turns back toward us, motioning through the window for us to enter.

"Holy shit," Keith whispers under his breath.

I don't stop. I don't think. I simply squeeze his hand.

Then we enter the conference room and the real work begins.

CHAPTER 19
EVIE

"You honestly believed your father killed himself?"

After sitting in silence in the car for so long, the sound of my lawyer's voice startles me. I've been staring out the window, watching perfectly normal people walk down the snowy streets of Boston, continuing on with their perfectly normal lives. I wonder if that's how I look to others; like I'm normal and functional, too, when in fact, I feel completely emptied out. Stacks of money. Fake IDs. Not exactly a treasure trove of dead wives, and yet, I'd been right: Conrad had been hiding secrets from me.

Which I want to think is only fair, because I hid my secrets from him. Except it doesn't feel okay at all. It feels awful and unjust, a final act of betrayal by a man I'd genuinely loved. True, I had my own suspicions. But then, maybe that's what love was for me. An exercise in mistrust.

"Evie?" Mr. Delaney prods again, his voice gentle.

I pull my attention from the window.

"My mom never told you?"

"All I've ever known is what she said that afternoon. That your father had been showing you how to handle the shotgun. There was an accidental discharge. She saw the whole thing from the kitchen doorway."

I nod. That was our story, and for sixteen years we'd been sticking to it.

"Do you think my parents loved each other?" I hear myself ask.

He doesn't answer right away, tapping his finger on the steering wheel. I always thought of Mr. Delaney as one of my father's friends. But all these years later, he continues to come around the house. Unmarried. Attentive to my mother's moods. Now I can't help but wonder.

"I met both your parents in college," he says now, surprising me. I'd known that he and my father went way back, but I hadn't realized it included my mother as well. "From the very beginning, their relationship was . . . volatile. And yet, the more they collided, blew apart, collapsed back, the more it seemed to work for them. You know your father genuinely loved math?"

I nod.

"Well, over the years, I've come to think of his relationship with your mom as his exercise in physics. She challenged him, in a wholly different way, and your father liked a good challenge. As for her . . . Your mother was never meant to live an ordinary life. Your father, in his overly intellectual, unquestionably brilliant, completely indulgent way, was perfect for her."

"The cocktail parties. University functions. Build the legacy. Protect the legacy."

Mr. Delaney smiles. "They fit together, Evie. Whether it made sense to outsiders or not, they were meant to be. And they both loved you."

I return to the window. My father loved me. I know that. My mom, on the other hand, is a different story. A genius husband had fit the exotic story line of her life. A daughter of slightly above-average intelligence, who taught math at public high school, not so much.

"You can talk to me," Mr. Delaney is saying now. "You're my client. Our conversations are protected by privilege. Whatever you say stays with me."

"And not my mom?" I can't help it; I sound bitter, maybe even petulant.

"Mum's the word," he says so quietly, I almost miss the pun. When I catch it, I smile, and he smiles back. It occurs to me that Mr. Delaney has been one of the few adult fixtures in my life. First as my parents' close friend and confidant, then as a substitute father figure, coming by the house regularly to check up on us in the months following the shooting. He'd been holding my mother together, though I hadn't thought about it back then. But Mr. Delaney had been the one who'd appear three or four nights a week, quietly making sure food appeared in the fridge, vodka bottles disappeared from the cabinets. He'd tried to get my mom to sell the house, then failing that, at least remodel. For me, he always said. She should do these things to ease her daughter's stress, help in my recovery.

She'd listened to him, certainly in a way she never would've listened to me. My father had been her world. Whereas she and I could never even agree on much of anything.

"We found him . . . dead, when we first arrived home," I murmur now. "Clearly, it had just happened. You could smell the gunpowder. And the blood . . . it was hot on my hair."

"I'm sorry, Evie."

"There was no sign of anyone else. No cars on the drive, no one in the home. And my father, those past few months, his mood had grown darker."

"On occasion, the genius in your father got the better of him. But he always came out the other side. He told me once, that was the power of fatherhood. Even when he felt he was failing at solving the great mysteries of the universe, he knew he would never fail you."

"I thought he had." Suddenly, I'm crying. I hadn't expected to. But all these years later . . . I haven't been carrying around just the shame of my secret, but the pain that my father chose to end his own life rather than stay with us. The father I loved so much. The father I would've done anything to make happy.

I turn back to the window, wipe hastily at my cheeks.

"You didn't pull the trigger," Delaney states now.

"No. He'd already shown me how to load and unload the Remington. I wouldn't have made such a stupid mistake. But as it was, Mom and I weren't even home."

"Was he expecting anyone? A TA, a fellow professor?"

"Not that he told us. When we left, he was holed up in his study, standing at a whiteboard, muttering away. You know how he could be. We called out to him that we were off to run errands. I don't even remember if he answered. We drove away. When we came back . . ."

Mr. Delaney nods. "You walked into the kitchen first," he fills in quietly. "Then came your mother, who took one look and fell apart."

"She told me what to say. She told me what had to be done. In the moment, I never questioned it. Maybe . . ."

"It's okay, Evie. I understand. You'd just lost one parent. Of course you went out of your way to make your surviving parent happy."

I'd never thought of it that way, but it made sense.

"You and your mother were together?"

"Yes."

"But according to what we just heard from the police, your father didn't commit suicide. There had to be another person in the house. Was the door open when you walked in?"

"The back door was always unlocked during daylight hours. Often because so many students were coming and going."

"I think you should prepare a statement. Write down in your own words what you can remember from that day. Then give it

291

to me for proofing. Ultimately, we'll deliver it to the police."

"So they can charge me in my father's murder as well?"

"Did you shoot your father, Evie? Remember, anything you tell me is protected."

"No."

"Did you shoot your husband? Again, anything you tell me is protected."

"No."

"But you pulled the trigger."

"I shot my husband's computer."

Delaney takes his eyes off the wheel long enough to give me a look. "Interesting. Well then, sounds to me like we have some work ahead of us."

"Why do I only love men who leave me?" I whisper.

"I don't know, honey. Some of us just aren't lucky in love."

Mr. Delaney takes me to lunch. A sandwich place he knows downtown. He doesn't fuss over me as openly as my mother, but he adds orange juice to my salad order and refuses to utter a word until at least a quarter of my food is consumed. His own choice is a rare roast beef sandwich with horseradish mayo. Once, I would've ordered the same. Now, in my delicate state, the sight of the bloody beef makes me nauseous. I do my best to focus on my lunch, take small bites, chew thoroughly. Even if I have no interest in sustenance, the baby does. Everything I do next, the whole rest of my life, this is what — this is who — my life will be about.

Again, I wonder if my mom ever felt that way about me.

"Why didn't my parents have more children?" I ask Mr. Delaney halfway through my salad. If my question surprises him, he's an experienced enough lawyer to hide it.

"I don't know. Have you ever asked?"

I give him a look. He grins back. The silver fox can be charming when he wants. Already, I'd noticed several female heads turning to admire the new lunch addition. Then they scowled at me, no doubt thinking I was his much-too-young trophy wife, because handsome men are never allowed to be merely friends with other women.

"Your father was nervous," he says at last, picking up a napkin, dabbing at his meticulously trimmed mustache. "When your mother found out she was pregnant, he was excited, but concerned. As he put it, no genius in history has been noted for their parenting skills."

"Was I a surprise?"

"Always."

I roll my eyes at him again. "I mean, did they want to have children?"

"I don't think they would've actively sought it out," Mr. Delaney allows after a minute, "but I would also say, you were the light of your father's life. Your turn." He looks at me. "Is your baby a surprise?"

"Yes. No. Kind of. We'd been trying once. But had mostly given up. And then . . ."

"I've heard that. Sometimes, not trying is exactly what a new life-form needs most. Did you love Conrad?" he asks me softly.

"Yes. No. Kind of."

That smile again, but a bit sad this time, as if he knows exactly what I mean.

"In the beginning," I hear myself say. "I thought he was everything I could ever want. Outgoing, funny, compassionate. He sought me out. He looked at me. He wanted to talk to me. He wanted to be with *me*. I know it sounds awful. Like an exercise in narcissism. But in my whole life, it never felt like anyone wanted me. Then, after my father died —"

"And you took the blame."

"Let's just say if I was the quiet weird kid before, I was the scary weird kid after." I shrug.

"You know, your father worried you'd be

gifted like him."

"He *worried*?"

"It's a lonely life, in case you didn't notice. His brain was exceptional because it didn't work like anyone else's. But it put him forever out of step with others. Even in elite math circles, he stood out."

"One of the greatest minds of his generation," I intoned. And suddenly, I feel like crying again, because I'd never wanted the genius, just the father, and I still missed him so much.

"If you loved Conrad," Mr. Delaney asks softly, "what do you think happened to your relationship?"

I can't answer right away. When I do, the words are hard to say. "I don't think I'm good at marriage."

"How so?"

"I don't know how to trust. I don't know how to . . . believe. The kinder Conrad was to me . . . the more I grew suspicious. I'd wonder what he wanted, what he wasn't saying."

"You thought he was being unfaithful?"

"I don't know. He was gone so often on business trips, but when he came home, he didn't want to talk about it. Life on the road is boring, he'd tell me. Let's hear about your week. Except I didn't believe he really wanted to learn about my week. He just didn't want to talk about his."

"You grew up in a household with adults who generally had an agenda."

I have to smile because I know exactly whom he's talking about. "My mom."

"Some men do like to hear from the women they love."

"I know. And I'd tell myself that. The problem is me. I believed my husband had secrets because, of course, I have this huge secret. But then, I'd notice little things, see little things . . ."

"Such as?"

"Conrad knew everyone. Every neighbor who stopped by, every fellow teacher of mine. He was a walking encyclopedia of names, faces, vital statistics. Except . . . no one knew Conrad. Where were his colleagues, family, friends? He'd told me his parents had died in an accident years ago. Our marriage was very small, at the courthouse because Mom —"

"Didn't approve."

"But month after month, year after year . . . All these people Conrad could tell you so much about, and yet no dinner with the neighbors, no guys' night out. He always had an excuse. For someone who appeared so outgoing, if you stepped back, peered at him from a distance, he was a loner. Separate from all of us. Even with me."

"Did you ever ask him about it?"

"He said he had me, he didn't need anything more."

"Romantic."

I look Mr. Delaney in the eye. "Is it? Because my knee-jerk reaction was that he was lying. So again, was the problem him or me?"

"Do you have close friends?"

I shrug, uncomfortable. "I have a colleague, another teacher at the school. She and I often have lunch together. But see, I know I'm antisocial. And frankly, given that I've spent my adult life being the woman who killed her own father, I have good reasons for being reserved. I admit to these things. Conrad . . . He came across one way, but over time if you paid attention . . ." I shake my head. "I felt sometimes he was less a person, and more a character in a play. He said the right things, but were they things he really meant, or just the next lines of dialogue?"

"You didn't trust him."

"I worried about it," I say carefully. "The inconsistencies between what he said and what he actually did. Add to that the whole locked office in the privacy of his own home. Yet, when I tried to bring it up . . . he'd make me feel petty. Like I was being paranoid. I really couldn't argue with that. They say liars are always the first to think others are lying. And let's face it, for sixteen years now, I've been one helluva liar."

"But you got pregnant."

I smile roughly. "Ever hear of desperately-trying-to-save-your-marriage sex? We got pretty good at it."

"All marriages are hard," Mr. Delaney tells me. I know what he means, but I'm not sure all marriages are the constant exercise in suspicion that mine was.

"By the end," I say softly, "I didn't believe Conrad anymore. He was lying. Maybe not about his love for me, which he promised was true. Maybe not about the baby, which he wanted so badly. He swore he'd be the best dad in the whole world. But he was also almost frantic on the subject. Something was up. I could feel it. Something was going to happen. The past few weeks, the tension in our home, all the things we suspected but couldn't say. I still don't understand it all. My husband was a liar I couldn't catch in a lie. And our marriage was on a collision course with something terrible I just couldn't see."

"The fake IDs?"

"I don't know anything about them."

"But you shot up the computer."

"One day, I found a document in the memory cache of the printer. Financial records regarding a great deal of money. More than even the cash Conrad had in that lockbox."

Mr. Delaney waits patiently.

"There were also monthly withdrawals. For what? What was this account? What was he funding on all those business trips?"

"Prostitutes? Drugs?"

"Maybe worse. I saw . . ." I can't bring myself to say it. I can't bring myself to see it again. I shake my head.

"You understand, Evie, the police are going to figure this out. When they do, they're going to say that Conrad's misdeeds are your motive for murder. Shooting the computer proves it — you were trying to cover your tracks."

"But I wasn't. At the time . . ." I shrug, feeling again the crushing weight of my dysfunctional childhood, followed by an equally dysfunctional marriage. "He's the father of my child," I say at last.

Mr. Delany doesn't need me to explain any more. "Still protecting the legacy," he murmurs.

"Some habits are hard to break."

"Do you have any idea who might have burned down your house?"

I shake my head. Which, now that I'm truly considering, sends a trickle of unease down my spine. In the shock of everything that's happened over the past forty-eight hours, the loss of my house has felt mostly like that — a loss. But after visiting the scene and talking to Sergeant Warren I'm starting to realize it's also a threat. Someone out there murdered my husband. Some unknown person torched my home to cover his or her tracks.

And for all my searching, all my questioning about the man I married, I have no idea who that person might be. Or if they're finished yet.

"Have you felt watched, threatened, in the past few weeks?" Mr. Delaney asks, as if reading my mind. "What about Conrad? You said it felt like something was up."

"He was tense. I wondered . . ." I can't put into words yet what I thought. The increasingly silent meals. The way I'd wake up some nights and find Conrad staring at me. The reason I had come home late from work that night, because if I arrived at the house any earlier . . .

I haven't been worried about some mysterious stranger out there. But increasingly, I had started to wonder about the man sharing my bed.

I shrug. Everyone wants answers. My lawyer. The police. I only wish I had some.

"Evie, whatever your husband did, it's not your fault."

"I'm a liar. I married another liar. And now, my baby . . ." My throat closes up. I can't speak anymore. Whether it makes any sense at all, at one time I did love Conrad. Then I lost him. And like my father, Conrad remains a mystery; there are so many things now I'll never know about him. I feel tired of it all. The pattern of my life is wrong, and yet I can't seem to break it.

"I want to know the truth," I whisper. "I want to know one thing to be true."

"About your husband or your father?"

"I'll settle for either."

Mr. Delaney regards me for a long time. "Then I think you're going to have to start asking more questions."

"How? Who? I don't know anyone to talk to Conrad about. And my father, that was sixteen years ago. You were his closest friend. If you don't know who might've shot him, how am I supposed to figure it out?"

"There is another person."

I have a sudden sinking feeling. "No!"

"Yes. If you really want to understand

what happened sixteen years ago, you should talk to your mom."

Chapter 20
D.D.

From the beginning, Phil had warned D.D. that she'd regret making Flora Dane a CI. The woman was a known vigilante, an avowed loner, and just plain reckless. D.D. always hated it when her mentor was right.

"So to recap," she said briskly now, sitting at the head of the table, "you" — she skewered Flora with a glance — "took it upon yourself to call an Atlanta FBI agent and invite her into my investigation."

"Technically, I invited her to assist in *my* investigation," Flora said.

Yep, D.D.'s confidential informant had definitely gone rogue.

Flora continued. "I have an interest in all this, too, you know. What was Conrad Carter's association with Jacob? Were there other men or predators he was meeting? Does this mean he was part of some larger network of sociopaths and I missed it? Then, talking to SSA Quincy and hearing about other missing women —"

D.D. held up a hand. She pointed at the other newcomer in the room, who appeared to be around thirty years of age, could've passed for a Tom Ford model, and was sitting a lot closer to Flora than strictly necessary.

"And you? What's your role in all this?"

Kimberly Quincy was already smiling, which meant this was going to be good.

To the man's credit, he planted both elbows on the table, leaned forward, and met D.D.'s stare. "My name is Keith Edgar. I'm a computer analyst, and, um . . . I run a forum for true-crime enthusiasts. In particular, we've been working the Jacob Ness case for the past six years."

"*You've* been working the Jacob Ness case?"

Kimberly Quincy's smile was growing.

"We've always suspected there were other victims. The degree of sophistication and planning that went into Flora's abduction . . . no predator gets that smart overnight."

If Flora was offended to be discussed as little more than a case study, she didn't show it.

"And you know this because you're a computer analyst?" D.D. pressed.

"No, I know this because I've done a great deal of reading on the subject —"

"Internet true-crime porn."

"And I work with a group of talented experts, which included retired BPD detective Wayne Rock."

That caught D.D.'s attention. She'd known Wayne before his retirement five years ago. Great man, brilliant detective, who had lost his battle with cancer just a few months ago. The whole department had grieved, herself included.

"Wayne also believed there were other victims?"

"Absolutely. Most predators follow a pattern of escalation. With a self-proclaimed sex addict such as Ness, he probably started young as a voyeur, then evolved to inappropriate touching, before engaging in full-fledged sexual assault, and finally, ultimately . . ."

Edgar gestured awkwardly toward Flora, who still remained completely expressionless. Briefly, D.D. felt her heart soften. This was Flora's life. To be forever defined by a monster, whether she wanted to be or not. For the two years D.D. had known Flora, the woman had always refused to discuss her past. So to be part of this conversation now, to have invited a feebie no less, was an act in courage, whether D.D. liked it or not.

"Which brings us to you." She switched her attention to SSA Quincy. "The agent who actually figured out Ness was a long-haul trucker and organized the SWAT raid. You must've recovered a helluva lot of evidence."

"Yes and no, that's the problem. Ness's rig offered up some hair, other DNA samples. But his computer — which, according to Flora, he logged on to daily —"

Flora nodded.

"— was suspiciously lacking in content. Not even porn."

"He always watched porn." Flora spoke up.

"Completely wiping a hard drive is nearly impossible," the computer analyst spoke up. "He must have used a tool or app. Let's see, we're talking 2010." Edgar paused, seemed to be considering. "I'm guessing SteadyState, which was a free Microsoft app that worked with all XP operating systems. Microsoft offered it as a home computer safety system. It basically reverted the computer to a prior clean slate every time the laptop was rebooted, effectively deleting any malware or viruses kids might have inadvertently downloaded while playing online. The app worked so well, many computer professionals used it as well, myself included."

Edgar regarded Quincy with open curiosity.

"Ness's laptop did indeed contain SteadyState," she volunteered tersely.

"Interesting. Because it takes some time and capability to set up the app. To pick which items on the hard drive should be cleared and which should be left alone each time the system is rebooted. That alone proves an interesting level of computer sophistication for a man who didn't even graduate high school. And you're saying you didn't recover a single book in Ness's truck on computer programming, Windows operating systems, anything?"

"Nada."

Edgar and Flora Dane exchanged a look. D.D. wasn't sure she liked it.

"Ness's cell phone?" D.D. interrupted now.

"No smartphone," Quincy supplied. "We recovered a cheap, prepaid flip with hardly any usage. Certainly no texts or anything useful."

"I don't remember him ever using a cell," Flora said. "I would've guessed he had no one to call."

"Meaning the lack of evidence *is* the evidence," D.D. filled in. "Someone must've taught Ness how to cover his tracks, both with this computer app, and the prepaid flip." She glanced at Flora. "But the only time you remember him meeting up with another person was the one time you saw Conrad at the bar?"

"That's the only person I saw. But Jacob would disappear for days, sometimes even a week at a time. I always assumed he went on drug binges. But he could've been meeting up with other buddies. Maybe he was going on mini crime sprees, I don't know."

"Don't you think he'd brag to you?" Quincy spoke up. "He spoke to you about a great many things. And wasn't above threatening you with replacement."

Flora shrugged. "Jacob bragged. If he'd spent days with another woman, whether victim or prostitute, he might say something. But . . ." Flora took a deep breath. "Jacob was clever. He knew who he was. From a very young age, he told me, he knew he was different from others. And he knew he had to hide it. He was very adept at self-preservation. If he'd found some group, started networking with other predators, even met them from time to time, no, I don't think he'd tell me. He liked his secrets, too. And it amused him when others underestimated him. Saw just a white-trash trucker, when he knew himself to be more."

"What about a Tor browser?" Edgar spoke up.

Quincy regarded the computer analyst coolly. "As a matter of fact, in addition to SteadyState, Ness's laptop also had the Tor browser."

"What does that mean?" Flora spoke up.

"Tor, a.k.a. 'the Onion Router,' is a browser that uses a peer-to-peer network that intentionally obfuscates source IP addresses," Edgar explained. He looked at D.D. "It's perfectly safe and legal. It also happens to be the primary browser used to access the dark web."

D.D. got it. "Where Jacob could very well have trolled chat rooms filled with other perverts such as himself, picking up all sorts of new tricks and forensic dodges, while rebooting his laptop each night, allowing this SteadyState to automatically clear all record of such site visits and chat-room logs." She glanced at Quincy. "And knowing all this, the FBI can't magically do anything to rebuild the computer's history?"

"The FBI has tried its magic," Quincy drawled drily, then turned to Keith Edgar. "Don't even think about it. No matter how brilliant a geek you are, I assure you, my geeks are better. Nor is the FBI in the business of sharing evidence."

Edgar sank down. D.D. started to remember how much she liked Kimberly Quincy.

"What about his trucking log?" asked D.D. "Don't long-haul truckers have GPS and computer monitoring and that kind of thing? Seems like that should be a significant source of data."

"Once again, the answer is yes and no," Quincy said. "The company Jacob worked for only kept the backup data for three months. So we know his last three months of movement, give or take, but as for the time he had his rig at his safe house to first load up Flora, nada. Likewise, even if we had a specific time period — say, Flora could pinpoint the week or month Jacob met your murder victim at the bar — we can't look it up. What we did find . . . Jacob drove the highways of the South with some side trips to cheap motels, et cetera. We also discovered gaps in the data, which leads us to believe Jacob may have figured out how to turn off his GPS and computer monitoring — and that's not easy to do. These systems are required by law and designed to track how many consecutive hours a trucker has traveled and basically demand driving breaks. You can't just turn them off with a flick of a switch, or all drivers under a tough deadline would do it. Again, a surprising level of electronic sophistication from a man with a ninth-grade education."

Quincy tilted her head toward Edgar, who'd first made the point.

"So what exactly is the plan here?" D.D. asked. "Go after Jacob Ness's principal hideaway? See if we can find new evidence there?"

Quincy and Flora nodded.

"And to do that, Flora has volunteered herself as what, a hypnosis subject? Because you know experts still don't agree on the validity of recovered memories, and juries just plain hate that crap."

"There are other techniques." Flora spoke up first. "I've done some research. The human brain works a lot like a computer. First, there's the matter of what data is recorded in the moment. Particularly in traumatic situations, some people's senses heighten and they see all. But most people actually shut down. They squeeze their eyes shut, cover their ears, try to block what's happening. They don't want to know. Meaning the data is incomplete."

D.D. arched a brow at her CI.

"I was a long-term victim," Flora supplied in response to the next logical question. "In

311

the beginning, maybe I did try to shut it out. I certainly don't remember many specific details of the first . . . assault. But over time, the . . . continuity" — Flora picked the word carefully — "made the events less traumatic and more normal. At which point, I had plenty of opportunities to note and record more . . . data. So it's not like I'm trying to recover one memory, which might be suspect, but a string of impressions I had months to form."

On the table, Edgar's hand moved closer to Flora's. Still not touching, D.D. noticed, but closer. In return, Flora's hand drifted slightly toward his. Fascinating. D.D. had never known the woman to even look at a member of the opposite sex. Now this: a true-crime buff. She hoped Flora knew what she was doing. And she hoped like hell Keith Edgar saw Flora as a person, and not just the object of a macabre criminal case.

"But there are other issues with memory recovery techniques," D.D. stated now. "To keep with your analogy, it's not enough for the data to be present. There's the small matter of extracting it without corrupting it with other information — the power of suggestion."

"I wouldn't do hypnosis," Flora said immediately. "I've been doing some research and that's my least favorite option."

D.D. and Quincy both eyed the woman.

"I would prefer a visualization exercise, grounded in known triggers."

"I'll bite," D.D. said. "What?"

"Smell is the strongest known trigger for memory. Therefore, some experts suggest starting a visualization exercise with what the subject knows to be true about the episode: say, the smell of urine-soaked pine wood." Again, the woman didn't flinch. "The taste of blood on my tongue. The feel of a sliver in my finger."

It took D.D. a moment to get it; then she wished she hadn't. "You're talking about sticking yourself back in the coffin? Recreating your own captivity, for the sake of a memory?"

Flora stared at her. Very gaunt now, D.D. saw. Very dark shadows under her eyes. "I think it's worth trying."

"And Dr. Keynes —"

"It's my decision!"

"I'll take that to be a no." D.D. turned to Quincy. "Did you know about this?"

"No," the agent said immediately. "And to be honest, I don't agree with it. Recreating trauma, particularly of that nature, risks sending you down the rabbit hole all over again. The psychological impact on you, where this might lead. It's not a good idea."

"We need to find where Jacob lived —"

"Not at the expense of your mental health," D.D. snapped. "He took enough from you. Don't give him any more."

"This is my choice. This is me fighting back!"

"This is you sacrificing yourself. First you wouldn't talk about anything, now you're risking a complete meltdown. You do realize there are options in between, don't you?"

"Such as?"

"Forget coffins for a second. For the sake of argument, we can try out your technique but go after a memory that's much less traumatic. How about the night Jacob met Conrad? You described it as a dive bar. You said you ate and ate. Nachos, chicken wings, beer? Country music on the radio, maybe you know a particular song? If you're going to use your five senses to attempt to trigger a memory, I think beer, hot wings, and country songs are a much safer place to start. With the assistance of Dr. Keynes, of course. Because this is way out of my league, and yours, too." D.D. gestured to SSA Quincy.

"You want more information on Conrad Carter," the federal agent filled in.

"That is the point of my investigation. But for the record, we made an interesting discovery today: Conrad Carter had hidden away half a dozen fake IDs. Not great ones, but good enough to get into a bar."

"You think he used the IDs as an alias when he traveled," Quincy stated. "Including when he met up with Jacob Ness."

"If Flora could remember what name Jacob called him, that would confirm our suspicions. But also, what exactly did they talk about, did any other names come up? You want to find Jacob's secret clubhouse — fair enough. But maybe the other way of coming after Jacob Ness is to identify the other members of the club. Especially if some of them are still alive . . ."

"They might be able to provide information on Ness, including his cabin hideaway." Keith Edgar spoke up.

"Based on what SSA Quincy is saying, they were probably the ones who gave Jacob the pointers on how to keep it hidden." D.D. looked at Flora. "What do you think?"

The woman frowned. "I don't know. I was drinking heavily that night. Meaning, the quality of the data recorded . . ."

"At a certain point you were drunk. Drunks have notoriously lousy memories."

"But I don't remember Jacob calling him

Conrad. I think it might have been another name. And that was in the beginning. Maybe there is more I saw, or noticed, than I think. If Jacob had help — and it seems like he must've — then, yes, I'd like to go after those men, too."

"Not just one predator, but a whole network of them." Keith Edgar sounded slightly breathless.

D.D. frowned at him. "Not so fast, big boy. This is an active criminal case. Civilians need not apply."

"He's not just a civilian." Flora spoke up quickly. "He's an expert on Jacob in his own right."

"Hey." Quincy tapped the table. "I believe the FBI wears that crown."

"I'm not doing it," Flora said, "if he's not around."

D.D. stared at her CI. Yep, Flora had definitely gone rogue. And was possibly love-struck? Except that didn't fit with the Flora she knew at all. Meaning . . .

More and more questions. Where would D.D.'s case be without them?

"He signs a nondisclosure."

"Done." Edgar spoke up immediately.

"We talk to Dr. Keynes and get his agreement."

"I'll do it." Flora already had out her phone.

"You should tell your mother," D.D. said, mostly because she was a mom and she just couldn't help herself.

She got back the answer she expected: a mutinous stare.

D.D. sighed. She didn't know if this was the best idea or worst idea she'd ever had. She respected Flora's strength but worried about her self-destructive streak. D.D. needed some kind of fresh approach to get her investigation going, but a "recovered memory" from a night spent binge drinking definitely felt like a stretch.

And yet, for the first time since D.D. had known Flora, the woman was willing to talk about Jacob. She was willing to look backward, at four hundred and seventy-two days of absolutely horrifying memories. There was a determination and resilience in evidence that D.D. had to admire.

If Dr. Keynes helped them, if they started with something easier than Flora climbing back into a pine coffin . . .

Maybe Flora could get the answers she now so desperately wanted. While Kimberly Quincy caught a new lead on six missing women, and D.D. found out what Conrad Carter had been doing on all his business trips and who, other than his wife, might want him dead.

It sounded simple enough. Which probably explained the sinking feeling in D.D.'s stomach. The best-laid plans . . .

Flora was still staring at her. SSA Quincy, too. Flora was going to do it one way or another, D.D. realized. She'd made up her mind sometime in the middle of the night. And once set on a course, she wasn't the type of person to let anything stop her.

"Fine," D.D. announced. "A trip down memory lane it is."

Flora hit dial.

CHAPTER 21
FLORA

When I walk into FBI headquarters two hours later with a bag of takeout nachos and chicken wings, no one gives me a second glance. Wearing my usual uniform of worn cargo pants and a baggy sweatshirt beneath a bulky down coat, I probably look like a delivery person. Keith, trailing behind me with a six-pack of Bud cans, earns several startled looks, but that's nothing compared to the attention Samuel gets just by waiting for us. My victim specialist, Dr. Keynes, has features that stand out in a crowd.

Compared to Sergeant Warren, Samuel was surprisingly agreeable to my plan. If anything, I had the feeling he'd been waiting for such a call. He probably recognized my refusal to talk about Jacob was a form of denial that couldn't go on forever.

Now Samuel moves forward. I get a clasp on the shoulder, a show of warmth from a man who knows everything awful there is to know about me, including the fact I don't do hugs. He shakes Keith's hand, and the two take a moment to size up each other. Neither says anything, but Keith still appears a little starstruck.

Samuel never initiates a conversation. His job is listening, not talking, as he once explained to me, but he's also intensely private. If he knows every terrible thing about me, it took me five years to figure out he was secretly in love with my mom. Even then, I didn't actually deduce anything; my mom had to announce they'd decided to start dating, but only if I was okay with it.

I'm not sure I ever gave permission. I think I was too busy standing before her with my jaw hanging open. I still can't picture my mom, in her free-spirit yoga clothes, driving a tractor around her organic potato farm, with a man addicted to Armani — but then, no kid wants to imagine her mom dating. I think they're happy. I guess I even hope so. But mostly, I don't want to know.

Federal buildings have a lot of security. Samuel is meeting us because of the beer, which the guards either don't like or surreptitiously hope to confiscate for later. Samuel takes one of them aside, murmurs a few words, and just like that, we're through. Keith continues his wide-eyed stare. I roll my eyes at Samuel and don't even bother to ask what he said. I've never seen Samuel not get his way. That and his cheekbones are like his superpowers.

Upstairs, Sergeant Warren and SSA Quincy are already waiting. They both have cups of coffee and are chatting away like old friends. Territorial pissing match aside, they seem to have mutual respect for each other, which makes my life easier. Individually, they are solid investigators. Together, I should have double the chance of getting answers.

I'm still very curious about D.D.'s earlier meeting with Conrad Carter's wife. Did the woman really shoot her own husband? Because D.D. implied the case wasn't as clear-cut as the news reported. I'm trying out some strategy of my own: assist with D.D.'s investigation now with this little trip down memory lane, then interrogate the detective on what she knows about Conrad Carter later.

Samuel has booked a meeting room. Much like the one at BPD headquarters, it has a wall of windows, which will allow the others to observe from the hall. For the "visualization" exercise, Samuel has already said it should be only him and me in the room. I'm supposed to relax, which is already nearly impossible. Having other people around won't help.

Now I open up the takeout and arrange the nachos and chicken wings in the middle of the table. Already, the smell wafts across the room. I wait for scent alone to transport me. I mostly feel like I'm standing in the middle of a federal building with soggy tortilla chips.

Samuel produces a glass. Keith does the honor of pouring out a beer. Again, we're trying to be as specific as possible. Jacob always ordered Bud, always in a glass. Final touch, country music. I have a vague memory of it playing in the background. I'm less sure about the song. Keith already Googled country's greatest hits from seven years ago and, while we were waiting for the food, compiled a playlist. He sets his phone on the table now and gets the party started.

Again, I wait to feel . . . something. Mostly, I'm self-conscious and awkward.

"We're missing something."

Four pairs of eyes stare at me. Not helping.

"Popcorn. There was popcorn in little red-and-white-checkered containers. And it shouldn't be this bright. No honky-tonk is this bright."

Keith heads for the panel of light switches. Samuel disappears without ever saying a word, meaning he must know how to get popcorn.

That leaves me with the two investigators. D.D. is eyeing the food in the middle of the table.

"I'm hungry," she says.

"You're always hungry," Quincy replies.

It's like they've suddenly become besties. This, I have a feeling, will not be as good for me.

Keith can't figure out how to dim the overhead bulbs. In the end, he shuts them off. Given all the light still pouring in through the glass windows, the effect works out nicely. At least it takes the edge off the room, makes it feel less sterile.

Samuel returns with a bag of microwave popcorn. He opens the bag, the smell hits, and for the first time I feel it. Like a door opening in my mind. I can smell the bar, the beer, popcorn, melted cheese. I pick up the glass, take a small sip, and then I can taste it, too. I'd been so thirsty, so hungry, so scared.

Fake-Everett. That's what I'd called him back then. Because he'd started my programming by taking away my name. No more Flora, just Molly. Molly in a hot-pink dress only a hooker would wear. And I was to call him by my father's name. I didn't even remember my father, but I had to believe he had loved me, so to call this beast by his name had hurt.

Everett, which I said out loud. Fake-Everett, which I used in my head, because silent rebellions were all I had left.

"Have a seat," Samuel tells me, and I realize for the first time the others have already left. It's just Samuel and me and beer and country music and the smell of popcorn and a memory of one evening, already trying to claw out of my head.

"Where are you, Flora?"

"Molly."

"Molly," he amends.

"I'm hungry. So, so hungry." I press a hand to my stomach. Then I pick up the first kernel of popcorn, tasting the saltiness of it against my tongue. Another small sip of beer. "He left me for the whole week," I murmur. "Each day hungrier and hungrier. But I couldn't leave the motel. If I did, he'd find me. He'd kill me. He told me so. And then he'd head north and kill my whole family. So I waited. Starving and starving. I waited."

Sweatshirt is all wrong. Too warm, too

comforting. I should be overexposed and shivering from the AC that always blasted away in the South.

No thinking. Doing. Shed the sweatshirt, followed by my long-sleeve top, until my arms are exposed in my gray tank top. Goose bumps ripple up across my flesh. Better.

"Where are you, Molly?" Samuel asks again. His voice is deep and rich. Hypnotic. It gives me a moment of uneasiness. I don't want to be under anyone's thrall. I don't want to surrender control. Not when I've spent all these years fighting to get it back.

My choice, my choice. Another kernel of popcorn, concentrating on the buttery goodness.

Hungry. I'd been so desperately, acutely, stomach-growlingly hungry. And that, as much as anything, takes me back.

"Two Buds," I whisper. "Fake-Everett lets me have a beer. He hardly ever orders me food or alcohol. Waste of money, he'd say. The beer is nice. I'm grateful to him."

"Are you sitting or standing?"

"I'm sitting. On a barstool. Fake-Everett stands behind me. Like he's protecting me. I'm his girl."

"What do you smell?"

"Popcorn. Oh my God, it smells so good! The bartender brings us some. Happy hour perk. I know the rules. I look at Fake-Everett. He nods. He's going to let me eat free food. My hand is shaking so hard I can barely raise it. One kernel. One single kernel."

On the table, my hand rises. Takes one single kernel.

"When you haven't eaten in a while," I whisper, "you have to pace yourself. Otherwise, you'll get sick. And I can't afford to get sick. Not when I never know when I'll get to eat again."

Another single kernel.

"Tell me about the bar," Samuel intones.

"The bartender?"

"Umm, white guy. Red flannel shirt over a black T-shirt. Busy. Nods at Fake-Everett once. Won't look at me at all. Glasses above his head. Pulling them down, pouring beers from the tap, sliding them down the bar. Scooping out more popcorn. Moving, moving, moving, always in motion."

"Name tag?"

"No."

"What does the bar look like?"

"Dark wood. Very shellacked. Shiny. But sticky. Popcorn all over the floor. Pool tables behind me. Clink, clink, clink. Lots of people sitting around the bar. Guys in cowboy hats, women in tight jeans. I keep tugging my dress up. I feel ashamed. I don't look at the bartender anymore. I don't want to know what he thinks of me."

"Is the beer sitting on a coaster? A napkin? Directly on the bar?"

I frown, squeeze my eyes shut, focus harder. "Coaster."

"What does it say?"

"Bud Light."

"Are there any lights behind the bar? Glowing signs?"

"Amber. Um . . . Abita Amber, glowing in orange and red."

"How's the popcorn?"

"Good! God, I'm hungry."

"Look around the room. What do you see?"

"I can't. Eyes straight ahead. Or Fake-Everett will get mad and I don't want him to be mad. Not till I've gotten to eat more popcorn."

"What about beside you? Can you see anyone beside you?"

"A man. He sits down. He looks at Fake-Everett and nods. Fake-Everett nods back. The man comments that I'm skinny. Fake-Everett says it's my own fault. I eat more popcorn. I don't look at either of them, but

I'm confused that Fake-Everett is talking to a stranger. He never talks to anyone."

"Can you describe the man to me?"

"Umm, younger. Early thirties, maybe? Fit. Not tall, but muscular. Dark hair, smooth shaven. He's wearing a blue T-shirt and jeans and I can smell him — soap and aftershave. Fake-Everett only ever smells like sweat and dirty clothes. The man stares at my chest. I pull up the top of my dress again. I hate the dress. Fake-Everett tells me I should be grateful when he gives me clothes. I'm not."

"What happens next?"

"A tray of nachos goes by. All chips and melted cheese piled with salsa and sour cream. Oh my God, they smell so good! The man sees me eyeing them and asks the bartender to bring us some. I'm pretty sure to share, but I don't dare ask. Fake-Everett has a hand on my shoulder. He's squeezing very hard. He's on something. His eyes are too bright. In this mood, Fake-Everett is very dangerous. I don't feel so good anymore. I'm nervous. Very nervous."

"Are the man and Fake-Everett talking?"

"The man is tapping the bar." My fingers move. There is a pattern. Same rhythm, over and over again. I can hear it in my mind. My fingers play it out on the table. *Tap, tap,*

tap, tappity tap. "I think he's nervous, too,"
I whisper. "But I don't know why. He keeps
staring at me. I just wish he'd look away."

"And then?"

"Nachos. They arrive. The man says we
can share. I look at Fake-Everett. I'm trying
to understand. He never talks to others, he
never shares. He tells me to show the man
some respect, be more appreciative. I don't
understand that. Something is wrong. This
whole . . . scenario. Something is going on.
The strange man, Fake-Everett, it's like they
know one another. And the man keeps tapping, tapping, tapping. I wish he would go
away."

"What does Fake-Everett do next?"

"Eats nachos. Scoops up big mouthfuls.
Smears sour cream and salsa on his face.
He doesn't care. He's a pig."

"What do you do?"

"I eat, too. Quickly. Drink more beer.
Something is going to happen. I don't know
what."

"And the man?"

"He doesn't eat. He ordered the nachos
but takes only a single chip. He just keeps
looking at me, and fidgeting. He orders
more food, but again, for Fake-Everett and
me, not for himself."

"What do you hear, Molly?"

The change in focus startles me. I return to tapping the table. The man's restless beat. Then, I'm humming, too. A Kenny Chesney song playing from the jukebox behind us. *Clink, clink* of pool balls.

And voices. Fake-Everett and the man. Heads closer together, murmuring while I grab another chicken wing and hastily gnaw away. I have a suspicion now. A growing feeling of dread over what's going to happen next. Must eat. Must eat as much as possible as fast as possible.

"Conner. Fake-Everett calls the man Conner.

" *'Told you she was pretty,' Fake-Everett says.*

" *'Too skinny,' Conner says.*

" *'Not at the rate she's eating now. Trust me, trained her myself.'*

" *'You're sure?'*

" *'Course. Deal's a deal.'*

" *'And the return?'*

" *'Same place tomorrow night. Parking lot. Don't want to make too big an impression, hanging out at the same bar twice.'*

" *'And she's agreed?'*

" *'Course. Girl knows better than to make fuss. You'll see.'*

"The bar lights flicker." Seeing it abruptly in my mind, I report the memory out loud.

330

"Closing time. We have to leave." My hand presses against my stomach. "I'm scared."

"What happens next, Molly?"

"The man, Conner, he pays the bill. Throws down a hundred without even blinking. When the man turns away, Fake-Everett grabs the money for himself. So fast, like a snake. I don't feel good. I stumble, walking out. The beer, the food, what I'm now sure is going to happen next."

"What's going to happen?"

"Fake-Everett . . . he sold me. Or rented me? But what they were whispering . . . Fake-Everett is going to tell me to go home with this man. I should be grateful. He's cleaner, younger, better-looking. But I think that's the problem. I know Fake-Everett. He doesn't share his toys. And I can already tell you, he doesn't like this guy. He doesn't like any man better-looking than him. He's playing some game. This Conner, myself, we'll both pay for it in the end."

"What do you mean?"

"Fake-Everett's already told me he's going to kill me and feed me to the gators. Conner touches me, Fake-Everett will kill him, too. Both of us. And take all the money, drugs, whatever it was Conner promised. Fake-Everett doesn't negotiate. He steals. He hoards. He is awful, but he's consistent. Conner doesn't understand yet. He's as dead as I am."

"Where is Conner?"

"Walking ahead of us. Straight into the parking lot. He has square shoulders. Strong, fit. Fake-Everett's fingers are digging into my arm. He's dragging me out of the bar. I can feel the rage coming off him in waves. I think he would like to kill me right now. Or maybe it's Conner that he hates so much."

"How do you feel?"

"Like I'm going to vomit. But I have to hold it in, time it right."

"For what?"

"Parking lot. The air is warm, humid. For the first time, I'm not chilled. Except now I'm breaking into a sweat. But it's okay. I know what I'm doing. I got this.

"People disappear, climb into their pickup trucks. Conner stops. Looks back at us. And then — I vomit. All over his shoes. He jumps back. Swears. Yells. Others turn, start to pay attention. Fake-Everett waves them off. I can still feel his anger, but it's softer. Conner is backing up. No one wants a puker.

"Conner turns away," I whisper. "He leaves without me. And I know Fake-Everett isn't happy, but then I also know exactly what to say. *You've been gone for a week. I just want to be with you. Only you.* Fake-Everett thinks he's so smart. He thinks he's the one in control. But I have my tricks, too.

"Fake-Everett isn't angry anymore. Fake-Everett takes me back to the motel. And I survive another day."

I'm tired suddenly. So exhausted my head slumps forward. I'm not thinking of popcorn or beer or country music. I'm thinking of the intense fatigue of all those minutes, hours, days. Never knowing if I would make it. Hating my life, but still not quite able to give it up. Eking out each moment because the will to live makes it harder than you think to simply let go.

Samuel's hand, solid on my shoulder. "Flora, open your eyes."

I do, but I still feel blurry, out of it.

"It's okay. Take a moment. You did good."

A bottle of water appears before me. I drink it gratefully, washing the aftertaste of beer from my mouth. I hardly ever drink, and certainly not Jacob's favorite beer. I'm shivering slightly. I realize I'm barely dressed and find my pile of clothes, pulling each layer back on.

The others are behind me, murmuring in low voices.

"Conner was one of Conrad's fake IDs," D.D. is saying.

"Abita Select Amber is one of the top-selling beers in Mississippi," Quincy supplies.

Keith says nothing. Comes to sit beside me. Remains silent, for which I'm grateful.

"The tapping," Samuel says. He rests his dark hand on the table, finds the pattern. It jars me a little, the sound from my head playing out in real life.

He regards all of us expectantly. "No military backgrounds?" he presses.

Keith suddenly lights up. "Oh my God. He was tapping in Morse code!"

"Exactly."

"What was he saying?" D.D. asks.

"He wasn't. He was asking a question, the same question, over and over. He was asking, 'Are you okay?' But Flora never answered him."

CHAPTER 22
EVIE

Before returning home, I convince Mr. Delaney to swing by CVS for some basic supplies. I find a gigantic purse. Cheap brown leather, covered in miscellaneous pockets and snap detailing meant to make it look urban cool. Definitely not my classic Coach Christmas gift from Conrad. My mom will hate it. I smile as I sling it over my shoulder.

I pick out a toothbrush, toothpaste, deodorant, light makeup. My mother has the bathroom fully stocked but I want my own toiletries. Brands I prefer.

I find myself in front of hair dye for a long time. Mr. Delaney has wandered off. No doubt trying to give me space. Alone in the pharmacy store aisle, I find myself thinking like the murder suspect I truly am. Maybe I should think beyond my preferred hair gel. What about a bug-out kit? New hair color, new hairstyle? Sunglasses, hat? If I ever want to leave my mother's house, it will require some subterfuge.

So I do it. A rich brunette to cover my ash blond. Then, while I'm at it, a cheap purple scarf, oversized sunglasses. Then I go a little nuts in the hair accessory section, from scissors to hair extensions to flowered barrettes. I don't know why I pick the things I pick, and yet it all makes perfect sense. Next up, pen and notepad. Then, even better, I stumble across a rack of prepaid cells. I select three. Again, not sure why. It feels right.

I need money. But my ATM card melted in the house fire. Maybe Mr. Delaney will take me to my local bank, where I can withdraw in person. Or loan me money? I feel uncomfortable, like I'm crossing some line; then I order myself to get over it. I can't be dependent on my mom and helpless in the face of whatever is going to happen next. Between retrieving my passport and financial documents from the safe, and now this little shopping expedition, I'm going to make it.

I head back to the checkout line. Mr. Delaney magically reappears. He already has a credit card in hand, which makes me feel self-conscious again. Then he spots the prepaid cells. Without a word, he returns his credit card to his wallet, extracts cash instead.

I think I get it. He doesn't want there to be evidence he bought the phones. In case they are recovered later at . . . what? The scene of a shooting? Another house fire? He doesn't ask. I don't tell.

"Nice purse," he says finally when we emerge from the store and I start transferring over my supplies.

"I need cash," I say. "And a new ATM card."

He drives me to the bank.

There, things get more interesting. I walk in, and the first teller across from me, some woman I've never met, immediately gasps. I actually stop and glance behind me, wondering what the fuss is about. Did someone famous walk in behind me? Nope. Next, I look down. Are my clothes covered in lunch? No. Then, finally I get it. She's gasping at me. A woman whose picture has been all over the news as a murderer.

I feel a lot better about my decision to buy hair dye. I only wish I'd bought more.

I square my shoulders, produce my passport, and get to work.

I know my accounts. I know what Conrad and I have and don't have in our joint savings. I'm not sure if the police can freeze the funds as part of their investigation — sounds like a logical enough thing for them to do — so I make a large withdrawal now. The woman fusses, says she needs her manager. I play it cool, officially having an out-of-body experience where I'm no longer a shy mathematician's daughter whose been shunning the limelight for her entire life but a regular La Femme Nikita. Yeah, that was me on the news. And if I was willing to shoot my own husband, just think of what I might do to you.

Then I wise up enough to turn sideways and show off my rounded belly. By the time the manager returns, I have the full pregnancy profile going on. She softens almost immediately. At least my future stretch marks have come in handy.

She tries to tell me there's a limit on what I can withdraw. Which is partly true, but not the paltry amount she's conceding to me. I keep my voice firm and polite as I walk her through it. This account is in my name. My passport verifies my identity. I am entitled to withdraw what I want to withdraw. Any questions, my lawyer is sitting in the car.

In the end, the manager counts out five thousand dollars. Stacks of hundreds. I find myself thinking of the metal box again,

Conrad's own stash of IDs and cash. It both confuses and saddens me. What was he really doing on all those business trips?

And why marry me? Why acquire a wife, then a child, if his whole life was just a lie?

As long as I'm in the bank, I order a new debit card to be sent to my mother's address. That customer service person is equally skittish to be around me. I keep my chin up, but on my lap my hands start to shake. I'm an introvert. This level of attention is difficult for me. Especially the way people look, whisper.

Forget Conrad. I feel like a sixteen-year-old girl who just shot and killed her father all over again.

I get my money. I get promises of a new card. Then I clutch my bag to my shoulder and flee the premises.

The moment Mr. Delaney turns down my mother's street, reporters rush forward. He is patient and firm. One slow, steady speed. The reporters quickly start giving way because he will not. It occurs to me that he's probably driven this gauntlet before, both given his line of work and given what happened sixteen years ago.

Did I come out of the house back then? I don't remember. I was so lost in my own grief. While I'm sure the media was terrible to my mother, asking for the gory details again and again, I'm also sure she got to vamp up her role of heartbroken widow. While I, the strange quiet kid, was let off the hook as a minor.

What did I do after my father's death? Sat in my room and stared at a wall, trying not to see his shattered chest. Sat in his office and stared at his whiteboard, trying to capture his last bit of genius. Then one day my mother said I was going to school, so I did. Because that's how it works in my family. We don't talk. We don't resolve. We just . . . move on.

Mr. Delaney turns into the driveway. Once we're on private ground, the reporters have to give up. I notice signs staked in the lawn: *No Trespassing.* Probably Mr. Delaney's handiwork from when he first arrived this morning. It makes an interesting counterpart to all the neighborhood Christmas decorations.

Mr. Delaney parks the car and looks at me.

"I'll be okay," I tell him.

"Two vodkas are okay," he says. "Five are too many." He's referring to my mother, who probably is a functioning alcoholic. Take away her vodka and she's unworkable.

Too much vodka and she's overly dramatic.

Conrad rarely drank, only the occasional beer. I realize now that's one of the things I liked about him. Growing up in a household where alcohol felt like a necessary evil, I barely touched it myself, and was happy my husband didn't either.

"Will you tell her about the lockbox discovery?" Mr. Delaney asks me.

"No. She already hates him enough."

"Do you know why?"

"A window salesman isn't worthy of Earl Hopkins's daughter."

Mr. Delaney smiles. "I don't think that's the case."

"Then why?"

"You should ask her yourself."

My turn to give him a look. But I'd told him I'd be okay and I can't make a liar out of myself now, so I pop open the door and step resolutely out of the car. Across the street, the reporters shout questions, hoping to get lucky. In front of me, my mother appears at the side door, vodka martini already in hand, though it's only three in the afternoon.

Last glance at Mr. Delaney.

Then, ready or not, here I come.

My first order of business is trying to gauge

how much my mother has already consumed. A jug of Ketel One sits on the
kitchen island, a peeled lemon beside it. She
follows my gaze, then raises her martini
glass in open defiance. Normally, my mother
waits till five o'clock sharp for her daily
habit, but she's never been great under pressure.

As usual she is impeccably garbed. Dark-
green wool slacks, a cashmere turtleneck
the color of oatmeal, a beautifully pleated
chocolate-brown vest. Given her beverage
and the waiting media, I doubt she's planning on going out, but in my mother's
world, there's no excuse for ever looking
other than your best.

Now she spies my new chunky, clunky
purse. Immediately, her brow furrows.
"What is *that*?"

"My new bag. Old one burned up in the
fire."

"Evie, if you needed a purse why didn't
you just say so? I have a number of Chanels
that would be perfect for you."

I don't answer the question, simply set my
purse on the kitchen chair closest to me.
Then I cross to the bottle of vodka, screw
back on the cap, put it away. In my world,
this passes for conversation.

"Did you eat lunch?" she tries now, going

on the attack as a concerned mom.

"Mr. Delaney took me for lunch."

"Did you eat? It's very important that you eat. The baby —"

"I had a very healthy, fulfilling lunch, thank you. Including OJ, hold the vodka."

She flushes, frowns at me again. "Did you find what you needed at your house?"

"I learned enough."

"Is it a total loss?"

I hate to say this. "Yes."

"Then, that's it; you'll stay here. Your rooms are ready to go, the nursery is nearly done. A woman in your condition can't be subject to undue stress. Frankly, all this nonsense about the shooting is enough."

For a moment, I think she's referring to my father, then realize she means Conrad.

"The police say Dad didn't kill himself." I don't mean to utter the words so baldly, but I don't know how else to deliver them.

My mom freezes. There's some kind of look on her face, but I can't read it. Horror, sorrow, confusion. All three.

"Why are the police talking about your father's death?"

"Because I told them the truth: I didn't do it."

"Evie Hopkins —"

Not my married name, I notice. Even half

drunk and caught off guard, my mom can still get her digs in.

"I didn't shoot him. We both know it. We lied to protect him sixteen years ago, Mom. Because we loved him. Because we couldn't bear to think he killed himself. But it's been sixteen years, and given what happened with Conrad . . . If we lied to protect Dad all those years ago, then I need us to find out the truth now, in order to save me."

My mom sits. Hard. Just collapses in the chair, vodka sloshing against the sides of her glass. For a moment, she looks lost, almost childlike, and it unnerves me. Then she takes a fortifying sip.

"I don't understand," she says.

"According to the police, someone else shot Dad. Someone had to be here in the house."

"But we didn't see anyone."

"Then the person left right before we entered."

"Are they sure? How can they know these things?"

"You watch TV —"

"I don't watch those shows —"

"Of course you watch those shows! Everyone watches *those* shows. Plus, I've seen them in your Netflix queue. This isn't the time for posturing, Mom. Now is the time for truth."

She glares at me. It makes her look more like herself. We both relax. She takes another sip of her martini.

"They're sure?"

"Yes, Mom. Dad didn't commit suicide." The words are harder to say than I thought. Again, my family has always been defined by the things unspoken. And *suicide* is such a sad, terrible word. We never talked about it. Just like myself at lunch, my mother gets a sudden sheen in her eyes. The weight of her own burden lifting after all these years. What could've been a shared burden, if only we'd been the type of people to share such things.

She looks away, drains her glass. Then, without another glance at me, gets up, crosses to the cabinet, and gets the vodka back down. I don't try to stop her. Some battles are too hard to fight.

"Everyone loved your father," she says at last, peeling off a curl of lemon rind. "He was a genius. Who doesn't love a genius?"

"Other geniuses," I answer. "Jealous professors, overworked TAs, flunked students."

She frowns again but, focusing on the preparation of a perfect martini, at least doesn't immediately dismiss my ideas.

"It's why your father threw the poker parties," she says abruptly.

I shake my head, not following.

"The academic world is competitive. For ideas, grants, students, funding. Your father didn't love that aspect. Especially in math, he saw everyone working alone. He thought ideas would be better if people shared their ideas and opinions. The university environment wasn't conducive to such things, he said. So, poker nights. Invite other professors, doctorate students, et cetera. Get everyone relaxed, having fun. Collaboration would naturally follow."

I nod. I never heard my father dismiss another colleague's ideas or talk down to a student. As professors went, I always thought he was ahead of his time. Or maybe, simply that secure in his own brilliance. But I hadn't known this aspect of the poker nights and it only makes me miss him more.

"There was a TA," she says abruptly. "Aarav Patil. Very promising, your father said. But a loner. He rarely attended the poker nights, no matter how many times your father invited him. And while your father wasn't one to go into detail with me, I could tell he was getting frustrated with Patil. I'm not sure the boy would've been his TA much longer."

"Okay." Belatedly, I realize I should be writing this down. Ugly purse to the rescue. I have my pad and paper. "Did this Patil know where we lived?"

"They all did. Your father was just as likely to have students over to his home office as the one on campus."

"What about professors?"

She takes her first sip of her martini but is contemplative now, less emotional. "I'm not sure. I never heard your father say a bad word, but that didn't mean others weren't jealous. There were things your father could just . . . comprehend. His mind . . ." She looks as me abruptly. "There was no else in the world like your father," she whispers. "No one else."

For the first time I get it, truly get it. She loved him. Probably as much as I did. We both loved him. And neither one of us has been the same since.

"I miss him, too," I say.

She just smiles, but there are tears on her cheeks now. I think I should stand up, give my mom a hug. But I'm too afraid she'll turn away. So I remain seated. She drinks her vodka. We both wait.

"You should talk to Dr. Martin Hoffman," she says abruptly, "the department chair. He's retired now, but sixteen years ago, he would've known everyone and what personalities might have had issues with others." She pauses a moment, then concedes: "And who might've been more ambitious. When your father died, that left a vacancy, of course, which had to be filled."

"Who got his job?"

"Katarina Ivanova."

"A woman?" It shouldn't surprise me but still catches me off guard. "Did my father know her?"

"Yes. He'd been mentoring her for the past year. He was . . . impressed." My mother's face shutters up, and in her expression, I learn a few more things about Katarina Ivanova: She was very beautiful and my mother hated her.

"I don't remember her from poker night."

"Not everyone could always make it." Or my mother hadn't wanted her around.

"But she'd been to Dad's home office?"

"Of course. That was how he worked."

"Thank you."

My mother looks at me. She still has tear tracks on her cheeks, and her fingers on the stem of her martini glass are trembling. "What good will come of this?" she asks me softly.

"I don't know."

"He's dead. We both paid the price. And

as for what happened Tuesday night . . . How can the circumstances of your father's death matter? You were a child. The records were sealed."

"The police are reopening the case."

"Because you stirred the pot."

"I have to know, Mom. I can't keep . . . being the same person, telling the same lies. Just once, I want to know the truth."

My mother smiles sadly. "You know what they say, dear: Be careful what you wish for."

CHAPTER 23
D.D.

"So what do we actually know about this guy?" D.D. asked.

They'd taken over the FBI's meeting room. Not D.D.'s favorite location, as she felt she was ceding more and more of her homicide investigation to the feds. Then again, she had two feebies at the table to her one BPD self. Add to that a rogue CI and a civilian true-crime buff, and this was getting to be the craziest investigative team she'd ever seen.

She didn't approve of crazy. Or the fact that she didn't know what to do next. She *always* knew what to do next.

Dr. Keynes did the honors: "Flora, did you ever see the man — Conrad or, I suppose, Conner — at another bar? Or perhaps meeting up with Jacob at one of the truck stops?"

"No. But Jacob would often take off on his own . . ."

There was a slight hesitation and D.D. caught it.

"What?" she demanded.

Flora wouldn't make eye contact with any of them. "It was shortly after that, Jacob returned to Florida with me. Where he became . . . involved in other business. Whatever he may have been doing previously, I think once he hit Florida, that became his full-time focus."

D.D. understood what Flora wasn't saying. Dr. Keynes and Kimberly Quincy should as well, meaning Flora's oblique reference had to do with the new guy in the room. Fair enough. Everyone was entitled to their privacy, and God knows a survivor of a sensational kidnapping case had to fight to keep hers.

"So Jacob had definitely made a connection with Conrad. Everything about what you described was hardly a coincidental meeting," D.D. stated.

"But Conrad's own intentions are unclear." Quincy spoke up. The FBI agent wore a frown similar to D.D.'s own. Clearly, she didn't approve of crazy either. "Was he there as a second perpetrator, or as some kind of self-appointed savior? Do you think he recognized you from TV?" she asked Flora.

Flora shrugged. "I doubt it. By that point, I'd lost a lot of weight. My hair was hacked off. Most of the time I didn't recognize myself in the mirror. Jacob had been taking me out in public for months, and no one ever looked at me twice."

"Did Conrad try to make eye contact, send you any other signals?" D.D. tried again. "Morse code isn't exactly the easiest way to establish contact. And risky, given Jacob was a long-haul trucker and had experience on the radio."

"I kept my gaze down. Jacob didn't like it when I looked up. Conrad might have tried something. I wouldn't have known. And Jacob never left us alone. He had his hand on my shoulder the whole time."

"When did you leave the town?" Quincy asked now.

"The next day. Up and out. Jacob was hardy. He could drink all night, still get up at four and start driving. He'd been off the road for a week. I imagine he had to get back to work."

"Motel Upland," D.D. provided. "Last time we talked, you thought you recalled a flashing motel sign that read Motel Upland. Something more for us to check out. Maybe we can even find a record of Conrad Carter or one of his aliases staying there or nearby.

Of course, it would help if we had a state and not just 'someplace in the South.' "

"Try Mississippi," Quincy suggested. "Given the Abita beer."

"I think Jacob promised Flora to Conrad, made some kind of deal." D.D. noticed Keith didn't look directly at Flora as he said this. He spoke evenly, his tone strictly professional. It made D.D. wonder if Flora would hurt him now or later.

"I don't think that's much of a stretch," Quincy said drily.

While Flora added, "You think Conrad intended to take me away. Jacob would've thought it was to abuse me. But maybe Conrad was really trying to rescue me."

"Interesting thought," Dr. Samuel mused. He nodded toward D.D. "Does Conrad have any history in law enforcement, military service? Time with at-risk kids?"

"Not even a volunteer at a soup kitchen," she assured him. "Which makes this all stranger still. But he did have a box of fake IDs. Meaning whatever he was doing in that bar, he was working 'undercover,' so to speak. The question remains, to what end? One predator networking with another? Or some lone gunman trying to save the day? But how would he know about Flora? And if this is really what he did, shouldn't there be some record of other girls he rescued, or crimes stopped? Certainly, his wife doesn't know about any of this. She appeared as shocked by the fake IDs and cash stash as anyone. Though again, she shot up his computer, which may prove his travel activities weren't altruistic after all."

"What do you know about his other aliases, the names on the IDs?" Quincy asked.

"Nothing yet. One of my fellow detectives, Neil, has been working on them. He's running each name through state databases with the license number, but given how common the aliases are, he's getting too much information. The few he's managed to whittle down to the 'right' Conner or Carter or whatnot, there's no attached credit history, criminal records, anything. He suspects the IDs are hollow — not representative of whole new lives, just literally a piece of plastic procured for getting into a club."

"But didn't you say Conrad had a connection to Florida?" Quincy pressed. "And Jacob was from Florida. Surely that can't be coincidence."

"I don't like coincidences any more than the next person," D.D. assured her. "But Florida is a big state. Conrad's family lived in Jacksonville. Jacob Ness's mother lived on the west coast, north of Tampa. They were hardly neighbors. On the other hand, Jacob drove all around on his job and Conrad traveled all around on his, so anything is possible. Neil will keep searching. But we just learned about the aliases today, so it'll take a bit more digging.

"I don't think we should worry about Conrad's reasons for meeting Jacob and Flora." Keith spoke up. "We can speculate about why Conrad came to the bar all we want, but at this time we lack adequate data."

An IT geek through and through, D.D. noted.

"The real question is: How did Conrad and Jacob make contact? You said Jacob had a cheap burner phone. Did you see him call anyone before you entered the bar?" Keith asked Flora.

"No. But he could've done it while I was in the bathroom cleaning up."

"But Conrad knew exactly how to find you. Walked straight over to you."

"I guess."

"Clearly the meet was planned in advance. By a guy who didn't really use his cell but had the Tor browser on his laptop."

Once again, Flora shrugged. The rest of

them simply waited.

"All the more reason to suspect that Jacob was active on the dark web and networking with other predators there. Now, Tor works to obscure a user's IP address by encrypting internet traffic while bouncing it through odd routes. However, it's not as anonymous as people think. A user's information is briefly unencrypted when entering and exiting the dark web, meaning there should be some recoverable information."

Quincy shook her head. "I already told you, the FBI turned the computer inside and out. Nothing."

But Keith wouldn't be denied. "To access anything, dark web, deep web —"

"What's deep web?" D.D. interrupted.

"Any site you need to log in to — banks, e-mail, e-commerce. Social networks, too, such as Facebook or Twitter. But there are members-only forums for just about anything and everything these days.

"Most people start on the deep web — visiting sites where they feel they're safe — then move on to the dark web. But either way, Jacob would have to have a username and password for some of these online accounts, which would be stored in his hard drive's SAM — Security Account Manager. Unless, of course, he remembered to remove that data. The Tor browser, for example, includes a screen asking the user if he really wants to save the information, as a way of prompting him *not* to store the info. Not all accounts are as helpful, however, and it's not uncommon for even the savviest IT guru to miss a stored password here or there." Keith stared at Quincy.

"I already said," the FBI agent bit out tightly, "our computer techs are the best in the business. As a matter of protocol, we ran the password cracker against the computer's SAM file and, yes, we discovered stored credentials for a single Gmail account, JNess. Except none of the recovered e-mails revealed anything of a criminal nature. Certainly nothing related to the dark web."

"What about a domain name? Most bad guys love to register vanity domains, Bad AssDude.com, whatever."

"No."

"Then he had another e-mail account," Keith stated. "He left the first as a reward for prying eyes, better hid the second. There are plenty of ways."

"Not that someone with Jacob's background should know about." Quincy clearly wasn't convinced. "You're giving him too much credit."

"But again, once on the dark web, the experts he could've met, the lessons he could've learned. Flora said he was clever and driven when it came to hiding his habits. And we're not talking about complicated programming. Get one tech nerd in a chat room, and the rest becomes paint-by-numbers security steps. Jacob would just need to do what he was told."

Keith spoke matter-of-factly. Flora looked interested, while Kimberly appeared even more pissed. At least D.D. was now having some fun.

"What would you suggest trying next?" D.D. asked Keith. The man did seem to know his stuff, and as long as the "best in the business" FBI techs were coming up empty . . .

"Work on figuring out a second username. Just because there's no record of one on his laptop doesn't mean we can't use old-fashioned deductive reasoning to come up with some possibilities. We could then plug and play those options on known websites till we get a hit."

"You mean given Jacob's own background and history." Dr. Keynes spoke up. "We determine what online identity would appeal to him?"

"We did every version of Jacob Ness possible," Quincy argued. "JNess Jacnes. NJacob, et cetera. Hell, one of our techs wrote an algorithm just to run all possible name combos."

"He'd never use his own name to access the dark web," Flora stated immediately. "Too obvious."

"We tried Everett, too," Quincy reported. "Fake Everett. Any detail we could glean from your interview with Dr. Keynes. Including your name, your father's name, even your brother's name. Jacob had a sly and cruel sense of humor. We all can agree on that."

"Hang on." D.D. raised a hand. "Forget username for a minute. Given this Tor browser, we can be sure Jacob was accessing the dark web?"

Quincy and Keith nodded.

"Meaning if Conrad was connecting with the likes of Jacob Ness or other predators — either as a fellow abuser or a naïve avenger — he'd have to be part of the dark web as well."

More nodding.

D.D. smiled. First real break all day. "Meaning, Conrad's wife may have destroyed his computer, but there should still be traces of his activities on the dark web, right? You said every time a user logged in and out, there's a moment when their data is unencrypted. Meaning, we figure out Conrad's username, log on through Tor, and . . ."

"We should be able to identify frequently visited sites, maybe even some chat rooms," Keith supplied. "Basically, identify this Conrad guy's username, or Ness's evildoer username, and the amount of data we could suddenly recover . . . Contacts, activities, identities of other predators."

D.D. started nodding. "I like it. Two subjects, two usernames, two bites at the same dark web apple."

Quincy had stopped frowning. "But do we have ideas for Conrad's username?" she asked.

"His wife might."

"Is she cooperating?"

"Not yet, but I have some ideas on that subject." D.D. eyed Flora.

"Monster," Flora stated.

"What?" D.D. didn't follow the transition.

"Jacob always referred to himself as a monster. *No one wants to be a monster.*"

D.D. was still confused, but Keith was suddenly nodding. "Loch Ness Monster," he murmured.

Quincy immediately sat up, expression intent. "Could it be that simple? His username is some play on Loch Ness? Jacob Ness the monster, Nessie the monster?"

"I don't think he'd use Ness." Flora again. "Too direct a tie. But that kind of sly inference he'd like."

"There are other creatures," Dr. Keynes provided. "Ogopogo, for instance. It would appear random, while having a secret meaning to Jacob that would fulfill his need to be silently superior."

"The sightings of the monster took place in Inverness-shire in Scotland," Keith rattled off. He turned toward Quincy. "Correct me if I'm wrong, but didn't Jacob's mom live in Inverness, Florida? A city named by a Scotsman who said the lakes in the area reminded him of the lochs of his homeland?"

Quincy nodded. "Jacob's mailing address was his mother's home in Inverness, Florida."

"There's a connection there." Flora again, looking convinced. "Inverness, loch Florida, L Inverness, something like that."

Quincy started to scribble on her notepad.

"There are some algorithms which could blow out all possible combinations," Keith began.

Quincy's turn to hold up a hand. "Quit

while you're ahead. All right, I got this. I'll get in touch with the techs, see what we can do."

"The office next to mine is empty," Dr. Keynes offered. "You can set up shop there."

The agent nodded her appreciation.

Flora looked at D.D. "What next?"

"Boyfriend goes home."

"He is not —"

"Civilian goes home," D.D. reiterated firmly. "You can catch him up later. But you and I have business. You're still my CI. Time to earn your keep."

"What do you mean?"

D.D. was already rising to standing. "Come on, you're with me."

"Where are we going?"

"I'll explain along the way."

D.D. headed for the door. Flora scrambled after.

CHAPTER 24
FLORA

"What do you know about arson?" D.D. asks me ten minutes later. I'm sitting in her car as she navigates through the snarl of downtown traffic. I'm not sure where we're headed yet but figure she'll tell me soon enough.

Boston is beautiful at Christmastime. The buildings decked out in huge holiday displays, streets lined with festive trees, poles covered in twinkling white lights. My mom loves this time of year. She's probably already planned the entire meal down to reserving some organic turkey named Fred who'd grown up free-range and was now completing the farm-to-table cycle of life. She's hoping Darwin will fly in from London to join us. While I don't say as much out loud, I hope he does, too. Otherwise it'll be myself, my mom, Samuel, I guess, and maybe a neighbor or two. Maybe I could ask Keith. Would that be too weird?

That's probably too weird.

"Earth to Flora. Arson?"

I belatedly pull my gaze from the giant tinsel snowflakes hanging from the streetlights. "I don't know anything about arson."

"Perfect. Then this will be a growth experience for you. Manila folder tucked next to your seat. Open it."

"Wait a minute. Is this about the Carters' house burning down? You want me to investigate their house fire?"

"Yes."

"This is stupid. I *don't* know arson. My time would be better spent chasing down more connections between Jacob and Conrad."

"I think we've already made progress on that front today."

I stare at her, closed file on my lap. "What the hell is going on here?"

"You're a CI. I'm giving you a job. Stop whining."

"I'm not whining, I'm telling you no."

D.D. takes her eyes off the endless row of brake lights in front of us long enough to arch a brow. "Conrad is connected to Jacob. Meaning whoever torched Conrad's house, possibly with the intent to cover up that connection or other significant information, might be yet another means of learning more about Jacob."

"Bullshit. You just want me out of the way."

"No. I want Jacob out of your head. Personally, I think you've given him enough real estate today. Don't you?"

The sharpness of her tone sets me back. I retreat in the passenger's seat. Whether I like it or not, I get her point. Ever since turning on the news yesterday morning, I've done nothing but obsess about Jacob. D.D. has a point; I could use a break.

Arson it is.

I open the file, peruse the contents.

"That's the report from the arson investigator, Patricia Di Lucca," D.D. provides. "Cause of the fire was a homemade ignition system prepped on the stove top, involving cooking oil and cotton, which then set ablaze the copious amounts of gasoline poured all over the house. Real low-end job. Materials all readily available. Cooking oil and cotton could've come from the house itself. Gasoline, given the amount used, probably was brought with the arsonist, as we're talking several gallons."

"When did this happen?"

"Fire was reported around two in the afternoon. Could've been set up earlier, say, one thirty, given the cooking oil needed time to heat up."

I start flipping through the papers. In addition to a formal write-up and a list of materials, the arson report includes detailed sketches of the home, the path of the fire, all sorts of visual aids. More photos and diagrams show the area of heaviest damage — where the arsonist clearly had poured a small lake of accelerant.

The office. Whoever the arsonist was, he, she, or it definitely had something against the office.

"Is that where Conrad was shot?" I ask D.D., pointing at the photo.

"Yes."

"You think the wife did it?"

She frowned, worried her lower lip. "I'm not sure. Maybe. Between you and me, detective to CI?"

This is a new conversation for us. I nod eagerly.

"There's an eight-minute gap. Reports of shots fired, then an eight-minute gap before more shots are fired. The police showed up for round two and discovered Evie holding the gun. She hardly protested when they arrested her, but was that shock from discovering her husband dead, or from pulling the trigger?"

"Clearly, she had the gun."

"According to her, she shot the laptop. Twelve times, to be precise."

"Why would she destroy the computer?"

"Wouldn't I love to know."

"She's not saying?"

"Not as long as she keeps hanging out with her lawyer. Damn defense attorneys."

"You think she was covering something up."

D.D. glances over. "I think you and I will be chatting with her sooner versus later on that subject."

"I get to meet her?"

"I think you *have* to. It may be the only way to get the truth out of her. Now, *you* tell *me:* If she shot up the computer, who burned the house?"

"I don't know."

"And *why* burn the house?"

"To cover tracks . . . destroy evidence, like you said."

"Evidence above and beyond the computer, which was already destroyed?"

"Did the arsonist know that?"

D.D. actually smiles at me. "Now you're thinking like a real detective. Okay, so you're looking at the report on burn patterns, right? Most concentrated area of damage was the office?"

"Yes."

"As of this morning, we know the office held two things: one, the computer; but, two, a metal lockbox filled with Conrad's fake IDs."

"You think that's what the arsonist was trying to destroy." I pause. "Why not just steal them?"

"Again, good question. My theory, the person couldn't find them. Remember, an entire forensic team swept through that house Tuesday night after the shooting without ever stumbling across the lockbox. In hindsight, I'm wondering if Conrad had a fake bottom in one of his desk drawers or filing cabinets. Those IDs mattered to him. Keeping that secret mattered to him."

"But someone else had to know," I counter immediately. "Otherwise, why burn down that house in an attempt to destroy them?"

Once again, D.D. smiles. "Flora, you just might be good at this. Someone else did have to know. And that person . . ."

"Might be another connection to Jacob Ness."

"Last page of the report," she orders now.

"It's a picture. Some skinny kid."

"Read."

"Rocket Langley. Twenty-year-old African American male. Really? Because he looks like he's fourteen. Okay, he's a person of interest in several fires in abandoned buildings, the warehouse district of Boston," I summarize. I skim farther down. All three fires involved gasoline as the accelerant, and the second was started by a cheap camp stove, which had a soup can filled with kerosene and a cotton wick.

"Arsonists are like serial killers," D.D. explains as she finally eases her car onto Storrow. "They have signatures, preferred methodology. Once they find their identity as firebugs, they don't deviate. Investigator Di Lucca put the elements of the Carters' house fire through the arson database and Rocket's name was what it immediately spit out."

"So we're going to arrest him?"

"Based on what? Being a 'person of interest' in an arson database? Without a history of prior arrests, an eyewitness report, or physical evidence that directly ties Rocket to the Carters' home, we have no grounds for an arrest. I could, of course, drag the kid down to HQ for questioning, but Di Lucca has already tried that. Rocket clams up tight, which is probably why he's never been charged with a crime. Just because he loves fire doesn't mean he's stupid.

"I'm going with a different strategy. I'm

going to drop you off in his neighborhood. Where you're going to track him down and talk to him. Shady character to shady character."

"I'm a shady character?"

"We both know you don't like to color inside the lines."

I consider the matter. "I'm going to have to kick his ass, aren't I?"

"See, you sound happier already."

D.D. drops me off a few blocks from Rocket's last known address. It's dark this early in December, and let's just say Rocket's neighborhood is a long way from the dazzling Christmas lights covering the Boston Commons. These row houses appear hunkered down in the winter gloom, half the windows boarded up, the rest covered in security bars. A lot of the poor neighborhoods in Boston have been bought up and renovated in the past few years. Rocket's isn't one of them.

D.D.'s right: This is my kind of place.

With my bulky coat over my equally shapeless sweatshirt, I blend right in. It's tempting to pull on my hood against the chill, but I don't want to reduce my peripheral gaze or muffle my hearing.

I stroll around the neighborhood for a bit,

getting my bearings. There are no lights on at Rocket's address, which doesn't surprise me. If I lived here, I certainly wouldn't hang out any more than I had to. Then again, I doubt the kid's out holiday shopping, so then what?

I consider my play as I roam from block to block. D.D. already revealed something interesting: no witnesses. If memory serves, the Carters' neighborhood is mostly white. Meaning some black teen was sniffing around their house and no one noticed it? I doubt that already. At least in his mug shot Rocket had aspiring hoodlum written all over him. Most people living in an urban environment are hardwired to pay attention to such things.

Meaning . . .

I try on various theories and ideas. One appeals to me the most. I tuck it away, just as I notice a neighborhood hardware store. Not many such places left, but this one gives me an idea.

Ten minutes later I'm walking around with a bag in my hand and new, local knowledge courtesy of the checkout clerk. Where do the local teens hang out? Again, in an urban environment, people know these things.

It's dark. Some ambient lighting here and

there from random windows where people are tucked in for the evening. There's a strange mix of both closeness and isolation in such densely packed areas. So many people, crammed together. And yet each in his or her own little world.

I don't envy their battles ahead. But I have my own.

I cross to the left, rounding the corner, and a gap appears in the building ahead. An awkward space wedged between two tenement housing buildings, like the hollow left from a lost tooth. Once, it had probably been a basketball court, or some kind of common ground. Now I behold the glow of what appears to be quite the fire roaring away in a centrally placed trash can. Around it, the flash of movement, glint of metal. Kids, on skateboards maybe. Or just hanging out. Way more of them than me.

At the same time, I become aware of a new presence behind me. I've picked up a shadow. Maybe D.D., who told me she'd be around, but I doubt I'm that lucky. I'd guess I have a new friend, someone cuing in on a lone white girl stupidly walking around his neighborhood.

I can't help myself: I smile. D.D. was right. My night is looking up.

■ ■ ■ ■

I walk straight to the trash can. The kids don't scatter. Why would they, when there's at least a dozen of them and only one of me? I don't make individual eye contact. More like a quick head scan. There, to the left, features hard to make out beneath a gray hoodie, is a long, thin face that matches the photo of my guy.

Perfect.

I don't speak. I don't pause. I reach into my bag, pull out the first item, and toss it into the fire.

Boom! The fire roars up, spitting flames and showers of deep red sparks. Now the kids scatter.

"Jesus Christ!"

"She's fucking crazy!"

But not my guy, of course. My guy remains standing right there, looking at the new and improved fire with total fixation.

"Want one?" I ask. I hold out my bag.

"What is it?"

"Kerosene-dipped pinecones. Basically a fire-starter kit from the hardware store. They come in several colors."

Rocket curls his lip at me. I can tell he's tempted, but a premanufactured fire starter?

Where's the fun in that?

"I also have bottles of vegetable oil."

Now I have his interest.

"Sure," he says, though I can tell he remains wary. But I'm thinking of the other thing D.D. said: Arsonists are like serial killers. Once they find their true selves, they can't go back. As Keith Edgar and his true-crime buddies would tell you, there's no serial killer out there who's ever been able to quit. What starts as a horrific crime becomes a terrible compulsion. And compulsions can be used against you by law enforcement — and by people like me.

I heft a small bottle of vegetable oil in his direction. He catches it effortlessly.

We both take a small step back. Then he oil-bombs the fire. More boom, now accompanied by a splatter and hiss. Whatever kids stayed earlier officially retreat. Fire might be cool, but hot oil is just plain dangerous.

Rocket smiles. I understand his grin. I've worn it enough times on my face.

"I'm trying to figure out how you did it," I say at last, voice conversational. There's still a presence behind me. I drift left, trying to get the form into my side view. Meanwhile, I help myself to another kerosene-dipped pinecone and add to the festivities. Rocket holds up a hand. I toss one in his direction.

His flares blue. I like it better than the red. Who needs Christmas lights when you can be doing this?

"I'm thinking pest control," I continue now, Rocket still staring at the flickering flames. "I mean, you walk into a neighborhood like the Carters', people are gonna notice. Especially lugging a few gas cans. But a young guy in a pest control uniform, walking the property with spray cans . . . People see what they want to see. Which is good for the likes of you and me."

My turn. I go with another small bottle of veggie oil. No cool colors, but I like the sizzle sound. This is fun. Maybe I should try for arson next.

Rocket still isn't speaking.

"You pick the back lock. No one to watch. Easy to do. Set up your stove-top ignition. Spray the 'pesticide' all around. Hell, if a neighbor saw you through the window, they wouldn't think twice. Very clever, I gotta say."

He holds up a hand. I toss two pinecones. This time, green and blue flames. We're both impressed.

"Too clever," I say, "for the likes of you."

Shadow behind me has drawn closer. I

slowly but surely unzip my jacket. I want ease of movement for what comes next. Not to mention, I never leave the house with empty pockets. Even now, I'm pulling out a small canister of my homemade pepper spray. Now, what *this* stuff could do to that fire . . .

Rocket finally looks at me. He's clearly reluctant to leave the flames. "I don't know what you're talking about."

"You did good work. The burn patterns, total destruction of the second floor, the way it collapsed onto the first . . . a thing of beauty."

"You a cop?"

"Nope. Just an interested party."

"Interested in what?"

"Hiring you. That's how it works, right? Your age, where you live, your world . . ." I gesture to the burning trash can. "This is what you're about. There's no way you and Conrad crossed paths —"

"Conrad?"

"The guy whose house you burned down."

"Who?"

"Exactly. You didn't care about him or his wife or their unborn baby. You cared about the fire. You were there for the burn, and how much better that someone paid you to do it?"

He frowns for the first time. As if finally seeing the trap. I don't give him a chance, though. I toss another bottle of vegetable oil in his direction and, of course, he has to catch it. Of course he has to throw it on the blaze.

"I'm not a cop," I say now. "But I saw a bunch of them pulled up in front of your house. Bet they're ripping apart your room now. Finding the uniform, the 'pest control' cans. Then, wow, you're going to have some explaining to do."

But I made a misstep because immediately Rocket shrugs, then returns pointedly to staring at the fire. The uniform, I realize, was probably soaked in gasoline and used to start this blaze, because what kind of self-respecting arsonist wouldn't burn up the evidence?

"I want to hire you. One grand."

He frowns, staring at the flames. I find one of the last pinecones, toss it in. Red. We both nod in fascination.

"Five," he says. "Cash."

"Don't got it on me."

"I'll tell you where to leave it. You drop off half, with the address. Afterwards, other half."

"Trusting of you."

He finally stares at me. In his dark eyes all

I can see are the dancing flames. "I like to burn things. All kinds of things. No one messes with that."

Good point. "It has to be discreet. You come up with the pest-control uniform, or did your last client provide it?"

"What do you care?"

"Has to be discreet," I repeat, voice steady.

He shrugs. "Depends on what I'm burning. Abandoned is easy access. Residential work, yeah, you can provide the props. Or, I've figured out what works over the years. Whatever."

So maybe his client had provided the pest uniform, or maybe Rocket is that clever. He certainly loves fire, and anyone who loves his job is bound to get better and better at it.

I still don't think this kid knew Conrad Carter or Jacob Ness. He was strictly the hired help. But he's also our first link to whoever it was who shot Conrad and then felt compelled to further cover his tracks by totally eradicating the house. My next step is clear:

"Give me the address to the drop site," I say. "I'll get you the money."

"Tomorrow," he says. "Already got plans for tonight."

"Which are?"

"Right behind you."

I don't turn my head. Rookie move, especially as I've been tracking my shadow for the past ten minutes. Instead, I plant my feet wide for better balance, whirl my entire torso, and whip the plastic bag with its remaining two bottles of vegetable oil at my attacker's head. Solid *thwack* as I connect.

The form, face hidden in the shadows of another hoodie, staggers back, grabs his head, clearly dazed. I dance forward three steps. I kick to the side of his knee, then snap the heel of my hand straight into his nose. He goes down, clutching his face, moaning.

I step back. I don't need to do anything more, prove anything more. I turn to Rocket. "I'm not a fucking cop. Now, give me the address."

Rocket appears stunned. Exactly where I want him.

From my pocket, I pull the burn phone I always carry on me. "Text now."

I'm not surprised when he produces a matching prepaid cell. His fingers fly across the surface. Buzz as the address is delivered.

I smile. "Pleasure doing business with you."

Then I toss my bag with the two remaining bottles of oil straight into the burning barrel.

Another roar and sizzle. When I walk away, Rocket is still staring at the flames, his friend moaning behind him.

D.D. picks me up four blocks later. I don't ask where she's been or how she found me. She has her skills, I have mine.

"Well," she demands.

"Hired firebug, definitely. Didn't even respond to Conrad Carter's name, and frankly, too much of a burn freak to have pulled this off without help. Canvass the Carters' neighborhood again, except this time ask about pest control. That's how he did it. Uniform, or what's left of it, is at the bottom of that burn barrel. If you look around, the pressurized spray canisters he used have to be around somewhere."

"Who hired him?"

"He wasn't *that* forthcoming. But" — I hold up my phone — "I have the address where I'm supposed to leave money for my future transaction. I'm guessing it's the same drop spot as Rocket used last time, given he appears to be a creature of habit."

"We can pull videos of the area from Tuesday night, Wednesday morning," D.D. fills in thoughtfully.

"Which should give you the client, caught on candid camera."

"Nicely done," D.D. informs me.

I just smile.

CHAPTER 25
EVIE

My mom makes some kind of French stew for dinner. Filled with lentils and greens and all sorts of things perfect for a growing baby, she informs me. Never mind that with every comment she makes me feel more and more like a broodmare.

I set the table. Three martinis in, my mother shouldn't be handling breakables. And it's only six P.M.

I need to get out of here, I think again. But how? Whom to call? Mr. Delaney? A teacher I sometimes sit with at lunch? I never realized how small my world is until now. How in keeping everyone out, I'd also shut myself in.

A knock on the side door. I'm so grateful for the interruption, I nearly knock over my chair standing up. "I'll get it!" I announce.

My mom appears mildly annoyed. I notice she's not eating her stew, just pushing lentils around in the bowl. This is what happens, I think, when you spend your afternoon filling up on vodka.

I head for the door. Sergeant D. D. Warren stands on the other side. She flashes her badge. Next to her is a younger woman in an oversized down coat and a gray hoodie. She looks like she'd be more comfortable on the mean streets of any major city than hanging out at an impeccably decorated Colonial in Cambridge.

I let them in.

"Evie Carter, Flora Dane. Flora, Evie." D.D. makes the introductions. I shake hands with the woman, who looks like she could benefit from my mother's stew even more than I. Her face is vaguely familiar but I can't place it. Someone who knew Conrad? Or one of his half a dozen aliases?

I feel the first trickle of unease.

In for a penny, in for a pound. I lead them to the table and introduce my mother.

In response, my mother scowls, reaches an unsteady hand for her martini. "Really, Sergeant, couldn't this wait? It's dinnertime, and meals are very important for a woman in Evie's condition."

Yep, nothing but a broodmare.

The Flora woman eyes me with renewed interest.

"Please have some stew," I mutter. *Please*

save me from this meal.

"Actually, we have a few things to discuss. Perhaps we could move into the front?" D.D. suggests. Works for me.

"I'll do dishes," I inform my mother because, again, she shouldn't be touching plastic plates, let alone Waterford crystal.

She only scowls, pushes more lentils around her bowl. She's depressed, I think. About our conversation earlier? The news her husband didn't kill himself? Or is this simply what midday martinis do to you? I've never known how to talk to my mom. I certainly don't have any answers now.

I direct D.D. and Flora to the side sitting room, with its greenery-swathed mantel and professionally decorated Christmas tree. My mom likes to have a theme for each tree. This one is Hark the Herald Angels Sing, meaning there is a lot of gold and, yes, a lot of angels.

As for actual sitting space, the room has a silk-covered love seat in stripes of pale green and pink. We all stare at it. It looks like something out of a dollhouse. The pile of matching throw pillows doesn't help.

I have to get out of this house.

"Can I take your coats?" I ask belatedly, because the sofa barely looks capable of holding two women, let alone their heavy winter coats. D.D. shrugs, unbuttons her long black wool coat. I notice the other woman follows more reluctantly. She's been taking in the room. Assessing. Again, the pinprick of unease. What is she doing here?

I don't know what to do with the coats. Walking to the coat closet in the main foyer will expose me to the reporters across the street. This is the problem with a nighttime siege — the house is nothing but a glowing fishbowl, putting both my mom and me on display. No doubt why D.D. used the side entrance. And why we're not seated near any windows now.

Finally, I pile the coats on the back of a wingback chair. I should sit, but I don't want to. In fact, I suddenly don't want to hear what they have to say.

"How are you feeling?" D.D. asks quietly.

"Like a bird in a gilded cage."

"Your mother brought you clothes for your arraignment." The woman speaks. She glances around the room. "I get it now."

"You were at my arraignment? Why? Who are you?" My tone is sharp.

"My name is Flora Dane —"

"She already told me your damn name!"

The woman regards me evenly. "It doesn't ring any bells for you?"

"Why would it? I've never met you before

385

in my life. Now, what the hell is this all about —" I break off. My eyes widen. The sense of déjà vu, that I'd seen this woman before. Flora Dane. Six years ago.

Oh my God, I know who she is. And I no longer feel a tinge of unease. I want to vomit. Hurl my mother's good-for-the-baby stew all over this fine silk-covered furniture. Because I'm sure I don't want to hear what she's going to say next.

"Sit," D.D. is murmuring in my ear, her hands on my shoulders. "Just like that. Head between your knees. Deep breaths. In, out, exhale all the way. Now deep in, hold, hold, hold, exhale. Two more times. You got this."

When I finally stop hyperventilating, I'm collapsed in the wingback chair with the coats. Both D.D. and Flora are now kneeling on the floor in front of me.

"What did he do? Those fake IDs, all his secrets. What did Conrad do?" I stare straight at Flora Dane.

"Don't you know?" D.D. asks me. "You're the one who shot up the computer."

"I had to."

"Why?"

"Protect the legacy." I'm not crying. I sound like a rote imitation of my mother, which is worse.

"You wanted to protect Conrad." D.D. eyes me. "The father of your child. From what, Evie? From what?"

"I don't know." That's the truth. He had secrets, I knew. And at least in my family, secrets can only cause pain. But that doesn't mean I know what his secret was.

Both women are eyeing me. I take a deep, shuddering breath, soldier on: "Have either of you been in a relationship with someone who travels a lot?"

They shake their heads.

"I loved Conrad. When we bought our house together, of course we each had to adapt. He snored. Left his shoes in the middle of the floor. Would enter a room chattering away, even when it was clear I was grading papers and needed to think. But you get used to those things.

"Except then he'd leave again. And I would sleep better without him. Appreciate being able to walk down the hall, get my work done faster. Then he'd return, and I'd have to reorient. You can't help yourself — inevitably, you're only in the relationship halfway, because it's only a marriage half the time."

D.D. and Flora wait patiently.

"It makes you look at your spouse more objectively than maybe the average married person. Analyzing things, noticing things. Like the way Conrad asked so many questions about my life, but never answered any of mine. The way he'd shut down sometimes, and I could tell something was bothering him, but he wouldn't say what. The hours he logged in his office. A window salesman? Still working at midnight? Then locking up the door to his own study when he left?

"I . . . I began to wonder. So I started snooping, which then gave him doubts. One day I found a page of a financial statement for a Carter Conner in Conrad's printer. At first I thought it was a mistake. But the account was from a bank in Florida, and I just . . . knew. He had a secret life. That's why he was always on the business trips. Why he never wanted to talk about them afterward. Why he was always locking up after himself. It's bad, isn't it?" I stare at Flora. "Is he . . . a predator, too?"

"I met Conrad," Flora says at last. "In a bar in the South. He was using the name Conner when he approached my kidnapper, Jacob Ness. It was clear they were expecting one another."

"Oh." I can't think of anything else to say. Instead, I clutch my stomach, as if covering my unborn child's ears, trying to block him or her from this terrible information. I'd known. Especially in the past year or so, I'd looked at my husband with a growing sense of dread.

"Conrad's a predator?" I whisper. "But he was so excited for our baby. He seemed genuinely happy." I don't know what it is I'm trying to say. "Do evil people love their children, too?"

"Did you know about the lockbox of IDs?" D.D. asks.

"No. And I tore that office apart trying to figure out what he was hiding. I never saw it."

"Conrad never talked about his trips?"

"No."

"How often was he gone? How long did he go?"

"One or two trips a month, usually three to five days. But not just to Florida. He traveled all over New England. I saw some of his tickets. He flew to Philadelphia, Virginia, Georgia. Some of his business travel was real. But I don't think all of it was."

"Did Conrad watch the news a lot?" Flora spoke up. "Say, follow national cases, maybe even watch a lot of true-crime shows on TV."

"He liked *Forensic Detectives.*" That sinking feeling again, except how could this get any worse?

"Why did you shoot the computer?" D.D. asks again.

"I had to."

"Where did you find the gun?"

"On his lap. I took it. From . . . him."

"He was holding the gun when you found him?"

"Yes."

"What did you think, Evie, when you walked into the study and found your husband's dead body? What was the first thought that crossed your mind?"

"That he shot himself. That all these years later, I still wasn't enough."

"What was on the computer, Evie? What was Conrad looking at when he died?"

"Pictures." I squeeze my eyes shut. I don't want to see them again. It was so much easier to forget, pretend it never happened. Maybe I am my mother, after all.

"What was on the computer?"

"Girls. Photos. Terrible photos. They look thin and horrified. Beaten. Young. Why would he be looking at something like that?" I shake my head. "He's the father of my child. And even knowing he had secrets . . . couldn't it have just been another woman? Maybe a gay lover? Even knowing something was wrong, even knowing I would regret digging, I never suspected what was on his computer." My voice is hoarse, hard to hear. I finally look at them. "I loved him. How could I love a man like that?"

"What did you do next, Evie?"

"I closed up the laptop. But the police were there. Already banging at the front door. There wasn't enough time to clear the hard drive, not properly. I couldn't . . . He's the father of my child," I say again.

"Protect the legacy." D.D. nods, as if she understands. Maybe, being the one who was here sixteen years ago, she does.

"I destroyed the laptop. Kept shooting until there were no bullets left."

"That was some good shooting."

I nod. "My father taught me."

"And you're not afraid of guns, are you, Evie, because you didn't shoot your father?"

"I didn't shoot my father. Or Conrad. I just . . . loved them both." I feel it now. The horrible weight of it all. To love so much, and it still wasn't enough. Was never enough. Seeing those images on the computer screen. *Horror* was not a strong enough word. It was like a knife to the heart. Not just because of what it said about him and how well he'd played me for ten years, but because of what it said about me, who'd had doubts, had known he was hiding things, and had stayed anyway.

"I knew he was a loser." A voice spoke up. My mother, standing in the arched entranceway, where she'd clearly been eavesdropping for a while. Her words were slurred. I stare at her dully.

"I know you hated him, Mom," I say tiredly. "I just assumed it was because he was stupid enough to want me."

"Window salesman," she grunts.

"Good news. Turns out he was a bit more than that."

She has her vodka; I have my bitterness. Maybe we deserve each other.

"You should know something," Flora says quietly.

She's still kneeling on the floor, clearly not the type to take a seat on a silk-covered settee. It makes me feel bad, to have a woman who's been through so much feel uncomfortable in my home. That this is that kind of place. That myself, my family, we are those kinds of people.

"When Conrad was at the bar, he tried to signal me. Using Morse code. Unfortunately, I didn't catch on and never answered him."

"What do you mean?"

"He was asking if I was okay. Tapping it out on the bar top."

I shake my head slightly, very confused now. "Why? I don't . . . Why would he do that?"

"I don't know. I was hoping you could tell me."

"When was this?"

"Probably seven years ago."

"Conrad and I were together. He went on his business trips. But that's all I knew. Often, I wasn't even sure where."

"Do you remember anything about the website he had pulled up on his computer? URL, anything?" D.D.'s turn.

"It was weird. Not a dot-com or dot-net, but dot-onion. I didn't know what that meant; I had to look it up. Apparently, it's a site on the Onion Browser; the dark web." My voice cracks slightly. I hear myself say, as if understanding for the first time: "My husband was surfing the dark web."

Flora and D.D. exchange a look.

"You never saw any other records bearing the names from his fake IDs? Just that one financial statement from the printer?" D.D. asks.

I shake my head.

"I don't suppose you kept a copy of that statement?"

"No. I didn't have to."

"What do you mean?"

I shrug. "I'm a numbers person. I don't need a statement in front of me. I can write out the account number off the top of my head. Including bank, address, and at that time, its balance of two hundred and forty-three thousand dollars and twenty-two cents."

D.D. whirls to my drunken mom in the doorway. "Get a pen," she orders sharply.

And I finally get to feel good about myself for the first time in days.

CHAPTER 26
D.D.

"All right. It's late, it's nearly the holidays, and I still have shopping to do. Let's get this done." D.D. had assembled her team back at BPD headquarters. Boxes of pizza sat in the middle of the table, surrounded by pots of coffee. At this time of night, comfort food and caffeine were two of the best investigative tools available.

Seated at the conference room table was the three-person detective squad who'd landed the initial shooting case: Phil, Neil, and their newest partner, Carol. In addition, D.D. was proud owner of one feebie, SSA Kimberly Quincy, and two wild cards, Flora Dane and — heaven help her — Keith Edgar, who had a laptop fired up and was clacking away wildly.

Odd team for an odd investigation. Yet, D.D. had that tingle in the base of her spine: They were on the verge of a breakthrough. Between Flora's conversation with the firebug and their candid face-to-face with Evie Carter, they were getting somewhere.

"Phil." D.D. nodded to the oldest and probably wisest detective in the room. "Tell us what you got on Conrad Carter's alias bank account."

"The account was opened eighteen years ago in the name Carter Conner at a local credit union in Jacksonville, Florida. Carter Conner matches the name on the Florida driver's license discovered in Conrad Carter's charred lockbox. The starting balance of the account was four hundred and fifty thousand —"

"Lot of money." Quincy spoke up.

"Yep. One initial deposit, which I'll get to in a second. Otherwise, Conrad, Carter, whoever we call him —"

"What do you mean whoever we call him?" Flora's turn. "Is Conrad or Carter or Conner his real name?"

Phil sighed heavily. "Everyone," he said. "Eat some pizza. And shut up."

They did.

"So, Carter Conner has an active account at the Florida First Credit Union. Since the initial deposit, he's been slowly but surely drawing down the balance. Cash withdrawals, always under ten thousand dollars."

D.D. nodded, understanding the reasoning behind that.

"Several withdrawals a year. So not a lot of money, but if you figure he was always taking it out in cash, a solid slush fund. Then three years ago, a new transaction shows up: monthly transfers of five hundred dollars to a separate account."

"Under one of his other aliases?" D.D. asked.

"Don't know yet. I entered the account info into our electronic tracing system but got back an error message. I'll have to call the bank manager in the morning."

"So what do you think he was doing with this money?" D.D. pressed.

"Good question. Neil, Carol" — Phil nodded to his two squad mates — "you're up."

Neil did the honors. "In answer to Flora's question, we asked the coroner to run prints, but we're pretty sure Conrad Carter is actually Carter Conner. That's his real name, real driver's license. The rest are fakes."

"Your murder victim," said Quincy, "was living under an assumed name? Good God."

"It's the money trail, the onetime significant deposit," Carol took over the story. "It got Neil and me thinking, where did that money come from? Sale of an asset, settlement check, lottery winnings? Because

Conrad never deposited again. Just that one check."

D.D. made a motion with her hand. "I'm assuming you have an answer."

"Life insurance," Carol announced. "He received a death benefit twelve years ago when both his parents were killed in a hit-and-run outside of Jacksonville, Florida."

"Evie said his parents had died," Flora murmured. Beside her, Keith frowned, clicked away at his computer, frowned again.

"Which is what got us looking," Neil said. "We couldn't find any death records for surname Carter. But we knew the aliases from the other driver's licenses. So we ran those last names. And sure enough, William and Jennifer Conner died in an MVA three months before Conrad opened the bank account."

"His parents are killed, Conrad receives the life insurance money, then uses it to open an account at a Florida credit union." D.D. stared at her detectives.

"We're just getting started," said Carol. She leaned forward. "William Conner, the dad, was with the JSO."

"Jacksonville Sheriff's Office," Quincy provided for the civilians' benefit.

"He worked in Major Cases, including

homicides, missing persons, assaults. And get this, the MVA that killed him and his wife wasn't an accident. Someone ran Detective Bill Conner off the road, knowingly targeting an officer and his wife."

D.D. was still having to process the details. "Conrad's parents were murdered?"

"Yes."

"At which time, Conrad deposited the life insurance payout from his parents' deaths, then headed north to live under an assumed name? Until someone gunned him down in his own home two nights ago?"

"Exactly." Carol beamed.

"That's it," D.D. said. "I'm having more pizza."

"I don't get it." Flora spoke up a minute later. Which was fair enough because D.D. wasn't convinced she understood everything either. "Why the alias? Did Conrad think he was a target? Like, whoever killed his parents was coming for him next?"

"Unknown," Neil said.

"Or," Flora continued now, "was Conrad a suspect in his parents' death? Was he running away from the police?"

"I doubt that," Quincy answered immediately. "He kept both an active bank account and a valid driver's license from

Florida. That's no way to hide from cops. Not much of a way to hide from a determined killer either."

The entire team was frowning.

"Conrad appeared in the bar with Jacob Ness seven years ago." Keith spoke up. "Conrad and his family are from Florida. Jacob and his family are from Florida. I still think there has to be a connection."

"The FBI has made some progress on that front," Quincy reported. "After our little powwow this morning, we started running Google searches based on some of the username ideas we discussed, across some of the online platforms we believe Ness would've frequented. In the end, we discovered an identical username on several social media sites as well as some more . . . specific . . . sexual fantasy forums. We're still building the user profile, but we believe Jacob's username is most likely I. N. Verness. Capital *I*, period, capital *N*, period, capital *V*, Verness. So it looks like first two initials, followed by a last name. But it's actually a shout-out to Jacob's hometown."

"And a county associated with another legendary monster." Flora was nodding. "That sounds exactly like him."

"Our experts will now flesh out a full

online profile of I. N. Verness, including specific site visits and website details. In turn, this will allow us to subpoena information from these sites. We're also running codebreaker software as we speak. I'm told within twelve to fourteen hours, we may finally have the answers to Jacob's online activities."

The FBI agent sounded triumphant. D.D. couldn't blame her.

"You said Conrad's father worked Major Cases for the Jacksonville Sheriff's Office." Keith again. "Is it possible he'd been investigating Jacob Ness?"

"Twelve years ago?" Neil shrugged. "Was Ness even on anyone's radar screen?"

"We didn't know about him till Flora's abduction," Quincy said. "At least not as a serial predator. Prior to that, he had a criminal record for assault. Upon release from prison, however, he disappeared from law enforcement radar screens."

"He was never going back," Flora murmured. "A man with his appetites didn't belong behind bars." She looked up at Quincy. "He didn't stop attacking women after prison. He just got smarter about it."

"Meaning a JSO detective might have been looking into him," Keith pressed.

"I'll call the Investigations Division chief,"

Neil conceded. "Given how far back we're looking, it might take them a bit, but there's gotta be a record of Detective Bill Conner's active cases at the time of his death."

"I'm thinking a big rig could certainly run a car off the road," Keith said. "That's all."

Personally, D.D. thought Keith Edgar saw Jacob Ness everywhere. Which was the problem with amateur sleuths — they often started with a theory of the case, then worked backward to justify their suspicions, versus letting the evidence do the talking. However . . . She leaned forward to address Neil. "When you're talking to the Jax commander, ask him if Conrad ever called with the same request. Or has made any follow-up inquiries about his father's work. It would help tell us where his head was at — searching for his parents' killer, trying to finish what his father started. I don't know. But we need to figure it out."

"If only his wife hadn't shot up the computer," Phil said now.

"She claimed she did it to protect her husband's reputation," D.D. provided. "When she walked in on the scene, Conrad was already dead, and the laptop was open with photos of . . . victimized girls on the screen."

"Sounds like motive for her to kill him

right there," Phil countered.

"Sure. But . . ." D.D. frowned. "I don't think she did it. The story she told Flora and me, coming home to the scene in the office, her instinctive need to cover for her future child's father . . ."

"Ah, but didn't you believe her story last time? Which turned out to be just that, a complete fabrication concocted by her and her mother?"

D.D. scowled at her former mentor. "I'm not saying we take her off our radar screen. Clearly, there was a lot going on in this marriage. But she did give us the financial lead . . ."

"All the better to direct you away from her."

"And there was an eight-minute gap between shots fired." D.D. skewered Phil with a look. "Say, the gap that would occur if a wife had come home right after the killer had fled, stumbled upon the scene, and for reasons of her own, took action against the laptop."

"You mean a mysterious killer who fled through a heavily populated neighborhood and left no trace, no witnesses behind?"

"You're a pain in the ass," D.D. informed Phil.

"Thank you." He helped himself to a fresh

slice, no doubt thinking he'd earned it.

"Which brings us to the arsonist." Flora spoke up, redirecting them. The woman looked tired, D.D. thought. She probably hadn't slept since first seeing Conrad's picture on TV. But she had acquitted herself well today.

"The suspected arsonist is a firebug. Obsessed with one thing only."

"He's not the shooter," Quincy filled in.

"If it doesn't involve flame, it would never hold his attention. His services are for hire, however."

"The shooter employed the firebug to burn down the house in order to cover up any evidence he might have left behind," Quincy said.

Flora nodded. Keith looked impressed by her new leading role. "Now, this arsonist, Rocket, isn't exactly big-time muscle. More like a local kid with a reputation for playing with matches. He's smart, though. Smarter than I originally gave him credit for. He's never been caught or charged with a crime, so while his services are available for hire, how you learn about him . . ." Flora's voice trailed off. She looked at Keith. "I was wondering about the dark web again. Earlier, you and SSA Quincy were discussing that Jacob was definitely using it. Evie says the images her husband had loaded up on his laptop were on an Onion site. This Rocket kid, how would someone know enough to hire him unless his . . . interests . . . appeared somewhere?"

"Entirely possible," Keith said. "The dark web is a known clearinghouse for everything from drugs to weapons to, yes, illegal services. For that matter" — he addressed the group — "you can also find a gun for hire on the dark web."

"Great," D.D. muttered. Most major criminal enterprises had moved online. A good detective adjusted. She still missed the good old days, however, when the felons were up close and personal, versus a computer screen away.

Flora was shrugging. "Since I located Rocket in his own backyard, we conducted our business mano-a-mano. I got him to give me the location of the money exchange. I leave an initial deposit and target address. He picks up, then goes forth in fiery bliss."

"You're going to hire the arsonist?" Quincy asked with a frown. "Shouldn't you just have arrested him and be grilling him for a description of his previous employer?"

D.D.'s turn: "Given his drop-box method, Rocket probably doesn't know who hired him. Safer for him that way. What matters is the handoff location. Assuming it's the same one he used last time, I've assigned two detectives to start tracking down all video surveillance in the area. Traffic cams, security systems, ATMs. If we're lucky, the drop box itself is covered by a camera. If not, we know the same person has to visit the area twice — first time for deposit, then final payment, within a short span of time. Not the easiest parameters for ID'ing a potential suspect, but we've worked with less.

"All right." D.D. looked around the room. "Phil, you're on deck to follow up with the bank. Neil, Carol, the Jax sheriff's department. Kimberly, you'll keep us in the loop regarding codebreaker progress. Flora, your job is to get a good night's sleep. Keith, I don't actually know what the hell you're doing, but the Inverness thing was good enough for now."

"I'm still chasing some leads," Keith said, completely straight-faced.

D.D. had nothing to say to that. She rose to standing. "Kimberly, you headed back to Atlanta?" Because the FBI agent could phone in any new findings.

But Quincy was already shaking her head. "Oh no. I'm staying. From what I can tell, this party is just getting started. And I'm not going to miss whatever happens next."

CHAPTER 27
FLORA

Keith and I walk out of HQ together. The sky above is pitch black, the horizon around us aglow with city lights. I have no sense of time. It feels like this night has been going on forever, but dark comes early in December, so it might be only eight or nine P.M.

Keith has his computer bag slung over his shoulder, his hands in his pockets against the cold. I like to exhale and watch the cloud of steam. I don't have a hat or gloves. I should be freezing, but I rarely notice such things. Sometimes I think rage is like a furnace, and I've been angry for so many years now, I'm perpetually heated from the inside out.

"I. N. Verness," Keith states finally. He smiles, and I realize he's happy. I've spent the day battling with demons from my past. But for Keith, this is simply a six-year-old puzzle that he's finally cracked. I decide to be happy for him.

"What happens now?" he asks me.

I shrug. "We do what the sergeant recommended. Go home, get some sleep, see what tomorrow brings."

"Do you sleep?" he asks, his voice genuinely curious.

"Not much."

"Night terrors?"

"I don't relax well."

"Do they pay you to be a CI?"

I frown. "No. Should I be paid?" I never thought to ask, and now I wonder if I missed something obvious.

"I don't know," he says. "But . . . do you have a job?"

"This and that."

"Focus issues?"

I sigh. He's pissing me off. I'm sure he doesn't mean it. People rarely meet survivors of major crimes, so of course they have a million questions, combined with an equal number of misperceptions. They assume I flinch at firecrackers or that I'm terrified of closed-in spaces. Or they once heard that I have a million dollars secreted away from a wealthy benefactor (maybe Oprah or Dr. Phil!) who was moved by my story.

I don't have or do any of those things. Nor am I the type who wants to talk about it.

"What did you think of the day?" I ask

him instead.

"Got off to a rough start —"

"Sergeant Warren doesn't like anyone."

"Good to know. But by the end, the breakthrough with the username . . ." He bounced up and down on his toes. "I'm excited. We're going to solve this one. All these years later, we're going to locate Jacob Ness's lair and, hopefully, evidence of six missing women. Amazing."

"Gonna tell your true-crime group?"

He appears offended. "I signed a nondisclosure."

"Make them pinky promise to keep the news to themselves."

"I signed a nondisclosure," he repeats, his tone firm.

"What will you do now?" I ask.

"I don't want to go home," he says. "I'm too wired. There are a few things I could research, of course. That this Conrad Carter is actually Carter Conner and his father a murdered cop . . ." He's nodding to himself. "Have some digging to do there."

I study him for a long moment. "Want to get a drink?" I hear myself say.

My newest admirer and/or possible serial killer breaks into a smile. "I thought you'd never ask."

Keith has an app for one of the ride-sharing services. He also claims to know a bar. I know plenty of bars myself, but probably not the type he'd feel comfortable frequenting. Not to mention that at quite a few of them, his computer would be stolen in minutes.

If I chased down the robber, took him out with a flying tackle and gallantly returned to Keith with his computer bag, would that earn me a look of adoration, or end the evening abruptly? In movies, everyone loves the kickass heroine. I'm less convinced the average man wants one in real life. Keith looks like he works out, but at the end of the day he's a tech guy. And I'm, well . . . me.

Keith takes me to Boylston Street. This is pretty Boston. With high-end boutiques nestled in between historic churches, the architecturally significant public library, and of course, dozens of restaurants and bars. Each window is framed in twinkling Christmas lights, while the ornate streetlamps are capped with glittering wreaths and the row of trees wrapped in dazzling holiday cheer. Keith leads me up four steps to an old stone building, very dark and subdued compared to its neighbors. Which should be my first hint.

We are greeted by a man in a tuxedo who could be anywhere between forty and a hundred. He nods at both of us, his face perfectly impassive. I note two things at once. Keith, in his cashmere sweater and finely tailored slacks, blends perfectly with the wood-paneled foyer. I do not.

Keith is already shedding his outerwear. I remove my ratty down jacket with more reluctance. I like my coat. It has many pockets, each a treasure trove of tools and resources for the vigilante on the go.

The maître d' holds out his hand. At the last minute, I can't do it. I clutch my coat to my chest. "I get cold easily," I say, to justify my decision.

Tuxedo man says nothing, merely turns, hangs up Keith's coat. Then he leads us into a much larger room, also covered in exquisitely carved walnut panels, and dominated by a gorgeous curved bar bearing a gold-flecked marble top. Around us is a collection of seating areas, some white-draped tables, some antique furniture pulled close for a more intimate feel. A fire crackles impressively from a massive fireplace against the far wall. Our host walks straight toward it, indicates a private arrangement of a single love seat with a spindly coffee table, then stares pointedly at my coat again.

If anything, I clutch it tighter.

"Thank you," Keith says. Our silent guide nods in acknowledgment, then disappears.

"What is this place?"

Keith has already taken a seat. His legs are so long he has to stretch them out at an angle to avoid the coffee table. I perch awkwardly on the other corner, not liking this seating arrangement at all.

"It's a private club. There are many of them around the city. Representing various Ivy League universities, special groups —"

"*Elite* groups."

"My father's a member. I picked this bar because I thought it would be quieter, a more private place for us to talk."

I'm not sure what I think of that. Private is good. But this . . . This isn't me. And if he was paying attention at all, surely he recognized that. Meaning this place was what? His way of showing off? Look at my success? Look at what I can buy you?

Mostly, I feel very uncomfortable and wish I'd gone hunting instead.

"What would you like to drink?" he asks.

"Seltzer water."

He doesn't comment, just flags down

another man in a white tuxedo jacket, this one bearing a silver tray. Keith orders seltzer for me, a single malt for him. I wonder if this is the kind of place women aren't allowed to order for themselves, or again, if this is Keith's idea of making a great first impression.

"Do you know the others in the room?" I ask.

Keith looks around. I've already taken inventory. The only obvious egress is the arched doorway through which we entered. I would guess the wood paneling on the surrounding walls disguises other options, and I have to fight the temptation to circle the room and feel out all the seams for myself.

"No," he says at last.

"Come here often?"

"No."

"But tonight, hanging out with a girl dressed like me" — I gaze down at my gray sweatshirt, worn cargo pants — "this seemed like a good idea?"

"No one cares," he tells me.

Which makes me scowl because, of course, *I* care, but like hell I'm going to admit that.

"If someone came up to you, how would you introduce me?" I press.

"Given you're someone who appreciates

your privacy, I would say you were a visiting friend."

"No name?"

"Only if you want me to."

I give him slightly more credit for this answer, then resume my working theory that he's a serial killer, and this is how he lures future victims back to his place. By pretending to be courteous and charming and sensitive. Ted Bundy with access to an elitist club.

"I'm not claustrophobic," I say abruptly.

He seems to consider the statement, and the second tuxedo man returns with a tray bearing our drinks. He also has a small bowl of what appear to be wasabi-coated nuts. After the pizza, I'm happy with my seltzer, lime wedge perched artistically on the rim.

Keith holds up a heavy crystal tumbler of amber liquid. We toast, not saying a word.

"People always assume I'm claustrophobic. You know, all that time in the coffin. Except that's the point. I spent so many days, weeks, in a pine box, I had no choice but to grow comfortable with it. Make it my home."

"I still wear scarves," he says at last.

It takes me a moment; then I get it. His cousin was strangled with a silk scarf. Touché.

I raise my seltzer in acknowledgment, allow myself to relax a fraction on the too-low, too-small love seat.

"Bring any of your true-crime buddies here?"

"No."

"Why not?"

"We generally meet at someone's house. When you're spreading out crime scene photos, it tends to disturb others."

"I think Jeeves could take it."

"Jeeves?"

"The guy who greeted us."

"His name is Tony."

"Really? That doesn't seem right at all."

He shrugs, takes a sip of his scotch. "Now who's typecasting?"

I almost stick my tongue out him. At the last minute, it occurs to me that would be childish, and I'm supposed to be the serious avenger sort.

"I think you can fit in this room," he says shortly, his gaze directly on mine. "I think you're strong and smart and can go anywhere you want to go and be anything you want to be."

"No."

The word comes out hard and matter-of-fact. Keith doesn't push it, just waits.

"I work at a pizza shop. Which, oh shit, I

415

was supposed to be at this afternoon. So from that alone, I'm not even a good pizza employee. I never finished college. I'll never get a degree."

"In the tech world, you'd be amazed how many business owners don't have them."

"But I'm not a techie either. I'm just . . . me."

Again, he waits.

"People think trauma is mental," I say abruptly. "I'm mentally scarred, damaged, take your pick. And with enough therapy, time, my mind will heal and, ta-da, one day I'll be all better again. But trauma isn't just mental. It's physiological. It's an adrenal system that's totally burnt out, so that I spend days at a time in fight mode." I realize as I'm describing this that one of my knees is bouncing uncontrollably. "Followed by crashes where I can barely get out of bed.

"I can't function in crowded rooms. I never take the T during rush hour. I can't stand the stench of other bodies. I'm hypervigilant to the point there's no way I could pay attention to a lecturer in a classroom environment, let alone start and finish an assignment. It's not in me."

"You stayed on track today."

"We moved around today. From idea to idea and building to building. I need that kind of action. Plus, I'm better when I'm with Samuel." I pause. "And I almost like D.D. Almost."

"So, the right people, the right mix of activities, and you can function. Ever thought of becoming a cop?"

"No way. Real policing requires a degree, for one. So that whole college thing is an issue. Plus, ask Sergeant Warren, the paperwork alone would kill mere mortals. It's the whole advantage of being a CI. I get all the fun, none of the legal responsibility. Besides, why should I become a detective, when it's only a matter of time before I convince D.D. to join me on the dark side?"

Keith nods. "Based on what I know from my detective friends, you have a valid point. Are you happy?" he asks me abruptly.

"I don't aspire to happiness."

"Why not?"

"It's just not something I feel."

"Survivor's guilt?"

"Maybe. Or again, burnt-out adrenals. Highs are hard to come by."

"Your family?"

"Love me despite me."

"Mine, too."

"You're an obviously successful computer guru. What's not to love?"

"My blog. My intense interest in violent

crime. They find it . . . distasteful. So do a lot of women, I might add. In the beginning, when I first mention my true-crime club, it sounds like a cool hobby. But then when they start to understand that it's real work, with photos of corpses and sketches of crime scenes and analysis of blood spatter . . . I enjoyed today," he says suddenly. "Today, for the first time in a long time, I didn't feel alone in a crowded room."

The way he says the statement, so quiet, so matter-of-fact, makes me catch my breath. Then, in the next instant, the alarms start ringing in my mind. It's too perfect. It's too exactly the right kind of thing to say to a woman like me. Almost as if he's been studying me. Which we both know, for the past six years, he has.

"I have to go." I put down the seltzer. My hand is shaking. I hate that. But then I snatch up my jacket and immediately feel better. The inside left pocket contains my homemade pepper-spray concoction. I reach for it without even thinking, let my fist close around it.

Keith is blinking, as if I've confused him. But I don't buy the act anymore. At least, I think it's an act. I don't know. I wish he didn't look the way he looked. I wish I didn't know the things I know.

The worst part of being a survivor: There's no security blanket anymore. You can't assume the worst won't happen, because it did. And none of your screaming changed that. Meaning that just because I don't want to believe this handsome, smart guy has nefarious intentions doesn't mean for a second that I'm safe.

"I'll walk you home," Keith is saying, climbing awkwardly to his feet.

"No, thank you."

"At least let me call you a Lyft."

"I'll be fine."

"Flora —"

I don't wait for him. I'm already weaving my way out of the room. In the dark foyer, the greeter, Tony, I guess, snaps to attention. "Nice digs," I inform him, before pushing through the heavy wooden door.

Keith catches up with me outside. Did he even stop to pay the bill? Maybe elite clubs don't bother with things as common as money. They just run a tab into perpetuity.

He grabs my arm. I whirl sharply, pepper spray out.

He immediately drops his hand, steps back. "I don't understand," he says at last.

"I'm not your puzzle to solve."

But I can already see in his face that I'm exactly that. His riddle to answer. His trophy to win. His prey to snare.

The look on my face makes him take a second step back.

"I just want to help," he states carefully.

"Why Jacob Ness?"

"The other missing girls, I already explained . . ."

"Not really."

"I. N. Verness. If my intentions were evil, would I have given you that?"

"Yes."

"Why?"

"Because all good predators bait the trap."

"I'm not —"

"Good night." Then, before this conversation can drag out any longer, before he can talk me into doing things I know I shouldn't do, I turn and race up the block. At the last minute, I turn back. I shouldn't. But I do.

He's standing exactly where I left him on the sidewalk. Staring straight at me.

He doesn't look angry. He doesn't appear frustrated.

He looks . . . lonely.

It's too much for me. I take off running again and, this time, keep on trucking.

CHAPTER 28
EVIE

I know it's morning when I wake up to the sound of the Cuisinart whirring away downstairs in the kitchen. Probably more green goo supplemented with flaxseed, coconut oil, probiotics, antibiotics, maybe a horse salve or two. All the better to grow the little genius that had better be occupying my womb.

I roll onto my side, already feeling sulky and rebellious. What is it about returning to my mother's house that immediately turns me into a five-year-old?

The clock next to the bed glows seven A.M. The sky is just beginning to lighten. I don't know how my mother can do it, knock back so many vodka martinis the night before and still be the first one up in the morning. It occurs to me, there's a lot of things I don't know how she does. Such as roll around this huge, empty house, day after day. Like find the energy to decorate each room with its own Christmas theme, when her only family, Conrad and me, hadn't even committed to coming over for the holidays. We probably would've. Arriving late and leaving early and clenching our jaws in between.

I'm going to have to learn this. How to live in a house all by myself. How to get up day after day, just me and my soon-to-be-born child. Does my mom think about my father every day? Does she still picture him in his study, which remains largely untouched? Or lounging in the front parlor, waiting for me to take up position at the piano? Or sitting on the front porch, puffing away on the occasional cigar?

I miss my house. Yet I don't know if I could've continued living there without seeing Conrad in every room. And I don't know what would've hurt more. Memories of Conrad laughing at his first attempt at laying floor tiles, which didn't go anything like the video showed, or dead Conrad, brains on the wall, gun in his lap in the upstairs office?

What was my husband doing? And what kind of woman marries a man like that?

I imagine I'll get another visit from the police today, and that as much as anything motivates me to roll out of bed.

I shower, taking my time because I'm in no hurry to face my mother or start the day. I don't have the answers when it comes to Conrad. Flora Dane met him in a bar. A kidnapping victim and my husband, meeting up in the South. I can't wrap my mind around it. Crazier, Flora thought he might have been trying to send her a message in Morse code. How did Conrad even know Morse code?

I feel like I've spent years trying to unravel the riddle of my husband. If I haven't figured it out by now, it's not going to happen. Instead, I have a different target in mind. My father. Maybe the first step to understanding what my life has become is to go backward, to try to solve the question of what happened sixteen years ago, when everything first went so wrong.

My mother gave me names of some of my father's colleagues from that time. I think it's time I give them a call.

I complete my shower, getting to use the toiletries I purchased yesterday, my own brands versus my mother's, and that minor show of strength bolsters me until I open the closet and contemplate the full lineup of brand-new maternity clothes, all in tasteful pale shades and in order from barely pregnant to hot-air balloon.

That's right, my mother is batshit crazy.

But also clever. The perfectly appointed house. The meticulously outfitted nursery. Just how far would she go to get her daughter back — or really, to get her future grandchild all to herself?

I never saw who shot Conrad. I have no idea who might have been in the house before me. I can't picture my mom opening fire on my husband any more than I could picture her aiming a shotgun at my father. But then, my mother has never been one to do her own work. That's what underlings are for. Particularly men, whom, from my earliest memory, she's been able to manipulate with a single crook of her finger.

I always thought my parents loved each other. But did they? All marriages have ups and downs. If she thought for a moment that my father was losing interest, might even leave her . . . Who was the female professor my mother mentioned?

I pick a heavy cable-knit sweater in a light caramel, because I'm suddenly chilled and not liking at all where my thoughts have taken me.

When I get downstairs, I discover Mr. Delaney at the kitchen island. He has already shed his wool coat, revealing a deep-blue sweater that is stunning with his silver beard and hair. My mom doesn't seem to notice, throwing what appear to be fistfuls of kale into the Cuisinart.

Mr. Delaney eyes me ruefully. "Breakfast of champions," he says.

"Please tell me you have Pop-Tarts somewhere on your person."

My mom pauses right before hitting the grind button to stare at us in horror.

"Never mind," I tell her. "Green is beautiful."

She smiles, returns to pulverizing.

I take the seat next to Mr. Delaney. "What brings you here this morning?"

"Just wanted to see how you were doing." But he's looking at my mom as he says this. I take in his sweater again, a color that he must know is flattering. Mr. Delaney has a bit of a reputation with the ladies, enough of one that he always jokes he's too busy to settle down. But is that true? He's never had one significant relationship that I know of. And yet he returns here, again and again, to the widow of his best friend.

And my mother? To the best of my knowledge, she's never dated since my father died. Sixteen years later, surely she's entitled to move on. Maybe the beautifully decorated house isn't for my benefit after all.

Do I mind? My mother, Mr. Delaney?

I can't wrap my mind around it. I'm adult enough to know my mom is self-absorbed, vain, and probably a functional alcoholic. I still can't view her as a woman who might be lonely, a woman with needs.

I'm never getting through liquefied vegetables now. I get up and make some toast. My mother frowns at me, then throws an entire cucumber into the Cuisinart. Does she think I'm giving birth to a rabbit?

I make three pieces of toast, butter them, slice them in half, then bring them to the table. My mother has finished with the Cuisinart and has moved on to furiously slicing fruit. She has yet to pause since I entered the kitchen, or even say good morning. There's something manic about her efforts. She's not just preparing breakfast. She's on a mission. I feel my uneasiness grow and look at Mr. Delaney again. I suddenly have a feeling I'm not going to like why he's really here.

Sure enough, once the fruit's been savaged and tossed on a serving platter, liquefied vegetables poured out for all, my mother arrives at the table, pulls out her own chair, folds her hands, stares at me.

"You have a trust," she says.

I stare at her blankly.

"Your father was a very successful man."

I nod, vaguely understanding this. "You once said he contributed to some major projects."

"He still receives royalties," my mother states. "Significant royalties."

I guess that explains the house, the clothes, my mother's lifestyle, which has never changed.

I'm still confused. "So you're setting up a trust for me?"

"We set it up when you were eight."

"Excuse me? I've *had* a trust? Since I was *eight*?"

I stare at Mr. Delaney because, of course, this has something to do with him. "I assisted your parents in finding the best attorney for establishing the trust," he says now. "As a criminal defense lawyer, it's not my area of expertise. At your parents' request, however, I agreed to be executor of the funds."

"So . . . you're the one who never told me I had a trust?"

"Actually, I assumed they had informed you." The look he gives me is faintly apologizing. I'm not buying it.

"They didn't."

"Well," my mother interjects, "like most

trusts set up for second-generation wealth —"

I'm second-generation wealth?

"— you don't come into the money all at once. Eligibility occurs in stages, as you turn certain ages. And given that we already had college resources set aside for you, and that we didn't want you inheriting too much money when you were still young and stupid, the first-stage gate . . . Well, you'd just met that Conrad. It hardly seemed the time to turn you into an heiress. How would you know what his true intentions were? Then, of course, you had to go and marry him."

I open my mouth. I close my mouth. I don't know what to say. My mom gives me a little shrug — as if to say, *So that's that* — and picks up a piece of cantaloupe.

I can't decide if I want to scream or throw things. So I settle for sitting perfectly still. I have money. Apparently, a great deal of it. And no one bothered to tell me. Forget Conrad. She just didn't want me to know. My mother, that selfish bitch, wanted to remain in control.

I turn to Mr. Delaney. "You figured it out. Yesterday, when I asked to go to the bank, you realized I had no idea."

He nods.

"You're the one who confronted her." I point at my mom. "You're the one who ordered her to tell me. Otherwise, I'd probably still be in the dark. Because if I have money, then I have independence. And heaven forbid" — my voice grows low and forbidding — "that I be able to take care of myself and my child."

My mother looks right at me. Takes a bite of toast.

"How much vodka do you have in that orange juice, Mom?"

"I did what I thought best. No need to be nasty about it."

I give up on her completely. She's never going to apologize or reconsider her actions. She doesn't have it in her. I target Mr. Delaney instead. "How much?"

"Roughly eight million dollars."

"Eight million dollars?"

"You can't take it out all at once," he warns. "There are some provisions in place. I can go over it with you later today."

"How successful was my father?"

"Your father was brilliant," Mr. Delaney says simply, as if that explains everything.

"But being a math genius doesn't necessarily translate to financial gain. Lots of geniuses die poor."

"Let me put it another way. Your father's

genius translated nicely to the expansion of computing power and a couple of Department of Defense encryption programs."

I feel like a gaping fish again. I had no idea. My dad was just my dad. The father I loved, standing at a whiteboard, dry-erase marker in hand, muttering under his breath.

There was applied mathematics, and there was theoretical mathematics. My father had been the theoretical kind, which my mother used to say proved he was a true genius. As if the applied kind were secretly selling out their intelligence for capital gain. But no, my father had ended up profiting. A lot.

I wondered what the applied mathematicians had thought of that. I wonder what his TAs and research assistants who probably helped develop some of the theories that then ended up being worth so much money thought of that. Let alone work that went to the Department of Defense.

I have so many things to consider. My mind feels overfull, near bursting. I'm sitting in my childhood home and yet it's like I've never been here. Never truly looked at my family, never seen any of us at all.

"I have some calls to make."

"You haven't eaten breakfast." My mother sulks.

I pick up the glass of green juice, which

has separated into silvery green at the top, swampy green at the bottom. I chug it down. Then, just because I am feeling childish and petty and pissed off, I wipe my mouth with the back of my hand.

My mother glares at me.

I turn to Mr. Delaney. "I need to speak to some of my father's former colleagues. I want to meet with them, today, in person. Can you help me?"

"Of course."

"You should know, the police came by yesterday. I spoke with them —"

"Told you!" my mother bursts out, eyes on fire now as she turns for Mr. Delaney. "I told you she met them without your permission!"

"As your lawyer," Mr. Delaney begins, his voice clearly placating as he attempts to split his attention between the two of us, "I advise against talking to the police. Or, if you feel compelled, let me set it up and be in the room. My job is to protect you, Evie. I can't do it if you won't let me."

"They talked to me, too. Sergeant Warren learned some things about Conrad."

"Such as?"

"He definitely had secrets and aliases. But maybe they weren't all bad." I stare at my mother. "Maybe, some lies are for good."

She sips her orange juice, which I'm now convinced is half vodka.

"I'm sure they'll get back to me today with more information," I continue. "Till then, I want to learn more about my father. Exactly who he trusted, what he was working on, sixteen years ago."

Mr. Delaney doesn't seem surprised. Following in my footsteps, he picks up his own glass of liquefied veggies and quaffs it down. "When do you want to start?"

"Right now."

I leave the room to finish getting ready. As I exit, I can see Mr. Delaney cross to where my mother is sitting, a hard set to her face.

"She does love you," I hear him murmur in my mother's ear, his hand familiar upon her shoulder. "Unfortunately, neither one of you is any good at saying it."

For a moment, I think she's going to shut him down. Then, briefly, she reaches up, enfolds her hand around his own. They stand there, a second, two, three.

When my mother looks up again, sees me watching them, her hand falls away. She glares at me, her gaze as hard as ever, till I give up and walk away.

CHAPTER 29
D.D.

D.D. awoke to the thunder of footsteps. She just had time to brace herself before the bedroom door burst open and Jack came plowing into the room, Kiko hot on his heels. Boy and dog hit the bed in a single flying leap.

"Two weeks till Christmas!" Jack roared. "Daddy says we can get a tree this weekend!"

Next to D.D., Alex groaned. Jack found the space between them and started his favorite morning ritual of bouncing. Kiko, on her spindly black-and-white legs, did her best to dance around her favorite boy, while tripping over Alex's and D.D.'s prone forms.

D.D. managed to turn her head toward her husband. "We're getting a tree this weekend?"

"Seemed like a good idea at the time."

"We are going to find a real grown tree and cut it down!" Jack fairly screamed.

"With a chain saw and everything. Then we're going to drink hot cocoa with whipped cream and marshmallows!"

"When he discovers coffee," D.D. said, "we're in real trouble."

She managed to unpin her arms from the covers and hold them out to her very exuberant child. In response, Jack collapsed to his knees, then pitched forward into her arms. He was still vibrating. He smelled of grubby hands, syrupy pancakes, and little-boy sweat. God, she loved him.

"Will a Christmas tree survive in our house?" she asked him.

"Of course! Kiko and I will take very good care of it."

"You can't leap on the Christmas tree."

"No!"

"You can't jump around the Christmas tree."

"Never."

"No throwing ornaments. And absolutely, positively, no *peeing on branches.*"

Jack stared at her indignantly.

"That last instruction was for Kiko," D.D. informed Jack. Since Jack was on top of her, Kiko had moved on to Alex and was attempting to lick his face, whether Alex wanted his face licked or not.

"What time is it?" Alex mumbled around

dog tongue.

"Round bottom six," Jack supplied.

"Oh dear." D.D. moaned. "I gotta get to work."

"No work!" Jack ordered. "Let's go get the tree."

"How about work and school today, tree tomorrow?"

Alex, one hand blocking his cheek from Kiko, arched a brow at her. First rule of thumb for a kid Jack's age was not to make promises you can't keep. Given the demands of D.D.'s job, that was easier said than done.

"I can figure it out," she assured him. "For that matter, I have a new fed playmate. Maybe I can make her work tomorrow."

"You have a playmate?" Jack asked. He'd calmed down slightly, curling up in her arms, head pressed against her shoulder. Kiko gave up on Alex, licked Jack's face instead. The dog was very gentle about it, as if she was grooming her puppy. Kiko loved Jack, too.

"A fed playmate?" Alex asked.

"SSA Kimberly Quincy. She has an interest in my victim, who we're pretty sure has been living under a false identity."

"What about the wife?" Alex asked.

"I still don't know. But I'm thinking that whatever happened Tuesday night was more than a domestic situation. Which is why" — she flipped abruptly, catching Jack beside her and tickling his sides while he giggled hysterically — "I gotta get to work."

"Gonna catch bad guys?" Jack asked. It was his favorite question.

"Oh yeah. And lock up a few from Santa's naughty list as well. We all gotta do what we can to help the big guy this time of year. Speaking of which, where's the elf?"

The Elf on the Shelf, which Alex had sagely brought home a few weeks ago and started moving around the house, was supposedly the eyes and ears of Santa. Reported all naughty, noticed all nice. Personally, D.D. thought a spying house elf was a little creepy. But Jack was all about keeping the elf happy, given that his future supply of Christmas LEGO bricks depended on it. Oh, the power of the holidays.

Not to mention, D.D. herself had taken up Googling photos of Felonious Elf on the Shelf, posed in various criminal acts, and/or at various crime scenes. Some of them made her laugh hysterically, which was probably inappropriate. Then again, she knew for a fact that Alex had already looked up how to make elf blood spatter. What either one of them was doing raising a child was the real question. And yet, here they were.

At the mention of Elf on the Shelf, Jack untangled himself from D.D.'s embrace and went tearing out of the room, Kiko in immediate pursuit.

"Does he ever walk?" D.D. asked.

"Not that I've seen."

"I could use that kind of energy on my case team."

"What do you think?" Alex said, referring to her case now that Jack was out of the room.

"I have no idea. You know how at the academy you're always talking about the importance of victimology?"

He nodded.

"This is one of those cases. Turns out Conrad Carter wasn't Conrad Carter at all. He's been living for years under an assumed name. Even met Jacob Ness in a bar in the South under an alias."

"The Jacob Ness?"

"Which is why I got a visit from the SSA Quincy. Then, just to make it really interesting, Conrad's father was a detective in Florida who died under mysterious circumstances."

Alex's eyes had widened. "That's one of the crazier victim backgrounds I've ever encountered."

"Hah. Wait till you meet my case team."

"You love this case, don't you?" He knew as well as anyone, the larger the riddle, the bigger D.D.'s fascination.

Now, she broke into a wide smile. "Honest to God, it's like Christmas has come early."

D.D. arrived ten minutes late to work. Supervisor's privilege, she decided. But in consideration of the fact that several of her detectives had no doubt pulled all-nighters, she arrived bearing gifts: a tray of four fancy coffee drinks with whipped cream and chocolate drizzles and peppermint pieces. Not just caffeine, but caffeine and intense amounts of sugar married together in a concoction designed to cause an immediate jolt to the central nervous system.

She set down her shoulder bag. Ditched her coat. Switched from her thick winter boots to her much sleeker black leather boots, which she'd decided to keep at the office and away from Kiko's evil clutches. Then, picking up the tray of chocolate minty goodness, she went in search of her detectives.

She found Phil first and presented beverages. He selected the cup closest to him and, without a word, took a hit, smearing whipped cream across his upper lip.

"When I'm done with Betsy, I'm gonna marry you," he said.

"Oh, you adore her, you big softy."

"I adore coffee. Whipped cream. Chocolate. What is this, a liquefied brownie?"

"Entirely possible. What do I need to know?"

"Video surveillance sucks."

"Fair enough. Walk me through it."

Phil caught her up on the techs' attempts to find footage of the arsonist Rocket Langley's designated drop site. As it was located in a major urban environment, the issue wasn't whether there were cameras, but how many cameras, where were they positioned, and were any of the captured images any good?

"Patrol collected the tapes," Phil explained. "Tech support started skimming for content. We have a photo of Rocket, so our first goal was to see if we could capture a shot of him in the general area. Which we did."

"Sounds promising."

"Yes and no. Drop site is a loose brick on the side of a building. Pull brick out, leave behind money, instructions, replace brick. There's only one camera angle that's any good for that side of the building, however. We caught Rocket walking up the street.

Full on, there's his face square in the lens, so that was excellent. But then that camera loses him. Security footage from a local business picks him up again, standing at the wall, but from that angle we can only see the back of his head. Rocket stood there so long we honestly thought the dude was urinating. I finally drove out there at four A.M., which is how I discovered the loose brick."

"Anything there now?"

"No."

"Okay. So you've located the drop site and at least spotted Rocket in action. What time and day?"

"Wednesday morning, seven A.M."

"And the fire was Wednesday afternoon?"

"Yeah. I think we caught him picking up the target address and down payment. So now we're going forward to late Wednesday evening/early Thursday morning to see when he picks up his final payment. Once we have that, we have two opportunities to catch Rocket's client — either when the suspect first leaves the address or when he drops off the final payment. It's taking a bit, though. Footage is dark and grainy. Combine that with random people bumbling about, and there are a lot of visuals to sort through. Hell, I think I've already ID'd several drug buys. It's not a quiet area."

"Smart thinking on Rocket's part. That much activity, his own comings and goings hardly matter."

"The kid's been a known firebug for most of his life. I doubt anyone in the neighborhood messes with him. Anyone who likes to burn things for sport is best left alone."

"He's got a reputation."

"He has a reputation *in certain circles.* Word-on-the-street sort of thing. Your CI might have been on to something last night. Rocket's hardly big-time. Meaning our shooter is either local, or Rocket already knows enough to advertise on places like the big bad web. Hell, even the mob has gone cyber. It's sad, really. Pretty soon, the department will be staffed by virtual cops programmed to ID virtual criminals. Where's the fun in that?"

D.D. rolled her eyes. "Given that we're not computer programs just yet, find me video of whoever hired Rocket the arsonist. A drop box is an old-fashioned system that will hopefully get us old-fashioned results. Sooner versus later, I might add. Now, Carol and Neil?"

"In the conference room. They've been working on Conrad Carter's background all night." Phil eyed her remaining coffee.

"Make sure you keep one of those for yourself. By the time they're done, you're gonna need it."

When D.D. walked into the room, Neil and Carol were just hanging up the department's speakerphone. They both appeared jazzed.

D.D. handed over coffees and took a seat. "All right, what'dya got?"

"Homicide, definitely. Conrad's parents' vehicle was run off the road shortly after eight P.M. One moment they're driving home from a local restaurant along a well-known route, next their car is rolling down an embankment into a canal. They were dead upon impact." Carol shook her head.

"Witnesses? Leads?" D.D. asked.

"Nada," Neil supplied. "We just spoke to Detective Russ Ange from the JSO; he personally worked with Bill Conner and has been investigating the MVA on and off for years. Road was rural, no cameras, but Ange is sure it was foul play due to damage on the rear fender consistent with impact. Height of the damage indicates a large vehicle, say, a truck or SUV. No paint, however, so maybe a chrome bumper. Unfortunately, there are a lotta trucks and SUVs in Jacksonville; without any witnesses, it's been difficult to get any traction in the case."

"Surely he's looked at Conner's active investigations? Suspects, criminals the detective has come into contact with over the years and had reason to hold a grudge."

"Detective Conner had a couple dozen open cases at the time," Carol reported. "Two are worth noting: First, a significant domestic abuse case. Asshole husband, rich, entitled, kept beating up his wife and, given that he was rich and entitled, didn't think her restraining order should apply to him. Situation had been going on for months. Detective Conner had taken a personal interest, meeting with the wife several times. Week prior to the accident, asshole husband showed up again, drunk, enraged, tried to break into the house. Detective Conner arrived at the scene. He and asshole had an exchange. Asshole ended up in the slammer for the night, with a black eye, and none too happy about it."

"Detective Conner punched the man?" D.D. asked in surprise.

"In self-defense," Neil clarified. "Husband took a swing at Detective Conner first."

"Okay," D.D. said. "But one way or another, I'm taking it the rich husband didn't care for some local cop's intervention into his self-perceived right to beat his wife?"

"Exactly." Carol this time. "Apparently, the husband, Jules LaPage, yelled some pretty nasty threats at Detective Conner during his arrest. Unfortunately, LaPage owned a Porsche, not a truck. Jacksonville detectives couldn't find any evidence he borrowed or rented a second vehicle. On the other hand, LaPage had no alibi either, so he hasn't been ruled out as a person of interest in the Conners' murders."

"What happened to LaPage?" D.D. asked.

"He violated the restraining order two weeks after Detective Conner's death. Shot his wife in the face. She lived. Barely. LaPage is now a long-term resident of the state. Still a smug bastard, though. According to Detective Ange, LaPage spends his days filing appeal after appeal. Ange believes it's only a matter of time before LaPage finds the loophole or uncovers the technicality necessary to overturn his conviction. LaPage has unlimited time and resources. Not like the JSO can say the same."

"What happened to the wife?" Because Detective Ange was right, anyone with enough determination and money could often beat the system. If Jules LaPage had been angry and arrogant enough to take out the cop standing in his way, there was no telling what he might do upon discovering the detective's son was still investigating the case all these years later. Which also made her more and more curious about what exactly Conrad Carter had been doing in his free time.

"Courtesy of the gunshot to her left jaw, Monica LaPage had to undergo several rounds of reconstructive surgery. She testified with the bandages still on, then took her new face and fled the state. General consensus is, the moment LaPage gets out of prison he'll go after her again."

D.D. made several notes. "Is anyone from the sheriff's office still in contact with her?"

Neil shook his head. "No, but according to Detective Ange, if she'd stayed in touch with anyone, it would've been Detective Conner."

"Does Ange know where she is?"

Neil shook his head again. "No, and Ange was pretty blunt that it was in Monica's own best interest to keep it that way. A man with LaPage's money can buy a lot of information, including from underpaid public servants."

"Meaning the sheriff's office itself could become the weak link. Has Ange heard from Conrad about the case?"

"According to Ange, immediately after his

parents' death, Conrad spent a lot of time at the JSO, talking to various detectives who'd worked with his father. He asked about all his father's active cases. Basically, like we just did."

"And presumably got the same answers?"

Neil cleared his throat. "Detective to detective, Ange let it slip they may have made some copies of . . . pertinent details . . . for Conrad. Bill Conner was the kid's dad after all."

D.D. arched a brow. In other words, the detectives at the JSO had duplicated case files for their friend's son. A definite procedural no-no and yet . . . Detectives were people, too. And sometimes, particularly after a hard loss, the rules mattered less than justice. Detective Conner's fellow investigators wanted it, and by the sound of it, his son, too. "So Conrad was actively investigating his parents' deaths?"

"Definitely."

"To the extent he took on an alias and ran away to Massachusetts?" D.D. murmured, then corrected herself. "Or discovered something dangerous enough, he had no choice but to get out of town?"

"Detective Ange had no idea Conrad was living under an assumed name in Massachusetts," Carol reported. "He says he heard from Conrad often in the beginning, but it's now been years. He assumed Conrad had moved on with his life. Ange also thought that was healthy and exactly what his parents would've wanted."

"So if Conrad was still investigating his parents' deaths, he was doing it on his own?" D.D. frowned. "But how did that bring him to a bar with Jacob Ness?"

"Second case of note," Carol spoke up.

"Two missing persons cases. Both female, white. One eighteen, in Florida visiting friends when she never made it home from the local bar. That girl, Tina Maracle, liked to party, so some debate whether she was truly missing or had just chosen to move on. Maracle had family in Georgia, however, and none of them had heard from her. While they may not have been the closest family in the world, three months without contact was unusual and they firmly believed something bad had happened."

"And the second girl?" D.D. asked, because this was interesting. Keith Edgar might have been on to something yesterday when he'd asked if Conrad's father had crossed paths with Jacob Ness. As Flora had pointed out, just because Ness hadn't made the FBI's radar screen didn't mean he was on good behavior. He probably had been actively abducting and raping young women. As someone who grew up in Florida, he would've been familiar with Jacksonville, and many predators started out close to home, before venturing farther afield.

"Second missing woman is Sandi Clipfell, age nineteen, who waitressed at McGoo's Tavern. Her shift ended at two A.M. Her habit was to walk home to her apartment just down the road. But that night, she never made it. According to her roommates, she was the steady type. Didn't necessarily love being a waitress but was saving up her money to go to school to become a dental hygienist. Sandi Clipfell didn't have local family but had worked at McGoo's for an entire year. Always on time, very reliable. She'd recently broken up with a short-term boyfriend but didn't sound like there was much drama there, plus, he had an alibi for the night in question. He also said she wasn't the type to simply cut and run. If she'd tired of her job, she would've given notice and settled up with her roommates before moving on."

"Any leads?" D.D. asked.

"At the time, Detective Conner was investigating regulars at both bars — looking for overlap between people who frequented McGoo's, where Sandi worked, and guys at the White Dog Tavern, where Tina Maracle was last seen. Detective Ange has continued to work the case since, and finally got a hit: A registered sex offender was in McGoo's the night Sandi disappeared, by the name of Mitchell Paulson. When Ange went to bring him in for questioning, however, the apartment was cleared out, and Paulson long gone. Ange put out an APB, but trail's been cold ever since."

"Did Paulson own a vehicle?" D.D. asked.

"A late-model Dodge Ram truck," Neil answered. "Bit of a beater. Could've had damage to the front bumper. No one would notice."

D.D. frowned. "Does Ange think he's the one who ran Detective Conner off the road?"

Neil and Carol both shrugged. "According to Detective Ange" — Carol spoke up first — "he's always suspected the abusive husband, LaPage. The accident seemed low-down and sneaky, exactly the kind of thing LaPage would do, plus, he definitely had a personal grudge against Detective Conner. Then again, something had to spook sex offender Paulson to make him violate his parole and split town. Meaning maybe he caught wind of Conner's investigation. And maybe that scared him enough to take the extra step of eliminating the detective working the case."

"Does Paulson have a history of violence?" D.D. asked.

Neil shook his head. "Just a thing for sixteen-year-old girls."

"The missing women are eighteen and nineteen. That's not exactly sixteen," D.D. pointed out.

"Ange doesn't claim to have all the answers; just a lot of questions, which apparently he shared with Conrad shortly after his parents' deaths."

"But he hasn't been in contact with Conrad in the past few years?" D.D. eyed her detectives. "Do you believe him?"

"Ange claims he wasn't that close to Conrad," Carol offered. "There was another detective, Dan Cain, who'd worked with Conrad's father for years, came over regularly for cookouts, that kind of thing. Ange's guess is that if Conrad was still in touch with anyone in the department, it would be Cain. He retired shortly after Detective Conner's death, but he's still around. Ange will track him down, then get us his contact info."

D.D. regarded both of her detectives for a moment. "So what do you think?" she asked them.

Neil answered immediately. "I think Conrad was investigating his parents' death. Meaning he was pursuing an incarcerated criminal with a lot of resources at his disposal, as well as a registered sex offender who may have been involved in the disappearance of two women."

"Not work for the faint of heart," D.D. said.

Carol took over. "LaPage, the asshole ex, knew Detective Conrad had a son. Apparently Conrad's real name was included in newspaper articles covering his parents' deaths. Given LaPage's threats against his father . . ."

"Conrad may have felt he needed to leave the area, even change his name?"

"All the better to protect himself while launching his own inquiry," Neil commented.

"But he never told his wife?" D.D. asked.

Carol shrugged. "Maybe he thought he was protecting her. According to Ange, LaPage is still working on his release and is still a rich asshole. Let alone, prison isn't exactly a stopgap. If anything, think of all the violent offenders LaPage has probably met over the past decade and offered money to, if only they'll do him one little favor upon their release . . ."

D.D. nodded. Somehow, prison seemed to be a breeding ground for criminal enterprise. Ironically enough, the county had probably increased LaPage's access to illicit resources.

Conrad's decision to move north and live under an assumed name was starting to make more sense to her. But it still didn't tell any of them what had led to his murder Tuesday night.

Photos of abused girls on his computer screen. The last thing Conrad had been looking at before being shot. Like Conrad's meeting with Jacob Ness, possession of such images could go either way. Conrad was either part of the problem, a sexual predator himself, or some lone-wolf operative, trying to make a difference.

D.D. knew who she wanted him to be, especially for his wife and unborn child's sake, but that didn't make it so.

"You think whoever shot Carter three nights ago might be the same person who ran his parents off the road?" Carol asked now.

D.D. shrugged. "We don't know what we don't know. We're just going to have to keep following the questions wherever they take us."

"Pretty damn scary ride," Neil murmured.

"Which apparently Conrad had been living for a long, long time. Find this retired JSO detective Dan Cain."

Both detectives nodded.

"And let's start digging into the missing sex offender, and what the hell, LaPage's terrified wife. But that inquiry —"

"Strictly on the QT," Neil filled in for her.

"Our best assumption: Conrad's father once got too close. Then, years later, his son, going down the same path . . ."

"Met the same fate. We need to find this bastard," Carol said.

"Agreed. Because whoever it is, the guy figured out Conrad's alias. Meaning he also knows about Conrad's wife and unborn child. And once you've killed three, what are two more?"

CHAPTER 30
FLORA

I can't sleep. All night long I'm plagued by terrible dreams where I'm running frantically down long corridors, only to turn the corner and find Jacob standing there. Except it's not Jacob, it's Keith Edgar, and he's telling me he'll take care of everything, which sends me careening away, running even faster.

I never make it to bed. I collapse on my sofa, where my legs twitch and my eyes keep flying open and I bolt upright like some demented jack-in-the-box.

My past and present have collided. I honestly can't figure out where old ghosts end and new demons begin. Is Keith Edgar just some computer genius who, due to a family tragedy, has a true-crime obsession similar to my own? Or is he too good to be true? The handsome guy who's been writing to me continuously since the day I came home, studying and perfecting the right thing to say so that one day, when we finally meet in person . . .

How many true-crime aficionados would love to brag they have Flora Dane as their girlfriend? Or maybe he is something darker, more sinister? The guy who got into studying killers because every thing about murder fascinates him? In which case, could there be any bigger coup than claiming Flora Dane as his first victim?

I'm being selfish, arrogant. Assuming I'm worth so much. Yet, total strangers stop me on the street to say, *Hey, aren't you that girl,* and, *Why didn't you run away the first time he left you alone,* and, *Doesn't that mean you must've liked him at least a little bit?* Sicko men write marriage proposals. Others think I'm the only one who can truly understand them.

Just because you're paranoid doesn't mean they're not out to get you.

At six A.M. I give up. Shower. Leave a message for my boss at the pizza parlor, claiming to be deathly ill and apologizing for missing my shift yesterday. Given how I feel, I'm not totally lying. This is the other thing I resent about Keith Edgar. Him and his whole *you can be anything.* What a load of shit.

If I could do better, don't you think I

would've by now? Instead of hanging out in a triple-locked apartment plastered with articles about missing persons cases. I'm not even a good pizza employee. And I don't want to write a tell-all novel or sell the movie rights or exploit my situation to make a quick buck.

Sure, I help other survivors. I assist the police. But six years later, I'm mostly still me, seeing monsters everywhere, and training every day to kill them.

I hate Keith Edgar all over again. Him and his elitist club and his quiet competence, which seems to argue you can fight predators and still lead an almost-normal-looking life.

I decide we need to talk. Which is why I grab my favorite down jacket, fill the pockets with all my latest tricks, then, hunching my shoulders against the cold, trudge down to the T station in Harvard Square.

It all seems like a very good plan. Till I knock hard on Keith Edgar's door. And SSA Kimberly Quincy opens it.

I feel immediately like I'm intruding on something, but I don't know what. Quincy doesn't say a word, merely opens the door wider. She doesn't seem surprised to see me. Maybe after yesterday's display, she thinks Keith and I are friends. Or more than friends.

She's wearing a pantsuit very similar to yesterday's ensemble, except today she has a dark-green fitted top beneath the short black blazer. Sensible heels, I notice, as she leads the way to the back of Keith's town house and I reluctantly follow.

They are set up in the dining room at a sleek, dark wood table. I note Quincy's long coat slung over the back of a chair, her computer bag occupying the seat. On the table, her computer is up and running, while across from her, Keith's hunched over a laptop. It doesn't look like his computer from yesterday. This machine is both larger and older-looking. I'm confused for a moment, then . . .

"Is that?" I ask Quincy, staring at the computer in rapt fascination. Keith still doesn't look up. He seems intent on avoiding me. That pleases me.

"Ness's actual computer? No. First rule of forensic analysis, you clone the hard drive so you're never working on the original. Granted, we made this replicate six years ago, so some of the external scarring is authentic by now."

"You brought the machine to Keith?" I

leave my next question hanging in the air. Why?

"He seems to know a great deal about Jacob Ness, as well as computers. I have profilers who can give me the first half of that equation and geeks who can give me the second half, but as for one person with insight into both psychology and technology . . ."

Quincy's voice trails off. I scowl. I don't want Keith to be that valuable to this investigation, never mind that I'm the one who involved him in the beginning.

"The geeks cracked the password?"

"We think. But that's only a piece of the puzzle. Are you familiar with the dark web?"

Quincy pulls out a chair, takes a seat without asking. Clearly it's up to me to follow if I feel so inclined. Across from us, Keith continues to type furiously, scowling at the monitor. Briefly, the FBI agent's gaze goes from me to him and back to me again. I don't think much gets by her.

"The evil underbelly of the internet," I say. "Its haunted house."

"Good analogy. The typical online experience, or open web, features legitimate businesses, interests, services. The dark web . . . the less reputable sort. Illicit drugs. Firearms. Assassinations. And, yes, human trafficking."

I take a seat.

Quincy leans forward. "One of our issues with Ness's computer was how clean it initially appeared. His use of SteadyState meant that every time he rebooted his computer, it automatically deleted any traces of websites he may have visited or content he downloaded."

I nod.

"Even knowing he must've been visiting the dark web — given the Tor browser — we couldn't make any headway with the one username we had. Keith and you, however, cracked that nut for us yesterday when you helped determine Jacob's 'real' username, so to speak."

"I. N. Verness," I fill in. "But you still need a password."

"To access sites on the dark web, absolutely. Which meant we were thrilled at four this morning when codebreaking software finally churned out the magic answer. Better yet, like a lot of people, Jacob seems to have reused the same password over and over again. Meaning now, a mere six years later, that computer right there, our Ness clone, is currently logged in to several markets and forums on the dark web. Hallelujah!"

Keith looks up briefly at Quincy, nodding in acknowledgment. The glance he throws my way is harder to interpret. Sullen? Hurt?

"But here's where it gets tricky," Quincy continues. "Even if we could re-create every IP address Ness ever visited six years ago, the internet — open or dark — changes all the time. Basically, we've finally arrived in the right country. But all the roads and landmarks are different. We have no idea where to go or what to do next."

"So what's he doing?" I ask, gesturing to Keith. "Learning the landscape?"

"Actually, I have other techs mapping out the terrain; one of them is an expert on the dark web and is continuing to cross-check Jacob's username with all the pages we know would appeal to a subject with his tastes."

"Porn, prostitution, human trafficking," I provide.

"Keith, on the other hand, I gave a different task. He's basically . . . wandering around. Seeing if he can get anyone else to approach with directions."

I don't understand right away; then it comes to me. "This is the first time I. N. Verness has been logged on in six years," I say slowly. "You're waiting to see if someone who used to do business with him, or hang out in a chat room with him, recognizes the name and initiates contact."

"Precisely. To the best of our knowledge, Ness kept his online identity secret, even from his fellow surfers. Meaning they don't know I. N. Verness was Jacob Ness or that Jacob is dead. They're simply seeing a visit from a long-lost guest."

"Won't the six-year gap scare them off? I mean, why now?"

"Fortunately, given that a lot of the activity on the dark web is illegal, it's easy to imply Verness spent the last few years in prison. Just got out. Not a new or interesting story, given the company. And of course, as someone who's been incarcerated, he's trying to get his bearings again."

I can't help myself. I move around the table and peer over Keith's shoulder. Up close, I can smell the scent of Keith's shampoo, see the ends of his hair still damp from his morning shower. I also sense the tension through his shoulders. My own stomach has tightened, as if readying for a blow.

I turn my attention to the screen. I'm not sure what I expected, but this appears so . . . banal.

"There are hundreds, if not thousands, of portals within the dark web," Keith says now, his fingers still moving as he scrolls down a screen too fast for my eyes to follow all the content. "One of the most famous, the Silk Road, was run by the Dread Pirate Roberts."

"Princess Bride," I murmur.

"Jacob Ness wasn't the only felon who prided himself on being clever."

"This page," I say, "it looks so boring." White background, menu items running down the side, with innocuous-sounding labels. Small photos of goods I have to squint to see, paired with brief descriptions. Frankly, it reminds me of scrolling through any old e-commerce site.

Keith has already moved on to another page, is scrolling rapidly. I don't know how he can take in data that fast. But then, my skill sets have always been more hands-on. And while I had a passing knowledge of things like the dark web, I'd never tried to visit or analyze it myself. I didn't have the computer expertise. Plus, I genuinely worried the stark reality of such a platform would completely overwhelm me. I had enough sleepless nights patrolling Boston. An entire virtual world of predators . . . Even I knew I couldn't take it.

"Post–Silk Road, these sites had to learn to be more careful. Many now appear exactly like a normal retail page."

"Obviously."

"There are backdoor portals that get you to the real page. Even then, sales items often appear under clever labels — hardware for guns, or you may have a prescription meds site that at first blush is completely legit, except if you click on the photo of aspirin, the jpeg file is much larger than it should be."

"Data is hidden in the photo. There's a term for that . . ." I search my mind.

"Steganography. Not all dark websites bother. But marketplaces dealing with child porn, human trafficking —"

"Jacob's kind of places," I fill in.

Keith looks at me. "They have the highest security features in place. They have to. They're hated even by other criminals who'd turn on them in a hot second. Which, of course, makes our job of retracing Jacob's virtual footprints that much more challenging. It's not just that he was walking around in bad neighborhoods, so to speak; he was touring the most sordid, dangerous back alleys possible, where everyone is suspicious and taking extra precautions."

I'm confused. "Given all that, how would Jacob even learn of such marketplaces? Know that clicking on this photo actually gets him that pornographic image? Is there like a web version of street smarts?"

"Welcome to forums — or chat rooms as some people call them. Ness had to belong to at least one to learn all the things he learned. Unfortunately, given the paranoia of the members of the more twisted forums, learning who, what, when, where, how, and why is that much more difficult."

"So what are you doing?"

"The dark web is a competitive marketplace, right? Illegal or not, the goal is still to make money. Hence customer reviews, rating systems, everything."

"Okay."

"I'm hoping one of Jacob's past business associates will find us. Start a private chat in a pop-up window, hey we haven't seen you in ninety days, welcome back with a free thirty-day trial . . ."

"Business is business," I murmur. I nod slowly. "You don't know all the forums Jacob visited or the members he might've 'chatted' with. So if you can't go to them, you're hoping one of them will come to you."

"Exactly. You said Jacob used a lot of drugs."

I nod.

"Those e-commerce sites have less security, believe it or not, so might be one place to start. But I think those deals had to be local, because to order off the dark web Jacob would need a PO box for delivery. Given his life on the road, always going from state to state . . ."

"He had mail sent to his mom's house."

"Exactly. Meaning he'd have to return there every time he needed a fix; and we know he didn't go there that often. As an illegal consumer, what other items would Jacob have been into?"

"Porn. And not child porn. But more like everyday porn." I grimace in distaste at the distinction. I tap the screen, where new images have appeared. "Wait. Is that what this is? But it looks like a gardening catalogue? Aren't those photos of different kinds of daffodils?"

Keith glances up. His expression is faintly apologetic.

"It's awful," he says.

I stare at the screen. "You said only the really terrible sites relied on steganography. The ones even other predators hate."

"It's awful," he repeats.

Meaning those daffodils aren't really daffodils. Young girls? Images of children for sale? He's right; the possibilities are too awful to consider. I sink down into the chair beside him. Just as a pop-up window appears on the screen.

Keith straightens, looks over the laptop monitor to Quincy. "We have contact."

The FBI agent marches over, takes up a position behind Keith's shoulder.

She reads the message, nods in grim satisfaction, then takes out her iPhone. She aims it at the screen and hits video.

"All right," she says. "Let's play."

CHAPTER 31
EVIE

Mr. Delaney insisted upon driving. I couldn't decide if he thought a woman in my delicate condition shouldn't be allowed behind the wheel of a car, or if he was just one of those guys who had to be in control.

I had wanted to meet with Dr. Martin Hoffman, the department chair during my father's tenure at Harvard. My mother had implied he'd know all my father's associates, so I thought he'd be the best place to start. Unfortunately, he hadn't answered his phone. I'd left a message but then decided I was too antsy to wait. I'd dialed Katarina Ivanova next, locating her office number on the department website. Interestingly enough, she'd answered and, after a moment's hesitation, had agreed — rather coolly, I thought — to meet with me.

I had looked up her photo online. She was indeed beautiful, thick, wavy locks of hair, darkly lashed eyes, golden skin. Everything my platinum-blond mother wasn't.

Personally, Katarina's photo sparked few reactions for me. Vaguely familiar. I probably had met her at one of the Friday poker parties. But I couldn't bring any specific memory to mind. Just the mildly shocked reaction that such a gorgeous woman was a Harvard math professor, an ironic generalization from a fellow female math geek who should know better. Just because I complain about the system doesn't mean I'm immune to it.

Now Mr. Delaney and I drive through Cambridge in comfortable silence. The Harvard campus isn't far at all, a matter of miles. Given the narrow, congested streets of Cambridge, it's probably a faster walk than a drive. But this time of year, with the frigid temps and slushy sidewalks, driving it is.

We make it another creeping half a mile; then I just can't help myself:

"Are you and my mom seeing each other?"

Mr. Delaney takes his eyes off the road long enough to give me an arched brow. The car in front of him stops short for a pedestrian darting across the street. Mr. Delaney slams on his brakes, then throws up an arm as if to keep me from flying through the windshield. I'm wearing my seat belt, not to mention we're barely moving, but I appreciate the protective instinct.

"Why do you ask?" he finally says.

"Why don't you answer?" I counter, having seen the lawyer at work before. "I'm not saying I care. I just want to know."

"Your mother's a beautiful woman," he concedes at last.

I nod in encouragement. Mr. Delaney and my mother. The more I think about it, the more I don't mind. It's good for my mother to have someone in her life. I know better than anyone that my father had been her entire world. The years since have been rough for her. I'm glad she has someone like Mr. Delaney in her life.

"I would be honored to be in a relationship with her," Mr. Delaney continues now, "if I was the kind of guy interested in a relationship with a beautiful woman."

It takes a moment for me to register what he has just said. The car ahead of us begins to move again. We edge forward. I feel like my head is in spin cycle, my brain the image of the whirling symbol on a smartphone as it struggles to load content. Wait a minute. Does that mean?

Suddenly, with a little click, I get everything I never truly noticed before. The incredibly handsome man beside me who never married, never had children of his own. Flirted shamelessly with every female in the room but never arrived or left with any one woman on his arm. I had watched ladies' interest in him and, given his charming smiles, assumed he was a player of the highest order. But again, for my entire childhood, then adulthood, no girlfriend, no serious relationship.

I feel ridiculously stupid.

"I'm sorry," I say.

He smiles gently. "It's not something I talk about. My parents weren't exactly open-minded on the subject."

"Haven't they passed away?"

"Old habits die hard. Close friends and associates know my preferences, but it's not something I advertise."

"I'm sorry," I say again.

"Whatever for?"

"Because . . . Because you shouldn't have to say who you are. You shouldn't have to feel self-conscious. And you shouldn't have to explain yourself to an idiot like me. Not that I care," I hasten to add, then realize that came out wrong. "I care about you," I correct. "I don't care about who you date."

"As long as it's not your mother?" he asks slyly.

"Ha. Please tell me I don't have to ask

about my father." I roll my eyes, clearly joking.

The look he gives me has me going wide-eyed.

"What? Wait! No way."

He starts to laugh, and just like that, I know he's played me. Good God, I have to start sleeping more, because every time I think I'm starting to understand my family, my worldview gets turned upside down again.

"Both my parents knew?" I ask, trying to regain my bearings.

"I understood who I was by the time I got to college. Your father figured it out first. As I said, it wasn't something I advertised. His complete and total acceptance was very dear to me, at a time in my life when I was still struggling to be comfortable with myself."

I almost say I'm sorry again, then catch myself.

"Your mother . . . She toyed with me for months. Had eyes only for your father, of course, but felt a need to keep me in the mix, most likely in an attempt to make him jealous. We didn't bother to correct her. It was too much fun to watch her work. I believe when I finally broke the news, she slapped me — for lying — then hugged me in sheer relief that there was a good reason

I hadn't yet succumbed to her charms. Your mother is a complicated woman."

"Tell me about it," I mutter.

"She does love you."

I shrug. "She is the sun. She will always be the sun. I can only orbit around her, and sometimes, that's really draining."

"She is who she is, just as I am who I am."

"Is that what the three of you had in common? My mother, who needs what she needs, whether she wants to or not. My father, whose brain worked the way it worked whether he wanted it to or not. And you, who preferred who you preferred, whether you wanted to or not."

"The three misfits," Mr. Delaney concedes.

It's hard for me to think of my parents that way. My father had always been the genius, while my mother has always been the gorgeous hostess, every frosted strand of hair. Add to that Mr. Delaney, the silver fox himself, one of the best criminal defense attorneys in Boston . . .

But before all of that, they were kids. Given my own awkward years, is it really so strange to think they had their own?

"Do you want to know another secret?" Mr. Delaney asks me.

"Yes!"

"Back in those days, I was a complete reprobate."

"A wild child?"

"They say inside every criminal defense lawyer is an excellent criminal, hence our ability to be so good at our jobs. I met your father outside a bar, brawling with another student."

"You were fighting? Like punching and hitting?" I take in his three-hundred-dollar cashmere sweater and can't picture it.

"Please, I was winning." His tone turns dry. "You don't have to look so surprised."

"Umm . . . Why were you fighting?"

"I don't even remember. Back then, I didn't need much of an excuse. Hot Irish temper. A great deal of misplaced rage. A need, I think, to prove myself a man in the more elemental ways, since there was one fundamental way I could not."

I can't help myself. "I'm sorry."

"All before your time. And everyone has to spend their days young and stupid. Otherwise we'd never figure out how to grow up."

"My father didn't mind you beating up the other kid?"

"The other student had been heckling him in the bar. Your father was so awkwardly cute about trying to thank me for taking

473

down his tormentor, how could I resist when he offered to buy me a beer?"

Now I'm not so certain about Mr. Delaney and my father anymore, and I'm not sure just how many new visions of my childhood I can take.

He smiles at me. We are at the campus, looping around it. From here we'll have no choice but to park and walk our way to Dr. Ivanova's office.

"I did have a crush on your father. In the very beginning. He may have known it, too. It was always hard to tell with him. Your father came across as socially awkward, disconnected. But later, if you asked him questions about an evening, a person, a situation . . . The things he saw. I used to catch my breath at the sheer stunning clarity of his insights. And I would wonder what a burden it had to be to see everyone, everything, so exactly."

"He saw me," I hear myself whisper. I look down at my lap. "He knew I was an awkward child, and no matter how many forced tea parties my mother arranged, I'd never belong with my own peers. He knew how much I needed the piano, something that was mine. He knew how much I needed him."

"Earl loved you very much."

"My father loved all of us very much."

Mr. Delaney smiles sadly, turns into the parking garage. "I can honestly say, he was one of the great loves of my life. And there isn't a day that goes by that I don't miss him."

Looking at his face, I believe him.

Dr. Katarina Ivanova glances up from her desk as I walk into her office. She looks older than in her website photo. Thicker around the face. She also doesn't look happy to see me. Her expression sours further when Mr. Delaney appears behind me.

Her office is small, nothing special. Linoleum floors, no windows, fluorescent lights.

She rises from behind her desk. She's wearing a dark cranberry-colored wool wrap dress that flatters her lush figure and rich hair. Clearly, Dr. Ivanova feels no need to apologize for being one of the only female professors in the math department. I want to like her for that, but her wariness has set me on edge. I'm already not sure I want to learn more about her — her and my father.

"Evelyn Hopkins?" she says, calling me by my maiden name.

I don't correct her. I'm here about my father, so when I'd called, using the name

Hopkins had made more sense.

"Dick," she says, nodding toward Mr. Delaney. If I hadn't just had such a revealing conversation with my father's closest friend, I'd be forming assumptions about how well Dr. Ivanova and Mr. Delaney are acquainted. Now I have no idea.

I take a seat. After a moment, Mr. Delaney joins me. Then the three of us stare at one another. Now that I'm here, I don't know what I'm trying to ask. What I need to learn.

"I have some questions about my father," I say at last.

"You said as much by phone." Dr. Ivanova has resumed her place behind the desk. She leans forward and plants both elbows on the clear surface. It thrusts her chest forward and, given the line of her dress, reveals quite a bit of cleavage. I wonder if this is to distract Mr. Delaney, or if Dr. Ivanova is one of those women who's used her looks as a weapon for so long, she's not even aware she's doing it.

I open my mouth to tell her the police have reopened his death investigation, then, at the last moment, change my mind. I'm not an expert in police work, but I know from watching countless cop shows that I shouldn't give too much away. If this woman did have something to do with my father's death, the fresh investigation into his murder would put her on guard. No need to go there just yet.

Then again, the real killer knows I didn't shoot my father. The real killer knows I've been lying for sixteen years. Is there something I can do with that?

Suddenly, I have a plan.

"You've seen me on the news?" I ask now, keeping my voice deliberately calm.

"You were arrested for shooting your husband."

"I didn't do it. Mr. Delaney, my lawyer." I nod in his direction.

Dr. Ivanova sneers slightly. Definitely no love lost there.

"He will have this cleared up soon enough," I continue. "In the meantime, I'm pregnant. Homeless."

She arches a brow.

"Oh, didn't you hear? My house burned down the other night."

Slowly, she shakes her head. Her expression remains shuttered. I'm not surprising her, and yet she's clearly feeling defensive.

"I'm suffering a reversal of financial fortune," I say, leaving out this morning's abrupt news about the trust fund. "I would like to remedy that situation."

She stares at me long and hard. She really is stunning. I could see my father finding her attractive. Her choice of dress alone hinted at an adventurousness no one would ever accuse my mother of. But would he stray? I always thought of my mother and him as being so much in love. Yet, like all couples, they had their differences. Then I have another, stranger thought.

If Conrad had met this woman, would he have strayed? Did he stray? Fake IDs, bricks of cash. How would infidelity even rate after that level of betrayal? But just the thought of it leaves me feeling slightly breathless.

Something must have shown in my eyes because Dr. Ivanova frowns at me. "I do not know what you are implying."

"He loved you." I keep it simple.

I score a hit. There, in her eyes. The words she wanted to hear. What all women want to hear.

"He never would've left my mother for you, but he loved you."

She glances away, but not before I see the sheen of emotion in her eyes. Beside me, Mr. Delaney says nothing. He's letting me run the show, unspooling secrets no doubt he already knows.

Sure enough: "Did you tell her?" She turns on him abruptly.

"She was a child. Of course not."

"Then how —"

"I'm not a child anymore. I'm a grown woman. Married. Widowed. I don't need to be told how the world works."

"What do you want?" she repeats.

"I know what you did. I covered for you all these years. The least you could do is repay the favor."

She scowls at me. "I don't know —"

"The police are reopening the investigation into my father's death."

Her eyes grow wide.

"In light of my husband's death, they have new suspicions they want to pursue."

"You didn't shoot your father accidentally."

"I didn't shoot him at all. And we both know it."

"What?" She sits backs from her desk abruptly. She appears genuinely shocked, which gives me pause. So far, I've been reenacting my own episode of *Law & Order.* Except in my script, now was the moment she confessed. Not stared at me in confusion.

"I know what really happened in the kitchen that day," I double down. "My mother was distraught. The truth would've further destroyed her. So I lied to protect her. But that doesn't mean I didn't keep some evidence of my own."

"You are ridiculous."

"Hair often gets left behind at crime scenes. Especially long dark strands. Embedded in so much blood."

She pales. Beside me, Mr. Delaney flinches slightly.

"The police can still run them."

"They won't believe you. You shot your husband. They know you for who you are."

"I didn't shoot my husband. I shot the computer. And the police believe me."

Now she's just plain confused. I don't blame her. I'm trying to keep her off balance. Turns out, I'm pretty good at this.

"Who shot your husband?" she asks bluntly.

"Who burned down my house?" I ask back.

She shakes her head, clearly starting to think I'm losing it. I need to wrap this up before she finds all the holes in the tale I'm haphazardly weaving.

"I know what you did," I state again. "I have evidence. But I'm also a woman down on her luck. Meaning, for the right price, I can make it all go away."

Now Mr. Delaney does turn and stare at me. Is he impressed or appalled? I don't have the courage to glance at him to find out.

"I do not know what you think you know." Dr. Ivanova scowls at me. "But I did not shoot your father. Yes, I slept with the man. He was handsome and brilliant. But I did not expect him to leave your mother. Nor did I want him to. He was much too old for me, and I have no need for marriage. I much prefer my life this way."

"But you two fought."

"We did not. We were two grown adults. We had appetites. We were greedy and then it was done. Well, except, of course, your mother found out. She was not happy with him. Though clearly it was not the first time she had learned such things. Your father worried for a bit. She was angrier than usual. What did he call it? 'The straw that broke the donkey's back.' "

"The straw that broke the camel's back."

"Yes, that. When I heard Earl had been shot, I assumed his wife had done it."

"My mother was with me."

For the first time, Dr. Ivanova smiles. It is a feline expression. "Please, your mother would never dirty her hands like that. And I've always thought she is much smarter than your father gave her credit for." Ivanova waves a hand at me, gesturing that she is done with me. "You do not have anything. If the police come, I will tell them the truth. Your father and I were lovers, a very long time ago. Then we were not, also a very long time ago. I do not shoot my exes. Frankly, I couldn't afford that many bullets."

She gives me a blatant stare. And just like that, my crime solving is done. She's won. I've lost. Game over.

I rise to standing, surprised to find that my legs are shaky. To be honest, I believe Katarina's claim that she had no reason to kill my father. Now I have doubts about my mother instead, which is worse.

I want to get as far away from here as possible. This morning has been disorienting. Maybe children aren't meant to know their parents this well. Maybe no one should look too hard at their childhood memories.

Mr. Delaney also rises to his feet. As I head for the door, he hesitates. I hear him murmur something to Dr. Ivanova. Maybe a final, parting barb. Whatever it is, she hisses in response, clearly unhappy with him.

I don't care anymore. I just want to get back to the car. And then what? Return to my mother's house? Watch her mix more martinis in the kitchen? Or ask her, finally, point-blank after all these years: Did you arrange for Dad to die?

I'm doubting things I don't want to doubt. And seeing things I don't want to see.

As we step outside the building, into the harsh chill of mid-December, Mr. Delaney's cell phone rings. He answers it crisply. "Delaney. Yes. Excuse me? What did you say?"

His footsteps immediately pick up. I'm rushing to keep up with him when he ends the call, pockets his phone.

"There's a fire," he says, his voice hard.

"Where?" Then, before I can help myself, "Mom?"

"She's fine. It's not your mother's house, Evie. It's mine."

CHAPTER 32
D.D.

D.D. wrapped up her meeting with Neil and Carol. Based on everything they had learned, it seemed logical that Conrad Carter had continued investigating his father's cases after his parents' deaths. That meant he'd been covering everything from how to hide Monica LaPage from her incarcerated-and-yet-still-vengeful ex-husband to pursuing the disappearance of at least two missing girls in Florida. Also, based on Evie's account of spotting a dot-onion site on her husband's laptop, Conrad had been using the dark web to do it. Which was where he'd encountered Jacob Ness, and arranged a meeting in a bar? Or where he'd met all sorts of predators, one of whom had ultimately figured out Conrad's true good intentions and felt compelled to kill the man? Or Conrad had simply learned something he shouldn't have?

They knew more, but they still didn't

know enough. Neil and Carol were to contact retired Jacksonville detective Dan Cain, who presumably had kept in touch with Conrad. They were also to make discreet inquiries into Monica LaPage's whereabouts. D.D. was already wondering — the monthly withdrawals from Conrad's account. Had he been sending financial support to the beleaguered woman, again, taking up where his father had left off in trying to help her?

So many questions.

In the meantime, D.D. headed back up to her office, where she could call arson investigator Patti Di Lucca. She wanted more information on Rocket, who appeared to be their prime suspect for burning down the Carters' home. Not to mention this whole firebug-for-hire gig. Had Di Lucca heard of such a thing before? Did it fit with her impressions of the scrawny kid? And how exactly would prospective clients learn of such services?

Clever in his own way, Flora had said about Rocket. In D.D.'s world, nothing good came from that.

She was just reaching for her cell phone when it rang. She took one look at the caller ID and smiled.

"Great minds think alike," she said, as she

took Patti Di Lucca's call.

"Though fools seldom differ," Di Lucca finished the proverb.

"Uh-oh. Does that mean I'm not going to like this call?"

"That depends. What are your feelings on a second fire?"

"Where?"

"Defense attorney Dick Delaney's town house. Reeks of gasoline — and I'm told the first firefighters on the scene discovered a burnt-out pot on the stove and thick smoke from cooking oil."

"Rocket Langley," D.D. breathed.

"I'm already on scene," Di Lucca reported.

"Any injuries?

"Nope. Residence was empty at the time the fire was started."

"Meet you there."

Phil had to park several blocks back from the scene of the blaze. Thick smoke drifted up in a dark column ahead, and D.D. found herself coughing the minute she stepped out of the car. The street near Dick Delaney's Back Bay town house was already choked with fire engines and emergency responders. Given the brownstones nestled shoulder to shoulder down the stately block, the BFD hadn't wasted any time knocking down the flames.

Phil and D.D. flashed their credentials, then ducked under the crime scene tape. D.D. found Di Lucca tucked behind one of the fire engines, taking refuge from the heat of the blaze. The sharply dressed arson investigator nodded at their approach.

"I still don't know anything more than I told you by phone. Scene's way too hot to enter. But the first responders all reported the smell of gasoline. Also, they spotted a clear burn pattern, which would be consistent with the use of an accelerant."

D.D. nodded while slowly turning in place. As befitting a notoriously successful defense attorney, Dick Delaney lived on one hell of an expensive block. The street was lined with imported automobiles, and every expensively restored town house appeared slightly grander than the one before. Huge wreaths decorated dark-painted doors. Pots of fresh Christmas greenery flanked front stoops, while the precisely manicured bushes were decked out in sparkling white lights.

"He's gotta be watching," D.D. murmured.

"Firebugs love to admire their own work," Di Lucca agreed.

"Any empty buildings in the area?" D.D. asked Phil, studying the row of windows across from them. This time of day, it was impossible to see inside. The windows merely reflected back the smoky sky. It was possible Rocket was standing at one of those windows now, the young kid staring down at them. Or he was hunkered on a fire escape, or tucked in the crowd of gawkers. So many possibilities. And yet she swore she could feel his eyes on her.

"Witnesses?" D.D. asked Di Lucca as Phil went to make some inquiries.

"Nothing. But not many people home this time of day."

"He blends in," D.D. said. "We have reason to believe he might have dressed up as pest control for approaching the Carters' residence. No one thinks twice about service people. Plus, gave him an excuse to walk around with giant spray cans."

"Smarter than I would've thought for a kid who's only ever been known to have an interest in abandoned real estate."

"We think he's expanding his skills — arson for hire. Getting paid for doing what he loves best."

Di Lucca sighed heavily. "Great, gangster turned entrepreneur. Just what this city needed."

A commotion in the crowd. D.D. and Di Lucca turned to see Delaney walking quickly up the street toward them. Evie trailed behind him, talking on her phone. Delaney came to a halt in front of the patrol officer working the perimeter. The patrol officer put up a hand to block his progress. Delaney uttered something sharp and the younger man nearly leapt out of way to let him through.

Evie looked up, spotted D.D. waiting for them. Something flitted across the woman's face. Guilt? Whomever she was talking to, Evie ended the call abruptly, stuck her phone in the folds of her coat.

"Mr. Delaney," D.D. called out, summoning them both over. She peered into the crowd as she waited for their approach. Again, nothing. But Rocket had to be around. She knew it.

"I'm sorry for your loss," D.D. said as Delaney and Evie halted before her.

"Was anyone hurt?" Delaney asked immediately.

"No," Di Lucca did the honors of answering. "A neighbor spotted smoke almost immediately; BFD was on-site in a matter of minutes. Unfortunately, it appears the damage to the structure is substantial."

Delaney shrugged unhappily. "Smoke

damage. Water damage. Forget the fire. I doubt anything is salvageable."

D.D. didn't say anything, just watched the criminal attorney.

He was staring at his home, but it was impossible to read his expression. Sad? Angry? Surprised? All three?

"May I ask where you were this morning?" She spoke up.

"Tending to my client." He gestured to Evie, who was gazing at the smoking building with open regret.

"And what were you up to this morning?" D.D. asked Evie. The silence dragged on for so long, D.D. didn't think the woman was going to answer. Then:

"Is it the same as my house? Arson?"

"We have reason to believe so," Di Lucca answered.

Evie gazed at the woman. "Did you investigate my house? The Carter residence?"

"Yes."

"Do you think it's the same person?"

"I can't comment on an active investigation."

"In other words, yes." Evie shook her head. "But why? Why burn down my house? Why burn down my lawyer's house? Why, why, why?"

"I was hoping you could tell me." D.D.

this time, regarding both Delaney and Evie frankly.

"I have no idea," Evie said, and she sounded so distressed, D.D. nearly believed her.

"Did you take anything from your house after the shooting?" D.D. asked her now.

"Of course not. The police arrested me. I didn't even grab my purse or cell phone."

"Eight minutes," D.D. said softly. "Eight minutes between the first round of shots and the second. Plenty of time to grab something and tuck it away."

"But I wasn't there during the first round of shots. I already told you; that wasn't me. I was just there for the end, to destroy the computer and try to save my future child more grief."

"Anything she would've taken" — Delaney spoke up abruptly — "would've been seized during intake at the county jail." He eyed Evie. "You were searched, I presume?"

She blushed, looked down. "Yes."

"Then she couldn't have had anything," Delaney informed D.D.

"What about you?" D.D. turned on him. "Did you meet her at intake?"

"No, we only spoke by phone. Our first contact was the next morning at the court-house."

"Someone must think you have something. Come on. First her house is burned to the ground" — D.D. pointed at Evie — "then yours. That's not a coincidence."

Delaney's tone remained clipped. "I'm sure it's not. But the connection . . . Honestly, Sergeant, I have no idea."

"Where were you this morning?" she tried again, this time going after Evie, who seemed the more cooperative of the two. Di Lucca was watching the show with obvious interest, but then her cell rang. With clear regret, she stepped away to take the call.

"We met with an old friend of my father's," Evie told D.D.

"Why?"

"I've been thinking. I know I didn't kill my father. Based on what you said, I also now realize he didn't kill himself. Which begs the question . . ."

"Good God, you're investigating your father's murder? What is it with everyone these days? Doesn't anyone understand that policing is real work?"

Evie stared at her slightly wide-eyed.

"Your husband was conducting an investigation, too. Did you know that?" D.D. pressed.

Evie shook her head.

"His parents' accident wasn't an accident.

492

They were run off the road. Possibly in connection with one of the two cases Conrad's father, a Jacksonville detective, was working at the time."

"He never said . . . He never told me —"

"He lived under an assumed name. He was hiding, Evie. Your husband was hiding. Do you know from whom?"

Now the woman was positively pale. "No."

"Did you ever talk to him about your father? Say you didn't shoot him?"

"No! Remember, I thought my father killed himself. So, no, I never brought it up."

"But Conrad was tense. You said you thought something bad was going to happen. You just assumed it had something to do with your marriage."

"He *was* tense."

"Did you ever notice anyone watching the house?"

"No."

"Strange phone calls, strings of hang-ups?"

"No, but Conrad was in sales. He was always on his cell phone."

"He was digging into something, Evie. He was on to something. I need you to think."

"I don't know! Just the computer. The images of those girls. Oh God, I thought he was a predator. I was so sure. But instead . . . His father was a cop?"

"Did you know anything about this?" D.D. whirled on Delaney abruptly.

"Absolutely not," he said stiffly. But her tactic had worked. She caught a flicker in his gaze before he had time to cover it up. Then, she got it:

"You ran a background. When Evie first met Conrad. The daughter of your deceased best friend meets a new man . . . Of course you did. And in doing so, you figured out Conrad wasn't his real name."

Now Evie was staring at Delaney.

The lawyer opened his mouth, looked like he was going to deny it all. Then, abruptly: "Yes. I ran his name. Evie's safety and well-being are my responsibility. I take my responsibilities seriously."

"What did you do?" Evie breathed.

Delaney sighed heavily. The jig was up and he knew it. "I confronted Conrad. I told him I knew his identity was a lie. At which point, he told me about his parents, his father's work. And we reached the mutual conclusion that it was in your best interest" — Delaney regarded Evie — "that Conrad continue to live under an alias."

"Who was he investigating?" D.D. demanded to know.

"He had two lines of inquiry. The first into

some missing girls. But he wasn't as concerned about that as he was the status of one Jules LaPage. According to Conrad, if LaPage ever got out of prison, he'd come for him. Hence the assumed name."

"Why would LaPage come for Conrad?"

"Because Conrad's father helped La-Page's ex-wife escape. He knew her location, and going through his father's papers, Conrad discovered her new identity as well. LaPage wasn't stupid. If he got out, the most direct line to his ex-wife would be through Conrad."

"He never said anything," Evie murmured. She was shaking her head slightly. "Never. Not once."

"It was his burden to bear. He didn't want you to worry. As the years went by and he never said anything more, I honestly thought the situation had worked itself out. LaPage was still incarcerated, so no news was good news. Perhaps Conrad was just being paranoid. It happens." Delaney turned to D.D. "When I heard the news about Conrad, the first thing I did was check on LaPage's status. He's still in prison, I assure you."

"But something had changed," D.D. said. "Evie already told us that. Conrad had become tense. Something was worrying him."

"I got pregnant." Evie shrugged. "If one of these guys he was investigating found him . . . there would be greater consequences."

D.D. shook her head. "It had to be something more direct than that. He found something. Serious enough someone didn't just kill him, but burned down your home. Except they're still worried. Why would they still be worried? So they went after your place next." She looked at Delaney. "Because you're Evie's lawyer, or because this person knows you learned the truth about Conrad?"

"I have no idea," Delaney answered coolly.

"Who did you speak with this morning?"

"Just a former friend of my father's," Evie volunteered. "Dr. Katarina Ivanova. She and my father were involved once. I thought maybe . . . maybe she'd grown jealous. She'd shot him."

D.D. couldn't help herself. "And?"

"I don't think Dr. Ivanova gets jealous. She just moves on to bigger prey."

D.D. frowned again. The more information she got, the less anything made sense. Evie's father's death. Evie's husband's death. Evie investigating her father. Evie's husband, investigating two different major cases.

A lot of stirring the pot of past secrets and current crimes. Any number of things could've risen to the surface. But what tied it all together? Two shootings. Two house fires. There had to be one connection.

Phil appeared beside her. "We have a sighting."

She didn't need to ask of whom. "Where?"

"Boarded the T three blocks from here. Green Line."

"Get MBTA on it," she ordered, referring to the Massachusetts Bay Transportation Authority police.

"Already done."

"You two" — she skewered Delaney and Evie — "sit tight. No more running around asking dangerous questions. We've got enough going on."

Then D.D. was on the move, phone in hand. She had one last tool to deploy. Someone who already knew Rocket Langley, who was intimately familiar with the city's subway system, and who could move faster and hit harder than any police officer could.

She called Flora.

CHAPTER 33
FLORA

Keith is typing furiously. From my angle behind Quincy's shoulder — the FBI agent is still videoing the computer screen — it's harder for me to make out all the words. Not to mention Keith seems to be using some kind of shorthand known by computer geeks and cybercriminals.

I catch snippets of the exchange. The usual long time, no see. Keith answering he's been on an extended getaway, which seems to serve as a euphemism for prison. Which is then followed by a stream of questions I don't get at all.

When Quincy murmurs some of the answers, I start to understand. The online target is trying to establish that Keith really has been incarcerated. Which prison, block, hey what'd you think of the corned beef? A level of specificity that never would've occurred to me, and without Quincy standing there, I'm not sure Keith could've handled.

He's sweating profusely. But he resolutely clacks away, building I. N. Verness's story of being gone from the game for a bit, but now out and ready for some action.

"Don't go to him," Quincy murmurs, placing a steadying hand on Keith's shoulder. Keith had just typed, *I'm interested in . . .*

"Make him come to you," Quincy continues.

My phone rings. I check the screen, see it's D.D., and take a step away from the table.

"Flora," I answer.

"Rocket Langley is back in action. Just torched Dick Delaney's house. No one was hurt, but uniforms caught sight of Rocket leaving the area. Hopped on the Green Line, headed in the direction of Lechmere."

I frown. "Do you have eyes on him now? Green Line is a major subway vein. Plenty of places for him to get off or switch lines."

"We have transit authority searching. But you've met him. You know how he thinks. I thought you might want to help."

I nod. So far, fighting cybercrime consists mostly of sitting around watching Keith type. I should be more patient. But I'm not. I prefer my action face-to-face.

"Why do you think he burned Delaney's place?" I ask now. "Isn't that Evie's defense attorney?"

"According to Delaney and Evie, they have no idea." D.D.'s tone is droll.

"First Evie's house, then her attorney's." I try to follow the thought. "Someone's trying to destroy something, but what?"

"Oh, it gets weirder. We're now relatively sure Conrad Carter was investigating two different Florida cases, one of which probably got his parents killed."

"Conrad is Batman? Turned into a lone crime fighter to avenge his parents' death?"

"I'm surrounded by nutjobs with no respect for law enforcement," D.D. agrees. "One of the cases involved two missing women, which may be what put Jacob Ness on Conrad's radar screen. Oh, and Dick Delaney, Evie's attorney, knew Conrad's true identity. Delaney ran a background check on Conrad when he and Evie started dating."

"Did Evie know about Batman, or did she just think she was married to Bruce Wayne?"

"I hate you," D.D. informs me.

But I have a thought now. I have no idea if it's any good or not, but I lower my cell briefly and check back in with Keith and Quincy.

"Hey, I have Sergeant Warren on the phone. We have a question. Has I. N. Verness gotten this dude to talk . . . product" — I hate the word even as I use it — "yet?"

"Getting there," Keith mutters.

"Can you ask about a mutual friend?"

Both Keith and Quincy stare at me. "Who?" Quincy asks.

"Conrad Carter. He's been using the dark web to conduct his own investigation into missing women. If this is all about human trafficking, and Jacob was using his name — I. N. Verness — to make connections on the web, then chances are he crossed paths with Conrad, right? That's why Conrad was in the bar meeting Jacob. Because his username — um, Jacob called him Conner at the bar — and Jacob's username had made arrangements."

Keith nods.

"I. N. Verness hasn't been logged on in six years. But Conrad was probably active right up till his death Tuesday night. So if we can establish what he was doing, who he last was in contact with, that may give us a bead on his killer, and maybe another connection with Jacob."

Keith looks up at Quincy. She nods. He starts typing again.

"I think it's the dark web," I tell D.D. by phone.

"*What's* the dark web?"

501

"Your connection. Jacob used it to perfect his crimes. Conrad used it to investigate crimes. Even Rocket Langley — I bet he's on it, as well. Services for hire, right? He's exactly the kind of vendor people on the dark web are looking for."

"Rocket has some loose-brick drop-box system for making contact."

"No," I correct the detective. "That's for getting payment. He's not sophisticated enough for Bitcoin. But he has a smart-phone, and he's gotta get clients somehow, right? Why not have a local flyer, so to speak, on the world's most invisible want ads?"

"It's possible," D.D. muttered. "Used to be the local hoodlum was just the local hoodlum. But for a kid Rocket's age, the internet is simply one more tool in his pocket. Why not use it to find new and improved ways to make fire?"

I turn my attention to Keith again. "How hard would it be for an arsonist for hire to set up an account on the dark web?" I ask him. "I mean is it just like preparing a business ad, but . . . well, secret?"

"Getting established as a vendor would take some doing," Keith reports from his seat at the dining room table. "For starters, there's a wait list."

This shocks me. "There's a *wait list* on the dark web?"

"Absolutely. And quite a few hoops a buyer or seller must jump through. Remember, the goal is to be anonymous, but at the same time, vendors have to establish credit and credibility. You don't want any idiot making promises they can't deliver. Or conversely, buying services they can't pay for."

"How is this done?" I ask Keith.

"New buyers must establish escrow accounts to guarantee ability to pay. And references are used to guarantee a seller's ability to provide services."

"Criminal vendors vouch for other criminal vendors?" The dark web sounds stranger and stranger to me.

"Something like that."

"Which means," I say, "someone else must be checking these references, verifying the escrow accounts?"

"All websites have administrators, even illegal ones. For that matter, these encrypted forums where Jacob would've met other predators — each have two or three moderators who know one another in real life. They trust each other, which forms the heart of the chat room. They then network and mine prospective new members, demanding evidence of illegal behavior such as a digital copy of child porn, snuff films, et cetera. This makes all site members equally guilty and therefore equally protected. For all the cyber in cyberspace, it's still a human system. You can't just hang out, chat, or trade on the dark web. A real person has to vouch for you. A real-life administrator has to grant you access."

I nod and feel it again — a tenuous connection forming, as delicate as the web I'm learning so much about. Conrad, spending year after year, hunkered over his laptop, dredging through the internet's worst of the worst. A particular kind of cat-and-mouse game with multiple targets. He was investigating two different cases. Missing women . . .

"What was his other case?" I ask D.D. now, my voice urgent. "Conrad's second investigation. You said missing women and . . . ?"

"A disgruntled ex-husband who shot his wife in the face. She lived. He went to prison. He's on the record for just waiting till he can get out and finish what he started. We think Conrad knew where the ex was hiding. Might've even been sending her some money to help out."

"Ex is behind bars?"

"Yes."

"So, evil ex can't look for the wife himself?"

"No."

"Vendors," I state. "Jacob used them. Conrad must've been exploring many of them. Pimps, predators, hired guns. Kidnappers. Hell, maybe even an arsonist or two. Like you said, behind every transaction is a real person, buying or selling. Now consider that Conrad has spent years on the dark web."

"A good ten to fifteen," D.D. supplied.

"Think of the network he himself must've started building under his various aliases. Providers of services who knew and trusted him, allowing him to dig deeper and deeper. Except he's not just looking at one crime. He's looking at all sorts of criminal enterprises. What if he figured something out? What if he figured *someone* out? Because as Keith is saying, none of the dark web can exist without actual people managing the works."

Long pause. "You mean like Ulbricht from the Silk Road."

"Maybe. But it doesn't have to be he identified some huge mastermind. It would be enough to reveal the principal at the local high school is actually the person running the child porn forum, or the nice lady up the block is a secret assassin for hire. It would explain the arson angle as well. If Conrad figured out an identity, the person in question might be worried Conrad documented it somehow. A notebook tucked in a drawer. A journal he gave to a known criminal defense attorney who's close personal friends with his wife."

A pause as D.D. considers the idea. "Not a bad theory," she says at last. "But given that it's also pure conjecture, it doesn't help us."

"Not yet. But give Keith some time. He can approach it from the dark web itself, using Conrad's various aliases to identify connections. He'll figure it out." I look at Keith squarely for the first time all morning. He arches a brow at the huge promises I just made in his name. But he doesn't shake his head. He'll do it. Meaning maybe I was wrong about him after all. Maybe there is hope for us. Maybe there is hope for me.

"We know Conrad knew Jacob," Quincy murmurs from behind Keith's shoulder. "If we use I. N. Verness to vouch for Conrad, and Conrad to vouch for I. N. Verness . . ."

Keith starts to nod. Quincy peers down closer at the screen. They are on it. Meaning my work here is done. I end the call with D.D., head for the door.

"Where are you going?" Keith calls out.

"I'm gonna catch myself a firebug."

I start with a map of the Green Line pulled up on my phone. It's a major artery, but then the Boston T system has many of them. Unfortunately, based on where Rocket entered the system, he would've passed through several major hubs where he could've exited the Green Line and entered any number of other ones. It takes me about thirty seconds to realize the possibilities are endless and I'm not going to get anywhere staring at a color-coded mass-transit map.

Instead, I start plotting points. Rocket's neighborhood. Where I'd think, having conducted his business, he'd head back to. A comfort-zone sort of thing, till the dust settled. Add to that, the location of his drop box. Having performed a major job, he'd also want to collect his fee.

Both of these points are in the exact opposite direction of Rocket's Lechmere-bound subway. Was he trying to be clever? Knew the police might be watching so deliberately tried to mislead them? Except if he's that smart, he'd know they'd be waiting for him at home, too. So maybe, in fact, he can't go back to the hood. He needs a safer place to hang for a while.

I decide to be brave. I dial not D.D. but her second-in-command, Phil, the detective voted most likely to be Father of the Year. He doesn't like me. I'm never sure what to make of him. I didn't grow up with a father, so I'm never sure if his perpetual scowl of disapproval is the real thing or a show of affection.

"Does Rocket Langley have a list of known associates?" I ask without preamble. "I'm staring at the T map, and he headed directly away from his neighborhood, which makes me think he may have another place to hang out."

"D.D. asked you to chase Rocket?" Yep, definite disapproval.

"I've met him before."

"And if you catch him?"

"I pinky promise I'll only talk to him. Unless, of course, he starts playing with matches. Then all bets are off."

"Rocket has an older brother and a friend from high school. Both live on the same block, however."

So much for that theory. "Do you know when he got the gig to burn Dick Delaney's town house?"

"Actually, we have two detectives reviewing every second of video footage, and the only activity we can find at his drop box is Wednesday morning before the first fire. If he was contracted to do a second job at Delaney's, we haven't picked up any contact yet."

I frown. Rocket had a system. Why deviate from it now? I'd made contact with him last night, but he had no reason to think of me as a legal threat. Instead, I'm his somewhat scary future client. So again . . .

I get an uncomfortable feeling. Lechmere. Headed toward Cambridge. Where Evie lived with her mother.

Her house.

Her lawyer's house.

Her mother's house.

"It wasn't one target," I hear myself whisper.

"Excuse me?"

"The initial drop. Rocket wasn't contracted to burn *just* Evie's house. He was contracted to torch three homes, the three places Conrad could've hidden a secret. His home, the attorney's home, his mother-in-law's home. Rocket is headed to Cambridge, where he'll hit Evie's mother's house next."

CHAPTER 34
EVIE

"You had no right!"

Mr. Delaney trails after me, holding out a hand in reconciliation. I'm not interested. I come up against a wall of gawking people, staring at the still smoking building, and feel my frustration double. I'm sick of crowds and media vans and people who treat my life like entertainment. I'm equally sick of my mother and Mr. Delaney, the two people who claim to love me but never tell me the truth.

I veer from the crowd, then think, *Fuck it.* I duck under the yellow perimeter tape. People part instantly as I shove my way through. I assume Mr. Delaney will stay behind. Instead, he plunges into the throng of people behind me.

"Just give me a minute."

"I don't want to hear it!"

"One minute!"

"No!"

But now we've burst through the sea of people. The sudden onslaught of fresh air stops me. Mr. Delaney grabs my arm.

"I'm not going to apologize," he says sharply. Which catches me off guard. "Your father was my best friend. When he died, I took it as my personal responsibility to look after you. I'll never apologize for that."

"You *lied* to me!"

"When?"

"That's lawyer-speak and you know it. Lies by omission. You never mentioned that I have my own money —"

"I thought your mother had told you."

"Really? As evidenced by my big house, my shiny car, my new clothes?"

"You were never into those things, Evie. Your mom is the one who needs appearances. You took a job at public high school where you could use your gifts to make a difference. I didn't *question* your lifestyle; I *admired* it."

I scowl at him. I want to hate this man. How dare he be nice to me now.

"You never told me my husband had an assumed name."

"It wasn't my story to tell."

"Bullshit! You want to keep me safe? I was living with an impostor and didn't even know it!"

"Conrad told me his reasons. In addition, I looked it up. His parents' deaths. His father's work. It all checked out. If he felt it was safer for you to continue to know him as Conrad — again, not my story to tell."

"I sat with you just yesterday. I cried about my marriage. I told you I thought the problems were all my fault. *I* had secrets, so I assumed my *husband* had secrets. *And you never corrected me!*"

There, the true source of my rage. That I really hadn't been wrong. That Conrad really had lied to me. And even if he claimed he had good reason — well, so did Mr. Delaney, and my mother, and once upon a time my father. Everyone had their reasons for lying to poor little old me. And I hated all of them right now.

Except I also wanted Conrad back, so I could throw my arms around him and tell him how sorry I was to hear of his parents. What a terrible burden that must have been to bear. I would've shared it with him. I would've helped him. We could've grown closer, dealt with it together.

Instead, we lived in a house full of secrets. Both of us fearing the other. Neither of us able to confess.

We loved each other. We hurt each other. And now Conrad is gone, and neither one of us will ever be able to make it right.

I wipe at the tears on my face. Mr. Delaney uses the opportunity to pull me in his arms and hug me hard.

"I hate you," I say, my words muffled against his heavy wool coat.

"I'm so sorry, Evie. If I could turn back the clock. If I could make things better for you."

"I am sick to death of regret."

"I know, honey. I know. Shh . . ."

I finally stand still, accepting his fatherly embrace. It occurs to me that I haven't been hugged in a very long time. Have had no one offer me comfort in what felt like forever. Our marriage had grown that strained. I've been that lonely.

"Did Conrad love me?" I hear myself ask, though I'm not sure I want the answer.

"Very much. He told me so himself. Before you, Conrad was totally fixated on the past. With you, he had a future."

Which had to terrify him as much as it terrified me. All the years of undercover work — I don't know what else to call it — digging into his father's past cases, taking on new identities to approach criminals such as Jacob Ness. How awful it must've been to dive into that world, seeing such horrors and depravity. Then come home and have to pretend everything was all right, he'd merely been out quoting custom window designs, nothing to talk about here. And all the while, still not finding whatever he was seeking, and still having to worry that one day, his other work might follow him home.

He'd been so tense these past few weeks. What had he finally discovered — and, dear God, how much had it cost him? His life, our house, now Mr. Delaney's house.

But it occurs to me just how dangerous my life has become. My husband shot. My home burned to the ground. My attorney's home incinerated. Conrad must've finally learned something, and just because I have no idea what that was doesn't mean it won't cost me and my baby everything.

I need to focus. I do still have work to do today. While Delaney was distracted with the fire, I'd made a second call regarding my father's death. And this time, I got results.

"I need to go," I say now, pulling away from Mr. Delaney.

"Are you okay?" he asks me quietly. He wipes at the moisture on my cheeks.

"You're the one who lost your town house."

He shrugs. "I'm also the one with two

vacation homes. Guess I'll be working on the Cape for a bit. Or maybe Florida."

I have to laugh. "Well, it doesn't totally suck to be you," I say. "As for me, I'll check in on Mom. If she sees this on the news . . ."

Mr. Delaney immediately tenses. "Go. Keep her company. And, of course, limit the vodka." He sighs. "Tell her everything is fine here. Just some property damage, nothing more. I'll come by first chance I get."

"Okay. I have a couple of errands I have to run first," I hedge. "But I'll call her, definitely. And if you get to the house before I do . . ."

Delaney looks at me funny. "What are you doing, Evie?"

"Nothing. Baby stuff. Just . . . maybe I don't want go straight from this to my mother and a bottle of vodka."

Mr. Delaney thins his lips, looks like he's about to argue. And he probably should, given that I'm lying through my teeth. But given all the lies that people have told me lately . . .

I wave goodbye. Then, before he has a chance to say anything more, I turn on my heels and head for my own little dance with danger.

This time Katarina is clearly annoyed when

I walk in. Not her office — for this conversation, we needed a less conspicuous location, hence a local coffee shop popular with Harvard students and jampacked this close to finals. No one pays me any attention as I wedge my way through the door, then work my way to the back of the overheated, overpopulated space. Katrina is perched at a table in the rear corner. With her long black coat belted around her waist, she looks like a character out of a spy movie. Which makes me?

"I already told you," she starts stiffly.

I hold up a silencing hand. "You already told me what you thought would make me go away. Now I want the real story. The one you and obviously Mr. Delaney know, but I don't."

She scowls. In my mind, I've already turned over our earlier conversation several times. In particular, the end, when Mr. Delaney leaned down to whisper something in her ear. Maybe it was paranoia, but it felt to me that all the adults in my life were keeping secrets. I didn't want secrets anymore. I wanted the truth, even if it hurt.

So I'd called Katarina again. Except this time, I told her I'd make her and my father's affair public knowledge, if she didn't talk to me again. I understood academia. Whether

516

Katarina had done something inappropriate or not, she still couldn't withstand the whiff of impropriety. Especially given the reopening of the investigation into my father's death, which would immediately shroud her in scandal.

"You didn't kill my father." My anger has made me bold. I like it.

She ceases scowling, appears more puzzled.

"You really didn't care that the affair ended."

I earn a single Slavic shrug.

"What about him? Did he care?" This is what I'd started wondering about after talking to her. So what if the affair hadn't been an issue for Katarina? That didn't mean it hadn't mattered to my father. Or my mother.

What was it Mr. Delaney, my parents' closest friend and confidant, had told Katarina? What did he know that I didn't?

"Your father had many affairs," Katarina said at last. That shrug again. "It was common knowledge. He was not a man who felt a need to follow rules. A mind as great as his own . . ."

"Did he love you?"

Her expression is surprisingly candid. "Men will say anything to get a woman into bed. As to what they actually mean . . . The other woman is always the last to know, hey?"

I can't decide what I think of her. "Do you think he would've left my mother for you?"

"No."

This time her answer is immediate and firm.

"That didn't bother you."

"No." Same tone.

"I don't get it."

She seems as genuinely confused by me as I am by her. "What is there to get? We met, there was a physical attraction. We scratched the itch. And the world moved on, as it always does. I am not a woman who wants forever. And your father was not the kind of man to leave his wife."

"He loved her?"

For the first time, Katarina purses her lips, appears thoughtful. "I believe so. Their relationship was . . . different. But again, Earl was not one to live by traditional rules. Your mother suited him. For that matter, he loved you, as well." Now she shrugs both shoulders. "A genius and a family man. They are not so easy to find."

"But you didn't want him."

"I always knew he was already taken."

"My mother."

Katarina doesn't answer as much as she regards me steadily. And in that look, I know what I was afraid to hear. The doubt that had been growing for hours now. My mom had been with me that day. But as Katarina said, my mother wasn't one to do her own dirty work. My volatile, reckless, overdramatic mom . . .

"She knew about the affair," I whisper. "You said my father told you as much. It was the straw that broke the camel's back."

"She came to see me."

I don't speak. Now that the moment has arrived, I am genuinely frightened by what I'll hear next.

"She told me to stay away from her husband. The whole 'how dare you' speech." Katarina sounds bored. "Followed by the 'if I can't have him, no one will.' "

"What did she mean?"

Katarina arches a brow. "What do you think she meant?"

I can't breathe. I think the coffee shop is too hot, too crowded. My mother, famous for her rages. If she really thought my father was going to leave her for another woman — especially one as beautiful and gifted as Katarina Ivanova. My mother, whose entire world had revolved around her husband, nurturing his genius, protecting his legacy. A widow was well respected. A jilted ex-wife, on the other hand . . .

"She couldn't have done it herself."

That steady stare.

"Who would she . . . How would she . . . I mean, this is my mom. It's not like she has a number for some hired shooter next to home repair."

Katarina finally smiles. "She does not need such a number."

"What do you mean?"

"She already knows who to call. Don't you?"

I can only stare at her in confusion. The gorgeous professor finally shakes her head. "You really do not know your family, do you?"

"I guess not."

"Do you still want to know the truth?"

"Yes."

"Then I'm not the one to talk to, for I honestly do not have the answers. Suspicions, yes. Answers, no."

I understand. Where I need to go next. Whom I must see next.

Katarina rises to standing. She is done with me. And most likely, based on my washed-out, shell-shocked features, she assumes I really will take it no further. People think they want knowledge. Until they have it, of course.

I watch her weave her way through the crowded room. The way certain men glance up, then look again. The smile she has for each and every one of them. She is beautiful, beguiling, and brilliant.

If I see that, my mother saw that, too. This new and unexpected danger to her heart, her family, her very identity.

I finally rise to standing. What I need to learn next can't happen here.

I'm just leaving the coffee shop when I first hear the sound of sirens.

CHAPTER 35
D.D.

"We got a problem." Phil hung up his phone, turned to D.D., who was just now climbing into the vehicle.

"Talk," D.D. demanded. They'd wrapped up the scene at the Delaney fire and were now headed for Cambridge, given Flora's suspicion that their arsonist, Rocket Langley, was headed for Evie's mother's house next.

"A series of fires have erupted in Cambridge."

"Rocket is already at Evie's mother's house?"

"No. Harvard campus. Trash-can fires. Three, four, five. I'm not sure. Calls are still pouring into the fire department. Details are sketchy, but it sounds like there's a series of fires all over campus."

D.D. didn't know what to say. "What are the odds our firebug was last seen headed for Cambridge, and now there's a string of

fires on the Harvard campus? Except" —
she glanced at Phil in confusion — "Rocket
is known for structural fires. Why the hell
would he suddenly be messing around with
something as petty as trash-can fires."

Phil shrugged. "Got bored? Killing time? I
don't know. I'm still not sure why anyone
likes fire so much. But I'm with you —
Rocket was last seen headed toward Cambridge. These new fires must be his handiwork. Too coincidental to be anything else."

D.D. shook her head. "As soon as this case
almost makes sense, it runs away from us
again. Burning Evie's house I can get. Torch
Evie's lawyer's house, sure. But trash-can
fires on a campus where Evie's father
worked sixteen years ago? That defies all
logic." She scowled, whacked the dashboard
of Phil's car, scowled again. "Any sightings
of Rocket?"

"Not yet. But the fire department is just
now arriving on-site. And given it's a college campus right before Christmas
break . . ."

"Tons of panicked students milling
about."

"I'll let Flora know," Phil said.

"Really? You're in charge of my CI now? I
thought you didn't even like her."

"She's had a couple of good points on this

523

case. Plus, she's already headed to Cambridge. Given the traffic we're about to hit, she'll be there way before us. And as you said" — Phil shrugged uncomfortably — "she knows what Rocket looks like. That helps."

"Fine. Manage my CI. See if I care." But D.D. was frowning again. They were chasing their tails. Worse, they were chasing a firebug's arson spree. A good investigator didn't just react to all the crimes going on around her. She got ahead of the game.

Three fire events. Evie's home. Dick Delaney's town house. And now a spree at the Harvard campus where Evie's father had once worked.

What the hell had Conrad stumbled upon? Because of all their avenues of investigation, the angle that made the most sense was Conrad's involvement with the dark web. All those years he'd spent running his own undercover operations. The level of trust and access he would've gained over time. The secrets he might have learned . . .

Since Phil was dialing Flora, D.D. did the next best thing: called Quincy. The fed picked up at the first ring.

"SSA Quincy."

"We got more fires — a string of trash cans all over the Harvard campus."

"That doesn't make any sense."

"Exactly. What have you and Keith learned?"

"Flora recommended we switch gears, see if we could use Jacob's username, I. N. Verness, to pick up traces of Conrad's activities on the dark web."

"Any luck?"

"Kind of. Conrad appeared to be shopping for an assassin."

"What?" That caught D.D. off guard.

"On the dark web, you really can buy just about anything. From human trafficking to murder for hire."

"Conrad was taking out a hit on someone?"

"Given the depths of Conrad's online activities, our preliminary theory is that he's spent years posing as a 'criminal of all trades.' Kind of a shadowy underworld figure, dabbling in drugs, women, all sorts of unsavory activities. Leading up to his death, where he talked about having some kind of serious threat that required a serious solution. He was looking for recommendations for wet work."

"He wanted to identify possible assassins," D.D. said.

"Clearly."

"Because he realized he was in trouble?

That maybe someone had finally figured things out and was coming for him? Or" — she had a second idea — "the missing ex-wife. If Jules LaPage had found her, his next move would be to hire an executioner. Maybe this was Conrad's way of trying to be one step ahead. Identify the major players, so he'd know if any of them got assigned that kind of hit."

"Either way, Conrad was researching hired guns. Then Conrad himself was gunned down."

"He got too close. Flora was right; he discovered something he shouldn't have. Dammit, if Evie hadn't shot up the laptop . . ." D.D. was frustrated again. She forcefully exhaled, got herself back on track.

"From a federal perspective," Quincy began.

"By all means."

"This is a cleanup operation. First the shooting, now all the fires. Someone is aggressively removing any and all traces of Conrad Carter and what he may have discovered."

"But why trash-can fires?"

"I have no idea. Except firebugs are like serial killers — they can't always control their impulses. Maybe your Rocket guy has gone from controlled burn to arson spree."

"Meaning he won't stop," D.D. began.

"Until someone stops him," Quincy finished for her.

D.D. shook her head. Just what they needed, an out-of-control fire-happy kid to go with their already-too-complicated investigation. Focus, she thought. Forget Rocket and trash-can fires. Think motive. Conrad, who'd spent years surfing the dark web. Meeting in person the people behind the cybermasks. Gaining trust. Building relationships. Year after year. What was it Keith had told Flora — the dark web was still a fundamentally human system? Real administrators who knew each other, forum managers who personally vouched for one another. And the assassin he'd been trying to hire? Maybe he'd also arranged to meet face-to-face?

"Gotta go," D.D. announced.

"We'll continue our work here," Quincy said.

"Keith any good?"

"Better than I expected. Interesting."

D.D. didn't have a reply for that. She ended the call, nodded once at Phil, and he roared away from the curb, hurtling toward Cambridge and the next danger to the city.

Chapter 36
Flora

I have just exited the T stop, climbing up into the slushy sidewalks and cold air of Harvard Square, when the first fire truck roars by. I track it instantly. Except the fire engine barely makes it three blocks before coming to a screeching halt, and I realize belatedly the sky is gray not from low-hanging clouds, but from plumes of smoke.

The sidewalks are a crush of activity. Groups of students moving away from the fire in an organized fashion, intermingled with lone gawkers who want to see what's going on. I decide to play gawker, too, pulling the hood of my gray sweatshirt over my head and burying my hands deep in the pockets of my down jacket as I shoulder my way toward the bustling firemen, already pulling hoses and shouting orders.

I had assumed Rocket was headed toward Evie's mother's stately Colonial in the residential part of Cambridge. But given the kid's penchant for burning things, I have to figure he's behind this latest danger, even if I don't understand why.

Which means he's around, somewhere. Watching.

Except then I identify the firemen's target and draw up short. I'm not looking at a building fire. Something big and ominous and impressive. I'm looking at a narrow cloud of smoke, followed by a sudden skinny burst of flame. Except there's another and another and another. Trash cans. I'm looking at four trash cans, spaced at random intervals, all on fire.

What the hell?

I think back to the first night I met Rocket, that particular trash can. And almost on cue, a new line of smoke rises in the distance . . .

I don't yell at the firemen. I burst into a run. It's Rocket. I know it. Working his way across campus, dropping firebombs as he goes. Why, I have no idea. But I've met the boy and this . . . this is exactly his style. Fire, beautiful and mysterious and everywhere.

Screaming. Chaos. None of the fires are big; it's the sheer number and randomness that are leading to panic. Trash cans bursting aflame here and then there and here again. Students are trying to scurry off campus as fast as I and various firemen try to push through. The firefighters need to hose down each trash can and stomp out embers. Me, I need to get to the head of the line, spot the source.

How is Rocket pulling this off? No way he boarded the subway with canisters of gasoline or a backpack of Molotov cocktails. Had he already stashed supplies nearby? A first stockpile for the lawyer's town house? A second buried behind a dumpster on campus? Is there another target?

I spy a figure moving ahead. Not running, but definitely moving in a brisk, direct fashion. Dark hoodie — not dissimilar to mine — pulled over his face. I don't stop to think if this is wise, or what I'm going to do if I draw too close and Rocket notices me. I trust in my training and the low buzz of adrenaline that's jolting through my entire system.

As I'd explained to Keith, it's hard for a girl like me to experience an up.

But this . . . this does it for me every time.

Rocket. Right in front of me. He turns just as I start to close the gap. For one moment we're eye to eye. He has a backpack slung over one arm. As I watch, he pulls out a small clear bottle. Alcohol. With a rag stuffed into its neck. A Molotov cocktail, just as I had expected, in a bag he must've stashed somewhere nearby. Meaning he knew he was coming here. All part of his plan. Burn down a lawyer's tony brownstone in downtown Boston, then head to Cambridge and light up a college campus.

Why?

My time for thinking is up. Rocket is no longer holding the Molotov cocktail; he's lit the fuse and is hurtling it straight at me. I yelp, dive left. The flaming alcohol hits the ground to my right, where lucky for me, it sputters out against the winter mush. I don't bother checking it. There are enough professionals on-site and my mission is clear. I clamber to my feet and start running. There, up ahead. I spot the dark hoodie again. Rocket, running pell-mell through a startled crowd of bundled-up students. The kid is crazy fast. In a straight-out sprint, I'm never gonna take him. Instead, I do my best to guess his direction, then race a diagonal intercept.

I'm just starting to gain on him, when he glances over his shoulder and realizes my strategy. Just like that, he veers left, farther away from me. I redouble my efforts, plowing through a huddle of students, leaping over a bench.

I land wrong, my right foot sliding out on the slushy ground. My shoulder hits hard, and briefly, I lose my breath.

"Are you okay?" someone asks.

Another: "What happened?"

I just shake my head, stagger to my feet, and take off again. Except I no longer see my target. Maybe there, around that corner. Wait, that coffee shop. That entrance to the subway.

I rattle down the steps as fast as I can, but belowground, on the waiting platform, I encounter a sheer wall of people. Heavy coats, obscuring hats, strangling scarfs.

I look all around, but it doesn't matter.

I've lost him.

CHAPTER 37
EVIE

When I first arrive at my mother's house and discover the media gone, I'm nearly disoriented. Where are the flashing bulbs, the screaming questions? Three days later, the silence is almost disturbing. What did I do to deserve this?

Then I remember the fire trucks in Harvard Square. Of course, a local fire. The media have moved on to bigger news. How kind of them.

I walked home from my meeting with Katarina. Only a mile and a half, and the kind of brisk trek I needed to put my thoughts in order. Still, when I reach the side door of the kitchen, place my hand on the knob, I can see my gloved hand is shaking.

All these years. All these years I considered my parents a great love story. And now this? My father had been cheating on my mom. Worse, she had known about it, and probably taken extreme measures to secure her own future.

Is that how she's lived in this house all these years? Because coming home that day to my father's body wasn't some terrible, shocking tragedy? Just a well-executed plan? That she then conned her own daughter to take the blame for?

I feel like such a fool. I've spent most of my life as nothing but a pawn for my mother. I was never strong or clever enough to have helped my father. Then I went on to marry a man who also kept me entirely in the dark.

All these years, I thought I was the one carrying around secrets. Instead, it's the people I love who've never trusted me with the truth. Who've manipulated me, over and over again.

I open the door and march right in.

My mother isn't in the kitchen. The vodka bottle is out, though, a fresh lemon peeled on the cutting board, meaning she couldn't have gone far. I pull off my gloves, hang up my coat, begin the search.

The sitting room with the impeccably decorated mantel: nothing. The ridiculous parlor with all its silk sofas: not there either.

Then I know.

I walk to my father's office. My mother is sitting, quiet and still, behind his desk. To judge by the empty state of her martini glass, she's been there a bit.

And she looks, at this moment, so small, so lost, so alone in the world, I lose my head of steam, just like that.

"This is where I feel him the most," she says quietly, not looking at me, but clearly knowing I'm in the doorway. "It's why I could never bring myself to change it. The kitchen was mine. But this room . . . Sometimes, I swear I can still smell him, his aftershave, the whiff of chalk from his fingers, the shampoo I bought him from Italy because it really did help thicken his hair. He swore only I cared about things like that, yet he smiled every time I got him a new bottle. Silly, all the ways we knew each other. Awful, to still miss him so much after all these years."

"You had him killed."

She finally glances up. Her expression is unfathomably sad. Again, not my mother at all. "What are you talking about?"

"Stop lying to me! I spoke to Katarina Ivanova."

Just like that, she deflates. "I was stupid," she mutters at last. "Vain and silly and upset. Your father knew that about me. He understood."

"Understood what? That given a choice

between him leaving you and him dead, you wanted him dead?"

"I didn't want him dead. I loved him! It was her. She was the problem. She needed to go!"

I'm so confused it takes me a moment. Then I get it. The whole *if I can't have him, no one will* didn't necessarily mean my mom had gone after my father, but after Katarina, the other woman. Who, being dead, still wouldn't have him.

"You hired someone to kill Katarina Ivanova? You tried to take out Dad's mistress?"

"I didn't go through with it. I just . . . had a weak moment. I was angry. Hurt. These things happen."

"Mom, you hired a hit man to murder a woman, and you call that a *weak moment*?"

"You don't understand! He was my world. My entire world! If he left me . . . I couldn't have lived with it. I'm not like you, Evie. I've never been like you."

"What did you do, Mom?" Because I'm still so confused. If she'd tried to kill Katarina, then why was that woman still alive and my father the one who was dead? And where in the hell had my mom found a hired gun? Who in the hell?

"I was upset. I'd read your father's e-mails

536

and it sounded like he was going to leave me. I became emotional. That woman . . . she had to go. But I don't know how to do such things. I don't even like guns. So I went to a . . . friend. Explained the situation. He tried to talk me out of it but when he wasn't looking, I swiped his Rolodex. Discovered what I needed for myself and made the call. Except then your father came home. He'd heard all about my confrontation with Katarina. He assured me he'd never for a moment been tempted to leave our marriage. He loved me and only me. I was the great love of his life. And then . . . things were good."

I struggle to grasp what she's saying. "So Dad plans to leave you, you plan to kill his mistress, but both of you decide you're perfectly happy together instead?"

"You've never known great passion, Evie. It's the real reason I didn't like Conrad for you. Oh, he was nice enough. But the way you looked at him . . . You were playing it safe. Again."

"Wow, I'm so sorry. My husband didn't cheat on me and I didn't try to assassinate the other woman, so clearly we had a boring marriage. I'll bear that in mind for the future."

"You don't have to sound so sarcastic,

537

Evie. I'm merely being honest. Frankly, I've never understood where you get all this anxiety from."

I stare at her empty martini glass and think that's an ironic statement.

"For a man like your father, with his ability to see what no one else could see . . ." My mother shrugs. "What are rules for a man whose own intellect exists outside of all preconceived notions? He wasn't just an extraordinary thinker; he was an extraordinary person. He didn't accept limits, and he didn't see how societal norms should apply to him. I loved him for that, just as he loved me. We were made for each other. And you" — she frowns at me slightly — "were our strange, introverted child, who never would've even made a friend if I hadn't forced you."

"I hated those damn tea parties!"

"Tough love, my dear. Isn't that what everyone calls it these days?" My mom lifts her martini glass, realizes belatedly that it's empty.

"Who killed Dad?" I grind out.

"I don't know. I'd made that silly call. So once your father and I patched things up, I had no choice but to contact the man again and say I'd changed my mind about Katarina. He just laughed at me. Said there was no such thing as a renege clause. Really? All contracts can be voided. It's just a matter of negotiation. He was rather stubborn on the subject, though, even when I promised him twice the money not to do anything. So that was it. I went back to our . . . mutual acquaintance, told him what had happened, and made him swear he'd make it right. I assumed that was the end of the matter."

"Except Katarina Ivanova is very much alive, Mom, and Dad isn't. Didn't you think it was strange? Didn't you wonder at all when you then came home and discovered your own husband shot to death on the kitchen floor!" I'm not asking the questions as much as I'm shouting them. I can't help myself. All the anger, rage, helplessness.

My mother simply stares at me. "I don't know what happened," she states. "I didn't know then. I don't know now."

"Who was your friend? How did you get the contact information for a hired killer?" Except in the next moment, I don't need her to answer. I know. I've always known. He told me so himself. A man with a violent past. Who then went on to represent most of the major criminals in Boston. Oh, the names he would have in his Rolodex. "Mr. Delaney," I whisper.

My mom acknowledges the name with a

small nod.

"Dick had assured me everything was handled. He'd called the person directly, agreed on a payoff to go away. Of course he lectured me on being so stupid. But in the end, nothing happened, all was made right. So that day . . . Walking through the door . . ." My mother's voice trails off. She's no longer looking at me, but I know what she's seeing. My father's body, splayed against the fridge. Such a great man, brought so low. And the blood, so much blood. When she speaks again, her voice is so soft I can barely hear her. "Walking into the house . . . I honestly thought your father had had one of his bad days. We'd been fighting, obviously. Maybe it had become too much for him and, well, he did what geniuses often do. I'd worried about him in the past. Done my best to keep his world right. It's not easy, though, being brilliant. Nor being married to one."

I don't believe her for a moment. Her words are too glib. Too casual. And her hand, still wrapped around the stem of the martini glass, is shaking.

"Did you ask Mr. Delaney about it? Had he really reached your hired gun? Made the payoff? Maybe your hired killer really was unhappy about you terminating his services.

I mean, seriously, a hired gun? Who believes they can truly negotiate with someone like that?"

My mother thins her lips. She appears less tragic, more mutinous. "For your information, I did talk to Dick about what happened. And he assured me everything had been taken care of. Besides, I hired the person to harm that witch, not my husband!"

"Did you pay the 'kill fee'?" I use the term ironically.

"No. Dick handled it."

"In other words, you don't know what happened next."

"I know my husband was alive! I know my husband said he loved me. I know everything was good again. And then . . . it wasn't."

I shake my head. I still can't believe my mother's naïveté, or that she'd be so foolish as to contact some professional killer to handle her marital problems. Then believe a second call would make it all go away. But I'm also confused about Mr. Delaney. What he'd done, or maybe, not done, sixteen years ago. Except he was my father's best friend. His first instinct should've been to help my father. Right?

I cough, feeling a tickle in the back of my

throat. I try to turn all the pieces of the puzzle around in my head. Cough again.

Then, for the first time, it comes to me. What I should've realized before, but I'd been too intent on my mother and her ridiculous story.

"Mom," I say, as my eyes begin to water. "Do you smell smoke?"

CHAPTER 38
D.D.

"That was Flora," D.D. said to Phil, hanging up her phone. "She spotted Rocket running across the Harvard campus with a bag full of Molotov cocktails and gave chase. She lost him."

"So this is definitely his handiwork." Phil regarded the firefighters marching through the snowy grounds, hitting first this trash can, then that trash can. In the chaos of students stampeding across the grounds, a few bins had toppled. Fortunately, the wintry conditions made short work of any errant flames. "Is it just me, or does this seem haphazard?" Phil continued now. "I mean, for a kid known for taking down entire buildings with gasoline-soaked structural fires, this seems more . . . child's play?"

D.D. nodded. She was struggling with the same thought. This hardly seemed up to Rocket's established standards.

Phil's phone rang. D.D. let him answer

543

the call while she stared at the various plumes of smoke wafting across campus. To give Rocket credit, he'd covered a lot of ground. Seemed like everywhere she looked there was some sort of small fire. Add to that, building evacuations, panicking pedestrians, and sorting out this scene would take the fire department the rest of the day.

"That was Neil and Carol," Phil reported in. "They just found Jules LaPage's ex-wife. Or rather, she found them."

D.D. waited expectantly.

"Carol reached out to Bill Conner's retired partner, Dan Cain. As Detective Ange had theorized, Conrad went underground almost immediately after his parents' death, keeping in contact with Cain while he worked his father's old cases."

"Batman," D.D. muttered.

"What?"

"Nothing."

"Of the leads Conrad was pursuing, he felt it was most likely that Jules LaPage had engineered his parents' MVA. Not that La-Page had personally done it. But using his considerable financial resources had hired it out. It was one of the reasons Conrad became fascinated by the dark web. He felt whatever happened to his parents, finding the actual driver would never be enough —

the person would just be one more cog in the wheel. Whereas Conrad wanted to understand the entire system, so he could use it to trace all activities to LaPage, whom Conrad continued to believe was operating a criminal empire while behind bars."

"Wouldn't be the first time."

"As we suspected, Conrad was helping out LaPage's ex, Monica. Sending her money. He and Cain both must have a way to contact her because, after Cain got off the phone with Carol, he dialed Monica direct, and she called Carol in minutes. Conrad had reached her about a week, maybe ten days ago. He believed LaPage had not only discovered her new identity, but had taken out a hit. She's been on the run ever since, living with a burner phone, waiting to hear more from Conrad."

"Except he never called her back." D.D. sighed heavily. "Okay. Let's take it from the top. Conrad has a whole second life on the internet, where he has spent more than a decade establishing himself as some shadowy figure. He spends his time working his way through the dark web, learning a little bit of this, a little bit of that. Comes across a Jacob Ness or two. Maybe has been getting to know various guns for hire, because those would be the kinds of contacts La-

Page would tap from prison. Till one day Conrad learns what he's been waiting to hear: A contract has been taken out on poor terrified Monica. LaPage is once again in motion, his ex-wife in his sight."

"He calls Monica directly, warns her." Phil picked up the story.

"Then sits around at home?" D.D. frowned.

"Maybe he was working contacts of his own. Is knowing there's been a transaction the same as knowing who's going to carry out the hit?"

"He needed more information," D.D. agreed.

"Except the hired gun must've found him first."

"And what? Walked into Conrad's own home and shot him three times with his own gun? That doesn't sound like any professional hit I've ever heard of. Hang on. Conrad isn't the only one who needed more information. We do, too."

D.D. pulled back out her phone, dialed SSA Kimberly Quincy. She walked down the block, away from the noisy din of the firefighters. Phil followed in her wake. The air smelled acrid. Later, she figured, she'd blow soot straight out of her nose. So many fires in a single afternoon. And somehow, she had the unsettling feeling they weren't done yet.

"Quincy," Kimberly answered her cell.

"D.D. here. Have a question for you and Keith. Okay, you're Conrad Carter. You're investigating an evil son of a bitch, Jules La-Page, who's currently locked behind bars, but who you're pretty sure engineered the death of your parents, and given the first opportunity will strike again to take out his ex-wife. So you set yourself up on the dark web, you learn the lay of the land."

"Does this story have a happy ending?" Quincy asked.

"I don't know yet. Conrad finally finds what he's been looking for: whispers of a hit being taken out. A connection to one of the hired guns bragging about a new job. I don't know. But Conrad called Monica La-Page over a week ago. He warned her to be on the lookout. Something tipped him off."

"Okay," Quincy said more thoughtfully. She was following the conversation now.

"So, what would be Conrad's next play? The whole point of the dark web is to be anonymous, right? Except it can't be completely anonymous. Flora was talking about escrow accounts, vendor reviews. At the end of the day, it's still people, offering services to other people. And someone has to know

547

what's going on. At least one real person."

D.D. heard a muffled sound as Quincy lowered her phone, then a distant exchange of voices. The fed was obviously hashing something out with Keith.

"So," Quincy came back over the line. "You're on the right track. The dark web is really just technology connecting real people to other real people. And, yes, it takes many key players to make that happen. IT gurus, for one — though, according to Keith, they spend more time coding than worrying about vendors. You'd have a management team. Who are actually funding individual sites, keeping their infrastructure running and paying the IT guys while coming up with new services, new payment opportunities, and more importantly, new security guarantees, which is the primary attraction of the dark web. And you'd have sales, I guess, for lack of a better term. Real people working from their own shadowy desks to recruit new shadowy vendors. It's a marketplace. You always have to be offering the latest and greatest."

"So if Conrad had learned a hired gun had recently taken on a new job, he could take steps to learn the hit man's identity. Starting with the site manager?"

More muted talking.

Quincy returned: "Conrad would probably want to make a financial offer of his own. For example, I'll pay you twice that amount to do a job for me right now. But if that failed, his next — and I gotta admit, it's a pretty clever play — would be to lodge a complaint against the vendor."

"Excuse me?"

"Keith just came up with it," Quincy said. "Remember, reviews matter. So if Conrad wanted to mess someone up, he could file a formal complaint against the hit man. I paid Vendor X and they didn't deliver. Or better yet, Vendor X is a cop. Now the site administrator has to investigate Vendor X. The site's credibility is shot until the matter is resolved."

"So Conrad contacts the site administrator. Vendor X cheated me or is a rat," D.D. filled in.

"The web manager will then have to open up a case review, just like in the real business world. Talk to Conrad. Talk to the hired gun. Sort things out."

"You've got to be kidding me," D.D. murmured. Forget the criminals on the dark web, what Quincy had just described was pretty much the same way complaints were handled at BPD. "In the course of this interaction, Conrad might've learned the hired gun's real identity," she guessed.

"Keith and I are only now retracing Conrad's virtual footsteps, but from what we can tell he'd established about as deep a cover as I've ever seen. Honestly, a professional agent couldn't have done as well. Ten years of lurking, Conrad didn't just visit the dark web. He became part of the landscape."

"Until he learned too much," D.D. said.

"Which cut both ways," Quincy amended. "Conrad didn't just learn a vendor's identity. A vendor, a manager, a customer — someone learned his."

And just like that, D.D. got it. The piece of the puzzle they'd been missing. She clicked off her phone. She stopped walking, stared Phil in the eye. Delivered the hard truth: "Phil. We've been idiots."

"Again?" he asked with a sigh.

"Investigative one-oh-one. Don't forget what you already know. We've gotten so caught up in the dark web and Conrad's mysterious double life, we forgot to factor in the basics: our crime scene."

"You were just talking about it. Conrad was shot in his own home with his own handgun."

"Exactly. Yet we've spent the past twenty-four hours spinning our wheels over hired assassins and dark-web vendors and shadowy criminals that go bump in the night. Really? How would a hit man know that Conrad kept his gun stashed in his own bedroom? How would a hit man gain access to Conrad's house, given that Conrad lives under an alias and has been on hyperalert for nearly a decade? Then, having accessed the house, and crept up the stairs and retrieved the hidden handgun, how does this ninja simply stand in the doorway of the study and shoot Conrad three times without Conrad ever putting up a hand in self-defense?"

"Conrad would've been on guard."

"Meaning Conrad never saw the threat coming," D.D. concluded for both of them. "He let his killer into his home. He thought nothing of it when his killer joined him upstairs in his study. He knew the person, Phil. Conrad had to have known and *trusted* his shooter; it's the only explanation."

Phil stared at her. "He finally identified the gun for hire contracted by Jules LaPage, and it turned out to be someone he personally knew? That seems far-fetched."

"Because I don't think it's the contract killer he identified. Or who identified him. I think Conrad stumbled upon a bigger fish. Not the vendor. The site manager. A person with a double life worth burning down the entire city to protect."

"Who —" Phil started, then stopped. "We *are* idiots," he said.

"Yep. We need to get to Evie's mother's house. Now!"

CHAPTER 39
FLORA

I can't keep roaming Harvard Square in hopes of spying an arsonist. For one thing, being the heart of a college campus, the area is swarming with kids in hoodies. Rocket blends right in. Also, with emergency response vehicles and news vans piling up, it's getting hard to move.

I don't like crowds. I don't like the feeling of bodies bumping, jostling, hemming me in. My heart rate is too high and that's not simply from chasing Rocket.

I discover a little side street and exit the teeming masses. I take a moment to breathe more easily, exhaling little puffs of steamy air. Shouldn't all these kids be on Christmas break? It's been too long for me; I don't remember how my own college calendar worked, let alone what a place like Harvard does. It makes me feel old — and, for a moment, adrift. The life I used to lead. The dreams I never returned to.

Okay, time to think like an arsonist. If I can't follow Rocket, how can I out-anticipate him?

He'll want money. Two big jobs in one day, he'll return to his neighborhood to pick up his cash. Phil told me the police had it under surveillance, however, so that doesn't feel like a good use of my time.

But wait — is Rocket done for the day? The criminal attorney's stately brownstone must have taken some finesse. No way a fancy lawyer didn't have a state-of-the-art security system — and no way a kid like Rocket didn't stand out in a neighborhood that upscale. So, a finesse job. Like disguising himself as pest control for the Carters' residence. He could've used the same ruse for Delaney, except the police sightings of him afterward didn't reveal any uniform.

Maybe a delivery boy? Pizza? He'd just need a cap to pull that off. In a city of twenty-four-hour takeout, no one notices delivery people either. He could've stashed the gasoline earlier, as many of those town houses have patios in the back. A kid as athletic as Rocket could definitely scale a fence.

Then exit the same way. Watch his handiwork. Bolt when the police presence got too high or he needed to get moving to his next job. Which took him to the T stop. A simple transfer to the Red Line and Harvard Square it is.

Where he must've stashed his Molotov cocktail backpack somewhere out of site. In this day and age of constant vigilance, no unattended bag could've been left sitting at a T stop or, for that matter, near a college campus. So he would've had to have scoped out everything first. Prepared his supplies, identified key drop sites. Then once the first fire started in Delaney's house, it was all go, go, go. Moving fast, leaving a trail of fire and chaos in his wake.

Which left me with the lingering feeling that he still wasn't done.

Then something came to me. Like a whisper in the back of my mind. The media craning for a closer look of the Harvard fire.

The media that used to be camped out in front of Evie's mother's house. Documenting everyone coming and going. Making approaching that house nearly impossible.

The media, now drawn away to a string of fires on a college campus that was clearly more exciting than curb patrol.

My first instinct had been correct. Rocket Langley is still after Evie Carter. And he set the fires around the Harvard campus to lure away the media and expose his true target.

Molotov cocktails for the foreplay. No doubt a fresh stash of gasoline for the main event. I start to run.

CHAPTER 40
EVIE, D.D., AND FLORA

By the time I pull my dazed mother out from behind my father's massive desk, then convince her to leave her martini glass behind, the smoke is noticeable. We pass through the doorway, then draw up short.

Thick black plumes roll out of the kitchen.

I remember what I'd heard about the fire that took out my own home. It had most likely started on the stove top, some kind of homemade trigger system utilizing cooking oil, which had flared up, igniting a trail of gasoline . . .

I eye the edge of the open parlor in front of us, and almost as if I've willed it a thread of flame appears in front of my eyes and darts along the perimeter straight to the front door, where — *whoosh* — it hits the mother lode of accelerant.

My mother and I both stagger back, trying to shield our faces from the sudden heat. The entryway is gone, consumed in a wall of flame, while to our right the kitchen flares with fresh heat while belching out black soot.

My mother moves first. She tugs at my hand, moving in the direction of the stairs. I try to resist. We go up, and then what? Fire climbs, heat rises. We will only be trapping ourselves on a different level. But on the other hand, both first-floor exits are now blocked. I give up and follow.

My mother doesn't talk. I can hear her ragged breathing as she hits the stairs, still holding my hand, still pulling insistently.

"Fire extinguisher?" I manage to gasp.

"In the kitchen."

Which certainly isn't going to help us. "We should . . . call . . . nine-one-one," I try next.

"How can they not know?"

Indeed, a fire already this big in a neighborhood with houses this close together, half of Cambridge has probably dialed by now. Given the intensity of the flames, however, the fire engines need to get here miraculously fast.

Keep climbing. Help is coming. I have to believe it.

I choke on more fumes, use my free hand to cover my mouth, and think immediately, *This can't be good for the baby.*

We make it to the second floor. My bedroom suite is to the right, but given how greedily the fire is burning in the entryway beneath it, we don't dare risk it. We head toward my mother's rooms instead, which are positioned over the kitchen. Halfway there, we pass the guest bath. I stop abruptly. My turn to tug at my mother's hand.

"Wet towels," I manage to choke out, the smoke growing heavier. "Wet towels . . . wrap around . . . our faces."

She gets it. For once in our lives, we move together. I'm throwing bath towels in the tub, she throws hand towels in the sink, and we're both running cold water, soaking through our piles. No more words. Working as quickly as we can. I throw the first dripping bath towel around my mother's shoulders to try to block the heat, as she pretty much slaps the smaller version on my face.

It takes a few minutes to come up with our new ensembles of cold, wet white; then we brave the hallway once again. Only to find the shadow of a man standing right in front of us.

My mother screams.

Me, I simply stare at what the man has cradled in his arm: my father's shotgun.

"There!" D.D. yelled, hitting the dash with her hand, just before Phil hit the brakes. "Rocket Langley. Just took off through that yard."

Phil didn't even get the vehicle pulled over. She already had the door open, was tumbling out into the snowy bank. Her phone was buzzing away in her pocket. She grabbed it out of habit, taking off in pursuit even as she heard Phil on the radio, calling for backup behind her.

"Rocket Langley torched the Harvard campus as a distraction," D.D. heard Flora exhale in a rush. "Evie's mother's house is his real target."

"I'm on Langley. In pursuit now."

"Okay. I'm almost at the house — shit! House is on fire. Repeat. Front windows totally engulfed. He got here first. Goddammit!"

"Are Evie and her mother inside?" D.D. demanded. There, Rocket's black hoodie, disappearing around the corner. She attempted to put on a fresh burst of speed, slid in the slush, and forced herself to move more lightly. This is why a Boston detective wore decent boots even in December.

"Car's in the drive," Flora said tensely. "A second car, too. Uh . . . luxury SUV. Lexus."

"Dick Delaney," D.D. muttered. "Listen to me, Flora. He's our shooter. He set this all up. If he's in that house, they're in double trouble."

"That's how Rocket did it!" Flora snapped. "I was trying to figure out how he could access such a prime target. Delaney set it all up for him!"

Up ahead, the firebug in question was gaining ground. The kid was young, fast, and all limbs. Just for a moment, D.D. really hated being a middle-aged woman who was none of those things.

But you didn't have to be fresher. Just smarter.

"Phil's called for backup," she gasped, watching the kid dart forward, working the next line of angles, preparing her play.

"I'm on it," Flora said.

D.D. clicked off, jammed her phone back into her pocket. Knowing it was her job to nab the arsonist.

And that she'd just sent her CI — a woman she respected, and even worried about — into the flames.

It occurs to me again that I don't know fire. For all my training, preparations, dangerous scenarios, this isn't something I know. How to *start* a fire in survival conditions, sure. But I studied fire as a tool, not as a threat for me to survive.

I shudder at the irony. I never worried about fire, because Jacob didn't like fire. Further proof that all these years later that motherfucker is still running my life.

I seize my rage. Good things can be forged from bone-deep fury.

The front of Evie's mom's stately Colonial is an inferno. Porch windows shattering, flames roaring up in response to the fresh influx of oxygen, dancing around what has to be some kind of fire-rated front door in pure frustration.

Fire is a greedy bitch, I decide. But like all beasts, it's a slave to its appetites.

With that in mind, I work on a strategy. Rear fire escape. Building has to have one. Cambridge loves its fire codes. Rooms must have a duel egress, meaning if there are bedrooms at the rear of the house, there must be a second way out.

Another glass window explodes. I reflexively throw up an arm as I dash around the side of the house. Out of the corner of my eye, I realize the neighbors are outside, watching the fire in horror.

"Call nine-one-one," I call out reflexively.

"Someone's in the second-story bathroom," the woman screams back. "I saw someone through the window!"

"Thanks!"

Then I spot it, a rickety metal fire escape. I hit the bottom rung and start to climb.

CHAPTER 41
EVIE, D.D., AND FLORA

I don't speak right away. Beside me, my mother stands perfectly still.

As Mr. Delaney steps through the smoke, heading straight for us. He's holding a handgun, I realize now. My eyes had been playing a trick on me, seeing the past when I need to be focused on the present. I'm not sure what kind of gun he currently has, but his grip is steady, his aim true.

"You're not supposed to be here," he tells me tightly, his voice already raspy from the smoke. "You said you had a meeting."

"I finished early." My voice sounds strange to me. Too normal. Too polite. Like this is any other conversation we've ever had. Like we're not standing in the middle of the conflagration, and that his comments alone didn't just reveal that while I wasn't supposed to be here, he assumed my mother would be.

"You killed my dad," I say.

Watching him now, the way he holds the gun, the way he moves comfortably through the house — how had I not seen it before? That day, I hadn't seen anyone leaving the house or scuttling down the sidewalk — all the more reason to think my father had possibly shot himself. Except, of course, there was another option — the shooter hadn't left the house. Maybe Dick Delaney had seen our car pull up and had simply moved to the front of the building, or even walked upstairs. He knew our house that well, my parents' oldest and dearest friend. He could've cleaned up in one of the upstairs baths while my mother was screaming, I was sobbing. Then once my mother had called him, he could've used the ongoing chaos to walk out the front door and walk back in the side door. Neither one of us had been paying attention.

But now . . . Now I feel like I'm seeing everything.

"My mom told you what she'd done. She admitted that much to me."

Delaney frowns. He seems agitated, but his grip on the gun is certain. The smoke is building around us, the fire growing closer. It occurs to me, he may have a pistol, but Mom and I have wet towels. Fire doesn't care about bullets, but it does hate getting wet.

"You always were impetuous," he snarls at my mother now. She still stands stiffly beside me. She's thinking something, but I can't tell what.

"You can't just call off a hit," Delaney says impatiently. "Good God, only you would be stupid enough to take one out in the first place, then honestly believe you could change your mind. That's not how things work with these people."

"You were one of them," I fill in now, speaking my suspicions out loud. "That's how you knew who to call. You were one of them."

"I did my best," Delaney says tersely. "I even paid the goddamn bill, once your mother saw the light, told the man it was for his trouble and he'd best go away. But I saw the look in his eyes. Hired killers don't simply quit jobs. I actually came here that afternoon to warn your father." Delaney glances at my mother. "Trying to kill off his mistress? Good God, you were always dramatic, but that was just plain crazy. Unstable. I tried to tell him. Because we all knew he wasn't going to change his ways." Delaney stares hard at my mother again. "Meaning what about the next mistress? Or the one after that?"

Now he positively glares at my mother.

"You tried to warn my father?" I ask, starting to inch backward, away from him, away from the blaze.

"He was cleaning his shotgun. Said Joyce had already confessed to it all. He was sorry for the trouble and expected there was some kind of reasonable solution that could be reached. When I tried to explain the severity of the situation, that you can't just hire a professional assassin then simply walk away, that it was one thing for Joyce to be possessive, quite another for her to be homicidal. Good God . . ." Delaney stops. Coughs raggedly. I glance quickly at his gun, but he still has it pointed at my mother's chest.

"He didn't believe you?" I ask. Because I didn't understand this either. My father was a very rational man. And there was nothing rational about a wife who tried to resolve marital disputes through contract killers.

For the first time, Mr. Delaney looks at me. What he says next comes out flat and hard: "He accused me of being jealous."

In that moment, I get it. Mr. Delaney. His close relationship with my father. But always as a friend, the outsider looking in, because my father had my mother, not to mention so many other women.

"He knew how you felt about him. How you really felt about him," I say. I'm saddened for this man and how much that had to hurt.

"He always saw everything," Mr. Delaney muttered roughly, which is answer enough.

"You loved him."

"It didn't matter! He had her. For your father it was always about her!" He jabs the gun toward my mother's chest. "So much so, that even when her actions threatened him, his reputation, his own mistress, for the love of God, even when I, as a good friend, tried to warn him no good would come of their increasingly volatile marriage, he didn't hear me. He laughed. He . . . He . . ."

"He rejected you." I can see it clearly. My father, who could be arrogant, who hadn't wanted to hear how his relationship with his wife might be wrong. Easier for him to turn on the messenger instead. Dismiss a legitimate warning as nothing more than the jealous ramblings from a friend he'd always known had more than friendly feelings for him. And Delaney, standing there, having come in good faith to talk about something he was the expert on . . . Delaney, who had loved my father, respectfully, from a distance, only to have his closest

568

friend turn on him.

I can see it. I can see all of it. And it hurts so much.

"I picked up the shotgun," Delaney says now, as if watching the movie in my mind. "At the last minute, Earl realized what I was going to do. We struggled. It went off." Delaney's voice falters. He and I both know no shotgun just "went off." It had to be pumped. It had to be fired. Into the torso of his best friend.

"He fell down. And I heard a car. Your vehicle in the driveway." He glances at my mother. "I wiped down the shotgun. Took off my shoes and tiptoed out of the kitchen. Upstairs, in Earl's bathroom, I rinsed my hair, hands, and face. Then I balled up my bloody clothes to be retrieved later and re-dressed in items from Earl's closet. You never even noticed."

My mother still isn't talking or moving. But I feel it now, a subtle pressure from her hand, tugging me closer to her. For a moment, I resist. Because I have to know the rest.

"Then I said I shot him, and you were home free," I provide now.

"I thought you knew." Delaney stares at my mother. "I thought you knew and asked Evie to confess to protect me. I kept waiting for you to approach me, make some kind of demand in return. But you never did. Then one day I realized, my best friend was dead." Delaney took a shuddering breath, coughed again from the rapidly thickening smoke now. "And I got away with it."

"And Conrad?" I whisper because there's more to this story; I know that now. More things I don't want to hear but have to know. I press the wet towel closer to my lips and nose. I can feel the heat growing. The fire is coming for us.

In fact, that's what I'm hoping for.

"You're on the dark web, aren't you?" I hear myself now. "A man with your past experiences, current contacts. What do you do? Run a site, a forum, something?"

"Even on the internet, it takes personal connections to vouch for, say, certain professionals." Mr. Delaney shrugs, as if this is the most obvious thing in the world. Maybe for him, it is. Maybe for my husband, all those years, all those aliases, logged online, it was as well. I know too much, I think, and yet still feel like I know nothing at all.

"Conrad figured you out," I venture. "Surfing the dark web, he came upon something."

"Ironically enough, he lodged a complaint

against a particular gun for hire. When I went to mediate . . . I realized from Conrad's e-mail who'd sent it. I knew then, it was only a matter of time before Conrad realized my role as site manager as well."

I stare at him. I don't care anymore about the smoke stinging my eyes, the intensity of the nearing flames, the feel of my mom tugging my hand. "Tell me," I order, my voice so thick I barely recognize it. "I want to hear it. Straight from you. Tell me exactly how you killed my husband."

"I didn't have a choice —"

"Tell me!"

"I waited till you were out," Mr. Delaney says slowly. "I went into the master bedroom and retrieved Conrad's gun, which both of you had mentioned before. Eventually he came home, went to work in his study. I appeared in the doorway. 'I never heard you knock,' he said. Then I . . . Then I did what I had to do. Then it was done."

"You killed my husband. You burned down my house."

"I did what I had to do."

"You burned your own house. Then this house? My mother's house?" I'm practically screaming. At least I think I am. It's hard to hear over the flames.

"She knows," he said. "And now you do,

too." He stares hard at my mother again. "Sixteen years ago, you didn't suspect?"

My mother doesn't say a word.

"But when Evie told the police the truth, you started thinking about that day again, too. If Earl hadn't shot himself, then there were only two logical solutions: The hired gun had come to the house, maybe to see you, and got in a confrontation with Earl instead. Or the only other person who knew everything that was going on had done it — namely, me. Of those two choices, who do you think you were going to turn on first?"

"You killed your best friend," my mother finally snaps. "He loved you!"

"You hired a contract killer to take out the competition. And he loved you still!"

"He was going to leave me!"

"No! You should've just been patient, Joyce. For the love of God, you weren't going to lose him."

"No. You took him from me instead."

Suddenly, my mom's grip on my hand tightens. Except this time, she doesn't tug. She yanks me backward. I stumble, falling halfway through the open bathroom doorway. Just as my mother, my platinum-and-pearls mother, ducks her head and charges.

She plows straight into Delaney, his pistol, the black smoke.

"Run, Evie, run!" my mother cries.

Then she and Delaney disappear into the flames.

You spend enough time chasing a dog to get back a precious black boot, you start to think like a dog. Spend the rest of your time chasing criminals, and you learn to think like a criminal.

Rocket was going over the wooden privacy fence across the street. D.D. knew it. He was counting on his youth and athleticism to launch himself up and over and leave his chaser in the dust.

D.D. couldn't beat him to the fence. Nor was she swinging over tall wooden structures anytime soon. Ten years ago, maybe, but now she'd be kidding herself.

What she could do was tap him, just enough. Vaulting took timing, balance, and a proper launch. Rocket knew how to start a fire; D.D. knew how to take someone out.

A last burst of speed on her part. Her lungs did not appreciate it and she made a mental note to get back to morning runs, even if it was snowy and cold and she hated winter. Sound of a vehicle up ahead. Rocket heard it the second she did. He made his move, a mad dash in front of the vehicle, which he most likely assumed would slam on its brakes — or, better yet, swerve and hit D.D. instead.

D.D. smiled.

Just as Phil turned right into Rocket's path, the kid slammed into the side of the hood. Then D.D. was on him, yanking both arms behind his back, as Phil flew out of the front and, weapon drawn, covered her.

"Just like old times," she gasped as she cuffed her prey. Being an administrative sergeant, this was her first takedown in a bit. It felt good, even if she couldn't catch her breath and was dangerously close to ruining the moment by vomiting.

"Anything for my partner."

Carol who? D.D. thought. She and Phil shared a smile. Then both of their attentions turned to Rocket, facedown against the hood.

"Who hired you?" D.D. demanded to know.

"Man, I don't know what you're talking about —"

"Yes, you do. And if you want any help saving yourself after today's fire show, you'd better start talking."

"I don't know his name," Rocket hedged.

"Sure you do." She leaned closer. "We know, Rocket. We know everything. Now the question is, who makes the deal first?

You? Or some criminal lawyer who played you from the very beginning and won't hesitate to throw you under the bus? Talk."

Rocket's eyes widened. "You know about Mr. Delaney?"

"Mr. Delaney? That's interesting. Keep going."

Rocket did. About burning a crime scene, then about the attorney who deactivated his own security system so Rocket could have access. Followed by the distraction fires to pull everyone into Harvard Square. Exposing his real target. A fucking awesome Colonial in Cambridge.

"Those old homes," Rocket said with a gleam in his eyes. "Man, do they burn."

Phil and D.D. exchanged a glance. They could hear sirens in the distance.

"Flora's already there," D.D. said.

Phil didn't need her to explain anything more. He threw Rocket in the back of his car, and they headed for the fire.

I reach the second platform of the fire escape easily enough. The metal is already heating up from the flames inside the home. Smoke pours up from the windows below me and I can smell the undertones of grease, like that night Rocket and I tossed bottles of vegetable oil into the fire drum.

The fire escape on this level leads to an old double-hung window. The neighbor had said she saw someone in the second-story bath. I'm tempted to shatter a pane of glass, reach through to unlatch the window and open it up. But at the last second I hesitate.

I'm not an expert, but I know fire likes oxygen. If I burst open a window and introduce a huge gulp of fresh air into an inferno, I'm pretty sure something bad happens.

I don't know if this is my best idea or worst, but I keep climbing. Third level of the fire escape. Much smaller window. A tight squeeze — but not a problem for a woman whose nervous energy keeps her on the emaciated side of skinny.

I have some experience smashing windows. Briefly, I think of another time, another place, another girl dying in front of my eyes as I desperately try to break us both out of a house. Then I force it from my mind. Elbow is your best tool. If you're a female in a hand-to-hand combat situation, an elbow is better than your fist any day of the week. Let alone what you can do with your knee, or the heel of your foot.

I turn my head away, count on my heavy coat for protection as I jab my elbow into the middle of the pane. Glass rains down.

Quickly, I shrug out of my down coat, wrap it around my forearms, and use it to clear the rest of the glass from the pane. Then, for good measure, I lay my jacket over the bottom sill as I shimmy headfirst through the narrow space.

I land with a thud. No graceful tuck and roll, more like ass over teakettle. But I'm in. I cough instantly, smelling the smoke.

Okay, now I just have to make it down a level, find Evie, her mother, whomever, and watch out for a homicidal defense attorney. I tell myself I've been in worse situations. But the fire still makes me uneasy. Rocket Langley is right: Flames have a lethal sort of magic all their own.

The door of the room is closed. I have a vague memory from childhood fire safety drills that I should touch the door with the back of my hand first before tugging it open. It's warm, not hot. I stand behind the door, then yank it open.

Nothing. But beneath me I hear an ominous sound. Sort of a scary cackle, like a witch, or blades of flame, sensing the fresh input of oxygen from above, and greedily changing course.

Quick, I realize. Whatever happens next, it'd better be quick. The fire will give me one shot at this. Then it's coming up these stairs one way or another. I'll be out first with whomever I can find, or that will be that.

If I survive this, I find myself thinking, *I really should call my mom.*

I head down the stairs, keeping my head down as the smoke builds. I'm not even at the bottom before my eyes sting and the smoke feels like a crushing weight against my chest. I rip off my hoodie and tie it around my mouth and nose, though I'm not sure that will help. I just hit the second-story landing when I hear coughing that's not my own.

My steps quicken, but again, I'm very aware of what D.D. said: If Dick Delaney is in this house, he's a threat as big as the fire.

Then, before I can move, a person emerges from the smoke down the hall and nearly crashes into me. She is weeping and coughing and . . . wet. Wet towels, I realize. Her head, her shoulders.

"Evie?" I ask.

"My mom," she gasps, heaves. "She went after him. Shoved him down the stairs I think."

"Your lawyer?"

"He killed my father. He killed my husband. Please" — *cough cough* — "find my mom."

"Okay, we're getting you" — short pause for my own hacking fit — "out of here —"

"My mom!"

"Evie! Listen to me. *You're* a mom!"

My statement startles her. Immediately her hands drop down to her belly, and I can tell with everything going on, she'd forgotten that fact.

"Your mom did what she had to do for you." *Rasp, wheeze, hack.* "Now you're going to do . . . what you have to do . . . for your baby."

"My mom hates me."

"No mom hates her daughter, Evie. Some of us just don't understand one another." I'm tugging her down the hall. Prattling a little because I need her to be moving and moving fast. I don't want her to look behind her. I don't want her to see the column of flame that just figured out there's an open window upstairs.

I don't want her to realize that if her mother really ran backward into that . . . there is nothing Evie or I can do for her now.

"You should meet . . . my mom," I rasp out. We can't go up. Pregnant Evie will never fit through that window. Which leaves us the second-story egress. A room at the end of the hall, I'm guessing. It's one thing to study a house from the outside. Another to be inside a smoke-filled abyss and still keep a sense of direction.

"She would love you," I continue. I pass a doorway on the right. Jerk it open. Discover a linen closet. Keep us moving.

"My mom's a farmer." I adjust my hoodie over my mouth. The smoke is so thick, cloying, stinging. "Her happy place is . . . nurturing a daughter who continuously puts herself in harm's way . . . bane of her existence. You . . . she could feed. Me. So sorry."

New doorway. Please let this be the one, because I hear a roaring sound now. Nothing good comes from that sound. Not to mention, my eyes are tearing so hard I can't really see. And the pressure on my lungs . . .

I falter, go down.

Oxygen. The greedy fire has consumed all the oxygen. We think we have air, but we don't.

Evie is tugging at me. She still has her wet cloth around her head. Smart girl.

I find myself wondering what it would be like to be an expectant mother. Have a baby to take care of. A life to grow, versus my daily mission of obliteration.

I think I'm going to pass out.

She slaps me. Actually slaps me. I sputter. Try to get myself up. I can't seem to do it.

"Fire escape," I manage. "Last bedroom. Window."

She nods. Then, she looks up, past my shoulder, and I see fear widen her eyes.

It's coming now, for both of us. But she can still make it.

I think my mother will like her very much. They will be happy together.

She's gone. I don't see her leave as much as I feel her absence. But it's okay. Because the heat is fierce now. Like a lover, licking at my face.

I think I hear laughing. And I know who is in those flames. Jacob. Walking through the fires of hell himself. Having the time of his afterlife. He always did love pain and suffering.

That, as much as anything, makes me start crawling again. Because I know in my heart of all hearts, no amount of good I've done in the past six years will ever be enough. The real reason I don't sleep, I don't eat. Because those flames of hell, they are waiting for me, too. Someday, I will join Jacob there. Just as he promised.

But not yet. Not yet.

Then, fresh air. I feel it, gulp it greedily. Evie, she's opened the window. She's found the fire escape. She and her baby are going to make it.

I have a sudden terrible premonition of what's going to happen next. Fresh air, hitting those flames.

I flatten on the floor, throw my hands over my head as if that will make a difference. Just as something flat and wet smacks against my arms.

"Run," Evie screams hoarsely in front of me. "Goddammit, move!"

She stumbles for the far window. I'm up, making a crooked dash. The roar the roar the roar. The searing heat against my back.

She dives awkwardly through the window. I think she's screaming. I think I'm screaming. But all I hear is the howl of racing fire.

I throw myself at the opening, falling against the frame.

Just as a hand snaps through the opening, grabs my wrist, and pulls hard.

"You will not fucking die on me!" D. D. Warren growls as she drags me through the window. The upper glass shatters. We flatten against the metal platform as flames explode above, and a spray of shockingly cold water shoots us from below, blasting back my hair. Firemen to the rescue.

I'm clutching D.D. Or maybe she is clutching me.

I think we are both now laughing.

But then we are both crazy.

"Evie?" I manage to ask.

"Phil's got her."

I don't talk anymore. We wait till the firemen beat back the flames enough for us to slide down to the ground. Then we lie in a puddled mess for a long time.

I look up at the sky. I think of so many things. Jacob, being sent back to the hell he came from. Keith, who is maybe more dangerous than I originally thought, but for entirely different reasons.

Evie. Motherhood. Mothers.

I make a decision. Then I close my eyes, because I'm simply too exhausted to think anymore.

Jacob is laughing again. But this time, I'm the one who lets him go.

CHAPTER 42
EVIE

When Flora said her mother lived on a farm in the wilds of Maine, she wasn't kidding. We have been driving forever. A good four hours at least, heading farther and farther north out of Boston.

Flora is at the wheel. It's my car, as she doesn't own a vehicle — but she's the pilot, as I don't know where we're going. Getting out of the city had been . . . interesting. Flora drives the same way she moves: quickly, impulsively, aggressively. I might have actually let the older couple cross the street, but hey.

Flora doesn't talk much. It's okay. These days, I don't often feel like talking.

Once Boston was behind us, she headed for Route 1 up the coast. Longer drive, but more scenic. It had been nice, watching the quaint towns and ocean views pass before us. Lobster rolls for lunch. She knew a place, total dive, which of course meant it had the best lobster in New England.

I settled for a simple garden salad. One month after our fiery experience, we are both recovering. Flora's throat still holds a rasp. I cough up black soot that makes me fear for my baby. Medically, however, we've both been checked up, down, and sideways. My health is good, my baby amazing. No more gentle swelling; I now have a firmly established baby bump and I couldn't be more grateful. Every day I start the morning talking to my baby. Letting him or her know how happy I am to be a mom. How I can't wait to finally meet in person. How much I'm already totally in love.

"And your daddy loves you, too," I always whisper. Because in my heart, I know that is true. Conrad had his secrets. But they were merely painful, not sordid. My husband was a good man. A great man, many might say, working quietly and discreetly for others.

Sergeant Warren tells me they're still piecing it all together, but with information from the Jacksonville Sheriff's Office and testimony from the ex-wife Conrad was helping keep hidden, the Boston PD had been able to track down several other women Conrad had assisted over the years. Flora could've been one of them. She doesn't talk about it. And I don't pry. We are both women who understand there's no point to the coulda, woulda, shouldas of life.

Flora makes the transition from Route 1 to another windy rural road, then another and another. She is humming slightly, her fingers tapping the wheel.

We've spent some time together these past few weeks, first at the hospital, then being debriefed by the police, then just . . . because. The day I was discharged from the hospital, she and D.D. seemed to have already worked out a plan: a month-to-month rental of a cute little home in Waltham. Maybe not the best location ultimately, given my job, but then again, I haven't been to work in months and, with the baby coming and no family of my own to say *do this, stay there, think about that,* the rental was as good a start as any.

Who knew there'd come a time when I'd miss my mother's overbearing ways?

I had lunch with the school principal and my friend Cathy Maxwell last week. It was awkward, as I expected. And yet . . . They were both so kind. *We're so sorry we didn't know. What can we do? How can we help?*

I feel like I've spent my life putting up walls, hiding behind my preconceptions while judging people for their own. I'm too shy to have real friends. And who would like some awkward woman most notorious for having shot her own father?

I told them the truth at lunch. About all of it. My dad. Conrad. The men I loved. The people I lost. The mother who died for me even though I'd gone most of my life feeling as though she didn't even like me.

They cried. They got up, gave me hugs. They asked about what I wanted to do with my future and, of course, I needed to think about my baby, but bear in mind I'm a gifted teacher and the students love me and they both hoped I'd come back to work, even if it wasn't until the fall.

I cried. I hugged them back. We scheduled a time to get together again, and it occurred to me, this could be my life. This could've always been my life. I just have to reach out. I have to keep some doors open.

Especially after losing so much.

Now, Flora. She's been working on me for weeks. I need to meet her mother. Her mother needs to meet me. We will love each other.

My first instinct, of course, was to decline. I don't want to be a bother, I've already taken up so much of Flora's time . . . So of course I forced myself to say yes. I'm not trying to replace my mother, I remind myself firmly. Because to picture her at all, her last determined rush into the flames, taking Mr. Delaney with her . . .

I still can't think about it. On my bad days, I'm angry. The whole thing was her fault anyway. The selfish, narcissistic witch, plotting Katarina Ivanova's murder in a fit of envy, then letting me carry the burden of my father's death for the sake of his legacy. Myself, even my baby — we were merely stage pieces in the theater that was her life. She dashed into those flames, I tell myself, because that was the dramatic thing to do, and she always loved a good drama.

My mother died. The police recovered her and Mr. Delaney's bodies at the foot of the stairs. Still tangled together. Completely and totally burnt to a crisp.

My mother died.

My mother told me to run. My mother charged Mr. Delaney and plunged them both into the inferno.

My mother died.

I just can't process it.

I'm rich. This is a different thought for me, too. A good one, because God knows my baby and I need the money. I've been working on finding a lawyer. Not a criminal defense attorney this time. Right after the fire, I didn't know what would happen: Mr.

Delaney had confessed to me that he'd killed Conrad, not to mention my father, but then he'd also gone and died, which made it my word against whatever the police believed to be the case.

Sergeant Warren told me not to worry. Delaney might have arranged to burn down his own town house, but not before removing his computer, valuables, and personal papers. The detectives found a treasure trove of information in his office. Including a confession he'd written years ago, then locked in his personal safe. Maybe an attempt to purge his sins, sleep better at night? I don't know.

Apparently, the computer experts would be tearing apart his hard drive for months to come, and with my help figuring out all of Conrad's usernames, they could now rebuild his own activities online, uncovering the very dangerous dance that Conrad had started, thinking he was thwarting a hired assassin, but instead unwittingly exposing himself and his activities to Mr. Delaney, who then decided Conrad had grown too dangerous to live.

I don't get to hear about it as much, but I've caught snippets of conversation between Flora and D.D. — the feds are reworking Jacob Ness's computer. In fact, they are using some of Conrad's usernames to track Ness's online activities during Flora's abduction. A local expert, Keith Edgar, is helping. I only know this because D.D. likes to say Keith's name to watch Flora blush. Interesting.

Flora is waiting for something. Wants something. From time to time she snaps at D.D., have you heard anything new, what the hell is Quincy doing anyway? D.D. counsels patience. She is clearly waiting for information, too. But I can tell she's much more worried about what the information will mean.

The truth hurts. I know that. Sergeant Warren knows that. Flora will figure it out, all in good time. And when she does, D.D. and I and maybe this Keith guy will be there for her.

My husband is gone.

We loved each other. We created a home together. We made a life together. And we lied and we lied and we lied.

I miss his smile. I miss the solid strength of his arms. I miss the look of wonder on his face when he contemplated the swell of my stomach, the mystery of our unborn child.

And now I will raise our baby alone.

I think I will teach. Return to my classroom and my brilliant, lazy, frustrating, hormonal, but never boring students. I feel like if I don't put one stake in the ground, one piece of something familiar, I will become completely untethered and float away.

Too much of my life has been lies. I get to own that. Too much of my life has been isolating. I get to own that, too. And too much of my life has been spent running away instead of running toward. I want something to run toward. My child. A community. Friends.

I think Flora and I are friends. She doesn't know it yet, but once my lawyer sorts everything out, Flora will be coming into an inheritance of her own. I'll disguise it somehow. Anonymous gift, legacy from a long-lost aunt. There's always a way.

But she saved me. I wouldn't have gotten out of the burning house without her. She saved me and she saved my unborn child.

My baby lives.

This, I can process. I can feel him or her each night, a swelling of my own body, making way for this new, incredible force. I can close my eyes and see each little finger and toe, resiliently forming, then growing, growing, growing. Arms, legs, nose, mouth, delicately curving ears.

My baby lives. We talk. We love. We share. No more lies. No more walls. My father was brilliant, my mother was melodramatic, my husband was a hero and a liar, my family was complicated.

No more.

I want to buy a cute town house in a normal neighborhood. Maybe one with a park nearby. And given my improved fortunes, I will have a nanny for the early years, then day care when my child is older. Or maybe I'll meet a nice older woman who'd love to help out a single mom living on the same block. I will host barbecues where I can get to know my neighbors' names, and let them learn a little bit about me.

And I won't stand in a corner anymore. I will step up. I will become part of the world I live in, even when it's scary. Because life is scary, but it still beats the alternative.

Flora turns down another road, then another.

She's not humming anymore, but her finger is tapping impatiently on the wheel. We're getting close, I think. I wonder if Flora knows that she is smiling.

Then a house bursts into view. Two stories, painted a charming yellow with slightly eccentric lavender shutters. The wraparound farmer's porch offers an array of benches, and rocking chairs with all sorts of brilliantly colored pillows, while the front door is a bright cherry red.

The car hasn't even parked when the front door bursts open and a woman I can only presume is Flora's mom comes hopping out, still pulling on her second boot. Half her hair is on top of her head, half is trailing down her back, and she is wearing so many different tops I give up sorting it out. She's grabbed some kind of man's checkered blue flannel shirt as her outer layer and is dusting what appears to be flour from her hands.

The parking area has been shoveled for our visit. Now Flora brings my car to a jerking halt.

"My mother, Rosa," she says, her voice still slightly hoarse. Time, the doctors had told her, had told me. We all need time.

But it's not her voice that matters. I'm looking at her face, and this is a Flora I've never seen. Younger. Lit up. Happy, I think again. But more than that, home.

This is Flora at home.

She already has the car door open, flying across the yard. In the passenger's seat, I slow, struggling with my seat belt. An inner instinct tells me not to rush. I don't want to miss what's going to happen next.

A pause. At the last minute, Flora's mom draws up short. I would swear she'd been about to fling her arms around her daughter, but then caught herself, as if knowing better.

For one moment, Flora's mother appears awkward, less certain. Yearning. She is staring at her child with clear, deep longing.

My own breath catches in my throat. I wonder if my mother ever looked at me like that. I'm already promising my baby I will always look at him or her with such love.

Then . . .

Flora closes the distance. Flora throws her arms around her mother and hugs her so hard, so tight. On and on and on.

Rosa closes her eyes. She squeezes back. Even from this distance, I know she is crying. And laughing and crying some more. I blame the baby hormones, but I'm crying, too.

I take my time easing out of the car. I cross the yard more carefully, aware of the snowy footing.

Flora has finally stepped back from her mom.

Rosa is teary-eyed but beaming. She looks at me. She smells of molasses and cinnamon and brown sugar, which are things I've been told mothers smell like, but I have never experienced it for myself.

"You," she says, "must be Evie."

ACKNOWLEDGMENTS

This book has been such an adventure! First off, my deepest appreciation to my editor, Mark Tavani, for keeping me focused and at the computer, even when the book was evil and all my characters hated me (which happens more than you think!). Not just anyone is cut out to deal with the cranky authors of the world. Thank you, Mark, for being the voice of wisdom for me.

On the investigative details front, a big shout-out once again to Lieutenant Michael Santuccio of the Carroll County Sheriff's Department for educating me on cold cases, prior shootings, and proper procedures for current arrests. Given this book also delves into the nefarious world of the dark web, thank you, Robin Stuart, for helping me understand all the cool ways to scrub a computer, and all the cooler methods forensic techs will use to rebuild a hard drive in the end. Rob Casella from Northledge

Technologies also educated me on cloud technology and multifactor identification. In the war of cops versus criminals, I'm happy there are such brilliant people on our side. Oh, please bear in mind that any mistakes in this novel are mine and mine alone. My sources may be experts, but I am just me.

Under the care and feeding of authors, the list is very long this year. First and foremost, thank you, Laurie Gabriel, for the warm reception from yourself and your family. Thank you to my posse, who always have my back: Michelle, Kerry, Genn, and Sarah. My deepest appreciation to my local family, Pam and Glenda, Bob and Carol, for taking such good care of me, especially this past year. And of course, love and affection for my real family, including my ninety-nine-year-old grandmother, who e-mails me weekly to make sure the book is getting done, and my teenage daughter who questions anything and everything but also makes me real chocolate cream pie so at least I have hope of surviving another day.

To my pub team, you are extraordinary. For my agent, Meg, thank you for all the extra guidance and heartfelt support. Finally, I couldn't have done this without the constant presence of my snoring elderly terrier, Ruby, or the youngsters, Bowie and Annabelle, crashing around the living room. Certainly, life is never boring.

Along those lines, several people joined the bookmaking fun by winning naming rights in this novel. Patty DiPiero won the right to a character of her choice, coming up with Patricia Di Lucca, arsonist investigator extraordinaire. Rhonda Collins won the annual Kill a Friend, Maim a Buddy Sweepstakes, nominating her friend Sandi Clipfell as the missing woman, presumed dead. Tina Maracle won the international edition, Kill a Friend, Maim a Mate, naming herself as missing, presumed dead. There are more books to write; who knows what will happen next? But thank you all for your generous support and I hope you enjoy your literary immortality.

To all my readers out there, thank you for your warm embrace of Flora and her particular journey. There is more to come. Hope you enjoy the ride.

ABOUT THE AUTHOR

Lisa Gardner is the number one *New York Times* best-selling author of twenty previous novels, including her most recent, *Look for Me.* Her Detective D. D. Warren novels include *Find Her, Fear Nothing, Catch Me, Love You More,* and *The Neighbor,* which won the International Thriller of the Year Award. She lives with her family in New England.